Myths & Magic

LEGENDS OF LOVE ANTHOLOGY

Published by
Dreamspinner Press
4760 Preston Road
Suite 244-149
Frisco, TX 75034
http://www.dreamspinnerpress.com/

Edited by Anne Regan
Cover Art by Analise Dubner http://www.dubnerdesign.com
Cover Design by Mara McKennen

ISBN: 978-1-61581-372-8
Printed in the United States of America
First Edition
October 2010

eBook edition available
eBook ISBN: 978-1-61581-373-5

Table of Contents

The 1002nd Arabian Nights Tale

Michael Gouda

THE Princess Scheherazade looked up from under her improbably long eyelashes and fluttered them at one of the harem ladies, who giggled and nibbled suggestively at a marshmallow. There was the hint of frankincense in the air, and everywhere the scent of gold.

In one of the cool corners of the courtyard where fountains plashed, the shade of Nikolai Rimsky-Korsakov hovered—and made orchestral notes. Cellos dripping honey, he thought, or if not honey, the sweetest of sherbet.

The Sultan Shahriyar, who had been driven mad by the unfaithfulness of a woman he had married, and as a consequence took a new wife every night, only to order her execution when the sun rose on the following day, now looked at the woman who had thus far escaped her fate.

Princess Scheherazade, her eyes made huge with kohl, seemed entirely at ease. Her long legs were covered with a rippling waterfall of peacock-blue silk, her hair hidden by an iridescent tumble of soft material.

Shahriyar, wearing those loose trousers that hid his masculine secrets from all save the ladies of the harem, lounged on brightly colored cushions and yawned, exposing white teeth.

Scheherazade smiled. "My Lord," she said. "I have entertained you for 1001 nights with my stories. Your promise was that my life should no longer be forfeit at the end."

The Sultan looked at her, his dark face serious, his fine Arabian nose jutting over thick, sensuous lips, his eyes eloquent, brown, and lustrous under cruel eyebrows. "Stories?" he repeated as if he had never heard the word before.

"My Lord, for 1001 nights I have regaled you with tales of djinns and peris, giant rocs and magic lamps, flying carpets, wicked Afrits and crooked Wazirs—and the fantastic adventures of sailors on and off the high seas."

For a brief moment the Sultan's eyes seemed to brighten. "Sailors," he murmured.

"And how they gained their true loves and married princesses."

"Oh, yes." He sounded depressed again.

There was a pause while several adipose eunuchs waved their fans and the still air, flavored with jasmine and mysterious Eastern scents (peppermint), was encouraged into a sort of slow motion.

"My Lord," pursued Scheherazade. "Have I not been successful in my task?"

The Sultan moved his head in a noncommittal gesture.

"But, My Lord," protested Scheherazade.

"Tyrants never keep their word," said the Sultan sadly, and a eunuch stepped forward, holding a large, curved scimitar in his right hand. His huge stomach wobbled threateningly.

"My Lord. I have one other story...."

The shade of Sir Richard Burton fluttered unobserved in another corner, endeavoring to sharpen a pencil. Equally transparent, his French competitor, the renowned Monsieur Galland, regarded him with jealous Gallic fury and prepared to take down his own dictation.

The eunuch glanced at his Sultan, who gestured him away with a languid forefinger. The Princess breathed a sigh of relief, and then continued in her low contralto voice, which always sounded as if she had been at the hashish pipe a mite too long.

"It is the story of Prince Hassan...."

"Aren't they all?" said Shahriyar, despondently.

"Le recit du Prince Hassan," scribbled M. Galland.

"And the Sailor," added Scheherazade, diplomatically.

“Et le Matelot,” added M. Galland.

Scheherazade cleared her throat. “But this was such a prince, a prince amongst princes.... His complexion was brown and ruddy, the chiefest amongst ten thousand. His head was as the most fine gold, his locks were bushy and black as a raven. His eyes were as the eyes of doves by the rivers of waters, washed with milk, and fitly set. His cheeks were as a bed of spices, as sweet flowers... his lips like lilies dropping sweet-smelling myrrh. His hands were as gold rings set with beryl; his loins as bright ivory overlaid with sapphires. His legs were as pillars of marble, set upon sockets of fine gold. His mouth was most sweet; he was altogether lovely.” Scheherazade paused and looked at the Sultan’s expression.

In his separate but parallel universe, Nicolai Rimsky-Korsakov listened to the melodic voice. Violin solo, he thought, though the huskiness of the voice could have suggested something deeper—clarinet, perhaps... or viola. Sir Richard, scribbling away, shook his head, suddenly bemused; the words seemed strangely familiar. The Song of Solomon, could it be?

Shahriyar’s eyebrows confirmed that this poetic description was not going down too well.

Scheherazade wondered for a moment if, after so many stories, at long last her abilities were failing her. She changed tack. “The broadest of shoulders,” she said with scarcely a pause. “Pecs you could die for, a washboard stomach—”

“What is a washboard?” asked the Sultan. The eunuch, who had to do much of the laundry, knew, but did not think it his place to explain.

“Perhaps more like a six-pack,” said Scheherazade.

“Qu’est-ce que c’est, un ‘six-pack’?” pondered M. Galland.

“And his thighs,” said Scheherazade, hurrying on. “Thighs....”

“...you could die for?” suggested the Sultan.

“Thighs of such strength and beauty... even the horse he rode was enamored of him.” For a moment she wondered whether the metaphor she had used hadn’t been a little over the top. Wasn’t there a prohibition in the Holy Books against relationships between men and animals?

An athletic Cornel Wilde, in faded 1945 Technicolor, flexed his own superb leg muscles and prepared to follow in the mustachioed, swashbuckling steps of Errol Flynn and Douglas Fairbanks Junior.

"Sounds a very paragon of youth," said the Sultan, eating a date.

There was a brief pause. "Unfortunately..." continued the Princess.

"Does there have to be an 'unfortunately'?"

"But yes, of course, my Lord. A lack of good fortune, a disharmony, unrequited love, an evil Afrit—these add the tensions. Otherwise, there would be no story. Who would listen to a tale where all was harmony and peace and everyday monotony?"

The Sultan's lack of comment seemed to constitute agreement, and Scheherazade continued.

"Unfortunately Prince Hassan was poor." She paused dramatically to see the effect of such a statement. She was not disappointed.

The Sultan's eyebrows rose into a startled arch. "Prince Hassan was *poor*? A prince, and 'poor'! A contradiction in terms if ever I heard one. By definition, a prince must be wealthy."

"So it would be thought... but death duties... capital gains taxes... depreciation... his father's unwise speculation on the stock market...." The Princess was vague. She wasn't quite sure of her facts here, but was fairly sure that the Sultan wouldn't know either. She hurried on. "So his father, the Sultan, told him to go abroad and make his fortune."

"Do I know this spendthrift Sultan?" asked Shahriyar suspiciously.

"No, Sire. His name was Suleiman, and he lived many generations ago. Anyway, the Prince dutifully took his leave and embarked on a ship leaving from the port of Haifa.

"The ship was small, little more than a dhow with two sails. The Sultan had done his best to furnish his son with accoutrements appropriate to a prince, but the sailors aboard looked with a certain amount of suspicion at this richly dressed noble who apparently could only afford passage in a two-masted dhow. They seemed a surly crew. The captain, a small, dark man with long mustaches and bowlegs, smelled of garlic, and the others were scarcely more attractive. Only the young sailor, Achmet, fair of form, fleet of limb, handsome of countenance, treated Prince Hassan with anything like the deference due to his rank, apologizing for the meanness of the food—mostly beans—and caring for many of his personal needs.

"The wind being from the desert behind them, they sailed North across that sea that barbarians from the West had called the 'Middle of the Earth,' though everyone knew that the Holy City of Mecca is the real center of the world. As the voyage continued, Prince Hassan became increasingly worried. The captain seemed to have little control over his men, and often at night they would get drunk and, he thought, cast envious eyes on the few golden ornaments that his father had been able to give him on his departure. His mind conjured pictures of them setting on him, stripping him and stealing everything, and then pitching his naked body overboard.

"On the third day, when by rights they should have been in sight of land, the wind changed, came from the West, grew stronger. Dark cumulus clouds, their bellies full of rain and thunder, rolled across the sky and the sea became choppy, with little whitecaps, then surged into high breakers, slapping against the sides of the ship so that it wallowed, and however hard it was turned, the rudder had no effect.

"Prince Hassan looked at the purple sky, the gray heaving waters, and felt his own stomach churn in sympathy. The force of the wind made the ship heave over so that water rushed in over the gunwales."

Rimsky-Korsakov rubbed his hands. He could work the Sultan theme into a tumultuous climax for the storm section, he thought, with harsh trumpets and crashes on the timpani echoing through the trembling strings.

Princess Scheherazade continued.

"'Lower the sails,' shrieked the captain, seeing that there was the possibility of a capsize. Several sailors rushed to the lines, but they were too late. With a crack that sounded like a musket shot, the main mast snapped and, together with the useless billowing sail, went overboard, taking with it three of the screaming men.

"With only the triangular stern sail, the ship was practically uncontrollable and tossed around like a dervish's turban, the planks groaning and screeching with the intolerable strain. It was then that the slim figure of Achmet appeared at Prince Hassan's side, as he stood gazing with staring eyes at the confusion that raged around him. 'The ship's breaking up, My Lord,' Achmet said. 'I think our only chance is to jump.'

"Prince Hassan had, of course, received all the education that befitted his rank—reading, writing, painting, expertise at chess and polo—but none of the essentials—wrestling, carpentry, haggling in the marketplace, and most importantly at this particular time, swimming.

"'I cannot swim,' he said. 'Save yourself.'

"This is no Prince," said Shahriyar. "He must know he is more valuable than a common sailor. He should demand that the sailor carry him on his shoulders through the waves."

Scheherazade sighed. It was obvious that the Sultan had no more idea than Prince Hassan how swimming worked. "It happened almost as you say," she said, "for the sailor clasped the Prince around the waist so that their bodies were held together and then leaped with him into the raging torrent.

"As soon as the Prince felt the waters close over his head, he feared he would drown and did the worst possible thing—struggling and gasping so that the salt water was sucked into his mouth and up his nose—and made matters worse. But even through all his agony, he felt the lips of the sailor against his ear and his voice saying, 'Do not struggle, Lord, or you will drown both of us.'

"Hassan did as he was told, and instead of the panic-stricken terror, felt a languor seep through his limbs. The arms holding him round his waist were strong and lusty, the body pressed against his was hard and virile, and the lips that had before whispered into his ear were now transferred to his own mouth, so that it seemed he could breathe through the other. He surrendered himself to the embrace."

"How is this possible?" asked Shahriyar, and the others, listening, also wondered the same.

"Achmet was no ordinary sailor," explained Scheherazade. "He was, in fact, a water spirit, and perfectly at home in the depths of the sea as well as on land."

"So Hassan was in no danger at all?"

"Not from drowning," said the Princess, ambiguously.

"And he took him to the nearest shore?"

"He took him to the Isle of Camaralzaman, of which Your Highness has obviously heard—an uninhabited island even to this day, with date palms and coconuts and crystal streams to slake the thirst and satisfy all hunger." She paused. "Save, of course, one that affects men most of all....

"At dusk, after the storm had died down, the prince was lying on his back on the soft sands. Most of his clothes had been washed from him by the storm and his chest was bare, the soft, brown skin open to the air, revealing two circular, erogenous islands perfectly aligned. His turban, though, was still on, bright scarlet against the yellow sand. Around his loins was wound a white breechcloth, but so loosely that his manhood appeared round the side and lay enticingly on his splayed thigh, as if wanting and waiting to be attended to. A gold bracelet clasped his left wrist.

"Achmet looked at him with eyes of longing. Eventually he could bear it no longer. He approached the unconscious body and covered it with kisses—hair, lips, chest, stomach, legs, feet, hands, and those more intimate parts that are normally hidden from view… the cavern of sweet darkness, the tree of regeneration, the eggs of procreation.

"When Prince Hassan opened his eyes, he felt his whole body tingling with sexual passion. He found he was mightily aroused as an eager tongue and tender lips probed his most personal and procreative parts and gentle fingers stroked and caressed his skin.

"Slightly bemused, for this was the first time he had felt such intense feelings, he looked up to see the handsome face of Achmet above him, and felt an irresistible urge to insert his erect manhood into a warm, moist place and there release his most precious juices.

"Achmet offered him two alternatives, and he chose the second, pressing in until he was absorbed inside the other, flesh into flesh, hardness into yielding acceptance, the two pieces fitting like a jigsaw together, as if there was no other place.

"And here Hassan achieved his culmination, pulsing his seed into the other, accompanied by a great gasp that sounded as if his life had expired… but in fact announced the beginning of a very new, very different one."

Princess Scheherazade stopped.

The evening shadows lengthened and dusk fell with Arabian suddenness. Slaves and eunuchs brought in oil lamps. Their flickering flames cast little pools of yellow light, and Sir Richard, accustomed to the more incandescent gas mantles—or even the newfangled electric lights—squinted in an effort to continue his writing.

No one spoke; there was no movement. Even the eunuchs ceased waving their fans for a moment, but the lights reflected more than just a casual interest in the Sultan's eyes, and it seemed as if he searched for something to say.

"Is that it? Doesn't he find a bottle with a Djinn imprisoned inside?" asked Shahriyar. "Doesn't he meet with a wicked Afrit who tries to capture his soul? Doesn't he escape on a magic carpet?"

"No, My Lord. He lived with the sailor on the island for the rest of their lives, in rural ease and domesticity."

"Has this tale a point?"

"Love is where you find it," said Scheherazade. "Wealth is not necessary for happiness."

The Sultan sighed. "Is that the very end?"

"That is the end, my Lord."

"But Achmet was a spirit."

"You would have preferred him to be human, and both drowned in the storm?"

"It would have been an acceptable tragedy rather than a fictional impossibility."

"What is impossible?" she asked softly. In the flickering lamplight, the Princess looked strangely androgynous—her hips slim as a boy's, her shoulders a little too broad, her cheekbones high, and, as the scarf slipped from her head, the hair short and curling—as black as the feathers on a raven's breast.

In all the 1001 nights of the telling of the tales, Shahriyar had not touched her, had not wanted to. The magic attraction had been in her fantasies. Now, after this last unnatural, perverse story, he felt strangely attracted.

He lifted her from the cushions and Scheherazade slipped into his arms, hers holding his body with surprising strength. He felt for—and missed—her breasts, for against him she was as flat and hard as a man. As their loins touched, he felt another hardness where there should not have been one. Shahriyar regarded the young man closely… for young man it was. His eyes were as the eyes of doves by the rivers of waters, washed with milk and fitly set. His cheeks were as a bed of spices, as sweet flowers, his lips like lilies dropping sweet-smelling myrrh. His hands were as gold rings set with beryl; his loins as bright ivory overlaid with sapphires. His legs were as pillars of marble, set upon sockets of fine gold. His mouth was most sweet; he was altogether lovely.

He gasped. "You are not a princess...."

"My Lord, my name is Hassan." His breath was cool and sweet against the Sultan's cheek. "Is this indeed the end?"

Shahriyar's manhood twitched. *It is only the beginning,* he thought.

Sir Richard smiled as he thought of how the metaphoric stays of his Victorian reading public would be affected should he ever include this last story in his collection.

"Zut alors.... Merde!" said M. Galland, raising his hands in Gallic mock-horror.

Cornel Wilde's mouth spread in his characteristic smile, which was so attractive to his audience. What he was thinking about, no one could guess—but when he shook his head, it seemed there was almost something of regret.

Rimsky-Korsakov said nothing. He was in the throes of composition. A tone poem, a symphony, a *ballet?*

Amongst the shadows, an even darker, rather large, fat shade appeared and blundered into a clumsy pirouette. A susurration shivered through the air.

"Vaslav Nijinsky would be so erotic in the part. But who could dance the sailor?" wondered Serge Diaghilev.

MICHAEL GOUDA was born and raised in London, England. He served in the RAF where, he claims, he lost his virginity. Then he went back to business. After a change of direction in his thirties, he left the world of commerce and entered that of education, becoming a teacher at a Comprehensive School in Worcestershire, England. Since retiring, he lives in a limestone cottage in the Cotswolds with a neurotic Border Collie. He also writes under the name of Michael Duggan.

A Fairy in His Bed

corinna silver & aundrea singer

"I'M DYING, love," the dear old lady said. Quinn moved closer to her, making sure he stayed where her fading eyes could still see him.

"I know," he said, stroking her cheek gently. He could sense it about her: a feeling of completion, like turning a page to the end of a book. She was lying on the grand bed in the master bedroom, the comforter pulled up nearly to her chin and the low beep of medical machines sounding in the background. He shifted so that he was yet closer to her, close enough to see the color as it faded from the sky blue of her eyes.

"You've been a dear friend, Little One," she said. Her smile crinkled the parchment of her cheek.

"As have you, Old One," Quinn said, returning her smile and using his special name for her. "I shall miss you, truly."

"Ach!" she admonished. "You'll get over it, sooner rather than later." Her smile widened. "Your kind is not made for sadness."

Quinn felt his smile waver. "I'm sad now," he said, and there was a catch in his voice. "I'll never forget you."

"I know," she whispered, and he could hear the end in the sound, like the crackle of dry leaves before the snows come. "I'm sorry you can't stay here."

He shrugged. "It is what it is." He winked to make her smile.

She looked fondly at him, and they stayed like that, enjoying the last moments of each other's company. Quinn felt his sadness ease a little. This was the right time for her to go.

They both heard the noise of the nurse as she moved about in the next room, and it seemed to remind the Old One of something. "Soon," she said, "my family will be coming from all over to descend upon this little house." Her eyes were intent. "They must not find you here."

"And they won't." Quinn nodded firmly. "I'll hide, just as you said."

"Good," she sighed, and her eyes drifted shut. "Take care, Quinn. Be happy."

"I will," he whispered, "I promise." But he knew she was already gone.

By the time the old woman's relatives had arrived, Quinn was well hidden.

IT HAD been one of the worst days Daniel Tibbits had ever endured—and that was before his stupid cats tried to kill him.

"God damn it!" Daniel swore as he climbed to his feet. He brushed uselessly at the wet snow that had ground into the knees of his pant legs. He glared at the three black-and-white cats, who were circling him unrepentantly, head-butting whatever parts they could reach and bawling at him as if Daniel had been away for months instead of barely an afternoon. Dewey sniffed at his pant leg, apparently none the worse for wear despite nearly being kicked as she tripped him. Daniel started petting her automatically, glowering the whole time. He hit the cold-stiffened cloth of his jeans a little too hard and winced, since he'd managed to scrape what felt like sixty layers of skin off his palms when his hands had hit the icy pavement. "This is exactly what I need," he snarled at the cats, squinting at his upturned hands in December's early dark. They were stinging, but at least he didn't see any blood. "With my luck, I'll probably get gangrene," Daniel muttered. At least his agent might get off his back if he didn't have any fingers.

"All right, already! All right! You're hungry, I get it!" he said to the yowling cats. "Can you at least let me get inside the house?" The cats, naturally, ignored him. "For Pete's sake, it's not like I never—ah, fuck." Daniel took a deep breath, and then closed his eyes as he let out a heavy sigh.

He'd dropped the teapot when Dewey tripped him, and it had smashed on the walkway. Of course.

Daniel sighed again. He rubbed at his face and pushed his snow-damp hair off his forehead. It was a standard "Brown Betty" teapot, the kind everyone sung about in kindergarten: short, stocky, and dark red-brown. The shards were still gleaming cheerfully, scattered in the freshly fallen snow.

"Fuck," Daniel said again. He picked up one of the larger pieces and used it as a receptacle for two smaller fragments. He started searching for the other bits, but the teapot had practically exploded on the front walkway. To do the job properly he'd need a broom, and some daylight. The dark shards were nearly impossible to see in the quickly deepening twilight.

"Fuck!" Daniel threw down the pieces he'd been holding, watching them burst against the concrete with vicious satisfaction. "That's my life, right there," he said. "And because I'm such a fucking hack, that's the best metaphor I can come up with." His mouth twisted in a bitter smile.

Daniel shook his head. "Stop feeling sorry for yourself." He trudged the rest of the distance from the sidewalk to the wooden steps of his front porch, fishing in his jacket pocket for his keys. The cats followed him eagerly, still giving the occasional mewl as if making sure he didn't forget them.

The house had been built in the 1920s. The floors creaked and all the doors stuck and the stairs were treacherous, but the lights Daniel had left on that morning were shining brightly through the windows and he knew it would be cozy and warm after the freezing night outside. Right then, it was all Daniel had to look forward to. He opened the door.

A short puff of warm air blew by his cheek.

He blinked, wondering what would have caused it, then immediately forgot it as the frigid night air bit into his face.

"Hurry up, come on!" he groused to the cats, who were now apparently happy to sniff around the open door for a few hours, letting in more frigid air and swirls of snow. Daniel had installed a cat port shortly after rescuing the three cats, but they never used it.

"Finally!" Daniel said as Dewey sauntered in with her tail twitching. "Homicidal fleabag." Dewey ignored the insult and trotted over to Huey and Louie, already at their food and water bowls. All six bowls were almost full, but the cats still paced back and forth in front of them, crying pitifully.

"Wait a minute, will you?" Daniel shoved the front door into the frame and locked it. He hung up his jacket and took off his boots, cursing to himself as he managed to step into every one of the cats' wet paw tracks on the way to the kitchen. "I should have left you all in the Tim Hortons parking lot."

He washed his hands, grimacing at how the soap and water burned the scrapes, then grabbed three bowls out of the cupboard, put them on the counter, and poured a generous helping of milk into each one. Huey started drinking from her bowl before Daniel was finished, ending up with a waterfall of milk down her face.

Louie, the fat pig, finished her milk first and started immediately crying for more. "All right, all right!" Daniel complained as he poured her a second bowl. She glanced at him but then looked away, her yellow eyes focusing intently on—nothing. Daniel followed her gaze, but all he could see was the shelf where he stored his dishes and the shadows underneath. She mewed at the shadow, and then jumped off the counter, landing with a heavy *thump* on the floor.

"Well, fuck you too," Daniel said, bemused. Louie walking away from a bowl of milk was unlike her. He went to pour the milk down the sink, but changed his mind. One of the cats would get it later.

Daniel's dismal mood had returned by the time he'd given the cats their milk, thinking of the smashed teapot outside and everything his mother had said before she'd given it to him and he'd finally been allowed to escape with the damn thing.

Nancy Tibbits had brought it all the way from Stratford-Upon-Avon in England, his one small piece of inheritance from his great aunt, who had just recently passed away. His mother had called him the day after she got back from the funeral, telling him about his gift and insisting he come see her immediately to get it.

Daniel was pretty sure that the teapot had really been a ruse to lure him to his mother's house. It had been at least four months since the last time she'd told him he'd never amount to anything, and she probably figured he was overdue.

It was Daniel's own fault, really. Paul, his "perfect" boyfriend, had just left him, Daniel had been miserable and lonely, and in a fit of moronic nostalgia for a childhood he'd never had, he'd called his mother and blubbered out his depths of despair to her over the phone.

Initially, she'd been surprisingly sympathetic. Then the lectures had started.

How could you have let such a fine man as Paul get away, Danny? he'd expected, since that had been the leitmotif of every conversation he'd had with her since Paul had sneeringly told him that he "didn't have time for a male cat lady who couldn't write a sentence without a breakdown", and Daniel had made the mistake of telling his mother about it. The *At least you could have been his kept man while you played at being a writer* was new, though, and even hours later he still felt as raw as the skin on his hands. She'd always wanted him to be a doctor, a lawyer, some kind of corporate peon… anything that she could talk about with her girlfriends over their brunch mimosas without embarrassment. She'd been ecstatic when Paul—the charming, gorgeous, and wealthy surgeon—had breezed into Daniel's life and given her, by proxy, the son she actually wanted. She'd probably been more disappointed than Daniel when Paul had breezed out again.

Daniel had finally made his excuses to leave. He'd just started the forty-minute drive back home when his agent had called and told him the publisher had moved up the deadline for the last book in Daniel's trilogy by a month. The same last book Daniel hadn't even managed to start yet. And if he failed on his contract, he'd have to give the advance back, which he was currently using for food, clothing, and shelter.

"And then I smashed the teapot," Daniel muttered. "All I need now is for my car to break down and I'd have a country song." He couldn't even laugh at his own joke.

He put the milk away and closed the fridge door harder than necessary. Then he looked over to the living room from the kitchen, where the tiny, rickety computer desk with his laptop on it was directly in his line of sight. Just looking at it was enough to make his pulse speed up with fear. But the cats were fed and he wasn't going to clean up the remnants of the teapot until tomorrow, so he had no other excuses not to go over there.

Daniel opened his word processor and pulled up his novel, trying to ignore how, in the last four months of work, he'd barely managed 3,000 words. He put his fingers on the keyboard, read over his most recent paragraph, then stared at the stark, white space he was meant to fill up with brilliant prose and waited for something to come to him. And waited.

And waited.

"God damn it." Daniel rubbed his closed eyes with his fingers. He'd been looking at the same spot for so long that his eyes were aching, and his head felt as blank as the computer screen, empty of anything even resembling inspiration.

Daniel had dealt with writer's block before, just like everyone else, but this was the first time he hadn't been able to force himself through it.

He reached over to turn off the computer and stopped. He heard a strange rustling sound, like dry leaves, behind his head. Daniel held his breath, searching with his ears for the strange noise to repeat, but there was nothing.

"Stupid." Daniel shook his head. He turned off the computer, all but slamming the lid closed. He shoved himself away from the desk, then went to the couch and flopped down. He picked up the remote and clicked on the television, then cycled through the channels.

There was nothing on, and he couldn't write, but it was too early to go to bed. Daniel sighed, tilted his head back against the couch, and covered his face with his hands. "Augh!" he huffed against his palms, feeling his chest tighten with his sense of failure.

He turned off the television, wondering if he should just grab his gear and hit the gym, when he saw something sparkling, gold and copper, on the upper right-hand side of the television screen. Daniel blinked, but it didn't go away. He looked over his shoulder, eyes searching the darkened room for something that could be shining like that. He scanned the bookshelf behind him, but there was nothing that should have made that reflection, nothing from the windows hitting the TV, nothing coppery or gold at all.

Daniel turned back to the television, but now it was completely black.

Shaking his head at his idiocy, Daniel turned the TV set back on. The science-fiction channel was playing a terrible movie he'd already seen twice, but at least it was something to distract him until it was actually late enough to go to sleep. And if it kept him from seeing shiny things that weren't actually there, so much the better.

He couldn't afford the antipsychotic medications, anyway.

HE COULDN'T sleep.

Daniel stared up at the ceiling of his tiny bedroom as the night settled around him. The conversation with his mother had Daniel thinking about Paul—again—and his thoughts weren't pleasant.

Daniel had already guessed he and Paul weren't all that compatible after Paul had been pissed off when Daniel rescued the kittens. They'd had vague conversations about moving in together, but Paul hated cats. He'd said Daniel was selfish for choosing the cats over him. That had been the end of their relationship.

The memory was depressing enough to have Daniel squeezing his eyes shut in a desperate attempt to launch himself into sleep. But it wasn't working.

"Fuck!" he swore and threw himself out of bed. He went to the bathroom and splashed some cold water on his face and then leaned on the sink, staring bleakly at his reflection. Pale blue eyes, nondescript brown hair, a face that was too long, lips that would look better on a girl. At least his body was buff, Daniel thought. He'd been spending a lot of time in the gym instead of staring uselessly at his computer.

He ignored the coppery sparkle in the mirror of the bathroom, chalking it up to his being overtired.

DANIEL didn't remember falling asleep, but he knew he had to be dreaming.

There was someone else in the room. It was a man—very, very obviously a man. He was naked, tall and lanky with hair that fell in soft, messy curls around his forehead and neck. The effect made him look both cherubic and dangerous, like a seraphim recently thrown out of heaven. His smile was as innocent and sweet as it was a direct, unmistakable invitation.

"What are you doing here?" Daniel asked, curious but unconcerned because he was so obviously dreaming. He sat up, letting the coverlet slide down his chest to pool around his hips. He felt languid and slow, like a cat curled up by the fire. Whoever this stranger was, Daniel was certain he meant no harm.

"I'm here to thank you," the man said, moving onto the bed. He had a British accent, which made Daniel smirk at himself, wondering idly what kind of Freudian significance there might be in this man sounding like his mother.

"Thank me?" Daniel asked vaguely. He was too distracted by the man to worry about the answer to his question. At first glance the man's hair had just looked like a warm chestnut brown, but now that he was closer, Daniel could see that it was actually a rainbow of browns and reds, like leaves in autumn. His eyes were a mixture of green and brown, flecked with gold. Daniel realized he shouldn't have been able to see the other man so clearly with only the streetlight barely illuminating the room, but it was as if the man was surrounded with light.

"You're gorgeous," Daniel murmured, distantly pleased with himself that he had such a great imagination. "What's your name?"

The stranger's laugh sounded like cool water rushing over smooth stones. "Quinn," he said in his lilting accent. He was pulling the coverlet back while he spoke, exposing Daniel's legs. "And you're gorgeous too."

"Thank you," Daniel said, which made Quinn laugh. Quinn had dimples in his cheeks, which only emphasized his veneer of innocence. "My name is Daniel."

"Hello, Daniel," Quinn said. "I want to kiss you now."

"Okay," Daniel said faintly. He'd gone to bed without a shirt, and Quinn's warm hands on his shoulders made him shiver. Quinn straddled Daniel's legs, nestling their groins together. He moved his hands to the sides of Daniel's face, then leaned in and finally kissed him.

The kiss was gentle as winter sunlight. Quinn smelled like cinnamon, Daniel realized: cinnamon and ripe apples, like wonderful autumn things. Daniel lifted his hands to Quinn's waist and then circled his arms around Quinn's back, luxuriating in the feel of the firm muscle and the strong ladder of his spine. He nudged his tongue into Quinn's open mouth and heard Quinn's contented sigh just before he felt the slide of Quinn's tongue against his own.

Paul's mouth had always been appropriately minty when they'd kissed, but Quinn's mouth tasted like sweetened milk, and Daniel knew instantly which he preferred. He moaned against Quinn's lips, bucking involuntarily. They were both hard, and Daniel's cock brushed Quinn's when he moved, sending a thrill of pleasure through him.

"Yes. Again," Quinn murmured delightedly and then purposely ground against him, making Daniel gasp and shudder.

"Wait, wait," Daniel panted, reluctantly pulling away. If Quinn kept this up, he was going to come in his pajama pants, and Daniel didn't want this dream to end that soon. He quickly lifted his hips and slid his pajamas down, hissing as the cloth moved over his groin. "Let me get this off."

Quinn gave him another of his blinding grins, then grabbed the cuffs and yanked his pajama pants the rest of the way off, pulling Daniel onto his back in the process. Quinn laughed at his surprised yelp, but was kissing him before Daniel could respond.

Quinn let Daniel roll them both until they were lying on their sides, facing each other, but Quinn kept his kissing at the same slow, gentle pace. He started thrusting against Daniel, angled perfectly so that their cocks met and rubbed deliciously, but he refused to go faster, no matter how Daniel tried to move in his growing need. Daniel's left arm was neatly trapped by Quinn's body, but he ran his free hand down Quinn's back and started kneading the curve of his ass. Quinn made some kind of happy, murmuring noise and returned the favor, effectively holding Daniel in place as they rocked together at the unhurried tempo he'd set, as if they had all the time in the world.

Daniel felt his orgasm rising like a slow tide, completely at Quinn's mercy, until all at once he was coming. He moved his head and panted against Quinn's neck, the scents of cinnamon and sex filling his senses as he rode out the wave. Quinn's lips reclaimed his, kissing him, wide-mouthed and sloppy, until Quinn shuddered and Daniel felt new wetness over his hip.

They lay together afterwards, Quinn rubbing Daniel's back. Daniel had his eyes closed, wondering vaguely how he could feel sleepy if he was already sleeping, but not willing to question it in case it made him wake up. "God, that was a fantastic dream," he muttered, and heard Quinn's musical laughter.

"Go back to sleep then, and maybe you'll have another," Quinn whispered. Daniel felt Quinn moving away and made a tiny whine of protest, but his arms felt too heavy to lift, his eyelids too weighted to open.

"Don't go," he pleaded.

He felt the briefest touch of soft, warm lips against his temple. He wasn't sure, but he thought he heard Quinn say "I'm not going anywhere" before he slid out of the dream and into sleep.

DANIEL grinned all the way through his morning routine, through breakfast, through feeding his demanding felines, and even through changing their litter box.

He was still grinning when he sat down at his computer, feeling relaxed and invigorated for the first time since he and Paul had broken up. In fact, he realized as he sparked up his red laptop, he actually felt *inspired.* Cracking his knuckles, Daniel pulled up his file and began to write.

Six hours later, his bare feet were ice-cold and his stomach was growling. Tearing himself away from the keyboard, Daniel nearly ran to the kitchen and threw some form of sustenance down his throat, ignoring the cats as they circled his legs in search of milk.

"Go away," Daniel said as he pushed Huey out of the way with the side of his foot. The bowl of milk he'd left for them last night at Louie's request was now empty, so Daniel didn't feel at all bad denying them yet another helping. He did fill up their food bowl, though, just because. Eating his haphazard lunch had given him another idea on how to start the next scene, and he didn't want to lose it.

Even the return of the strange rustling sound from behind his head didn't break his concentration.

It was dark by the time he looked up again, his stomach growling over another missed meal. Daniel checked the computer's clock and was surprised to realize how late it actually was.

"Damn!' he exclaimed with a wide smile, and immediately checked his word count. He'd written over 10,000 words in one sitting, and he hadn't even broken a sweat.

Daniel meandered into the kitchen and grabbed something else to eat, idly wondering if he should pack it in for the night. *Pack it in!* Daniel thought, chewing on the hunk of cheese he had scooped out of the refrigerator, and suddenly he knew how to begin the next chapter, *and* he had solved the plotting dilemma he'd accidentally created for himself at the end of book two.

Stuffing the cheese into his mouth, he jogged back to his computer desk and started typing before he even sat down, laughing at how easily his book was progressing. At this rate, he'd have it done well before the new deadline.

It was two a.m. by the time he looked up again.

"Damn!" Daniel repeated, blinking to relieve the eyestrain from nearly eighteen hours of typing, and he was hungry—again—but he was still smiling, nearly giddy with both exhaustion and what he had accomplished. "Time for bed," he said with a yawn and stretched his arms over his head, feeling his spine *pop* with the movement.

He stood, weaving a bit from the sudden change in posture after sitting for so many hours, and wandered into the kitchen, idly scratching his stomach as he went.

Something flickered copper and gold out of the corner of his eye and Daniel shook his head. His eyestrain must be worse than he thought.

The cats all seemed to be somewhere else at this early hour of the morning, so Daniel was blissfully alone. He rummaged through the fridge, looking for something to take the edge off his hunger before bed. He made himself a sandwich and ate it over the sink, then pulled out the carton of milk, smiling to himself as he did. Normally Daniel wasn't that into milk, and he disliked warm milk most of all, but his dream lover's mouth had tasted like milk mixed with honey, and now Daniel had a craving. Besides, he thought, warm milk was meant to make you sleepy, and if going to bed meant he could have a repeat of last night and more time with "Quinn," he wouldn't mind feeling sleepy at all.

He poured himself a cup, elbowed open the microwave, and put it in, shutting the door solidly behind him. Daniel looked at the buttons for a moment, trying to decide if he should nuke the milk for longer than a minute, when he thought he saw something fluttering inside.

Daniel blinked, looking closer and wondering if one of the stupid cats had managed to jump inside when he wasn't looking. The glass in the door of the microwave distorted his view of the interior, but Daniel could just make out something fluttering around his cup with gold and copper wings.

“Oh my God, it’s a bird!” Daniel exclaimed. One of the fucking cats must have caught something and brought it inside. The poor thing was most likely wounded and probably frightened half to death. Thank God he hadn’t started up the microwave already. That would have been a disaster. Daniel popped open the door immediately.

There was a doll-sized man in the microwave, standing behind the cup. His hands were held up to his mouth, milk dripping from his chin. His tiny eyes were round with shock, his butterfly wings trembling in agitation.

Daniel slammed the door shut, feeling his own eyes widen to astronomical proportions. He stumbled backward, banging against the island in the middle of his kitchen. His head smacked against a pan suspended from the rack hanging from the ceiling, making the rest of them clang together loudly.

“Ow,” Daniel said distractedly, gaze still firmly fixed on the microwave. From this distance he couldn’t tell if anything was moving behind the glass, but he knew what he had seen.

Or thought you saw, his brain corrected helpfully. *It wasn’t real. You’re just tired.*

“I’m just tired,” Daniel repeated out loud. He took a step toward the microwave. “I just need to open it again and I’ll see that it’s really empty. And then I’ll go to bed.” Wincing, he opened the door.

The microwave held nothing but the cup of milk.

“Oh, thank God,” Daniel breathed, incredibly relieved that he wasn’t losing his mind after all. He picked up the cup of milk and put it directly into the fridge. There was no question of his drinking it now.

“Bed,” he repeated, and headed upstairs.

He brushed his teeth and threw on his pajama pants, nearly diving into his bed like a child afraid of the monsters supposedly hiding underneath. Daniel pulled the coverlet up to his chin and closed his eyes, banishing all thoughts of butterfly-winged, doll-sized men out of his mind. “I just need sleep,” he said, forcing himself to relax.

Dewey mewled at him.

"Shut up," Daniel said and rolled over.

Dewey mewled at him again, and then Louie jumped on the bed and stepped on his side with all her substantial kitty weight.

Daniel grimaced. "Get off!" He shoved at her, and Louie dug her claws into his side and yowled.

"Fuck!" Daniel swore and rolled onto his back to dislodge her. Louie narrowed her yellow eyes at him and yowled again, sticking her nose directly into his face. "Jesus, Louie! Get off!" Daniel yelled and pushed her away. And that was exactly when Huey launched herself out of nowhere and landed squarely on his stomach. Daniel was out of bed in an instant.

"Okay, okay!" he said to the three cats, "I get it! You don't have to kill me!" Rubbing his stomach, he stomped downstairs, cursing the cats with every step. So they hadn't had their hit of milk today—it wasn't worth *this* kind of punishment.

Daniel went into the kitchen, nearly tripping over Dewey, who had placed herself between his feet, meowing loudly with every step. "Damn it!" he shouted, "I'm getting you your fucking milk! Okay?" He yanked the door of the fridge open.

The doll-sized man with the big butterfly wings was lying on his side on one of the shelves, tiny arms wrapped around his tiny legs and his wings curled around him. Minute vibrations were running through him, making his wings shake. His eyes were closed and he looked half-dead. His skin was tinged an unhealthy blue.

"Jesus Christ!" Daniel cried. He could feel the adrenaline rocketing through his system, screaming at his brain to *shut the fridge door and run!* And for a second Daniel nearly did.

But the man—or whatever it was—was in a bad way, too weak from the cold to be any kind of threat. No matter what this thing was, Daniel knew that if he closed the door it would die, and Daniel would have killed it.

Before he even finished the thought, Daniel reached in and scooped the little creature out, cupping it gently in both his hands. Its skin was cold to the touch, its wings fluttering feebly against the palms of his hands. It felt light, nearly insubstantial, as if its soul might already have left its teeny body, and Daniel felt a wave of remorse so strong that a lump formed in his throat.

"Please don't die," he breathed as he cupped the creature closer, holding it against his bare chest. It was almost exactly what he had done nearly a year ago when he'd found Huey, Dewey, and Louie as tiny, freezing kittens in a dark and cold Tim Hortons parking lot.

"Don't die!" Daniel repeated, slamming the fridge shut with his knee and bolting for the stairs. He needed to warm the little guy up, and as fast as possible.

Daniel went straight to his bed and climbed in, holding the creature gently but firmly against his skin. He tucked the coverlet around them both, putting it over his head for good measure. He couldn't see, but he could feel the little guy lying on his chest, a cold, slight weight over his heart. If he concentrated, Daniel could feel the continual flutter of those incredible wings, and he took it as a sign that the man might still be alive, even though he hadn't moved at all.

Daniel closed his eyes, focusing on the feel of the creature under his hand, and prayed for its survival.

THE sunlight streaming through his bedroom window woke him.

Daniel yawned, blinking in the harsh daylight. He wasn't sure what had woken him, but he'd been having a really wild dream about a tiny man with wings....

"Oh, my God!" Daniel rocketed upright, frantically searching the sheets. He hadn't intended to fall asleep, and he didn't even remember closing his eyes, but the tiny, winged man wasn't on Daniel's chest anymore, and Daniel was terrified that he'd crushed the little creature in the night.

But there was no little, broken body where Daniel had been lying and nothing under his pillow. Daniel turned to search the other side of the bed.

There was a man there, smiling sleepily at him.

Daniel let out a yell and launched himself right out of the bed, landing heavily on his ass. He scrambled backward until he hit the wall, never taking his eyes off the stranger.

"Daniel?" The stranger was sitting up, blinking at him with big, surprised hazel eyes and pushing curls of myriad shades of red-brown off his forehead. "Daniel? Are you all right?"

Daniel had frozen in the midst of levering himself to his feet. His mouth was moving, but no sound came out.

"Daniel?" the man asked again. He shifted closer. "Daniel?"

Daniel blinked, looking at those wide eyes. Recognition trickled like a stream into the desert of his brain.

"*Quinn?*"

The man beamed. "Good morning."

"YOU'RE a fairy," Daniel said. It wasn't the first time. He put the mug of tea on the table, only slopping a little over the side because his hands were shaking.

"Yes," Quinn said simply. He took the tea with a warm smile, cradling the mug and breathing in the steam. "This smells wonderful."

Daniel smiled wanly and sat down across from him at the small kitchen table, after nudging Louie off the chair. He had to push Dewey aside so he could put his own mug down, but she just glared mildly and closed her eyes again. It was past eleven o'clock in the morning, but he was still wearing the pajama pants he'd fallen asleep in the night before while trying to warm up the fairy. Quinn was wearing a pair of Daniel's jogging pants, which hung low at his waist and were too short at the ankles. He didn't have any clothing; fairies didn't stay outside in winter. He had been in Daniel's house since the teapot had broken two days before, hanging out and sharing the cats' milk.

Daniel sipped his coffee, part of him still reeling at the situation. "And you hid in the teapot my mother gave me?"

"Yes." Quinn nodded, but his expression said that he was beginning to wonder about Daniel's intelligence. "My Old One—Aunt Elaine, I mean." He corrected himself with a bit of embarrassment. "Aunt Elaine was dying, and she told me to hide so that none of the Big Folk would find me. I didn't know the teapot was going to go away." He beamed. "But I really like where I am now."

Daniel twitched another smile at him. "You haven't seen very much of it."

"I know, but I'm really looking forward to it! I've never been in a city before." Quinn was still beaming, as if ending up as part of a carry-on item on an Air Canada flight was the best thing that had ever happened to him.

"Right," Daniel said. He rubbed the back of his neck and then took another sip of his coffee, mostly to buy himself some time. The initial panic Daniel had felt in his bedroom had subsided, but his heart was still thumping double time. Part of him—far too big a part—was ecstatic at finding out that the spectacular lover of his dreams was *real*, even if "real" meant that he was a fairy who could make himself no bigger than Daniel's hand. And grow wings… beautiful copper and gold butterfly wings that allowed him to fly.

Daniel had stopped believing in fairy tales a long time ago, and now he had one sitting across from him, drinking stale chamomile tea. "I don't know if there are any fairies in Toronto." There might be, Daniel suddenly realized. Hell, until an hour ago Daniel hadn't known there were any fairies in the world at all. Maybe the city was full of them.

"We can find them," Quinn said. He sounded extremely unconcerned. Daniel was sure he had completely failed to grasp how dire this situation was. Quinn stretched, showing the strength in the smooth muscles of his bare arms and chest. "But even if we don't, I still have you."

"Yeah," Daniel said. He tried to ignore the thrill of joy that Quinn's words ignited in him, but he couldn't help grinning back, feeling himself light up at the naked affection in Quinn's eyes. He dragged himself back to the dilemma with an effort. "But this isn't your home—you should be in England! I need to figure out a way to get you back."

He couldn't ignore how little he wanted to do that. Quinn had been in Daniel's life for barely forty-eight hours, but already Daniel was having a hard time imagining life without him, without that gorgeous face and sweet smile, or the way Quinn took genuine and uncomplicated pleasure in everything, from the tea he was drinking to petting Huey, who had decided to claim his lap. Daniel thought of the way those same gentle, long-fingered hands had moved so confidently over his body that night….

He squirmed in his chair, hoping Quinn wouldn't notice the evidence of where Daniel's thoughts had gone. But Quinn was just petting Huey, his eyes on the table. Daniel realized he suddenly looked sad.

"I don't want to leave," Quinn said. He looked up at Daniel again. "I like it here. I want to stay with you."

Daniel blinked, then had to clamp his jaw shut so he wouldn't blurt out how Quinn didn't have to leave, how much he wanted Quinn to stay with him as well, because that wasn't fair to him. Quinn was a *fairy*. He didn't belong in Canada, no matter how much Daniel might want him to stay. Daniel swallowed. "I don't think—"

Quinn shook his head, his face suddenly adamant. "No, you don't understand—I *can't* leave! Not until I've given you your wish!"

That entirely derailed what Daniel had been going to say. "What?"

"Your wish!" Quinn repeated, all smiles again. "You saved me from the winter box—anyone who saves a fairy's life gets a wish!"

"I do?" Daniel asked. This was completely unexpected. "You mean, like, anything I want?"

Quinn nodded solemnly. "Yes. Anything you want."

"Wow." Daniel blinked. The potential was staggering. "What should—"

Quinn slapped his palm over Daniel's mouth. It smelled like cinnamon and apples. "No!" He shook his head again, eyes enormous. "The wish has to come from *you!* You mustn't be influenced!"

Daniel stared at him until Quinn pulled his hand back. "Okay..." he said slowly, his eyes on Quinn's still-anxious face. "Can I ask for world peace or something? Because I want—"

"No!" Quinn covered Daniel's mouth again. "Don't do it yet!"

Daniel raised his eyebrows.

Quinn moved his hand again, looking embarrassed. "Sorry. But a wish is precious. You need to think about it, decide what you really want."

I really want you, Daniel thought, but that was selfish. And now Daniel was remembering the fairy tales he'd been read as a child, stories that might well have been true. They always said to be careful what you wished for.

"All right," he said, nodding. "I promise I'll think about it."

Quinn's delighted smile made Daniel want to kiss him. "So I'll stay until you decide!"

"Yeah," Daniel said, smiling back. He hated how happy that made him. "You can stay until I decide." He looked at Quinn, and his long, graceful, nearly naked body. "But first, we need to find you some clothes."

IT HAD been the most incredible week of Daniel's life.

Daniel smiled to himself as he walked along the sidewalk to the local Starbucks and thought about Quinn. He didn't know what stroke of luck had brought the fairy to his house, but he sure didn't want it to end. Not only was Quinn incredibly good-looking—hell, Daniel thought with a grin, the boy was *gorgeous*—but he was also clever and kind and interesting to talk to. Quinn took joy in everyday things. And the sex! Daniel shook his head incredulously as he walked, feeling his grin grow even broader. Never in his wildest dreams had he ever thought he'd have sex this good on such a consistent basis.

Daniel stopped at the corner to cross the street, and as he looked down, he saw the unmistakable purple color of a ten-dollar bill lying half-hidden in the snow. He bent and picked it up, not even surprised at his find. That was another thing about having a fairy in the house—an unending supply of good luck.

In fact, Daniel's luck had definitely been on the upswing ever since Quinn had arrived. First his mother had called to tell him that she'd been invited on a cruise over the holidays and therefore he wouldn't be able to spend Christmas with her. Daniel had tried not to sound too delighted when he told her not to worry, and that they'd catch up when she got back. Then it had been his agent calling, saying that his publisher had reverted back to the original deadline for his third book, since no one would be working over the holidays anyway. After that, it had been a series of small, yet terrific things. He'd found a watch he'd thought he'd lost forever; one of his best friends from university contacted him on Facebook after nearly ten years of being out of touch; there was a sale on his favorite shampoo at the drugstore. Finding a ten-dollar bill on his way to Starbucks, therefore, was starting to feel almost normal.

And he'd been writing like crazy. At this rate his book would be finished in less than a month.

Daniel was still beaming as he held the door of Starbucks open for an elderly woman. The past week had also been his most productive since his creative writing classes in university. He and Quinn had gotten into a routine of sorts, where Daniel would leave for the library sometime after amazing morning sex, and then write his brains out for about eight hours, before coming home via Starbucks to a sparkling clean house and Quinn, who sparkled even more with an apparently unending supply of happiness.

It was a relationship better than Daniel had ever hoped for, he realized as he collected his drinks from the barista, went out the door, and headed for home. Quinn was everything he'd ever wanted in a boyfriend: bright, funny, and full of joy. *And when my mom gets home,* Daniel thought as he took a sip of his caramel mocha, *I might even take Quinn to meet her.*

He stopped dead in his tracks, reusable coffee mug halted halfway to his lips.

Take Quinn to meet his mother? What the hell was he thinking?

Reality hit Daniel like a brick. Quinn was a *fairy,* for Christ's sake! He'd come to Daniel's house *hidden in a teapot!* How the hell could he introduce a fairy to his *mother?*

Daniel started walking again, but significantly slower than before. Quinn was a fairy. A magical being who belonged in the forests and glens of England, not trapped in some semi-detached house in Toronto, thousands of miles away.

It felt like the caramel mocha was curdling in Daniel's stomach.

Quinn was trapped in his house. *Trapped in his house!* Why hadn't Daniel noticed it before? Why hadn't he even thought about it?

The only reason Quinn was in Daniel's house, cooking and cleaning and making Daniel lucky and having sex, was because Daniel was taking his own sweet time coming up with a wish. And the only reason Daniel had even been granted a wish was because he'd taken Quinn out of the refrigerator after accidentally sticking him in there in the first place.

Daniel had enslaved Quinn through his indecision as surely as if he'd put chains on those well-shaped ankles himself. He was exactly as selfish as Paul had said he was. Daniel had just been too stupid to even realize it.

And Quinn—smiling, loving, caring Quinn—had let him do it.

Daniel thought he was going to throw up.

In seconds, he knew what he was going to do. Turning abruptly, he emptied both cups onto the sidewalk and headed back up the street. Quinn's accidental enslavement was going to end today.

Even if it broke Daniel's heart.

DANIEL raced back home. This was going to be the hardest thing he'd ever done in his life, but he knew he had to do it. He had to make things right; for his own self-respect, and most importantly, for Quinn. Slavery was wrong. Even accidental slavery, where you didn't even know what you were doing to the other person. Daniel had finally gotten a clue and now he had no more excuses.

He ran into the house, leaving his coat on and ignoring how his boots left drops of melting snow on the clean wooden floor.

Quinn turned to him from where he'd been doing something in the kitchen, all bright smiles and wonderfully messy autumn-colored hair.

"Daniel!" he exclaimed, taking a step toward him. "You're home!"

"Yeah, I am," Daniel said lamely. He took a step back when Quinn tried to embrace him. He wasn't going to force Quinn to do that anymore.

Quinn looked at him, those perceptive, multihued eyes widening in concern. "Is everything all right?"

"Yeah, sure," Daniel said. He rubbed his face. "No, no, it's not. Look," he said, opening the bag he had with him and pulling out a small Canada Post box and a yellow mini box cutter. "You can't stay here. I finally figured it out, and I'm *really* sorry, but you can't stay. Not anymore. Hell, I'm sorry you had to stay this long."

Quinn was still looking at him, his handsome face drawn in lines of concern. "What?"

"I bought you a box!" Daniel said, hearing the note of desperation in his own voice. "I thought you could hide in it, and I'd mail you back to England, okay? You'd be there in four days. Five days, tops." He held out the box in front of him. "See?"

Quinn blinked. "You want me to go home?" He looked dejected, as if Daniel had just said something terrible.

"Well, yeah," Daniel said. He licked his lips. "I mean, I finally figured it out. It's wrong for you to be here. It's *wrong,* and you should go home." Quinn's heartbroken look didn't change, and Daniel felt like there was a knife twisting in his chest. "We could put granola bars in it, for your trip!" Daniel said hurriedly. "You like those, right?" He held out the small blade. "You wouldn't be trapped in there. I bought you an Exacto knife for when you arrive."

"Oh," Quinn said, dropping his gaze. He ran one long-fingered hand through his thick curls. "If that's what you want."

No! Daniel wanted to shout. Quinn leaving was the last thing in the world that he wanted, but it had to be done. "I want—I want you to go," Daniel said, feeling like the words were choking him. "I want you to go home."

Quinn looked up at him again, confusion and sadness apparent in the deep hazel of his eyes. "But what about your wish?" He paused, blinking, and Daniel could almost swear Quinn's eyes were wet. "Is *this* what you wish? For me to go home?"

"No!" Daniel said too quickly. He could feel his heart skittering around in his chest. He knew he should have said "yes", that would have been the easiest way to solve this, but he couldn't say it. He didn't wish for Quinn to leave; there was nothing he wanted less than that. "No," Daniel repeated more slowly, "no. Don't—don't worry about my wish." He put his hand on Quinn's forearm, wanting so badly to pull the other man into his arms and pretend this whole horrible conversation had never happened. "You've been, well, amazing. I don't need anything else."

"Okay," Quinn said again. He swallowed. "I suppose… I suppose I'll go?"

"It doesn't have to be right away!" Daniel said. "I mean, we could have dinner together, or something? I could post the box first thing tomorrow…."

Quinn was shaking his head. "No, Daniel," he said softly. "I think it would be best if I left now." With slow grace Quinn walked to the door and put on his boots. The three cats had appeared from the living room and were now meowing pitifully; Quinn bent and gave each one a fond pet farewell. Quinn then put on Daniel's old coat and wrapped his scarf around his neck. He turned to Daniel, and his eyes were definitely bright with tears. "Good-bye, Daniel," he said as he opened the door. A gust of freezing air blew into the foyer, and Daniel shivered.

"Wait!" Daniel cried, horrified at the idea of Quinn going out alone into the cold night. "What about the box?"

Quinn smiled, but it didn't reach his eyes. "I'll make my own way," he said. And then he was gone.

"Good-bye," Daniel whispered to the closed door. It felt like his heart had frozen as surely as the ground outside.

DANIEL'S life pretty much went to hell the second Quinn left.

Well, it wasn't so much that his life went to hell, exactly, as it was that Daniel constantly felt like hell and couldn't seem to do anything about it. He couldn't sleep at night, and then he couldn't get out of bed in the morning. Shaving seemed a waste of time, just like eating. If he went to the kitchen, he was reminded of Quinn standing there, eyes shining and face bright with happiness as he exclaimed delightedly about the breakfast cereal Daniel had bought or the way butter melted on toast. Everything Daniel bothered to make to eat just tasted like cardboard anyway. The idea of drinking milk made him want to throw up, so the cats got it all. Plus all the tuna fish and the sandwich meat left in the refrigerator. Daniel felt miserable, but at least the cats were happy.

His agent, however, was not. After making such a great start on the new novel, Daniel's inspiration had dried up again as suddenly as it had come. Working on his laptop was as difficult and painful as it ever had been. His agent tried everything, from screaming to cajoling to outright bribery, but Daniel wasn't touched by any of it. When she finally suggested psychiatric medication, Daniel hung up on her. She took the hint and left him alone.

It was even worse than when Paul had left. At least then Daniel could still sleep, and eat, and take a shower. Now, it was like he'd been scraped empty inside, every scrap of inspiration and happiness taken out of him when Quinn had walked through the door.

And to make it worse, he still saw the flap of little copper-and-gold wings out of the corner of his eye. He was so miserable that his mind was playing tricks on him.

"Fuck it," Daniel muttered and got up from the computer desk where he'd been sitting and staring at the empty white facsimile of a page for the last two hours. He was still wearing his pajama pants and a ratty T-shirt that probably could use a wash, but hell, it was winter and no one would see it under his coat.

He had to get out of the house and away from the ghost of Quinn or he really was going to go as crazy as his agent already thought he was.

Daniel threw on his boots and jacket, jamming a hat on his head more to hide his greasy hair than for warmth. He grabbed a couple of bucks from his wallet and headed out. It was mid-December now, only a few days before Christmas, and the street was festooned with colorful lights and sparkling ribbons, turning the city into a bit of a winter wonderland. Daniel scowled. Sparkle made him think of Quinn.

He turned toward the Starbucks, hoping that a walk and a coffee might alleviate his mood. It hadn't helped the last two times he'd tried it that week, but today might be the first, if he was lucky.

But he wasn't lucky, not anymore. Not since Quinn had left.

"Hello!" a woman said as she passed by him. She stopped walking to smile. "How are you, Mr. Tibbits?"

Daniel stopped and looked at her. She was short, with long brown hair cut squarely across her eyebrows. Her glasses were large and partially hid her brown eyes. She looked a bit mousy, and Daniel didn't recognize her, but she was beaming at him as if they were old friends.

"I'm sorry, do I know you?" Daniel asked.

"Oh, no, you don't know me," she said, and blushed. "Not really. I've seen you around, of course, but…."

Daniel tried not to glower. "And?"

"Well, it's just that Quinn talks about you so much!" the woman said with a small laugh. "And you look exactly like he said you did.

Well, a bit less, ah...." She let her voice trail off, her expression one of complete embarrassment.

"Scruffy?" Daniel finished for her, because he knew it was true. He flicked a smile at her. "I haven't shaved."

"Oh," she said again. "Well, anyway, it's nice to finally meet you, Mr. Tibbits! I'm Alice Mackey, director of Sunlight Place, down the street." She put out her hand. "Quinn speaks very highly of you."

"Sunlight Place?" Daniel repeated, shaking her hand automatically. "You mean the nursing home?"

"Yes," Alice said, nodding brightly. "Quinn's been volunteering with us, and I must say, he's just fantastic with our residents! He calls them 'Old Ones'. Isn't that cute?"

"Wait," Daniel said, blinking. "Quinn is volunteering with you *now?* You mean he's still *here*?"

"Why, yes," Alice said. There was obvious confusion on her face. "He's been with us for about two weeks now. Did you think he'd gone somewhere?"

"Uh, no. No, of course not," Daniel said, but his mind was racing. He'd sent Quinn home two weeks ago, offering him an all-expense-paid trip with Canada Post back to the UK. But if Quinn was still volunteering at a nursing home, and still in Toronto, then clearly he hadn't gone anywhere at all. But why wouldn't he take the opportunity to return home?

Daniel felt his heart speed up. Did that mean Quinn really hadn't *wanted* to go home? Did he actually want to stay here?

"Uh, sorry, I've got to go," Daniel said, interrupting Alice in mid-sentence. He turned and bolted for home without waiting for her reply, boots skidding over the snow.

"QUINN!" Daniel bellowed as soon as he entered the house. "*Quinn!*"

There was no answer.

Daniel dropped his coat on the floor and ran into the middle of the living room, his boots dripping everywhere. Everything looked exactly the way he had left it: the empty coffee cup by his computer; the pile of unopened mail and unwanted solicitations left by the phone. Even the socks he'd taken off and dropped by the stairs two days before were still there in a crumpled black heap, untouched by anything but the cats.

But suddenly, it all was different. He could *tell*.

"Quinn!" Daniel shouted again. "Show yourself! Damn it—*I know you're here!*"

A shiver of copper-and-gold flashed by the corner of Daniel's eye, and suddenly Quinn was standing in front of him, human-sized, every inch of him—from his wonderfully tousled hair to the tips of his long toes. He was gorgeous and glorious and completely naked, a fact that Daniel couldn't help but notice even as he forced himself to look at Quinn's face and ignore the leanly muscled body standing a mere hand's span away.

Quinn looked very angry. "What do you want?" he demanded, arms crossed and beautiful mouth scowling.

You. Daniel swallowed. "Why are you still here?"

"Because it's winter," Quinn said as if Daniel were three kinds of idiot. "Fairies don't live outside in winter."

"No," Daniel said, shaking his head. "Why are you *here?* In Toronto? I thought you were heading back to the UK!"

Quinn glared at him. "That was *your* plan, Daniel. Not mine. I wanted to stay."

It felt like all the breath had left Daniel's lungs. "What?"

"I wanted to stay," Quinn repeated. "I told you I was happy here."

"But you'd only been here for like, *fifteen minutes!*" Daniel said. "How would you know if you were happy?"

Quinn looked at him like he really was stupid this time. "Because I know," he said. He tilted his head. "Don't you know when you're happy?"

Daniel blinked. He'd never thought about it before. "You make me happy," he blurted.

Quinn smiled but then frowned almost immediately. "Then why did you send me away?"

"*Because I'd trapped you here!*" Daniel shouted. "With that fucking wish! You were cooking and cleaning and keeping house like some glorified housekeeper, just waiting for me to make up my fucking mind!" He grabbed Quinn's forearms, trying to make him understand. "I made you my slave, Quinn! And I didn't want to do that anymore. I didn't want to do that to you!"

Quinn looked at him. "I wasn't your slave."

"Yes, you were!" Daniel insisted. "You were cleaning and—and *everything!*" And of course, the "everything" meant the incredible, wonderful, amazing sex that Quinn may or may not have actually wanted. "And you didn't have a choice! If that's not slavery, what is?"

"I wasn't your slave," Quinn repeated.

"But—" Daniel started, getting ready to explain again, but Quinn shook his head.

"No, Daniel, you don't understand. I'm a *fairy. We cannot be enslaved.*"

Daniel blinked again. "What?"

"Magical beings can't be enslaved," Quinn said slowly as if Daniel was even stupider than he'd first thought. "I stayed here because I wanted to. And I cooked and cleaned because it made me happy."

"Cooking and cleaning for me made you happy?" Daniel asked. He could feel his heart start to bang, stumbling into a hopeful rhythm.

"And the sex!" Quinn said with great enthusiasm. "I really liked the sex too!"

Daniel started to laugh. "So you *chose* to stay here?" he asked. "And it wasn't because you were waiting on my wish?"

"Of course not!" Quinn said as if it were obvious. "I could have been anywhere while you were making up your mind. Like the nursing home. There're lots of warm places for a fairy to wait. Did you know that Old Ones like to keep their rooms very warm?"

"Oh my God, Quinn!" Daniel said, pulling the other man into his arms. "I missed you so much!"

"I missed you too," Quinn said, hugging him back just as fiercely. "Please don't send me away again."

"I won't," Daniel said, "I promise." He was so happy he didn't know if he should laugh or cry. “You can stay as long as you want.”

“Wish it,” Quinn whispered, and the longing in his voice was palpable. “Please, make that wish. For me.”

“I wish you’d stay as long as you want,” Daniel said immediately.

“Thank you,” Quinn said, and kissed him.

And as Quinn led Daniel upstairs to Daniel’s—no, *their*—bedroom, Daniel decided he would introduce Quinn to his mother after all.

CORINNA SILVER has been writing short fiction for the amusement of herself and others since 2002. When not pounding away at a computer at her day job, she enjoys hanging with her husband and children and talking to Aundrea Singer on the phone, wishing they lived in the same city.

AUNDREA SINGER was born in Canada and has been an avid fan of sci-fi and fantasy since her mother read Lloyd Alexander and Madeleine L'Engle to her at a terribly impressionable age. Despite this, she was well into adulthood before giving up her aspirations to normalcy and embracing her geekatude—whereupon she naturally fell in love with an engineer and moved to Texas. She started telling stories before she could write and will always be enthralled with how words can be used to create entire universes. She is grateful to her husband that she is now able to write full time.

Aundrea still lives in Texas with her much-beloved husband, three cats of varying levels of insanity, and the most wonderful little boy in the entire world. Her penname is a small homage to her parents, her heritage, and her husband, as well as a salute to the gaming buddies she left behind.

Aundrea blogs as taste_is_sweet on livejournal.com, and you can contact her at aundrea.singer@gmail.com. She loves getting email.

Kissing the Dragon

Heidi Cullinan

EVERY night when Bao Fischer closed his eyes, the dragon came.

He would fall asleep and drift off into a thick, white nothingness, his body so heavy that he simply stepped out of it, and then out of the mist came the dragon. It had no wings, but in the dream this made it seem *more* like a dragon. Its eyes were wild and bright and slitted like a reptile's, and it had a great broad lump on the top of its head between its ears—ears that, in fact, looked a bit like those on a cow. It had horns like a stag and claws like a bird, though when it lifted its feet, Bao saw it had pads there, like a cat. It was covered head to tail in fishlike scales, except for its belly, which had a hard, impenetrable shell. And at its chin was a long, string-like beard that swayed with the dragon's movements.

Every night the dragon would lumber out of the mist, slithering and sliding its great length across the empty landscape, and every night it stared at Bao, its demon-eyes burning hot and yellow as it waited. But that was all that ever happened. It just came, and it stared, and after what felt like an eternity had passed, the dragon would shake its head, turn, and walk back into the mist again, and Bao would wake, not knowing who he was except that he had one mother of a headache.

Today, as the thin morning light cut through the blinds on his bedroom window, Bao lay once again staring up at the ceiling, waiting for his headache to abate and his memory to return. The memory loss had upset him the first few times, but he was used to it now. Actually, in a way, it was nice. For those few minutes he wasn't anyone at all, just a man in a bed, his head pounding. He usually tried to use the time to reflect on the dream and try to make some sense of it, and he did so now once again. This dream had been different—subtly so. Bao lay still awhile, trying to suss it out. He shut his eyes and played it all over again in his head, like rewinding a movie. The mist came, the dragon came out of it, and it stared at him, and it held out the white orb—

His eyes came open. *There*. That part had been new. But he had no idea what an orb had to do with anything. A yellow-white, opaque orb, like a pearl.

And as if some timer had gone off, the forgetful-dream state vanished, sluicing away like water off his consciousness. In its place came memory.

And depression.

Bao. Bao-Bo Fischer. His memory returned, and with it the flotsam his identity dragged along. Bao, junior communications coordinator at Lampton Insurance Company. Bao, who owned a condo just outside downtown St. Louis, a condo whose value had dropped by almost a quarter since he bought it—thank you very much, recession. Bao, whose practical little Mazda needed a new timing belt.

Bao-Bo Fischer, who hadn't gotten laid in almost a year.

Snorting in derision, Bao gave himself the finger as he passed the mirror.

But his own image reflected there lingered in his mind as he entered the shower; and as it had every night since the dreams had started, that image upset him. He felt like he was thirteen again, when his body had become his enemy and cooked up daily cocktails of acne and hormonal impulses that were bad enough for any male, but to have to be a gay *Asian* had been the last straw as far as Bao was concerned. He felt that way now, once again too conscious of his identity.

That awareness colored not just his perception of himself but his impression of others, making him acutely conscious of every glance and quirk of lips, every nuance of word and expression, making him feel judged and alien, even more than usual. As he hurried down the stairs of his condo he saw the pretty blonde woman from 2B; logic told him a smile was just a smile, but his dream-colored eyes insisted she was looking down on him, judging him, discarding him because he was not white. When he stopped at the convenience store to get gas and had to go inside to pick up windshield-wiper fluid, too, he tried to tell himself the clerk only *seemed* to speak loudly and slowly to him, doing that bizarre thing people did sometimes to foreigners, as if English being their second language made them stupid. He told himself that he was just paranoid, but every morning the sense of being different returned, and if anything, it was getting worse.

The irony was that, outside of his genetic makeup, Bao was one hundred percent American. Technically, he was Korean, yes, but he'd been adopted—at *birth.* He had been raised by white people in a town full of white people. But that didn't matter, not to the people who looked at him and judged, and it had always been that way because he *looked* Asian. It didn't matter that his only advantage over his peers was that he could probably find Korea on a map. It didn't matter that he knew more Illinois and Missouri history than Korean. When he was a kid, instead of the traditional A-B-Cs of the Phoenician alphabet, his parents had painted Korean characters on the walls of his bedroom and filled his shelves with books about his native country. As soon as he'd figured out what they were, Bao had made them paint over the characters and he'd given the books to the library. Bao didn't *want* to be different. He didn't feel different, except when he looked in a mirror or when other people treated him as if he were foreign. Bao hated his "heritage," and he wanted to put it firmly behind him.

The dragon dreams, though, were screwing with his head. He may have avoided his native culture, but he knew enough to know it was an Asian dragon that was haunting him. He'd looked it up, and he knew that it was supposed to be some sort of guardian spirit, but if it was guarding him, it was lousy at it, and it had poor communication skills to boot.

Ruminating over the dreams and the chaos they caused inside him did no more good this morning than they had any other, and Bao pushed them firmly aside as he pulled into the parking garage for his building. The last thing he needed was to have stupid Asian dragons dragging him down at work. And as he got into the elevator and realized what day it was, he smiled, forgetting about dragons and dreams entirely.

It was Tuesday. Which meant Hottie would be working at the Starbucks counter in the lobby.

It was probably stupid to have a crush on a barista. Maybe not stupid to have a *crush,* but very likely Bao shouldn't look forward to seeing him like he did. A twenty-seven-year-old man should be above such things, and an Asian loser-boy *really* should know better, because this guy was completely perfect. He was, essentially, everything Bao had ever wanted to be, with some bonus features thrown in to make him absolutely enthralling. He was white, and he was tall. He was muscular, but not too much so. He had—God, Bao loved this part—*red hair.* Not bright, but just a hint. Enough to be completely exotic to Bao. The hair looked absolutely stunning with Hottie's hazel eyes.

He had the best smile too. It made Bao's heart skip a beat every time it was aimed at him, and when he came around the corner, he found his pulse had already increased in anticipation. There Hottie was, tall and lithe and gleaming, the morning sun catching the back of his hair in a halo through the plate-glass window. He looked good enough to fucking eat. In a few drunken masturbation sessions, Bao had imagined doing exactly that: tasting every salty inch of Hottie Barista.

Bao didn't know the man's real name because, aggravatingly, the barista never wore his name tag. But whatever his name was, Hottie was there today, as Bao knew he would be, and he not only had a smile for Bao, but he had his drink ready and waiting for him too.

"Right on time," Hottie said, still beaming, still absolutely fucking gorgeous as he handed the cardboard cup to Bao. "*Grande* caramel macchiato, no foam, extra cream."

"Thanks." The word came out slightly breathless. Bao took a sip, and then gave the barista a thumbs up and a grin. "Perfect as usual."

In his fantasies it was always at this point when they would connect. The man would smile back at Bao, and the smile would go on a little too long, and Bao would realize that the barista was a little breathless too, that he had the caramel macchiato ready not because Bao always left a dollar tip but because he was secretly in love with his 8:50 a.m. regular customer, that he was simply trying to find the courage to admit his attraction. In that moment, with them both smiling and the contact going on a little too long, Bao would know for sure, and he would pause long enough so it looked like the thought was just occurring to him, and he would ask what Hottie was doing that night around five-thirty, and would he like to go out for a cup of coffee that he hadn't had to make? Or maybe to dinner? Because there was this great pizza place just around the corner.

In Bao's fantasies, that was how it happened. But just as he did every day, once Bao had declared the drink perfect, the barista lowered his gaze and made a show of wiping up the counter that didn't need wiping. In short, telegraphing, *I am not interested in you beyond your cup of coffee and your generous tip. Go to work, Asian Boy.*

Feeling ridiculously let down, more so even than usual, Bao made a sad salute with his cup and stuffed his dollar into the tip cup. "Have a good day," he said, then went back to the elevator and to work, sipping his macchiato and wishing desperately that he were white.

BAO'S supervisor was waiting for him.

Jael Jorgensen was sitting on the edge of Bao's desk, his feet sticking out of the tiny cubicle and halfway across the narrow "hallway" that connected the cubicles of the communications department. When he saw Bao approaching, Jael pushed his lanky form off the desk and tucked his hands into his trouser pockets as he loomed over his underling. The gesture pushed the lapels of his jacket back, making him look like a magazine ad.

"Bao. I've been waiting for you. We need to talk about the new systems profile." Jael hooked his thumbs in his belt loops and tipped his head to the side. "You were supposed to have that done by now."

Bao set his teeth, but he didn't avert his eyes from Jael. "I've been working on it all week. I put in overtime."

"These are difficult times, Bao. We all have to work even harder than before." Jael unhooked his right hand from his belt loop to wave an admonishing finger at Bao. "I have my eye on you. Remember that as you're working."

Because there was nothing left to do, Bao nodded curtly and waited for Jael to leave so he could get to work. But Jael lingered a moment, studying Bao, or at least making a pretense of doing so. Too late Bao realized his supervisor was letting the small audience he'd gathered grow, which meant he was going to belittle Bao again. Jael really got a high off that sort of thing.

"You disappoint me, Bao," Jael said, his voice full of paternal empathy that might have worked if he'd meant it, or if he hadn't been three years younger than Bao. "I need people on my team that I can count on. Is there something going on in your personal life? Someone keeping you up a little too late at night?"

There were a few snickers from the cubicle behind him. Bao's orientation wasn't a secret, but it *was* the butt of many of his unenlightened colleagues' favorite jokes.

Bao pressed his teeth together so tightly that he risked shattering one of his crowns, then forced his jaw to unlock and his mouth to slide into a brittle smile. The new systems profile was a bitch, and Jael knew that. Of course, *he* didn't do any actual work on it, just yelled at everyone else, so why should he care what management wanted was impossible? All he cared about was getting another feather in his cap and taking another step toward senior staffing. Bao itched to point this out, to lash out at Jael, to tear him down the same way he was tearing down Bao. And in his mind, as his fury surged like an angry sea, he saw the dragon appear, orb in hand. *I could do it too,* Bao thought. *If I said something, I* would *best him. I'd win. I should say something. I should say something right now.*

But when Bao lifted his head and saw Jael gleaming, handsome and assured and perfect, the rage receded, and Bao lowered his eyes again. "I'll have it on your desk by the end of the day, Mr. Jorgensen."

"I hope so, for your sake." Jael shook his head again. "And here I thought Asians were supposed to be efficient." He clapped a hand briefly on Bao's shoulder, then sauntered back down the narrow hallway toward the posh comfort of his private office.

Bao stared at him, his teeth pressed tightly together again. It took him longer than he would have liked to calm down, too, because people were still whispering and sniggering behind him. God, but he hated them, hated them all, hated this job, hated this life—

A movement out of the corner of his eye interrupted his internal tirade, and when he turned to look at whatever it was, he stopped, all his impotent rage bleeding away as shock took over instead. Then he blinked, and looked again, but by then it was gone, of course, because nothing had been there.

But for one strange moment, he'd sworn he'd seen a scaly tail sliding into a cubicle.

BAO quickly lost himself in his work on the systems profile, forgetting not just the silly hallucination but also the humiliation at Jael's hand. It was hard work, and what Jael wanted *was* impossible, but it was the sort of thing Bao truly enjoyed working on. By two o'clock he thought he almost had it. He decided to go downstairs and get a second latte as a reward for his hard work.

To his delight, when he stepped out into the lobby he saw that Hottie was still working.

To his horror, he saw that Jael was waving a *venti* coffee cup in the barista's face and shouting at him.

"I told you *no more* than a quarter inch of foam. Are you *deaf* as well as stupid?"

"I'm sorry, sir." Hottie's ears were red, as were his freckle-spackled cheeks, and his eyes were downcast, fixed on the counter as he tried to slide away toward the espresso machine. "I'll make you another one right away."

"I *told you* already, I'm *late*. I don't have *time* for you to make me another one." He reached out and took rough hold of the barista's chin. "And you will *look* at me when I'm speaking to you!"

Bao didn't think; he just surged forward, heart hammering against his ribs and blood pounding in his ears. How *dare* Jael touch him? How *dare* he! He felt the angry tides rise inside him, and this time he didn't stop it, didn't even try, just stormed up to Jael, grabbed his arm—

—and felt his fury turn to foolishness as Jael turned his fire on Bao instead.

It was not that Bao had no spine. It wasn't because he was raised to be meek, either. His parents, actually, would be shocked to see how Bao deferred to his supervisor. The problem was that Jael was just so… perfect. So everything Bao wasn't. Blond hair that always behaved and adapted to whatever the latest style was. Blue eyes that pierced. A beautiful mouth, a perfect body: he was a walking Abercrombie & Fitch ad. And Bao couldn't seem to make himself see past it.

"What do *you* want?" he sneered, his benevolent but arrogant boss mask down.

Bao choked. "Your report," he said, hating that his voice was shaking a little, but he couldn't stop it. "It's almost ready."

"*Almost*?" Jael put his hands on his hips and gave Bao a withering look. "If it's *almost* done, why the fuck are you down here pissing around with coffee?"

Behind the counter the barista was still blushing hotly, but he was glaring at the back of Jael's head as he hurried through a second latte.

And as Bao watched, a dragon passed behind the counter, almost knocking over the "Starbucks Recommends" chalkboard.

Bao blinked, and then he stared. What? *What?* He blinked again, and again, but yes, there was a dragon there. It was about four feet high and twelve feet long and walking on four legs, and it was weaving around the coffee stand as if that were very normal dragon behavior.

He had to be dreaming, Bao decided. None of this was actually happening, and he was still in bed, dreaming. One of those lucid dreams. A really, really lucid dream.

"Are *you* deaf, too, Bow-wow?" Jael snarled.

But Bao, still stunned by the sight of the dragon, did not respond. The dragon was still there and was eyeing the open container of whipped cream with interest, and it robbed Bao of the power of speech. Red and glistening, the dragon's scales glinted in the overhead light and its antler-horns made the "order here" sign suspended from the ceiling sway every time they brushed against it. The dragon turned its head, and Bao saw its yellow, slitted eyes watching him, and Bao could not have turned away even if Jael had threatened to set him on fire.

Listing its head slightly to one side in a rakish manner, the dragon winked.

The dragon's tail brushed up against the barista, and Bao gasped when he watched the barista startle, turn, and then freeze in shock as he saw what was behind him.

Holy shit, Hottie could see it too.

"*Listen here, Fischer,*" Jael shouted, and he reached out to take rough hold of his face.

But when Jael touched him, the dragon roared. White mist erupted from its mouth, engulfing them.

The barista shouted, the building shook, and then they were gone.

Everything was gone: the Starbucks stand, the building, the whole world, everything. Bao stood in the white nothingness of his dreams, but he was wide awake, and this time he knew exactly who he was.

And he was terrified.

The dragon stepped forward, bigger than it had been in the Starbucks stand, bigger than a city bus, bigger than anything Bao knew to compare it to. It simply waddled forward on great paws, its claws scraping against whatever it was Bao was standing on, and when it was mere feet away from Bao, when he could have reached out and touched it, when he was gagging from the harsh, chemical smell of its breath and wilting under the steam of its nostrils—*then* it stopped, and it spoke a single word.

"*Believe.*"

And then it was gone. Bao stood alone in the nothingness, trembling—naked, because somehow his clothes hadn't come along for the ride—reeling with shock and terror and disbelief. The mist was gone, and he was standing, naked, in the middle of a barren, rocky patch beneath a black and starless sky, and Jael was looming over him, fifty feet tall, slick with oil and fire and suspended by an absolutely huge pair of black and silver wings.

Bao stared up at him, his brain well beyond its ability to process this, and said, "I'd like to wake up now, please."

The Jael-shaped beast beat its fiery wings and laughed, a cruel and hollow sound. "This is no dream," it boomed, and reached for him, a great, perfect flaming hand sweeping down to crush him where he stood.

And then something pulled at him, dragging him backward over the rock.

It was Hottie.

"Come *on*!" the barista shouted, jerking them first left, then right, practically yanking Bao's arm off as he leapt behind a boulder and into the narrow opening to a cave.

"What—?" Bao shouted, but his question was cut off as the barista pushed him backward into the dirt, knocking the wind out of him at the same time the Jael-beast pounded its great fist against the mouth of the cave, shattering the wall of rock and sending rubble down all around them.

BAO thought that a cave collapsing on top of him would be a very good time for him to wake up from his dream. That was not, unfortunately, what happened.

What actually happened was that he gagged and choked on silt and dust and felt the stinging pain of a thousand scrapes and minor cuts along his legs, his arms, and worst of all, his bare ass as the barista shoved them both tighter beneath the wedge of an overhang. The red-haired man's body was tight against Bao's, shielding him—the man's body that, Bao couldn't help but notice, was just as naked as his own.

They huddled together, the barista clutching at Bao's shoulders and Bao at the man's waist until the rain of rubble ceased. When it was finished, they coughed for a few seconds, and then, tentatively, the barista lifted his head and looked at Bao.

"Are you okay?" he asked.

Bao just blinked up at him. He wasn't sure where the light was coming from in here, but there was some sort of faint, bluish glow that outlined the man's face in light and shade, making him look even more beautiful. *And he's naked. Those are his hips beneath your hands, his smooth, glorious hips, his legs pressed against yours. And that's his cock against your belly.*

Shutting down that line of thought lest he show Hottie just how very okay he was, Bao swallowed and said, unsteadily, "I think I'm going crazy."

The barista laughed, and there was that smile, crooked and a little strained, but it was the smile that Bao had fallen for months ago, and it had the usual effect. Bao tried to pull back, though this only made things worse; not only was there no room to do that, but the movement only aggravated his arousal.

"Sorry," he murmured, mortified, pulling his hands off the barista's hips and shutting his eyes to hide his mortification. "I don't—" He gasped as the barista shifted against him, and he couldn't help it; Bao pushed his hips back, chasing the sweet friction. When the hands on his shoulders tightened and his thrust was met with an answering rhythm, he couldn't help it. He groaned and placed his hands on the man's hips again.

"Don't be sorry." The barista leaned down and nuzzled the side of Bao's face, lips brushing his ear. "I've wanted to do this for months."

Months? "Why—?" Bao asked, then stopped and shivered as the other man's tongue stole inside his ear.

"I wasn't sure before," the barista whispered, then nibbled again. "God, you're so hot."

Bao let his hips give in to the rhythm they were seeking. *I'm hot. The hottie thinks I'm hot.* "But you're sure now?"

The man laughed, but it was a sorrowful sound. "I figure at this point either you're going to kill me, or I'll suffocate inside this cave, or get eaten by that asshole outside. I'd rather go out having given in and touched you."

Even with the ring of doom around his confession, Bao felt himself sliding under the barista's words. "I don't want to kill you," he whispered.

He felt the man's smile against his cheek and the slide of his now very erect cock against his hip. "Good."

Bao slid his hands up his lover's back. "What's your name? I've been dying to know."

The man groaned and shook his head. "It's stupid, that's what it is."

Bao snorted. "My name is Bao," he said.

The man lifted his head and looked down at Bao curiously. "Like the dumpling?"

Bao sighed. "I'm adopted. My parents wanted to give me a name that reflected my heritage. Their book told them it meant 'precious'. My full name is Bao-Bo. 'Precious wave'." He grimaced. "Or 'wet dumpling'."

He could see the other man smiling in the dim light, but for the first time in his life, he didn't mind someone finding humor in his name.

"Abner," the man said.

Bao lifted his eyebrows. "Oh?" he said, trying to sound casual. It didn't work.

Abner sighed. "I told you it was stupid."

"No, it's—" *Odd,* Bao admitted to himself. He scrambled for a save. "Well, it doesn't mean dumpling."

"It makes me sound like I'm eighty," Abner complained. "It was my great-grandfather's name. But do you know how hard it is to get laid in the twenty-first century with a name like *Abner*?"

The mention of sex ended the levity for Bao. "So you were interested in me all this time?"

Abner laughed, bitterly. "Oh, God. I had such a crush on you that I was sure I'd only make a fool of myself if I tried to do anything besides give you your macchiato."

"Had?" Bao echoed, his fingers sliding against Abner's naked hips.

Abner's hand slid up to Bao's cheek and he looked down at him with a soft expression that made Bao melt. "Have."

Bao looked into those beautiful hazel eyes and shook his head. "This has *got* to be a dream."

"If it's a dream, it's one for me too." Abner's thumb caught at the corner of Bao's mouth, and his gaze, full of heat, drifted down to watch the lips part beneath his prodding. "Which I can't say I've ever heard of before."

"But this is so… impossible." Bao shivered as Abner shifted his hips and made their cocks slide over one another. "Oh, God, that feels good."

"Basically," Abner said, still moving slowly, "I figure this is either a dream or some sort of other dimension."

"You seem rather calm about it," Bao observed, but with his eyes closed as he matched Abner's rhythm. He couldn't move much, but he could move enough to make it count. *God,* it felt so good.

"Well, I'm a gamer," Abner confessed. "We pretty much live our lives hoping something like this will happen. Except we figure we'll be given a sword or some magic power to help us along. I'm kind of still hoping for that, actually. But if this isn't a dream, which I guess is still an option, either we're already dead in some messed-up afterlife, or this is an alternate dimension. We're going to find some way out of this, or a way to survive within it. Though I'm not sure how we do that in a cave with a monster outside, so for now we sit tight."

"And in the meantime"—Bao thrust up against Abner and gasped—"we fuck?"

"Yeah." Abner opened his mouth over Bao's jaw and nipped him briefly. "You okay with that?"

"Not much room to maneuver," Bao said, but his hand was already sliding between them, trying to find Abner's cock. He couldn't see it, but he could feel it.

"Room enough," Abner murmured, humping more insistently now as his mouth trailed up and down Bao's jaw. "Bao, you feel so good."

Bao found Abner's cock and took hold of it, exploring it for a few seconds, running his thumb over the glans, the slit, the length—and then he pushed his hips up and caught both their sexes together, casing them as tightly as he could within his fist, making Abner gasp and moan as their thrusts began in earnest.

"Wanted—" Bao shut his eyes tight as the pleasure of the friction shot up into the back of his teeth. "I wanted—this—so long—"

"Me too," Abner rasped. "Didn't think a guy like you would—*Bao! Ohgod!*"

Bao nuzzled Abner's cheek, seeking skin to kiss. "Guy like me would what?"

"Want a guy like me," Abner answered, then moaned and dug his fingers into Bao's neck. "You're so smart. Handsome. *Hot*. Successful. I'm just… coffee shop loser—*oh fuck, Bao, oh God!*"

Bao was kneading Abner's ass with his free hand, first massaging the fleshy globe, then sliding his fingers into the crack to tease him. Abner was humping him roughly now, his hands braced against Bao's shoulders in the narrow space.

"I want to come all over you," Abner whispered. He dragged his lips back to Bao's chin. "I want to kiss you. So hard. I want to kiss you while we come together in this fucked-up pile of rocks."

Bao almost laughed, but he didn't because his heart was still too full. *A guy like you. Hot. Handsome. Smart.* He turned his head, caught

Abner's mouth, and nipped sharply at his bottom lip. "Do it," he whispered.

Abner groaned, took hold of Bao's face, and thrust his tongue inside.

It was probably weird to be fucking when the world had turned upside down, when dreams had come to life and made whole office buildings disappear, when he was about to be crushed to death by rock if the cave shifted again. Bao acknowledged, briefly, that he probably should have been wondering why his clothes had gone, where it was exactly *he* had gone, why Jael was some fifty-foot-tall freakish fire monster, and how the hell he was going to get out of this. Yes, those all would have been sensible courses of action. But holy shit, Abner might look like the nicest boy-next-door anyone had ever seen, but he had a really wicked tongue on him, and it was thrusting roughly into Bao's throat while Abner rocked their hips into a harder and harder rhythm. Abner swallowed Bao's moans and growled deep into Bao's mouth in response as Bao tightened his hand around their cocks, slid his fist up and down their lengths with one hand, and continued to probe into the hot musk of Abner's slit for the pucker of his ass with the other.

There were more sensible things to do right now, yes, but Bao wasn't interested in sensible. He was interested in coming his brains out against the sleek, slightly muscled chest of his crush. Of Abner.

Who thought he was *hot.*

Soon the kiss stopped as they began gripping one another roughly, grunting and gasping and murmuring, "Oh yeah—oh yeah—*oh God!*" and then they were coming, first Bao, roaring his pleasure into the skin of Abner's neck, then clamping his mouth down and sucking hard as he breathed through his orgasm, feeling the hot spray of semen cooling between their bodies, against his hand, against their cocks, sticky and wet. But when he sucked a little too hard, Abner cried out, then gasped, his voice going very high and soft as he bucked, froze, then spilled his seed as well, spraying up over Bao's chest, his nipples, and the planes of his abdomen, coming so much that it ran over the sides of Bao's body and tickled against his back.

Oh, fuck, but it was *great.*

Bao did laugh then, softly, smiling against Abner's naked shoulder, licking the freckles he saw there as he waited for his lover to catch his breath. Abner was right. Whatever this was, there wasn't any point in getting worked up over it. And if this was a dream, he didn't ever want it to end.

He slid a semen-slick hand up their bodies and shut his eyes, savoring the moment.

When his hand skimmed over Abner's waist, his lover tensed, which amused Bao, because Abner hadn't been ticklish at all before, and then he heard a whispered, terrified, "Bao!" and he opened his eyes and turned his head to see what was wrong.

The cave was gone. They were back in the white mist, still naked and twined together, but they were in that void-like place that Bao had seen in his dreams, the place where the dragon met him.

The place, he acknowledged, when blinking didn't make the huge, scaly head or demon-yellow eyes go away, where the dragon was right now.

BAO and Abner were still twined in one another's arms, and they were still full of dust and scrapes from the falling rock, but all the rock was gone. All that was in the world were the two men and the dragon that had been haunting Bao, except it was even bigger now than it had been before. A single eye was so big that one of its eyelashes was as long as Bao's arm. Its breathing sounded like a bellows, and even the most gentle exhale was a great wind to Bao and Abner, sending a wave of heat over their bodies.

"Shit," Abner whispered.

Bao's hands sought Abner's hips again, this time to anchor himself in his terror. "I keep dreaming this dragon. Dreams I *know* are dreams. And then today I started seeing it in the office. And I saw it again before we came here. Wherever here is."

Abner's eyes were wide, and he was clearly terrified, but he looked intrigued too. "Bao, are you Korean, by any chance?"

Bao tensed. "I'm *American.* I'm *Presbyterian.*"

"But is your ancestry from Korea?" Abner dogged.

"Yes," Bao admitted reluctantly. "But I haven't been there since I was four months old."

Abner was staring hard at the dragon now. "Bao, this is a Korean dragon."

Bao tipped his head backward and gave the dragon another look. It just looked like a big Asian dragon to him. "How can you tell? *You* aren't Korean."

"I've read a lot about Asian culture." Abner glanced at him, looking abashed. "It's kind of my thing. When I was a kid, I drove my parents nuts because I insisted I was born on the wrong continent. I wished I was from Korea. Or Japan. Or China. Or Indonesia. Anywhere but here." He looked back at the dragon, less scared all the time, just interested. "See, he has a longer beard and four toes." His eyes widened. "Bao—*Bao!* He has a *Yeouiju*!"

Bao braced on his elbows and swiveled his body around to get a better look. The dragon's size had reduced significantly, its head now only as tall as Bao would have been if he had been standing. It was holding out its right claw, and in the middle of it was a milky, yellow-white, and glowing sphere, just like in Bao's dream.

"That's a dragon orb," Abner whispered reverently. "Legend says that anyone strong enough to wield one is omnipotent and can create at will."

Bao glanced at Abner. "You really believe in this stuff, don't you? It doesn't upset you at all that we've been sucked out of our lives and into this place. You believe in this. In the dragon, the orb—everything."

Abner's ears turned red, but he nodded. "It's either that or I have to accept a world where I'm never going to be anything more than a Starbucks barista and a loser who spends his weekends gaming."

Bao forgot the dragon entirely and looked up at Abner, amazed. So the hottie barista he hadn't thought he was good enough to ask out thought *Bao* was too good for him, wished he were Asian, and never thought he was going to amount to anything.

In short, he was Bao, the Caucasian version.

"What are we supposed to do with a dragon orb, Abner?" Bao asked.

Abner laughed nervously. "*I* can't do anything with it. There's no way I'm strong enough."

The dragon huffed like a cow, except there was a distinct chemical nature to its exhale, and Bao craned his head to watch as the dragon set the orb down into the white mist. Once the *Yeouiju* was released, however, it changed; it was now a thick, white scroll with five Asian-looking characters written on it. Bao had no idea what they said.

Somehow it was no surprise that Abner did.

"Those are the five elements!" he exclaimed, and the next thing Bao knew, Abner had released him and was moving tentatively closer to the scroll, alight with excitement. "Metal, wood, water, fire, earth. Oh! Bao, I wonder if this is something to do with the zodiac!"

Bao sat up, keeping one eye on the dragon. It was still there, still the same size, but it had retreated about twenty feet. "You mean like Aries and Virgo and Taurus?"

Abner waved an irritated hand. "No. *Chinese* zodiac. Boar. Dog. Tiger. Ox." He nodded at their guardian. "Dragon." Pointing to the symbols, he turned to Bao. "The zodiac corresponds to the elements, depending on the year. They're yin and yang too. Like, I was born in July of 1985, so I'm a yin Ox, and my element is wood."

None of this made any sense to Bao. "I was born in January of 1983. What does that make me?"

Abner shut his eyes and moved his lips as he did some mental calculations. "You'd be a yang Dog, and your element is water."

Bao didn't see what good this did them, or what the connection was. "Is there a zodiac sign for 'big scary monster'? Or just dragon? Because that must be what Jael is."

Abner shook his head. "He can't be a Dragon. They're only every twelve years, and he's not old or young enough. I'm betting he's a Tiger."

"I know he was born in 1986, and I think he's a Sagittarius," Bao offered.

"Ha!" Abner pumped his fist in triumph. "I was *right.* Yang Tiger." He made a face. "Fire. No wonder he makes me so nervous. Fire burns wood."

But water puts out fire, Bao thought. *So why does he intimidate me so badly?* He pursed his lips. "You know, it's fine that you believe in this stuff, but frankly, it's all a bit too weird for me."

Abner raised an eyebrow. "Oh, but a dragon that appears in my coffee stand and sucks us into an alternate dimension is fine with you?"

"It's not *fine* with me, no," Bao said, irritated. "But when it's staring me in the face, it's hard to ignore. Anyway, I don't understand how it would help even if I did believe in it. What does the zodiac have to do with these characters? What I want to know is where *are* we, and why are we here? More importantly, how do we get back?"

Abner blushed. "Sorry. You're right. I shouldn't geek out. I mean, it's an amazing adventure for me, but you'll want to get back to your life."

Bao felt abruptly embarrassed. "Well, it's not *that* great of a life."

"Oh, come on!" Abner gave him a rueful look. "A guy like you has to have it all. If I get back, I'll probably have to start ducking your hottie boyfriend."

What? Bao became acutely aware of the semen drying on his skin. "I don't have a boyfriend."

Abner looked interested for a moment, and then turned abruptly back to the scroll. "Well, you want to get back. So let's figure this out."

Bao felt like he'd screwed up somehow, but he didn't quite understand it and didn't know what to say, so he crouched down beside Abner and studied the markings.

"The first thing," Abner said, bracing his elbows on his knees as he squatted before the parchment, "is to figure out why we're here. I mean, the dragon is obviously a spirit guide. I would love to think it was mine, but you're the one dreaming about it. The problem is that you don't believe in it, so you probably don't have much information to put in the kitty."

"Well," Bao confessed, "I have been dreaming this white place. A lot. And I saw the dragon in the office before I came down to get coffee. And last night I did dream of that orb thing."

Abner turned to him, eyes alight. "This is *great*! I don't suppose it's ever said anything to you?"

"Believe." Bao looked over at the dragon, which had all but vanished into the mist. "It said, 'Believe'. And it winked at me."

"Hmm." Abner rubbed his thumb thoughtfully over his lips. "And then we have the five elements of the Chinese zodiac. So I'm thinking this is kind of a broad scope, a Korean dragon and Chinese symbols. And that explains why I'm here: maybe I'm like your guide, your sidekick. Since I know all this stuff, I mean. Whatever it is, I'm just glad I got to come. This is *cool.*"

Bao stared at him, feeling strange and oddly humbled. He'd crushed on Abner, he knew, because the barista had seemed like the man he wished he could be. And clearly Abner had done the same over him. There had been nothing about the real men beneath. And yet, as they stood here, naked except for each other's sperm—he was really having a hard time letting go of that image, and it made him slightly hard again just to think about it—as Bao began to see the person behind the crush, the self-conscious, geeky-shy but enthusiastic man that Abner was, his bright outlook, his sense of kindness.... Well, it wasn't just a crush anymore. Bao was attracted now to the man he was starting to know.

And suddenly he wasn't in such a hurry to leave this place either, dream or otherwise.

As if feeling Bao's gaze on him, Abner turned and blushed. "Sorry, was I geeking out again?"

Bao smiled. "Yeah. But I like it." Abner blushed deeper. God, but Bao loved that. His smile turned to a grin and he reached out and touched the other man's hand. "You're not a side-kick, Abner."

"Too presumptuous?" Abner asked, in a whisper. He was looking down at their joined hands. His cock was also bobbing just a little as a tentative erection reformed.

Bao couldn't answer, so he just smiled and squeezed Abner's hand. Abner smiled back and held onto Bao's hand as he regarded the symbols again.

"I'm thinking this is like a puzzle. I think it's like the dragon said, that you're supposed to learn something, and probably you're supposed to defeat Jael. Who probably isn't actually your boss, but is taking on that form because it intimidates you." He paused. "Well, I guess since it's really me here, it could really be him too. And if that's true, we need to figure out why he's so powerful. Is it his ability, or yours, making him so strong? Your belief in him, or his own strength?"

"Why would that make a difference?" Bao asked.

"Because if it's your belief powering him, you can defeat him by cutting off the source of his power, which is your belief that he's stronger than you. Of course, the problem is that the only way to test this theory is to face him and see if it works."

"We'd have to find him first," Bao pointed out. "And I don't know how to get back to where we were." *Thank God.*

Abner shook his head. "This place doesn't seem to work like that. So far it's changed around us at critical points. If my theory is right, if it has to do with you, it's going to change when you're ready for it to do so. When you want to challenge Jael, he'll appear."

Bao held up his hands. "I don't want to challenge Jael."

But a shadow was already falling over them, and they turned together to see the monster that Bao's supervisor had become looming over them.

"Or," Abner said weakly, "he could just show up on his own."

THE Jael-monster was even bigger than he'd been the last time. Bao thought it was particularly cruel that he wasn't just big and scary but beautiful too. His supervisor was even more sculpted, even more gleaming than usual, because now he was lit everywhere by fire. It licked the edges of his skin, his hair, his lips, and his great, huge wings. Jael was monstrously huge, as big now as their office building. Looking up at him, Bao felt smaller, uglier, and more ineffective than ever.

"You have to face him," Abner said. "He's your demon, so only you can take him down."

"How am I supposed to do that?" Bao asked, craning his neck as he scraped his gaze up and down Jael. It lingered on his supervisor's groin, which—since Jael was as naked as he and Abner were—gave Bao a very erotic if somewhat magnified view. Yep. Jael was perfect everywhere. Bao looked at the huge cock, perfectly formed, perfectly shaped, twice as long as Bao was tall, and he felt aroused and defeated at once.

"I don't know," Abner said. "I think only you can answer that one." He drew Bao sharply back as Jael advanced on them. "Just try something," he urged, panic creeping into his voice.

Try what? Bao couldn't ask out loud, because they were busy dodging the Jael-monster now, both his feet and his reaching hands, and all under the gale-force wind that the beating of his wings pushed upon them. They could gain no ground, because every time they switched direction, so did Jael, and no sooner were they heading for open space than Jael's giant foot was blocking their path and his hand was swooping down to scoop them up. After a few rounds of this, Bao and Abner were running out of breath.

And soon Bao discovered another problem: they were running out of space too.

Bao finally caught a break and feinted right before jerking hard left into the thickest part of the fog. For a moment it seemed he'd won. And then he was slamming into something and bouncing back against Abner before knocking them both to the ground.

"Walls," he gasped, rubbing at his sore nose. "This place has *walls.*"

Abner scrambled to his feet. "We've got to keep moving." He was heaving for breath, and he looked scared, but he gave Bao a brave smile and squeezed his hand as he helped him up. "You can do it. I know you can."

But *Bao* didn't know it, chiefly because he didn't know what the hell he could possibly do against whatever it was Jael had become. And after a few more rounds of dodge-the-feet-and-hands, they were seriously slowing down, and with nowhere to hide.

"Believe in yourself," Abner rasped as they used the time it took Jael to turn around to try and catch their breath. He squeezed Bao's hand again, but his grip was starting to get weak. "Believe that you can best him. That might be all it takes."

Might. Bao, mouth as dry as paper and his chest burning as he tried to take in more air, looked up at Jael and tried. He really did. He tried to tell himself that he could do this, that he was strong enough or good enough to take his boss down. But it was about as effective as those times when he'd been twelve and he'd tried to levitate his pencil across the room. It just didn't work. He *wasn't* better than Jael. He could never defeat him—not as a supervisor, not as a monster, not as anything, ever.

Jael turned, reached down, and caught Abner, hefting him into the air. Bao cried out, and Jael laughed as he reared his arm back.

"*No!*" Bao cried, the pain of loss mixing with the pain of overused lungs. He reached out his hand impotently, but he was not thinking of his diminutive size now or his lack of power, just his fear for his lover. "No!"

Jael looked down at him, grinned, threw his arm forward, and let Abner fly.

And so did Bao.

He didn't think, didn't even really try; he just lifted up from the ground and flew, shooting like a rocket past Jael's huge, meaty hands, into the mist, aiming at Abner's flailing body. Bao's heart was pounding against the back of his throat, but he focused on Abner, willing himself closer, to fly faster.

And then he was beside him, and with a glad cry Bao reached out and took Abner in his arms.

"Bao!" Abner cried, holding fast.

"Hold on," Bao told him. "I've got you. Hold on."

"I won't let go," Abner promised.

Bao had no idea how he was going to land. But then he decided that, since he'd leapt into the air and flown, he could land as well. And maybe Abner was right: it was as simple as belief. Because the next thing he knew, he was arcing down, like when he was a kid and he jumped off swings on the playground. He could not see the ground, covered in mist as it was, but he could sense it, and he could feel it when he landed. It didn't hurt at all.

He kissed Abner hard and fast on the mouth before he gently let him down. "I was so scared," Bao whispered, and kissed him again.

"Me too." Abner's hands were on Bao's shoulders, but he was looking at Bao oddly. Specifically, at his hand.

"What is it?" Bao asked, and turned to see what he was looking at. His eyes went wide.

There was the dragon orb, glowing warm and yellow in his palm.

BAO stared down at the orb. It felt warm in his hand, the sphere glowing a soft yellow-white, and staring into it, Bao felt the chaos within him quiet. At the same time, it created a strange emptiness inside him, a sense of space that he wasn't entirely comfortable with. Big. The space inside the orb, or the space it created, was big. Bigger than Bao wanted it to be.

"You're using the orb," Abner whispered, awed. "Is that how you saved me?"

"I don't know," Bao confessed. "I don't know what happened exactly, or how. All I knew was that you were going to die, and I couldn't let that happen."

The confession made him feel exposed, and he glanced at Abner to see how he reacted. To Bao's surprise, Abner looked surprised, and soft. Bao watched him school his expression, though, before he spoke. "So you just flew up into the air? No dragon? No orb?"

"I just flew," Bao confirmed.

Abner had been making a study of his own hands, but now he lifted his eyes to Bao without lifting his head. "So you were thinking about Jael? You realized how you were better than he was after all?"

Bao considered lying. It would be so easy, to just let that be the excuse. But as he stared at the orb, as he watched the subtle play of white smoke beneath its surface, he knew it wouldn't help, and it might hurt to lie.

He cleared his throat. "No. I was thinking about you, like I said. That I didn't want him to hurt you."

Abner blinked, and Bao watched carefully this time, catching the softness, the tender spot his words warmed in the other man before he looked down again. Abner was flustered now, and Bao felt something catch in his chest as he watched how deliberately Abner worked to move the compliment away from himself.

"Oh. Right. Because you didn't like seeing someone get hurt." Abner cleared his throat. "You're a good person, and that's what did it. Your sense of justice over his sense of selfishness, or meanness."

Why was it so hard, when he could see, right there in front of him, that Abner felt the same way? Why did the truth stick in his throat?

Because it's scary to believe you're worth something, when the whole world seems to tell you that you aren't, a quiet voice within him answered. Or maybe it came from the orb. And he realized that the voice was the same as the dragon's, and they all tumbled together: the orb, the dragon, and that voice within himself.

Believe, they whispered in unison. *Believe in you. Believe you are worthy of the life and love you yearn for, or you can never have it.*

New levels of panic and fear rose in Bao at the thought. Believe in himself. Oh, that was easy for them to say, wasn't it? Dragons and orbs and inner voices, not feeling the pinch of fear, the burn of real life. The weight of it, and the loneliness.

What freed his tongue in the end, what gave him the strength to believe, was nothing within him, but rather the lost look on Abner's face. No, Bao did not quite believe in himself yet. But he believed in Abner, in the kindness and affection he'd received from him, in this place and in real life. And that was enough.

"No," Bao confessed, a little shakily. "It was because it was you, Abner. I didn't want him to hurt *you*."

See, this was why Bao hadn't wanted to confess the truth, because Abner didn't look touched. He looked wary. "But you don't know me! Why—?"

Bao laughed, a little bitterly. "Abner, I've had a crush on you since you started working at that Starbucks. I never used to buy coffee at all, but one day I really had a headache and needed a latte, and there you were. Now I know your schedule and I make sure I come when you're there. I'm disappointed when you aren't."

When Abner just stared at him, surprised and still confused, Bao thought, *To hell with it,* and told him everything.

"At first I just liked you because you were so much of what I wanted in a man," Bao explained. "You were tall, you were handsome, you seemed nice, and—yeah, you were white. At first it was more about what I wished *I* were than about you. But then you *were* nice. And—" He stopped, as saying this out loud made some of his reasoning unravel. "Okay. So probably it was still about that. Probably I was projecting. But you know, I do that on a lot of guys, but it was you where it really stuck. And now, here you've been helping me, and you're—I don't know, you're different, but in such an interesting way. You're into gaming and you know Chinese characters, and weird things happen to me when you smile at me. I feel a little crazy, like I could do anything. And maybe that's all just my fancy still. I don't know. Maybe this is just me, over-romanticizing everything. All I know is that when I watched you sailing out into the mist, all I could think of was that I'd just barely gotten to know you and that I would do anything, give anything, to save you so that I could keep getting to know you, this man who seems so amazing. And that's why I flew."

Bao was red-faced when he finished, and he felt horribly foolish and exposed as he waited to see what Abner would do with his confession.

For a long, awkward moment, he did nothing, just stared at Bao as if he weren't quite certain what to think of him. Bao held still, naked, afraid, and living his worst nightmare: Bao, stupid old Bao, the adopted Asian, Bao, the perennially uncool, Bao, exposed at last as a fool. He clutched at the orb, trying to take solace in it.

And then the moment ended, and Abner was speaking.

He shook his head, blushing as he closed his arms over his naked chest. "Bao, I'm nobody. Why would you think stuff like that about me?"

"You aren't nobody," Bao corrected him, then smiled as the orb warmed and began to lighten in his hand, and then he added, "Neither am I." He palmed the orb thoughtfully. "That's the secret. It's like you said: I need to believe in myself. But you're along in this, Abner, not to be my reference librarian or my sidekick." He made himself look up at Abner for the rest, even though it made his cheeks pink. "You're here to be my partner. The one who helps me believe in myself. The one who *shows* me I'm not a nobody, that I'm more than Jael makes me believe I am, than the world makes me believe I am. You're the one who helps me, but not as an assistant. As someone beside me."

Abner was flushed from the praise, but when he smiled there was nothing shy about the gesture. "Is this the sort of partner who kisses you?" he asked.

"God, I hope so," Bao replied, a little breathless. His heart was beating faster too.

Abner, still smiling and eyes dancing now too, reached out and took Bao's hand, but his thumb grazed over Bao's wrist. "Maybe a partner who pushes you down on the ground and gives you the most amazing blow job you've ever had?"

The blood that had been pounding in Bao's ears rushed directly to his groin, where his erection rose up in silent hope between them. Abner laughed and reached down to take it lightly in his hand.

"I take it that's a yes?"

"You mean—right now?" Bao asked, hissing a little as Abner began to stroke him.

"Did you have somewhere else you were supposed to be? Something else to be doing?" Abner asked, amused.

God, that hand. Bao gripped his shoulder. "I thought we were supposed to figure out how to stop Jael or give me confidence or something."

Abner laughed, wickedly and brushed a kiss against his lips. "I'll give you a very *confident* blow job."

Bao groaned and grabbed Abner's head to draw him closer. The orb vanished from his hand as he reached out, but he didn't care about it just now—he kissed Abner hard and full on the mouth and pressed their foreheads together.

"You are, you know," he rasped. "You *are* wonderful." Bao shivered, clutching at Abner's neck as his thumb flicked over Bao's glans. Reaching down, Bao stilled Abner's hand so he could finish, and made himself look his lover in the eye. "You're kind. You're funny. And you're very, very smart. I don't care if you're Asian or white or purple with green stripes. You're Abner. I won't think about an eighty-year-old man when I hear the name anymore. I'll think of you. And I'd love to scream out your name in the height of passion."

Abner kissed him tenderly. "I will be aroused by dumplings," he said quietly, "until the day I die."

Bao kissed him back, drawing his face closer with one hand and urging Abner's hand back into action with the other. They sank to the ground, which swallowed them in mist; when Abner pressed him back, the ground felt soft, like a bed. They rolled, kissing, touching, thrusting. Abner was hard now too, and their cocks thrust in time to one another. Bao liked it, but he wanted more this time. He wanted to see Abner. He wanted to see him everywhere, to touch him, and yes, he wanted to taste him too.

He slid his mouth down Abner's chin, suckling his neck as his fingers traced circles over his lover's chest, memorizing the planes and the soft places, and then, when Abner was lost to the sensation, Bao lifted his head and let his eyes feast too. He *saw* the skin as well as felt it; saw the pale beauty of it, and the freckles, and the places where Abner's skin was so translucent he could see his veins. Then he bent and kissed those veins, swirling his tongue over the little patch of hair in the center, sliding down his sternum to his lover's belly. It was not a hard body, not a six-pack. Just a belly, soft and tender, and—Bao thought wickedly as his tongue explored the cavity of Abner's belly button—it was quite tasty.

But when Bao's exploring hands and mouth drifted even further south, Abner stopped him.

"No," he said. "No—turn. I want to touch you too."

And so Bao slid his body around so that they lay side-by-side, faces to groins. He took in the beautiful sight of Abner's ruddy cock, full of blood and heat and arousal, and then he closed his eyes as he felt Abner take his own sex in hand. For a moment he savored the erotic feel of it, first of his lover's touch and then the sensual, skilled heat of his mouth, and then, with a contented sigh, Bao bent forward and gave as good as he was getting.

As the sex turned gritty, as hands began to clutch at hips and asses, as tongues dipped down to lave balls in addition to shafts, as Abner, after crying out in surprised pleasure as Bao pushed a dampened finger inside him, braced a shoulder against Bao's thigh and applied his mouth to Bao's own opening.... What Bao would remember forever was that when they were bucking against one another and shouting out in rough, primal pleasure, when they were together this time, Bao felt a tenderness, a deep, oddly calming connection, not just to Abner, but to himself. When he came, pushing hot and hard into Abner's humming throat, he saw the orb appear in his mind's eye, and this time he could see inside it, could see something swirling inside the smoke—himself. He saw Bao-Bo Fischer, strong and proud and beautiful.

Believe.

They had barely caught their breath when the ground around them began to tremble, and this time it didn't surprise Bao when Jael appeared, larger now than he ever had been. He was a living wall of fire this time, the blaze consuming him, not just falling from him, though it did that too. The mist scorched and blackened where his feet fell, and soon small fires had broken out around them.

Jael had returned.

BAO didn't tremble, he didn't freeze—he just reached for Abner and kissed him hard and fast on the mouth.

"I can do this," he said, still breathless, but from passion, not from fear. "But it's going to take me a little time to sort it out."

"How can I help you?" Abner asked.

Bao looked up at the man-mountain between them, at the impossible beast Jael had become, and he took Abner's hand. "I don't know yet," he admitted. "But I think I can do this if you stay with me."

They rose as one, and Bao tried to draw strength from him, tried to use the confidence that Abner had gifted him with, had shown him how to find in himself, but he might as well have been trying to grasp the mist. He still felt like Bao. When Jael reached down, bellowing a roar before the wind of his wings began to flatten them to the floor, when the force of it ripped Abner out of his hands and sent him skittering away, Bao realized with a sick heart that, as much as he wanted Abner as a partner, as much as his lover had given him, this part he must do on his own. He had to believe in himself before he could take on the monster. And that belief had to come from himself alone.

He pushed to his feet, and he saw the dragon striding toward him, smaller than he'd ever been; he was, in fact, the same size as Bao. And as in his dream, the dragon walked up to him, blinking its yellow eyes as it waited, while in the distance Jael roared and Abner screamed and Bao stood there, lost and helpless, the spirit guide of the ancestry he did not want waiting patiently before him.

The dragon. The Korean dragon.

His spirit guide.

His self. His orientation, his culture, his history, his future: that was what this dragon was. This dragon was Bao. His self.

His self that he did not want.

Except, as Bao looked at the dragon, at his self reflected, at the power and magic and wonder that did not need anyone's permission to be, that simply was—the power to fly, to grow, to change, to be, beautiful or ugly, to simply *be*—as he stood there, suddenly Bao did want it. He wanted it very, very badly.

Heart aching, Bao took the dragon's face in his hands, and he kissed it on the mouth.

It began in him like a pulse. When he drew back, the dragon was gone, and he held the orb in his hands—bigger this time, and hotter, and much, much heavier. And then Bao realized his hands were not his hands at all, but claws. When his lips parted to gasp, he realized that they were camel lips, and that his tongue was thicker and fatter and forked, and that there was a heat, a spark inside his throat: his fire. Except it was not fire, it was power. Pure, blinding power, a power all his own. All he had to do was figure out how to use it. As the world turned yellow around him, as his body lengthened and hardened and covered with scales, Bao's heart pounded inside his chest, and he thought, *Me. The dragon is me. The dragon is not just me, but I am the dragon too.*

He had seen the dragon grow.

And he could fly.

He could feel the earth shake as Jael came back, but by that time Bao was already growing, his body expanding with every step he took as he circled around the sound of Jael's footfalls, not running at him and not running away, just moving around and around him in a circle, enclosing him. Because he was big enough now that, even as he rounded his enemy's massive feet, he could see his own tail curling ahead of him in the distance.

Water. Bao's beard twitched in thought as he continued to circle. Abner had said that water was his element. Jael was fire. In the dragon's body, Bao could feel the magic, the power that came not *from* the orb but was channeled through it, the power within him to change this place, to manipulate it—just as Jael had. Jael, not just in his own confidence, but that which Bao and Abner had given him.

Water puts out fire. Bao could feel the element all around him, could feel how he could use it. But what would it do to Abner?

Wood floats on water.

Bao kept growing, faster and faster now, and with him came a sea, water he called from the mist, from the air, from the sacred place where water began. He felt the dragon rise within him, a dragon born of water. All around him it rose, putting out the flames that Jael had started, and very quickly it was putting Jael out too. Inch by inch, his enemy was extinguished, roaring in fury, lashing out in protest, but now that Bao had claimed his power, the flames did nothing to him, only went out on contact. And all the time Bao grew greater and larger, stronger and more confident, and soon he and his ocean were as high as Jael's neck, and the monster was screaming. The wings fell away, burning cinders that turned to mud upon the water, and Jael flailed and screamed, frantically trying to get away from Bao.

Bao the dragon paused, unwilling to extinguish Jael completely now that he was so helpless. He turned his great head from side to side instead, searching for Abner, afraid he would not find him, that his ocean had drowned him. But no, there he was—no dragon, no beast, just a very wet man floating in a hastily made ship. He was clinging to the side, looking spent and terrified, but when he saw Bao, he grinned, and waved. Bao smiled, and because he could not wave back without causing a tidal wave, he winked.

Then he cried out as he saw the small ship go up in a terrible ball of flame.

Rage and despair made Bao swell—he reached out to the ship to dampen it, to stop the flame, and in so doing the whole world became water. The flames went out, both on the ship and within Jael, and the last Bao saw of his supervisor was a very small, terrified man sinking out of sight. But Bao ignored him, too consumed with searching for Abner, crying out for him, swimming through the blue-green expanse for him, terrified, absolutely terrified that it was too late, that he was gone.

No, he cried, and reached out with his heart.

And then there he was—Abner, floating, right before Bao, inside his orb. Was it Abner's orb? Bao's own? He didn't know, and he didn't care, only laughed and cried in relief and reached for him. When he touched the surface of the orb, it sucked him in, and for one brief second he knew pure bliss: happiness, completion like nothing he had ever known before and never would again, not this hot, not this complete, not this total. It shook him, and it grounded him, and it changed him.

And it woke him.

Because in the next second there was no orb, no ball, no Jael, no Abner, and no dragon; it was just Bao, sweating and breathless, sitting bolt upright in his bed as rain pelted against his bedroom windows.

For one moment he despaired. It had only been a dream, after all.

And then the power—his power—surged inside him and he thought, *No.*

BAO rose from his bed and threw on his clothes without really seeing them. He got in his car and drove through the driving rain, not sure where he was heading at first, but as he let his instinct guide him, he found he was headed back to work, to the office. They would be there—both Abner and Jael. Somehow Bao was absolutely certain of this.

And they were. In so many ways it was exactly the scene it had been before the dragon had appeared—Jael shouting and Abner cowering—and it made Bao pause, worrying that this, too, might be a dream. But he pushed the fear aside. No. This was the real world: he knew the difference between the two now. Here he'd been stuck at a red light and had realized halfway into downtown that he'd failed to use the toilet when he'd woken up, and he'd had to stop on the second floor and use the bathroom before coming down the rest of the way. Somehow it was still Tuesday, or perhaps it was Tuesday again.

But perhaps he was just now waking up for the first time that Tuesday. Perhaps he was about to go into the lobby and make himself a terrible fool.

Except as he saw Abner and Jael, he knew this was not the case and would not be. When he saw the barista, this time there was a knowing in his eye, a look that went deeper, a heat that burned him even from here, and a familiarity you did not give your casual patrons. And Jael looked at him with a hatred that went deeper than the usual disdain. The look of the defeated.

Somehow it had all been real. But this new reality was fragile too. All it would take was for them to slip back into their old patterns for the waking dream to end.

Bao wasn't going to let that happen.

He saw the dragon slide behind the counter, but this time when it looked at him, he smiled and winked back. Then Bao took the orb between his hands and claimed the life, the identity, and the self he was always meant to have.

"Jorgensen," Bao called out, interrupting Jael mid-tirade, "what the hell are you doing?"

Jael turned at him and started to sneer, but Bao cut him off.

"Why the fuck are you down here being a dick when everything is going to hell upstairs?"

Jael stopped, arrested. "What?"

Bao pointed to the elevator. "They're looking for you. I heard them say something about cutting middle management positions."

Jael went pale. *"What?"* he cried, then, without even picking up his coffee, took off like a bat out of hell for the stairs.

And Bao and Abner were alone.

Abner was flushed; Bao hoped it was from nerves and not just from the blister of Jael's abuse. He hoped that his dream had happened, somehow, that he was not as alone in this as he was afraid he was. He hoped Abner had dreamt it too, or better still that it all had been real and someday, when they were very old, they could remember it and smile. But as he looked at the man who had been his lover in a dream world, the man whose heart had touched him, he knew it wouldn't matter. If they had to start all over again, they would.

He had strength enough for that. Abner was worth it. And so was he.

"Can I help you?" Abner asked, his voice shaking. He reached for a cup and forced his gaze on it. "The usual?"

Bao reached out and stopped his hand. "Abner," he said quietly. Hopefully.

And Abner melted, dropping the cup and clutching their hands together in his own. “Bao—” He looked up at him, uncertain again. “That’s—that’s right, isn't it? You’re Bao? And you—”

“Turned into a dragon in your dream?” he suggested. Bao smiled as he added, “And made love to you in a cave? And in a very delicious sixty-nine?”

Abner made a sound that was half-laugh, half-sob. “God! I thought—I woke up, so it had to be a dream, even though I wanted—” He clutched at their hands and drew them up to his lips. “Bao. *Bao.*”

His name, Bao decided, had never sounded so sweet. And the dragon strength swelled within him, carrying him over the counter—the old-fashioned way, because he had to climb it—and then Abner was in his arms.

“Would you like to go out sometime?” Bao asked, as their bodies nestled together like old friends. “Dinner? A show?”

Abner pressed a little tighter to him. “Sex after?”

“That’d be fine with me,” Bao agreed. And smiled. “Or before. I’m not particular.”

Abner smiled back. “Me either,” he said, and took Bao’s face in his hands.

When they kissed, Bao could see the mist again, and he saw the dragon too—two dragons, beautiful and unique and strong in the center of the mist, embracing.

And he believed. Now and forever, in Abner, and in himself, Bao believed.

HEIDI CULLINAN has always loved a good love story, provided it has a happy ending. She enjoys writing across many genres but loves above all to write happy, romantic endings for LGBT characters because there just aren't enough of those stories out there. When Heidi isn't writing, she enjoys cooking, reading, knitting, listening to music, and watching television with her family. Heidi also volunteers frequently for her state's LGBT rights group, One Iowa, and is proud to be from the first Midwestern state to legalize same-sex marriage.

Visit Heidi's web site at http://www.heidicullinan.com and her blog at http://amazoniowan.livejournal.com/.

Something Pipeth Like a Bird

david cheater

SUMMER evening in the Shephelah hills of Judea arrived as a welcome relief. The arrogant gaze of the sun slipped behind the hills and the flowers opened to the dewy breeze. It was the time for the singing of birds.

For Yosef ben Nathan Ha Ro-eh B'Layla, it was the time of day when he would have to round up his family's stupid sheep so that the waking jackals wouldn't get them. He was so bored with his life, he felt like screaming his frustration in a way that would have rivaled the roaring of young lions.

Or so he supposed. Nothing as exciting as fighting a lion had ever happened to him. One of his older brothers had joined the Queen's army and had written home about the siege of Damascus. Another brother had gone to the Holy City to study with the Pharisees. *He* was stuck looking after smelly, dirty animals.

Yosef sat daydreaming that one day he would be like King David, who had also started life as a shepherd. That he would be famous as a warrior, a scholar, and a lover. He mused as the fires of the sunset calmed into the star-sprinkled night. And that's when he first heard the music.

At first he thought that it had to be fragments of birdsong carried on a breeze. But all the birds had grown silent at the first notes. And no bird had a melody that went on and on instead of repeating the same few notes. The song was cheerful, with a regular rhythm. Yosef was curious, and went to the crest of the hill to try to see where there were other people in the loneliness of the Shephelah.

And from the summit of the hill, under the light of the rising moon, he saw where the strange music must be coming from. The next valley had the ruins of a small fort built around a well. A ruin that was so old no one remembered whether it had been built by the Jews or by the Philistines or even by the ancient Amorites. It was a place that had been long abandoned and unclaimed.

At least by B'nai Adam, humankind.

Yosef turned and ran back down the hill. The Prophets and the Writings both spoke of the ones who shared the Earth with humans. As Eve was the Mother of All Who Live, so was Lilith the Mother of the Djinn. Her daughters were women with the wings and feet of owls, who claimed the stillborn and the women who went mad after giving birth. Her sons were the Hairy Ones, the Se`irim, who danced in the deserted towns. Unlike the angels, who were made from light, the Djinn were made from flame and smoke. They had free will, like Humanity, but the Holy One had given dominion over the Earth to the Humans rather than to the Djinn. And the Djinn envied and hated Humanity for it.

It was unwise for a mere shepherd boy to attract the attention of one who played songs in an empty house, even a shepherd boy who had just recently fancied himself as stronger, handsomer, and braver than King David.

On the other side of the hill, Yosef turned in the direction of Jerusalem and said his first prayer in days.

"In the name of the Lord, G-d of Israel, I call Michael at my right hand. I call Gabriel at my left hand. I call Uriel before me. I call Raphael behind me. I call The Presence above me."

He repeated the invocation twice as fast as he could, racing through the words his father had taught him. When he finished, he realized that he could no longer hear the tempting music on the wind. Vowing that the very next day he would move the sheep to a safer valley, he curled up by the campfire with a rock under his head and went to sleep.

Masul bin Layla al-Sa`ira was so bored with his life that he felt like screaming to the indifferent winds. Over the last few centuries, his brothers and sisters had left their home to settle in with strangers and follow strange ways. Some brothers had gone north with the Hellenes, to spend their days drinking wine and chasing after tree spirits. Others had gone to the desert lands, to build themselves palaces out of molten gold.

One of his sisters had the bizarre notion of going to the far north, giving herself the lower body of a fish, and spending her days trying to sing sailors off their boats into the cold water.

Masul would rather spend his time learning how to play the pipes that his cousin Pan had given him. While his kind had great immunity to harm, Masul preferred comfort. Spending centuries immersed in half-frozen water or blast-oven heat, just because one could, seemed like exceptionally unpleasant ways to spend eternity.

Masul walked out of the crumbling buildings into the air of a night scented with roses. As the heat of the day faded, the grass softened with dew. That's when he heard the Invocation.

In the next valley over, someone had tried to summon the Four Elements and the Spirit. They hadn't done a very good job of it, but the effort intrigued him. Humans were rarely any good at magic, especially in these parts. Even though the Prophet Solomon (may peace be upon his head) had been the greatest of wizards, the rest of his tribe treated the higher arts with horror. To even feel someone trying intrigued Masul. He called up his invisibility and went to have a look.

Halfway down the neighboring hillside was where Masul found a young Judean settling in to sleep. He was truly a delight to gaze at.

The Human youth was wearing a worn linen robe that clung to his body rather more snugly than he might have been aware. He had the curves and lines of a young gazelle, slender and firm. His skin was the dark gold of thyme honey. His hair was thick, loose curls of shiny obsidian. His nose was long and straight as a dagger blade above a mouth that was lush and curved. The youth smiled, caught in a pleasant dream, and Masul felt delight. Masul knew from experience that the hands of men who handle sheep were soft, strong, and gentle.

As the stars circled through their nightly dance, the hills grew cold and the youth shivered in his sleep. Masul was inspired to concern. Since he was barely affected by either cold or heat, he had no need of the cashmere blanket abandoned long ago in the ruins. He fetched it for the youth, who curled around it with a sigh, falling into a deeper sleep.

He spent the night watching the youth sleep and left only when the stars faded from the sky in the hour before dawn.

Yosef woke in the morning more slowly and feeling more calm than he had for months. It took him a minute to realize that he now had a blanket. That brought him to full awareness quickly enough. He knew the stories about the danger in accepting gifts from Djinn, and the other stories of the dangers of rejecting their gifts. Since the coming evening would be Shabbat, he had the right to round up the sheep and drive them back to his family's village so that they could all rest. Certainly one of the elders would know what to do.

The annoying, smelly animals were not too difficult to direct in the morning before they were awake enough to act out their stupidity. As soon as a shepherd can get a portion of the flock heading in the same direction, the rest will follow, lest they be shamed by appearing to think for themselves.

It was only a little past noon when Yosef arrived at his family's village. He locked the sheep into a yard and filled their water troughs by carrying a bucket from the well twenty-three times. Only then would his parents greet him and welcome him back into their house.

He told them of the previous night, the music, and the appearance of the blanket.

Yosef's father Nathan stroked his beard and thought. After some deliberation, he spoke to Yosef.

"What will cause the least possible offense is if you treat the blanket as a loan. Shake the dust from it and return it to the habitation of the Djinn. Bring a gift of the food of the Djinn and leave it there upon the blanket."

"What is the food of the Djinn, Abba?" Yosef asked.

"The Holy One, blessed be He, has decreed that the Djinn are to have that which is discarded by humans. We will give you the gift."

Yosef went to the Mikvah to immerse himself, since contact with the Children of Lilith could be assumed to put one in a state of ritual impurity and it was always best to take extra care before facing the Holy One. After the end of Shabbat, Yosef's mother packed for him the bones from roast doves, dry crusts of wheat bread, the rind of cheese, pits from fine olives and an amphora that had held honey wine. Early the next morning, Yosef set out to return the gift, silly sheep in tow.

It was well past noon when Yosef reached the hillside from two nights before. It was the worst part of the summer day, when the sun was pitiless and the air was thick and still. Even the bees retreated to their hives and the snakes to their holes. This was also the safest time of day to approach a Djinn.

Yosef carefully stepped over the broken cobblestones and thorny vines leading into the deserted courtyard. He laid the blanket on the ground with great care and arranged the remnants of a rich meal upon it. (He had asked his mother about including the cheese with a meat meal. She pointed out that, since the kosher laws were not observed even by Righteous Gentiles, it was unlikely that unnatural spirits borne from disobedient Lilith and demons would bother.)

Yosef felt as if someone were watching him from the shadows. He spoke clearly and slowly.

"Oh, you who are the Child of Lilith, the first woman. You who are the servant of Solomon, King born of a king and Prophet born of a prophet. I give you thanks for the loan of this fine blanket and return it to you with a gift meal."

He walked with dignity until he was well out of the ruin, and then broke into a clumsy dash.

Masul had been watching from the shadows. He was surprised at the actions of the youth. Humans tended to react in one of two ways: either they would accept the gift as their due without bothering to thank, or they would reject the gift with horror. This action was unexpectedly thoughtful.

And upon seeing the youth in daylight, Masul appreciated that his dark brown eyes were as large and liquid as the eyes of a deer. His voice was high and clear, though still masculine.

Masul feared that he would be spending yet another night mooning over the lad, but for now, he would feast. He approached the blanket and sat before it. He recited the blessings over food and drink.

The bones sorted themselves into skeletons before becoming steaming roast doves, stuffed with grain and leeks. The crusts of bread became full loaves. The honey wine bubbled up from the bottom of the dry jug. And the pits reconstituted themselves as plump black olives, rich with oil. For many years, Masul had been living off the bare memories of ancient meals that grew thinner and less substantial each time he recalled them. This would be the best meal he had eaten for ages.

Yosef, on the other side of the hill, sat down to his midday meal. Usually, he was able to carry enough food from his parents' house to last for two weeks, until he could return, but that was when he hadn't had so much else to carry. For this week, dried dates and bread along with whatever wild plants he could find would have to suffice.

That night, when the piping started, Yosef took out the beeswax that his mother had given to him, along with clear and unequivocal warnings, and considered putting it into his ears.

He had thought about nothing else the entire day. What harm would it do merely to listen to the music? Whether or not he could hear it, the music would still be there. Why would his hearing it attract the attention of the Djinn? Wouldn't he and the flock be a lot safer if he could hear the howling of jackals, in case they should attack? He ignored the part where his mother had told him that if he were close enough to hear the music of the Djinn, he was too close. If he could hear the music, he was supposed to block his ears just long enough to get at least one valley farther away, all the time praying to the Holy One to send angels to protect him. He put the beeswax back into the pocket of his robe.

Masul was in an exceptionally fine mood. He told himself that it was purely the enjoyment of a good meal, yet his fancy kept drifting to a slender form with curly hair and deep brown eyes. He decided to wander through the hills—not searching for the lad, of course, just taking the blanket as a precaution. He was well aware that if his family were there, seeing him acting like a goose girl sneaking off to peep at a prince, they would laugh their heads off, quite literally. His brothers and sisters would flap their big ears like the wings of owls and have their disembodied heads swarm around him, cackling manically, through the night.

Under the gracious moonlight upon the gentle hills of the Shephelah, Yosef dreamt of mysteries. So many things that hid from the brutal eye of the sun lived their lives in the shadows of the night. White flowers opened themselves, like shy brides removing their wedding veils, to be visited by softly droning insects. Mice quietly searched for seeds and dew, while trying to be alert for the soft flutter of owls. For the night held both gentle wonders and stealthy predators.

Walking over the crest of the hill, Masul saw the campfire of the shepherd boy and dropped the last of his pretense concerning this night stroll. He went directly to the campsite where the handsome youth sprawled in sleep.

The flicker of the fire painting Yosef gave the only color to the silver and black of the night. Masul stood watching the youth sleep. The shimmer of the firelight gave the illusion of expressions dancing over the lad's face. As the fire died down to embers and the night grew cold, he started to shiver and stir in his sleep. Masul snuck over for one last, closer look, and to regift the lad with his blanket.

The soft weight of the blanket settling on Yosef jolted him out of his quickly forgotten dream. He started, and opened his eyes to see the form bending over him. Their eyes met.

Yosef saw, in the last glow of the embers, a young man of around his own age, holding a blanket. In the glow of the dying fire, the youth's hair was copper and gold, curling at the edges. His eyes were the blue of the fire's heart, the blue of the hottest, clearest summer's day. His nose was strangely short and broad. His face was round, with ears that stuck out just a bit too much. His body was stout and muscular, more like that of one of the Hellene or Etruscan merchants than the slender grace of the Judeans. He was different from anyone Yosef had seen before, yet somehow, pleasant to look at.

Masul was startled when the shepherd boy awoke and looked at him. He saw, not the fear or revulsion that he had anticipated in the other's eyes, so deep and dark, but merely curiosity. The youth sat up and touched Masul's face, breaking his focus. Masul yelped, dropped the blanket, and ran back toward his safe and empty ruin.

"Wait!" Yosef called after the fleeing figure. The local scribe had warned him that the Djinn were shadows whose touch burned like ice, but the face Yosef had touched had been no phantom. His skin had been as soft and warm as Yosef's. If he were a Djinn, why then did he run away from Yosef?

Yosef disentangled himself from the blanket and pulled on his sandals. Whoever it had been had run out of sight, but there simply weren't any other places for him to have gone than the ruin in the next valley. With a quick glance at his huddled flock, which had yet to have been attacked by any of the supposed dangers he was there to guard them from, Yosef folded up the blanket and walked toward the next valley, the moon at his back.

Once on the other side of the hill, Masul slowed down and started thinking again. He knew he was being silly, exceptionally silly. What harm could a Son of Adam do to a child of Lilith? He-Who-Cannot-Be-Named had given dominion over the Earth to Humanity out of some misguided pity or as a test to the obedience of the Djinn. He ought to turn around, go back to that shepherd boy, look him directly in his big, brown eyes....

An image rose in Masul's mind of the curiosity in the youth's eyes turning to horror or disgust when he got a closer look at Masul. This made his bones grow cold. *This* was the way the Human could hurt him. A haughty glance would slay him as surely as an arrow to his heart. A sneer would be deadlier than an iron sword. He turned around and saw the silhouette of the shepherd boy with the blanket in his arms on the crest of the hill.

Yosef looked down the slope and saw the stocky figure of his benefactor standing still, halfway down the hill. He felt a strange satisfaction that the other young man was moving neither away nor toward him. Yosef could choose whether to meet him or to turn around and walk back to his campfire and the silly sheep. Usually someone else would be telling him what to do, when to go and when to stay, when to talk and when to listen. As is written in the Book of Wisdom, "For everything there is a season. There is a time enough for every purpose under heaven." This was the time to take a risk and accept the consequences.

Masul watched the shepherd boy's cautious walk down the hillside. Each step was a glide forward, making sure that he would neither tread on a snake nor trip on a stone. But there was a sure confidence in the movement forward, even in the shadows.

Yosef reached the stranger, who was standing so silently and still in the night. So many things he thought of saying and discarded. Finally, he said the simplest.

"Peace be upon you. Thank you for the blanket. I'm called Yosef."

It had been so long since someone had spoken to Masul that his first thought was of how much the language had changed over time.

"And to you, Peace. I'm called Masul."

They were both silent for a moment, unsure of what to say next. Yosef decided that, since whatever he asked would sound stupid, he might as well go ahead and ask.

"Are you an Angel?"

Masul laughed. "No, I'm a Djinn."

Yosef said, "I thought that Djinn were supposed to be made out of fire and of smoke. But I touched you...." He reached out his hand and ran it through Masul's hair. "...And I touch you without being burned."

Masul reached out and touched Yosef's face. "And you are supposed to be made out of mud, but your flesh doesn't feel dead and cold."

Another pause, as they stood looking upon one another in the moonlight. Yosef asked another question.

"So, tell me. The story about Father Israel wrestling with an Angel until sunrise, was that one of you?"

Masul snickered, "Wrestling, wrestling? Yes, it was one of us, but that is not what they were doing."

Yosef shrugged with a coy smile. "I was going to ask if you'd like to wrestle, but if you'd rather not...." He turned around and headed back to the campfire over the crest of the hill. He had reached it before Masul caught up to him, sputtering.

Yosef walked back to the campsite and laid the blanket on the ground. He turned back to Masul, teeth flashing in the moonlight with his grin.

"The ground is flat here and I moved away most of the rocks before I tried to sleep. It's a more comfortable place for you to show me how to not-wrestle."

Yosef was not all that ignorant; anyone who spends a significant amount of time around sheep can observe that rams do not necessarily care whether or not it is a ewe. What Yosef lacked in experience, he could compensate for with enthusiasm and stamina.

Yosef woke the next morning with the sunrise and took the opportunity to observe Masul. The Djinn was rather hairy—and hairy in some unusual places—but it was definitely human, not animal-style, hair. His feet, not hooves, were wide and large. His body hair was copper while the hair on his head was like spun red-gold. His skin was inhumanly pale—like that of a mercenary soldier from distant Gaul who was a friend of Yosef's brother—and it was dappled with tiny, darker spots he'd later found out were called "freckles."

Quite endearingly, like any human male Yosef had ever seen, he snored gently, and drooled in his sleep. Yosef pulled on his robe and sandals, said the morning prayers, then lay down again beside Masul and curled up against the warmth of his body.

Masul woke to the sting of sunlight on his skin. He yelped and thrashed around for his clothes. Yosef handed them to him.

"Why so modest?" Yosef asked.

"It's not modesty. Sunlight will burn me and make me sick," Masul said.

"I have heard of that, with albinos. Is that why your skin is strange?" Yosef asked.

"My skin is not 'strange'. It's quite normal for my people. We are people of the night and the shadows. Your people belong in the hot sun; mine don't!"

He got dressed in his tunic and rushed back to his ruin. That evening he woke to the baaing of sheep and a shepherd boy waiting outside his door.

And so, Masul allowed Yosef the Shepherd into his house and into his life. During the day, Yosef would take the sheep to graze in the nearby hills and valleys; while the nights—ah!—the nights were made for love.

But this broken world is a world of change. As the months passed, the days grew shorter and the hills cooler. The sheep grew fat and groaned under the burden of their fleece. The end of summer heralded the beginning of a New Year. At the Festival of the Harvest, Yosef would take the sheep away from the Shephelah to their winter quarters and come to the ruins no more. Masul prepared himself for his return to loneliness.

On their last night together in the ruins, Yosef packed his own belongings in one bag, and then packed Masul's in a second. He took Masul by the hand and informed him in a firm voice that if he could put up with the stupid, smelly sheep for a summer he could take the chance of meeting Yosef's family, who were nowhere near as stupid or as smelly.

How could Masul resist? But that's another story.

DAVID CHEATER was born in Ottawa in 1961. The fact that the year reads the same upside-down has never ceased to amuse him.

He grew up a military brat. He has lived in Nova Scotia, New Brunswick, Newfoundland, Ontario, and Lahr, W. Germany, where he became fluent in German.

When he returned to Canada in the mid eighties, a new political party announced that immigrants to Canada ought to respect the pre-existing culture and learn the language properly. He promptly went to the Native Canada Community Centre and studied Ojibwey (Anishnaabewowiin) for two years. He spent a few years working for a Native AIDS organization afterward.

David spent two decades working in the LGBTTTIQ community formally known as Queer. His favorite jobs were as DisAbility coordinator for Pride Toronto and a Sign Language Interpreter for a Queer Moslem Conference as a Gay Orthodox Jew. (It's a pity that the language he knows is ASL and the only person requiring an interpreter used BSL.)

Currently, David works in various Jewish cultural organizations. He spends most days at the Speculative Fiction research library studying post-Soviet Fantasy literature while wishing that his Russian were much better.

Greenleaf's Blessing

M. King

"NO, NO, no… stupid boy!"

The old man's hand connected sharply with the back of Rhynn's head, sending stars spinning across his vision and pain shooting through his skull. The pouch he had been holding fell to the worktable, disgorging a shower of headily scented dried herbs over the scarred wooden surface. Rhynn reached up and rubbed the sore patch on his crown.

"Ouch! I'm sorry, Master."

Wemmick sighed and leaned heavily on his stave, peering down at the pestle and mortar before Rhynn.

"There, you see?" He pointed one gnarled finger at the spilled herbs, some of which had fallen into the mixture Rhynn had been preparing. "What are you doing, putting this in? It's all ruined now. What have I taught you about the principles of magical substitution, eh? You must always work first by…?"

Rhynn stopped rubbing his head and frowned at the mortar. The astringent smell of copal resin filled his nostrils as he tried to remember his lessons.

"By… by the planetary element, Master?"

"Yes!" Wearily, Wemmick lowered himself into the battered wooden chair beside Rhynn, adjusting his well-worn brown cloak around his shoulders. Rhynn always took care to keep the cottage warm—not a hard task when there was a cooking fire in the grate every day, and the heat of the summer swelling to burnished ripeness outside—but the old man still keenly felt the chill. "And horehound is not under the dominion of the sun, is it? Unless, perhaps, I have lived long enough to see the very heavens altered."

Rhynn stifled a smile. For all his stern discipline and high expectations, Herb Mage Wemmick had always proved a good master. He tempered his teaching with kindness and patience, which was more than many young men Rhynn's age could expect. Even now, despite the wasted ingredients, a trace of humor lingered beneath the herbalist's words, and Rhynn knew he was not truly angry.

"No, Master. I should have used… cinnamon bark?"

"Aye." Wemmick nodded. "That would have done well. Else, oak leaf or mistletoe. But this…." He poked a finger into the ingredients Rhynn had been grinding in the mortar. "Bah. This will not do. A Thousand-Named Solar Incense cannot be tainted with an herb of the moon. It brings entirely the wrong influences. But, since you have the horehound pouch about you, go and fetch me the coltsfoot, marsh mallow, dried ground ivy, and the vial of Oil of Roses."

Rhynn rose from his seat, counting the list through in his head. "Yes, Master."

He crossed to the rank of tall cupboards and wooden racks that covered the wall opposite the inglenook, and Wemmick closed his eyes, sitting as still and silent as a carved god.

"Not that one, boy! The *ground ivy*."

Rhynn's fingers faltered on the little earthenware pot he had grasped, and he set it back on the shelf. He glanced over at his master, wondering how Wemmick could possibly know which was which, just from the sound the pots made. Maybe it was some altogether stranger way of telling. The man had, after all, been Herb Mage in these parts for as long as anyone remembered, and the role brought with it a certain powerful mystique.

Any fool—as old Wemmick was fond of saying after a glass or two of spruce beer—could know enough to put a dock leaf on a nettle sting, or chew a bit of willow for an aching back, but their craft was more than that. Since Rhynn's twelfth summer, Wemmick had been slowly sharing with him those secrets: how every plant, no matter how plain or dowdy looking, had its own uses and its particular powers. There were so many rules and facts to memorize—what plant was governed by which planet, which sign of the heavens, and how that changed what they should be used for—not to mention the hard rote of learning which ill was cured by what recipe.

"That's right," Wemmick said, his eyes still shut, as Rhynn's hand closed on the correct jar. "Now. What shall the preparation be used for, and what shall the quantities be?"

Rhynn juggled the three clay pots close to his chest, praying he wouldn't drop anything to the hard-packed dirt floor. The rushes and strewing herbs that softened the ground beneath his feet would prove no saving barrier to the earthenware jars. He reached for the stone bottle containing the Oil of Roses, a costly ingredient that Wemmick bought each year from a peddler who came through in the spring. He was nearly as old as the Herb Mage, and Rhynn had grown used to watching them haggle the price for an hour or more, bickering with the weight of years behind them, like an old married pair.

"Um.... 'Tis a cure for coughs, Master. To soothe the pain and rawness, ease the hacking, and bring up the foulness in the lungs. Three parts horehound, two apiece of coltsfoot and marsh mallow, and one of ground ivy, all to be bound up in a blue silk cloth and boiled in water the moon has touched." Rhynn glanced at his master, waiting for the nod of that gray-topped head that would signal he was right. He wet his lips, anxious to please the old man, but still eager to learn. "But... I don't know what the Oil of Roses is for."

Wemmick smiled as Rhynn set the pots and jars down upon the table.

"For earaches. Mix it with the horehound and drip it in by means of a raven's feather. Takes the pain clean away. The Widow Olafson's youngest has been sorely troubled by such hurt. So much so the woman fears he'll go deaf."

Rhynn raised his eyebrows. "The Widow Olafson? But... you paid the peddler more than one gold piece for the Oil of Roses, and—"

"And the price does not matter," Wemmick said curtly. "You know that, boy."

Rhynn looked down at the table. "Yes, Master."

The old man must know what people in the village said about him—and about Rhynn too. They were pleased enough to come to the cottage's door at all hours, should they need healing, but they still whispered behind their hands in the market, and drew their children out of Wemmick's path when they met him on the road. The widow was one of the worst. She, like so many of the people now, had taken to the new religion of the monks and their abbeys—dour, stern, and austere, preaching abstinence and obedience—and though Rhynn did not begrudge anyone their faith, he hated the judgmental hypocrisy that came with it. What right had she, or any of them, to call his master the names they did? Rhynn knew. He'd heard them, when Wemmick sent him down to buy food, lard, or cloth and thread for herb bags. He heard the whispers, the mutters of witchcraft and sorcery. And these were the same people who had depended on the Herb Mage their whole lives—no distaste for magic and the old ways then, when they were sore or bleeding and needed help.

He said nothing, and began to sweep up the mess he'd made on the worktable. If it were up to Rhynn, the Widow Olafson could take her puling, squalling brat up to the abbey, and let their prayers right him.

"It's not the way we work, boy," Wemmick said, as if he'd read the thought from the inside of Rhynn's skull. "What must be done is done, and there is no payment for it. The act is not weighed against anything but the simple fact of what is needed, and that is where we take our art."

Rhynn carried the handful of spilled herbs over to the fire. The flames grumbled and spat low in the grate, but as he tossed the dried leaves on, they flared bright, releasing an intense, woody odor. Rhynn shivered and brushed his palms together.

"I know, Master. I'm sorry."

"Ah, you're young." Wemmick lifted the stopper from the stone bottle, and a strong scent of rose, rich and luxurious, reached Rhynn even from across the narrow room. "You've been learning at my knee for ten years, and you think you've thought your way through all the problems and injustice in the world… but you're still learning, boy. And you'll go on learning as long you live. But, mark this: There are greater depths in all things, Rhynn. Even in yourself. And, until you know the full breadth of a thing, you can never begin to change it."

Embarrassed by those odd, grand words, Rhynn looked down at his feet. The firelight danced on the worn toes of his thin leather shoes, and he supposed it must be the heat of the flames against the already balmy day that brought such warmth to his cheeks.

"'s, Master," he mumbled.

"Go on, then," Wemmick said, glancing up at him, his gruff tone belied by the look in those sharp, merry blue eyes. "I'll see to these preparations. Get out of my sight, boy. Take yourself off for the afternoon."

"Thank you, Master."

Rhynn bobbed a clumsy but grateful bow, and was already darting for the door before Wemmick called out, "Why not go down to the pond, eh? There should be plenty of Herb Robert fit for gathering. Bring three bags back, will you?"

"Yes, Master," Rhynn promised.

Obediently, he grabbed a handful of the thin cloth bags that hung on a peg by the door, and slipped from the cottage into the bright summer sun.

After the dimness within, the harsh light streaked his vision with hot, blue shadows, and Rhynn screwed up his eyes, the pain sharp and sudden. He began to walk, his vision adjusting, and the sun was pleasantly warm on his skin.

The cottage lay a way back from the rest of the village, shrouded by trees, just one narrow dirt track running from its humble plot down to the crossroads and, from there, to the easterly end of the settlement, where the houses were fewer in number. Down the slope that led away from the cottage, some of their thatched roofs were visible between the patchwork of trees and shrubs. Rhynn turned and headed away, taking the other fork of the narrow path, the village at his back and, ahead of him, the great tracts of forest that lay between the settlement and the river. Despite his affection for the old man, he was glad to leave Wemmick's dark little cottage and head out into the sunshine. The cottage had been Rhynn's home since his twelfth summer, when the aunt who had raised him—a thin-faced, severe woman, full of vinegar and that new, dour religion of the abbeys—had determined it was time for him to repay his blood-debt to the Herb Mage.

Wemmick had saved Rhynn from the fever that had claimed both his parents when he was but a baby. No one had thought he would live, and Aunt Elinora in particular had never seemed all that glad of the fact that he had. His life, Rhynn decided, was better with Wemmick than it might have been in so many other places. He did owe his life to the old man, after all, and next to that, what was the consequence of spending each day doubled over a cooking fire, or perpetually smelling of hog's lard, soot, and dried herbs?

Rhynn let the breath whistle through his teeth as he walked slowly toward the pond. It was the vague, tuneless kind of jollity that suited a day like this, with the sky a clear, clean blue, and the tall, feathery grasses tickling the skirts of the hedgerows. He counted off the plants and their uses as he passed. Cow parsley, celandine, chickweed… no Herb Robert, though. He would have to go all the way down to the old pond—not that it was a hardship.

Rhynn smiled to himself at the thought of his master's kindness, and headed up to the overgrown track that led to the pond, a favored spot for most of the village's youth at one time or another. As he drew nearer, Rhynn heard water splashing, and automatically slowed his gait. The thick greenery that grew between the tree trunks afforded a kind of screen, allowing him to peer down the slope to the pond without being seen.

He stepped into the lee of an old, high-arched willow tree, its trunk laced with lichen and its leaves hanging to the brush like a great brocade curtain. Below the track, someone was swimming in lazy strokes across the pond, nothing much visible of them but flashes of tanned skin rhythmically cleaving the water, a sudden contrast to the dark surface.

Rhynn held his breath. He knew that figure as well as he knew his own—it was Vareth, one of the few boys from the village who had ever consented to be his friend. Rhynn remembered the day they met; how he had looked up from his childish scrawls in the dirt and seen the face of an angel gazing back at him. Blond hair, blue eyes, an upturned nose spattered with freckles, and a wide grin that spoke of unlimited mischief to be had… a promise that Vareth, with his irresistible love for pranks, had always lived up to.

Rhynn moved to call out to him, but something stilled his tongue and, laying his palm against the willow's trunk, he stood quiet for a moment, just watching. They would come up to the pond together sometimes, and swim or just laze on the banks, watching the sun sparkle on the water and the iridescent dragonflies glimmer in the sultry air. Vareth seemed to prefer that, in recent years, to the madcap scrapes they'd gotten into in the past, and Rhynn had almost mourned the loss of those silly, childish times. Almost… because he could never quite feel sorry for any time spent with Vareth, even if he was doing nothing but listening to his friend breathe.

Now, Rhynn watched him swim to the edge of the pond and rise from the murky water, his naked body gilded by the sun, every curve and angle of his flesh glistening in the fresh light. Vareth stood half a head taller than Rhynn, the work he did as the miller's boy lending an enviable broadness and strength to his back and shoulders. The muscles stood out as he stretched his arms above his head, completely unself-conscious in what he took to be his solitude.

Rhynn wet his lips with a nervous tongue, trying to banish from his mind the thought of each tiny rivulet of brackish water running down that firm, wide chest, tracing in tender lines the slim waist and narrow hips.... He leaned forward, his breaths short and tight, craning to snatch a better glimpse of Vareth's nudity without exposing himself to discovery. He knew it was wrong—a dirty, shameful thing, to peep like this—but Rhynn had grown used to scrabbling for snatches of such pleasure.

He pressed closer to the tree trunk, losing second after second to the whirl of fantasy inside his head. The tree's unyielding hardness was no comfort to the ache in his body. Long-held frustrations seethed into an uncomfortable pinch in his breeches as he watched Vareth's handsome form, and every inch of Rhynn's flesh seemed to yearn for the simplest of touches. A hug, an embrace… a kiss.

They had been friends for years. Friends, and never anything more.

Even after all this time, Rhynn had never dared reveal his secrets to anyone. He was already an outsider, distrusted in the village, and marked out by that same taint of sorcery that clung to the Herb Mage's cloak. What sense was there in driving away the few who did deign to talk to him?

Rhynn took a deep breath, willing the dizziness to leave him, wishing he could gaze down at Vareth and see only a friend, not a wonderful, forbidden, intoxicatingly tempting promise, so far out of his reach that it was painful to look at him—and yet impossible to look away. For a moment his plea seemed answered, for Vareth glanced up to where Rhynn was hidden, and his face split into a grin as he raised one brown, sinewy arm and waved.

"Rhynn? Is that you?"

All the desire and emotion ebbed out of him, as suddenly as water spilled from a broken bowl, and his mouth worked hopelessly around a dry, empty shout, barely a murmur leaving his lips. Rhynn cleared his throat and stumbled from his haunt behind the tree, lifting his hand in recognition.

"Vareth! I didn't think it was that cold today."

He started down the track toward his friend, a little ashamed of the bravado. In truth, Vareth was better endowed than Rhynn, but he wasn't about to admit his envy… or his desire.

"Hoi! Cheeky." Vareth grinned, hands on his hips, his body still damp when Rhynn tripped the last few feet from the bottom of the track and down to the pond's muddy banks.

It was a quiet, secluded hollow of a place, fringed with long grasses and towering weeds, the arching shapes of trees clasped around it like the fingers of cupped hands, and, in their center the old pond lay, its dark surface a still palm, crisscrossed with lines of duckweed.

"Come on, then," Vareth said, jerking his head at the water. "Are you swimming?"

Rhynn drew breath to refuse, but paused. His master *had* given him the afternoon off, and the day was warm. His gaze met Vareth's, and a sly smile spread across his lips.

"I'll wager you tuppence I can beat you across the pond," Vareth added.

"Then I'll take your money," Rhynn boasted, pulling his shirt over his head and tossing it to the grass.

Vareth laughed and, bending down, dipped his hand into the cool, black water, flicking it up and splashing Rhynn before he twisted away and plunged back into the pond.

"Rotten cheat!" Rhynn called, failing to be even remotely angry as he grinned at his friend's receding shape, already making for the far bank.

He dropped his breeches, wishing he could feel as free with his body as Vareth, and followed him into the water, only wincing a little at the coolness of it on his sun-warmed skin. Rhynn had been swimming in this pond most of his life, and he navigated its hidden depths with ease, veering away from the reaches of sharp stones or sucking silt, and unfazed by the tickle of weeds or minnows against his flesh.

He was fast, and soon caught up to Vareth, who reached out to splash him again, in the sense of good-natured competition. Rhynn fought back, and the pair of them were soon splashing and dueling within an arm's length of the far bank, a challenge that lasted until Rhynn—with a roar of triumph—plunged from the water first.

"I win!" he cried, but the victory was short-lived.

Vareth launched himself at Rhynn with a playful growl, arms locked around his waist and head against his chest, wet hair and hot breath dragging on Rhynn's skin. The force of the tackle—and the sensation—knocked him off balance, and Rhynn fell backward, Vareth's weight bearing him down beyond all control until they toppled to the pond's sloping, muddy bank in a tangle of limbs, splashing, and laughter.

They wrestled and tussled with each other, the trailing streaks of duckweed and algae painting their bodies. Rhynn moved to get up, but Vareth's hands shot out, pinning his arms to the silt. He slid his knees further apart so he sat astride Rhynn's body, and not even the cool, slime-speckled pond water lapping between them could mask the heat of his naked thighs, or all the weighty promise of what lay at their junction. He was still laughing, his face bent low and close, but Rhynn's mirth faded fast next to the uncomfortable reality of his friend's nearness.

He wriggled, splashing helplessly in the inch or so of water in which he lay, terrified his body might betray him at any moment, that Vareth would find him out and be disgusted, embarrassed… ashamed of him.

Unless *he* wanted it too. The thought barely occurred to Rhynn, because things like that just did not happen. The world did not throw him those kinds of chances, and yet here was Vareth, pinning him in the wet mud, with his wet mouth so close, so aching to be kissed.

Once he'd admitted the impulse, Rhynn could barely breathe, able to think of nothing else, able to see nothing but Vareth's face, mud-smeared and scattered with droplets that beaded his forehead, nose—and those incomparable, bowed lips—like small, delicate pearls. He was sure Vareth must feel it, must *know*, though he showed no sign.

They stayed like that a little while, and the laughter seemed to fade from both of them as if it was the most natural transition, the most ordinary thing in the world for their faces to draw nearer, their mouths to gradually move toward each other in a gentle and inexorable progression.

Rhynn knew he couldn't have drawn a breath had he tried. His head thrummed with a whirl of flashing colors and deafening thrills of panic and excitement, too disparate and jagged to even be fully formed thoughts. His lips burned, his cheeks hotter than flames, and the moment seemed so surreal he was sure it couldn't be truly happening. Rhynn closed his eyes, waiting for the beautiful second that would bring his friend's mouth to his. He was barely aware of craning up to seize Vareth's lips against his, too caught up in the blissful knowledge that, after so long, he finally had a true friend, one who understood what he'd ached for all this time, and one who—

"Rhynn! What in the Devil's name d'you think you're doing?"

It was over so fast, like a rude awakening from a dream, the perfect details already fading as fast as mist scalded off by a vicious sun. Vareth flung himself back, landing rump-down in the murky water and splashing farther away, his face twisted in shock and horror.

Rhynn could say nothing. He blinked, his lips no longer hot with desire but rubbery and cold, his face now scalded with an altogether different flame. His throat tightened until the breath wheezed in him, and the world seemed to crack into shards.

"I…."

Vareth scrambled to his feet and lurched to the bank, seizing his clothes and rapidly dressing. His muttered curse words were not too quiet for Rhynn to hear, and they sliced into him with the deft ice of knives. Rhynn rose unsteadily, his legs wobbly and his stomach threatening to revolt.

"Vareth…."

"Don't," Vareth warned, his voice hard and his face pale as he laced his breeches, his shirt tugged haphazardly over his head. "Just… don't, you hear?"

That hurt. It hurt worse than anything Rhynn had ever known; a physical agony with steep, slippery sides, pitching him into its endless, isolating depths. He was acutely aware of his nakedness, of standing there nude and exposed, ankle-deep in the old pond, the air in tatters around him.

He gritted his teeth, clenching his jaw for fear of loosing the bile that rose in his throat and, wordlessly, staggered out to pull on his clothes. Rhynn's fingers shook on the laces, but he dared not halt or slow, knowing all the while that Vareth was standing there, watching him with such a hard look upon his face. The weight of tears prickled behind his eyes, yet he held fast and did not allow them to fall, fighting to keep the dignity he so wished he hadn't betrayed. Voices seemed to taunt Rhynn from the depths of his own head. What a fool he was for having—even for one moment—imagined himself to not be alone, for having imagined that his friend had felt the same way as he. Such a thing would never, *could* never happen. He yanked his shirt over his head and, not pausing to tidy himself, blundered back up the track, away from the old pond, away from the pain, and away from Vareth's accusing stare.

Rhynn walked faster and faster, his stride eating up the ground until he broke into a ragged, loping run, a desperate pelt without direction or conscious thought. The tears came then, blinding him even as he swiped at his eyes with the heel of his palm, hearing the gasping, sobbing breaths ripped from his chest like the gulps of a horse run to death.

Rhynn ran on and on, deeper into the forest than he had been before, though he took no heed of which way he turned, the path long since abandoned behind him. The towering arches of trees reached high above him, their canopy a mantle of black, interlocked fingers mottled with webs of leaves. The light that filtered down to the dank, musty ground had a strange, thick cast to it, as if it had been passed thirdhand through mirrors, reflected and refracted until it became a curious copy of itself, no longer clear or true.

Eventually, Rhynn's breath failed him and he fell to his knees beside the great, decaying trunk of an old oak, long since perished due to some storm or, perhaps, the ravages of time… if time did indeed reach this far into the forest. Sniffling and glancing about him, Rhynn was not sure whether it did. He shivered, recalling the bedtime stories of years gone by: of princesses captured by wicked witches, and foolish maidens snatched by fairies after they foolishly wandered between standing stones.

Rhynn blotted his eyes on the back of his hand and rested against the fallen tree, trying to catch his breath—and his sanity. Old Master Wemmick said that stories like those were fools' gargles and nothing more. Believe in magic, he always said, but not in superstition. Rhynn sniffed, and thought ruefully of the three bags of Herb Robert he was supposed to take back to the cottage. He'd left the bags down by the old pond, he realized. Not that it would matter. If he could ever find his way back to the road, much less the Herb Mage's cottage, worse than his master's disapproval would probably be there to greet him.

Rhynn rose cautiously to his feet and looked around him. Trees pressed in on every side, the forest floor thick with shed leaves, turned dry and crisp in the upper layers and, beneath that, given to dense, intoxicating decay. This was no gentle, well-tended copse, like the woods just beyond the village's boundaries. Somehow, he had come into the dark heart of the place, to the depths of the forest where not even the corpses of trees were truly dead. Rhynn held his breath and listened to the sounds that throbbed through the dank air: the clicks and chirrups of insects and unseen creatures scuffling through the undergrowth, and the soft creaks and sighs of the trees themselves. They almost seemed like words, half-lost on the thin echoes of a breeze.

He walked slowly, trying to take note of the direction he took, but it was hard to even guess which way was which. The light, filtered down through the canopy, lent everything a weird, greenish air, like the cool, deep cathedral quiet of a riverbed. Rhynn began to fear he would never find his way out, and his thoughts turned both to the coming night and the things that would stalk it. There could be boars, wolves, bears… who knew what, just waiting for such easy prey as him.

Rhynn shivered and walked on, his fingertips grazing the rough trunks of the trees he passed. He tried to memorize each one of them, imprint them on his mind as a map of sorts, and fell to counting off their names in the ways Master Wemmick had taught him.

"Here's black alder," he murmured to himself, squinting up at the leaves, "which Venus rules. The bark is dried and boiled in vinegar, whence it doth kill lice and purify all that it touches. There, the spread of mighty oak, that is the child of Saturn. Use to stay all fluxes of the blood. A-and here, sycamore, whose bark seals together at once the lips of open wounds…."

The words sounded hollow, his voice shaky and timid, but the litany gave Rhynn comfort. He kept going and, at length, came upon a small clearing, dominated by the great, twisted body of a fallen tree.

Rhynn stopped, his first thought that he'd taken a wrong turning and ended up back where he started, but this was not the same place. As he looked at the fallen tree, he saw a shape, outlined in shadow, just beyond the claw of its upturned roots. Rhynn blinked, sure he must be going mad. For a moment, it had almost looked like—

"Who enters my forest?"

The voice was a man's, or seemed to be. It was clear and authoritative, but neither loud nor challenging. It came to him across the clearing like a clarion, and the hair rose on the back of Rhynn's neck. The shape flickered, its edges fuzzy with all the indecisiveness of a thing seen through water, and he strained to make out who it was that had spoken.

"M-my name is Rhynn," he stammered. "I mean no harm. I've just lost my way, and—"

"You name us," the voice said, seeming to echo from the very fabric of the trees. "You *know* us. We feel it in your touch."

Rhynn's fingers curled defensively into his palms, and he edged forward a little over the dry carpet of leaves.

"Please, I mean no harm. Might I see who you are, sir? I'm apprentice to Herb Mage Wemmick, from the village back… well, back that way, I think. I'm lost. I never meant to…."

"Hush, mortal. Be still and do not be afraid."

Rhynn pressed his lips tight together, terrified despite everything that calm, warm voice said. What did it belong to, that called him "mortal"? He stared at the odd, shadow-laden shape by the fallen tree and, as he watched, it seemed to shiver, its form becoming clear in one long, awful moment that made his eyes itch and his mouth turn dry and slack.

What had been nothing but a shadow became a man… or something that very much resembled one. He—for Rhynn had no idea what else to call this extraordinary being—stood easily six feet high, and he had both arms and legs, a head and torso, and all the other things that marked out a human being, but there the similarity ended. He was formed, it seemed, entirely of the living, beating heart of the forest.

Though he was broad-shouldered and as elegantly made as the finest of princes, his figure stately and impressive, Rhynn could trace in every limb, every muscle, the shape of a tree's bough, the twist of vines and subtle stems, and the rustle of soft, verdant leaves. His hair hung down to the center of his back, as full and delicate as the sweep of a willow, and he regarded Rhynn with a face that, from across the clearing, appeared to be a finely wrought carving, like the well-polished knots on the trunk of a young birch.

He wore no clothes, as such, but his body was draped in a patchwork of mosses, lichens, and leaves that seemed to be less garments than an actual, living part of him. Rhynn knew he was staring, but he couldn't wrench his gaze away. The man, the… whatever he was, raised one great arm, tendrils of moss and vines trailing from it, and curled his attenuated, twig-like fingers, beckoning gently.

"Come. You are welcome."

Rhynn licked his lips and, unable to resist, drew near to the strange being. Close up, he was even more incredible. A tall, beautiful man, not hewn from wood, not made up of many ill-fitting, unjoined parts, but his entire body one amazing, flawless whole. He was the green life gushing from the earth, the sap rising in the spring… the wild heart of the greenwood.

The mingled scents of leaf mold and dark earth, of sharp pine resin, fresh bark, and warm rain enveloped Rhynn. He longed to reach out and touch the man's broad chest and arms, to feel whether blood-heat beat within him. His skin, if that was what it was, was not cracked or ragged, but smooth-layered, like the banded russets and browns on the bark of a young yew. What on a man of flesh would have been the delicate blue tracery of veins, on him were thin trails of greenery, fresh shoots trailing his arms and neck. His face, too, bore the same patterning of deep, earthy hues, the high, proud angles of forehead, nose, and cheekbones giving way to a mouth that Rhynn was sure must be flesh, for it seemed to hold all the sensuality of skin.

He wondered, briefly, why those thoughts did not shame him. Had he not, just hours ago, fled from all the embarrassment and disgust that an outcast such as he was due? Yet here, in this place, so far removed from anything that could be real or sane, Rhynn could muster nothing of the fear he'd felt with Vareth, and none of that awkward humiliation

"Forgive me," he murmured, his gaze drawn to this remarkable creature's face, and to the eyes that burned at its center: great, pupil-less voids of dark fire shot through with stars… like staring into the very essence of time itself. "I… I don't know what…."

"I have many names," the man said, and his voice brought such comfort to Rhynn, throbbing right through the core of his chest like a warm balsam, as if no pain could ever penetrate there again. "They call me Old Tom, Old Greenleaf, The Watcher, Jack-in-the-Green.... I am the Waldgeist, the spirit of the forest, and its guardian. All that this place is, I am, and all that I am, it is. We are one, the wildwood and I. We see with the same eyes, the same heart. And we see you, Herb Mage."

A fearful gasp broke from Rhynn's throat. "No, I am not— I'm but Master Wemmick's apprentice. I don't…."

"Ah, yes." A low, rumbling sound that Rhynn supposed must be a laugh echoed from the spirit, and all around the clearing the leaves rustled, as if touched by a summer breeze. "We forget. There is so much time. So… many years."

Old Greenleaf reached out one of those curious, elongated hands and touched Rhynn's face, his moss-wreathed head tipped to the side like a bird's. Rhynn did not flinch; he was not, he realized, afraid. Those bark-shrouded fingers were surprisingly warm, gentle, and smooth against his skin.

"And yet, you are very like him."

Rhynn frowned, confused. "Like Master Wemmick?"

"Aye."

As soon as that careful caress ended, Rhynn found he missed it. He tried to shake the feeling, embarrassed by it, but he couldn't deny the peculiar, comforting sense of peace and calm he gained from this place—and its guardian.

"You know my master?"

"I did." Greenleaf sighed, and it rippled through Rhynn like a physical sensation, a warm breeze across water. "We knew all those who held to the old ways, once. There was a time, not so long past, when their songs rang through the forest… but we do not hear them so loudly now.

Those who truly know us are few, and their voices are but whispers. Until you came."

Rhynn frowned, confused. Those great, terrible eyes seemed to gather him in, as if the spirit was assessing him, weighing every part of his soul. He drew himself up, finding he was neither afraid nor outraged. Rhynn's only desire was for Greenleaf to be pleased with what he saw—that he should be everything his master would want him to be, and all that *he* wanted to be, besides. Even so, he trembled a little beneath the spirit's gaze. Rhynn shut his eyes, not wanting his nervousness to betray him.

Within the darkness inside his head, the sound of his own breathing seemed loud. Every noise from the forest around him—every rustle of the leaves, every flutter of a bird breaking cover, even the gentle creaking of the trees themselves, alive in growth and spirit—seemed loud, and the dark, damp, musky scent of the forest enveloped him. It grew heavier, and Rhynn shivered at what felt like warm breath skating across his cheek. He yearned to open his eyes, but something held them closed; perhaps apprehension of what he might see, or perhaps fear at breaking whatever spell held him in its grasp.

"Don't be afraid," Greenleaf said softly, "it is but a gift. Will you take my gift?"

Wordlessly, Rhynn nodded. He didn't know what the spirit meant—yet his body responded without the need for thought or analysis. The breath wavered in his chest, his flesh prickling with anticipation.

It was a strange, perplexing sensation. Amid the crackle of leaves and the groan of timber, Rhynn was aware of Greenleaf moving. He clenched his hands into fists, the tips of his fingers digging into his palms, and willed himself to stay still, fighting the urge to run.

Though Rhynn had known little of lovers' caresses in any form, there was no mistaking the feel of the spirit's attenuated, elegant fingers wrapping themselves around his ankles. He tensed, still hiding in the dark world behind his eyes as Greenleaf slipped off his thin leather shoes, leaving Rhynn's bare feet to bury themselves in the thick mulch of the forest floor. The dry, crumbly mass of leaves was unexpectedly soft, and he wriggled his toes experimentally. The breath caught in his throat as the instantly recognizable pressure of hot, human lips grazed the sensitive skin of Rhynn's insteps.

The spirit was kissing his feet.

Gently, first one, then the other—two kisses, sweet and soft gifts that Rhynn could not help but accept with love and a blissful sense of trust that bloomed in his chest, more intense than any longing he had felt before.

Blessed be the feet that brought you to me.

The voice seemed to echo at once from the very fabric of the forest, and also from deep within Rhynn, as if the words were not spoken but simply existed, like the memory of things already said, a truth already admitted.

He quivered as Greenleaf's clever, magical hands deftly unlaced his breeches and drew them down, exposing his most intimate parts. Despite the warmth of the day, the air came as a cool surprise, and Rhynn gasped. Immediately, he felt the spirit's touch on his thighs, soothing yet also stoking the heat that rose in him, pooling like liquid mercury in the base of his belly.

Rhynn's clenched fists began to tremble as Greenleaf kissed his knees, and that familiar voice ran through him, calming as balsam.

Blessed be the knees on which you kneel, for you know what is truly sacred.

He had to look. The lips that brushed his skin felt so warm, so real. He had to *see*…. Rhynn took a deep breath and opened his eyes, unclenching his hands as he gazed down at the figure kneeling before him.

Greenleaf had changed. Where a figure of unearthly, inhuman proportions had been, cloaked in the green of the forest, Rhynn now saw a beautiful, proud man. He was still tall and broad, even hunched down on his knees. His face was still a perfectly hewn sculpture that held eyes dark as a velvet sky riven with the specks of newborn stars… but he *was* a man.

It seemed as if the bark and moss had fallen from him like a coat and he had stepped from the shell, his skin smooth and fresh, his scent that of earth dampened by rain, mixed with the sharpness of rising sap and fallen leaves.

Yet he was not human. It was the little details that gave him away; those eyes, for one, plus the faint glow that seemed to swell beneath his skin, like a barely contained sunrise, and the fact that his hair was still the dark, rich green of moss. The knowledge hammered at Rhynn's brain, together with the last shred of rational thought that screamed he should flee the clearing, should… what? Return to the cottage, perhaps, and try to cling to the routines and mundanities of everyday life, forever regretting that he hadn't stayed?

No, that would not do.

Greenleaf raised his face, looking up at Rhynn with those impossible black, shining eyes, the fire of a thousand heavens sparkling across their surface. His handsome, somber mouth curled into a slow, seductive smile, and he reached out, gently taking Rhynn's hands. He threaded his warm fingers through Rhynn's, pulling his arms a little way out from his body, each hand clasping its twin close, palm to palm.

Blessed be all with which you create, the tools that give life, love, and power.

The words throbbed through Rhynn as the most intimate kiss engulfed him; wet heat and the tender, delicate embrace of a hot tongue on his shaft. He sighed, his knees weakened, but it was over before it had begun, and a soft cry of disappointment left him as the spirit pulled away.

Rising, Greenleaf let go of his hands and stood before him, his full height making him more than a head taller than Rhynn, the breadth of his muscular frame more apparent than ever. Barely realizing what he was doing, Rhynn reached out, needing to touch, to feel, to caress that warm, smooth skin. The heat of that firm, strong chest seared his palms, and his fingers traced the irresistible swells of a body it felt as if he had always known. The more he stared at the spirit's beautiful form, the more it seemed to shift and change. One moment, the skin seemed to be as pale as birch, the next as deep as mahogany, its surface etched with a fine, silky grain, like a stave of polished holly.

His touch roved, and Greenleaf did not deny him. He bent his head, the powerful muscles of neck and shoulders bunching between Rhynn's fingers as another kiss—dropping with all the softness of dandelion down—met the center of his chest, quickening the beat of his eager heart.

Blessed be your heart, for it is wise and true, and holds the wisdom of the gods.

Rhynn tipped his head back, luxuriating in the feel of that rose-sweet mouth trailing up his chest, up the slim column of his neck, and butting against the hard line of his jaw. The spirit's great trunks of arms enfolded him, and Rhynn breathed deep, the scent of the forest floor—that warm, musky spice—filling his lungs.

Blessed be your mouth, which, in truth and love, speaks the sacred names.

A firm, warm hand cupped his cheek, and brought his lips to Greenleaf's. For the briefest of seconds, Rhynn looked into those black, star-chased eyes, and a wave of complete adoration engulfed him. It was a curious thing, greater in its depth and intensity than anything he'd ever felt, and it seemed to stem from the pit of his soul.

Never had he felt so safe, so cherished, so utterly accepted.

The memory of Vareth filtered dreamily through Rhynn's mind and—as his mouth melded with the spirit's—a pang of regret gnawed at him, for the friendship he had certainly lost, as well as the love that had never been. Yet even that pain was short-lived. As Rhynn thought of his friend, and wished things could have been different, the regrets seemed to evaporate like dew, and he found he could feel no shame, no anger… only a deep, sweet peace.

He lost himself in Greenleaf's embrace. The kiss lasted until he grew dizzy, and then a little longer, and Rhynn leaned against the spirit's broad body, glad of the strong arms wrapped around him. He closed his eyes, his cheek pressed to the spirit's chest.

Time did not seem to matter in the forest. That much Rhynn had already learned, but what Greenleaf proceeded to teach him eroded almost all he knew of the world beyond the trees. He might have been an innocent in experience, but Rhynn's enthusiasm outweighed his clumsiness. As the spirit embraced him afresh, a ruthless desire flowed through his body, his limbs moved by a new, sudden passion. Rhynn laced his fingers into the strange, ferny falls of Greenleaf's hair, cleaving himself ever closer to the spirit's form, which, even if it was not fully human, was more than man enough for what he sought.

Those arms—at once both flesh and some darker, older sinew, like the gnarled roots of ancient trees—bound him tight, and Rhynn lost the rhythm of his breathing in a ceaseless round of kisses, each deeper than the last. Lips seared his cheeks, his mouth, his closed eyes, brow, jaw;

they traveled south, peppering his neck like a fall of leaves, even as his flesh was held tight against a firm, obdurate form that so nearly mirrored his own. Every angle and swell of his body met the answering pressure of another's, chest for chest, thigh for thigh, belly for belly and, below that, a new and indescribable pleasure stoked fresh flames in Rhynn's heart.

His mouth earnestly pressed to Greenleaf's, Rhynn's touch roved the spirit's body, and his hips thrust his eager, hungry shaft against the answering pressure of another proud staff.

There was so much more to it—this new barrage of sensations—than the fevered explorations he'd enjoyed alone. Where, by himself, Rhynn had only ever experienced a wash of satisfaction that, though intoxicating, remained local, the pleasure he felt now flooded his whole body. He seemed totally enfolded by the spirit, completely encapsulated in a perfect sphere of delight that left him light-headed and loose, his pulse thundering and every nerve fizzling with uncontained bliss.

They could, he supposed, have either risen to the heavens or tumbled to the ground, fallen head over heels and tangled in each other through the leaf mold and tree roots. He had no conception of space or time, nor any notion of what was real and what was fantasy… if the twain had ever been sundered.

Rhynn's last thought, before he peaked into a blinding, almost painful ecstasy, was that none of this might be real. For all he knew, he could have been struck upon the head and, even now, be lying in the mud and silt by the side of the old pond.

That image set itself in his mind and he fought to drag his eyes open, fixed on the sudden recollection of the dark water, and the sun-gilded body of one whom he'd thought was his friend….

No such vision greeted Rhynn—just a blur of greens and browns, and the strong, almost overpowering smell of the forest, stirred with a long, drawn-out sigh, like a low wind rustling through the creaking boughs. He reached out, his hands closing on nothing but air as, slowly and inexorably, he slipped into a peaceful, comfortable sleep.

Blessed art thou, child of the forest: dear to its heart, marked with its love.

RHYNN did not know how long he slept, but when he awoke, the lazy afternoon sun was filtering low through the leaves, dappling the undergrowth with thick, golden light. He was slumped against the fallen oak tree, its damp, musky smell strong in his nostrils, though there was no sign that any other being had ever been in the clearing.

Cautiously, Rhynn ran a hand over his head, but found no bumps or bruises. He rose unsteadily to a sitting position, patting down his shirt and breeches and finding himself all laced up and as tidy as he'd been when he left Master Wemmick's cottage. He ran his tongue around the inside of his mouth and tasted nothing but the rime of sleep and torpor, which left him supposing, however loath he was to entertain the thought, that the whole thing had been no more than a dream.

Puzzled, and still somewhat woozy, Rhynn reached out a hand and pushed against the fallen oak, intending to steady himself as he stood. At once, a shock ran through his arm, his palm hot against the rotting wood.

He gasped, and looked sharply at the tree. The bulk of the thing had already begun to decay, the bark peeling back to reveal its darker inner pith. Beetles and woodlice burrowed deep beneath the surface, working away at the business of devouring the corpse. Yet, as Rhynn touched the oak, it seemed to shiver under his skin and—from those dark, thick-lipped wounds—tiny shoots of green began to emerge.

Fighting the urge to pull away, curiosity prevailing over fear, Rhynn brought his other hand to the fallen tree. With a soft, sighing groan, the bark peeled back a little farther, and tendrils of delicate, tender green curled from within its ravaged outer shell.

Rhynn watched, astounded. Could that really be his doing? He snatched his palms from the tree, and the shoots stilled in their growth, the first furled hints of leaves curling at their tips. Breathing hard, he stepped back, but stopped at the sound of his feet meeting something other than dry leaf mold.

Rhynn looked down, and saw narrow blades of grass—a vivid green against the muted brown tones of the forest floor—edging out from under his shoes. As he lifted his foot, he could plainly see the imprint of his shoe in the brush, lined with fresh new growth, incongruous and verdant.

He turned, and didn't stop running until the canopy overhead began to thin and the creak of the trees, which sounded so awfully like the laughter of an unseen but familiar figure, subsided into quiet. Rhynn didn't look back to see whether he left a trail of new turf behind him but, as he finally emerged from the forest—and it was so much easier, it seemed, to find his way than it had been before—those strange effects seemed to have ceased.

Bent double, at last trying to catch his breath, Rhynn panted. Sweat dampened his shirt, his head and lungs throbbed, and violent streaks of blue slashed his vision as he tried to sort the real from the impossible. Slowly, gulping the warm air and feeling the sun soothe his clammy skin, he started back toward the road. He would head for home, and perhaps try to find the words with which to tell his master what had happened… or what, at any rate, *might* have happened.

Rhynn glanced nervously behind him as he walked, but his steps seemed to leave nothing more than dents upon the ground. Had he simply imagined the new shoots springing from the fallen oak? Perhaps he'd imagined all of it, though that thought did not sit comfortably alongside the memories that jostled in his head.

It had felt real. That sense of incredible love and acceptance. Such a thing had to be more than a phantasm, but Rhynn didn't know.

Sure, he'd dreamt of love often enough—the sweetly chaste kind, and the kind that still echoed in his blood, thrumming with the imprints of Greenleaf's caresses—but never quite like this. He'd never pictured a love that could be so wide and all-consuming, and yet leave him so lonely… for he was lonely, now that the forest lay behind him, and nothing rose ahead but trekking back to the cottage, his skin grimy with the traces of sweat and the echoes of passion.

Rhynn stopped, wanting to sag to his knees in the middle of the path and weep, but it would have done little good. He felt different, that much was true; as if his body was no longer entirely his own, but a house in which other guests might trample, seeing and touching more than he gave them permission for.

Yet, in itself, that didn't feel wrong.

Rhynn walked slowly—pushing himself onward, back toward home—but he walked tall. A peculiar pride etched his steps, and a smile trembled behind his lips as he thought of how this strange day had changed him.

It was heading into dusk when he arrived back at Master Wemmick's cottage, the silvering of the air taking the dull heat from the day at last. Rhynn made out the old man's figure against the open doorway, backlit by the dim firelight. He'd already lifted a hand and waved before he realized Master Wemmick was not alone.

A tall, black-cloaked figure stood beside the door, almost blending into the lengthening shadows. With a pang of dread, Rhynn recognized it as the Widow Olafson. He cursed under his breath as the woman turned, and he could have sworn her gaze pierced into him like a steel-fletched arrow.

"And, pray, do you make it a habit, sir?" the widow demanded of Wemmick, her small gray eyes never leaving Rhynn as he sloped nervously up the path. "Allowing your boy to run wild all the day, looking like a ragged jackanape?"

Master Wemmick leaned heavily on his stave, his cloak pulled tight around him and his lined face dark with, Rhynn suspected, the effort of being polite to the woman. As he drew closer to the cottage, he saw she held a cloth bundle, which he assumed held the preparations for her brat's ailments. Her scrawny, red-knuckled hands wrapped tight around the pack, and Rhynn supposed he ought to feel more charity toward her; she was, after all, a mother, and probably worried about her child. It didn't make it any easier to dredge up a respectful smile and a bow.

"Good day t'you, Mistress. Master. I'm sorry I'm late back, I—"

The widow's tight-lipped mouth buckled into a smug sneer, her thin, stern cheeks puckering as she evidently decided some inner prejudice of hers had been proven right. Wemmick lifted one crooked hand from his stave and shook his head.

"No matter. Go to the garden, make up four sticks for burning. Sage, rosemary, and thyme. You know how it's done. Quickly, boy, Mistress Olafson doesn't want to be standing here all night."

Rhynn nodded, and darted toward the little willow gate at the side of the cottage, his antipathy at least a little forgotten. Small bunches of those herbs, tied up and burned, were supposed to both help ease pain and breathing, and to prevent a sickness spreading throughout the house. It could well be the widow's child was sicker than he'd thought. Perhaps it was that which prevented her from entering the cottage, rather than any moral opposition to their kind.

"Oh, and Rhynn?" His master's voice stopped him as his hand touched the gate, and he turned, waiting for extra instructions. "You've a visitor."

Rhynn frowned, confused, but he nodded and went on with the errand, not wanting to prolong the widow's presence here.

Still… a visitor? Who would come to see him?

He pushed the little willow gate shut behind him, his fingertips lingering on the smooth wood. The herb garden adjoined the gable end of the cottage, facing south and garnering the majority of the sunshine. Rhynn enjoyed working out here, gathering roots, buds, flowers, or whatever else his master needed from the plants he had, in many cases, tended since they were nothing but seedlings. As the mingled scents of herbs washed over him—woody, clean, fresh, and pleasantly familiar—he found himself thinking quite suddenly of Old Greenleaf, and the hidden, secret memories of the forest.

Rhynn's body flushed with warmth, and he felt the heat of the remembrances blush in his cheeks, a shiver skimming his skin. He blinked, pushing the thoughts away, but not from embarrassment. He would return to them later, he knew; take them out, dust them down, and hold them close again, like treasured keepsakes.

He smiled and crossed the narrow, paved path to where a raised bed of sage and thyme stood, shaded a little by the cottage's wall. There was a definite comfort to being here, among the plants. At the end of the garden, rosebay and staves-acre stood tall, their great spikes of flowers blazing with color. Low-trained cordons of pears and apples fenced in the beds, and the dappled foliage of sowbreads and lungworts glimmered duskily beneath the taller, brighter plants.

Rhynn laid his hand gently against the soft, downy leaves of the purple sage. The words came easily, for he'd said them countless times before.

"Humbly I greet you, and ask of you permission to take that which I seek."

It was one of the earliest rules Master Wemmick had drilled into him as a young boy. Life was in all things, and had to be respected. No one had the right to take without asking, and so he must always ask, and never take more than he needed, or more than the plant could give. They were simple but important rules, and Rhynn knew them as easily as he knew how to cut, mill, or grind, or how to plant, sow, and reap.

He fancied he felt the sage bush's leaves flutter against his skin, which was not unusual. Master Wemmick had taught him to discern the signs of permission, as well as to ask it. Rhynn bowed his head and, using the edge of his thumbnail, snapped off four young, greenish tips of sage.

The same procedure yielded a fat bunch of thyme sprigs, and Rhynn turned his attention to the handsome, stately rosemary bush that grew beside the woven willow fence. He touched his fingers to the slim, pointed leaves, their fragrance drifting up to greet him, and could have sworn that a pulse beat beneath his touch.

Dear to its heart, marked with its love.

Rhynn blinked, trying to shirk away the musty, odd recollections. Now, with the evening light tinting the whole garden with pinkish, golden tones, every leaf seemed gilded, every breath laced with magic.

"Do they talk back to you? The plants?"

Rhynn flinched, gasped in surprise, and then felt foolish for it, fresh heat flaming in his cheeks. Over by the cottage's sun-drenched wall, leaning against a patch of bare plaster and framed by the glaring blue spears of staves-acre, stood Vareth.

The light flared off his hair, his skin golden-brown and his eyes creased against the sun, no more than chinks of azure in his unblemished face. His shirt seemed very white, its lacings open to reveal the slim, hard column of his neck, tracing a solid, densely packed line between the angle of his jaw and the top of his smooth, broad chest. He held out his hand—offering the three thin, cloth herb bags that, in his haste, Rhynn had discarded down by the pond.

"You left these… earlier."

Gradually, Rhynn realized that he was staring, and his mouth was open. He swallowed hurriedly and licked his lips.

"Uh, I…. I mean, thank you. I didn't—"

He reached out, the gesture clumsy and awkward, and his fingers brushed Vareth's as he took the bags. For one tiny, fleeting moment of contact, it seemed to carry an enormous importance. The touch blazed through Rhynn, galvanic and shocking, and he felt as if the very air was alive, brushing against his skin like a million grains of sand.

He searched Vareth's face for some hint of explanation, but the slabs of sunlight sliced between them, blinding him with thick layers of gold. As much as he wanted to know what was happening, Rhynn didn't want the moment to end.

"I didn't mean what I said," Vareth murmured, lowering his gaze. "I'm sorry."

Sorry? Rhynn thought back to those drawn-out, bottomless minutes, when the world had cracked around him and he'd hurt so much he'd wanted to run—*had* run, and never looked back. He didn't want to forgive Vareth. He would much rather have stayed angry, been cold and cutting, or even pretended that it mattered so little he didn't even remember the incident… but none of it would have worked.

Right now, Rhynn could hardly breathe. He wanted nothing more than he'd wanted at the pond, nothing more than he'd wanted in all the years he and Vareth had been friends. He knew that now, knew the shape and the depth and the breadth of it. All that, and yet he couldn't voice any of it. His tongue felt fat and flabby, his mouth dry, and he couldn't force a single word past his lips.

"Rhynn? You believe me? I didn't mean to be so cruel. I was… surprised, that's all. It was stupid of me. I acted badly, and I don't deserve you to forgive me, but—"

Vareth stopped, pushing away a little from the wall, his face caught somewhere between remorse and desperation. He half-raised his hand, the movement over before it had completely begun, as if he'd thought better of it… thought that Rhynn wouldn't want him.

Rhynn blinked, shook his head, and turned back to the rosemary bush. He had to concentrate. The Widow Olafson was still there at the front of the cottage, and Master Wemmick needed him to prepare the herb bundles. Rhynn reached into the pocket of his breeches and pulled out a spool of thin cotton thread. He put his palm to the rosemary once more, and murmured his petition.

"Rhynn. Please…. I didn't know. That was all. I want us to be friends. I want us to—I didn't mean it," Vareth finished, lowering his voice, the words thinning under the weight of the things he seemed to want to say.

Rhynn stared hard at the rosemary plant. Carefully, he plucked four soft branches from it and laid them lengthwise in his palm, biting down hard on his lip as he wove the sage and thyme around each stalk to create the sticks for burning. It was a fiddly, awkward task, knotting each one at the base with the cotton and keeping the weave tight and even. Rhynn cussed under his breath as he dropped the herbs to the path, and immediately knelt to gather them up.

He hated, in that moment, being so aware of Vareth's presence, and longed for the cool, quiet stillness of the forest. A light breeze rose, odd against the day's stagnant heat, still held in the paved pathway and the gable wall that shielded the garden from sight. It rippled through the leaves, mixing up the fragrances of a dozen different species, and Rhynn frowned, sure he detected the trace of a voice on the air.

He looked up, and found Vareth kneeling to help him gather the herbs. The front of his shirt bagged away from his chest, affording tantalizing glimpses of his skin, yet he seemed to be fixed entirely on the dropped tips of greenery that lay between them. Rhynn licked his lips, the pulse pounding in the base of his throat.

"You didn't answer me," Vareth said quietly. "Do they talk back? The plants?"

He glanced up at Rhynn and smiled, so much tentative warmth and apology in his gaze. Rhynn had never seen anyone look more vulnerable.

"Sometimes," he managed. "If you listen."

"Oh."

They were both looking at each other, yet it seemed that their hands met by design on the sun-warmed paving. The soft points of rosemary leaves prickled at both their flesh, and Vareth's mouth tightened, as if he wanted to speak but had thought better of it. His gaze flickered for just a moment, and Rhynn breathed in, embraced once more by that woody, musky scent of the forest.

It was true, he supposed. There were greater depths in all things, and once their truth was acknowledged, their true beauty shone through. He understood that now; he knew who he was, and what he wanted to become, and he owned at last the power that lived within him.

Slowly, he leaned forward, recognizing the nervous stiffening of Vareth's frame and accepting it, giving him time to adjust. The answering pressure of his friend's hand against his came as an assurance, and Rhynn closed his eyes, shifting those last few inches until it finally happened, and the world halted upon its turn.

Vareth let out a small, soft sound of surprise. His lips were smooth and firm, his breath hot on Rhynn's face. He leaned into the kiss, the chaste warmth of his mouth giving way to a wet, velvet heat as the tip of his tongue touched Rhynn's.

Dizziness tugged at Rhynn's senses, the starlit black world behind his eyes whirling and pitching with disbelief. He felt, he thought, Vareth's fingers clasping his, and the touch of his other hand against his cheek, cupping his jaw. Rhynn relaxed into the embrace, wishing it could never end, even as his lungs began to cry for air.

When at last they parted, he wanted nothing but to see Vareth's face, and the acceptance and trust Rhynn found in those bleary blue eyes and that rumpled smile filled him with relief. Vareth's hand was pressed to his neck, his thumb slowly stroking Rhynn's jaw and—as Rhynn moved to speak—Vareth touched the warm, firm pad of the digit to his lips.

"Shh."

He understood. It was new. It would take time and adjustment but, here in the languid, dimming light of midsummer, that didn't matter. They had crossed the first, and greatest, bridge.

Rhynn glanced down, expecting to see Vareth's brown hand in his, and watched in surprise as the rosemary sprig in his palm, with all the ease of a cat stretching on a warm patch of dirt, began to bend and change its shape. The slim, pointed leaves lengthened and—like gentle, silken ribbons—wound out from the center of his hand, around his fingers and Vareth's, binding them to each other.

Vareth inhaled sharply, but he didn't pull away. Rhynn flexed his fingers experimentally against these strange, tender chains. Easy enough to break, he supposed, should he choose. Yet, somehow, he doubted he would want to. He leaned in again, seeking Vareth's mouth and knowing when he found it that, in time, they would share all the wonders of the wildwood, and explore its mysteries together.

M. KING resides in a damp, verdant corner of Southwest England, where she may usually be found behind a keyboard and a vat of coffee. A former Arvon Foundation Award winner, she is an inveterate scribbler and teller of tales and has never yet met a genre she didn't like.

Her work features flawed and fascinating characters, vibrant storytelling, and worlds to lose yourself in time and again, with titles ranging from horror to fantasy, humor to romance, erotica to tear-jerking drama… and more.

On the very rare occasions she isn't writing, M. King enjoys taking long, muddy walks with her dogs—otherwise known as the hairy chaos monkeys—reading, dabbling in her herb garden, and falling off horses. Just not all at the same time.

Visit her web site at http://www.thenakednib.com. You can contact her at lavengra@yahoo.com.

On Wild Wings

Connie Bailey

CHUNEH Stride-Sky was already awake and almost dressed for flight by the time the first faint pewter glow of dawn touched the rim of the world. From his vantage, he could see the peaks of the snake-spine mountain range thrown into stark relief, black on silver, as the great, shining eye of the heavens opened on a new day. Light began to filter into the steep-sided valley and a stirring, bugling sound filled the air. The trumpeting rose in a resonant blend of many distinct timbres and melodies blending into one hymn to greet the return of the sun after Her long journey through the night. Though Chuneh had heard this song every morning of his life, it still moved him, making his blood race and his thighs ache for the saddle. The mood was especially joyful on this Day of Rebirth that marked the end of Snowmas and welcomed the season of Flowertide.

Eager to be about his duties, Chuneh stamped his heels down into the heavy boots of fireproof hide and snatched up a handful of nuts and dried fruit from a stone jar. As he turned back to the open entry of his dwelling, he felt on his face the cinnamon-scented breeze that heralded the arrival of his fellow scout. Chewing quickly, he finished his breakfast and went to stand once more on the edge of the stone shelf that formed his porch. Below his ledge, rocky slopes patched with green fell sharply away to a river like a rivulet of molten silver. Above him, casting him in the shade, hung the winged bulk of the dragon, absurdly graceful despite its great size, almost implausibly supple in the sinuous play of muscles. A ripple of iridescence ran along polished scales as the dragon's narrow wedge of a head lowered until it was level with the man's face.

"I greet thee, Greatheart."

Chuneh smiled as warm, fragrant vapor wafted over his skin along with the honorific. Dragons chose names for their comrades-in-arms and, as such things went, Chuneh could not complain overly about his. Greatheart was far too grand for him, but at least he was not called Sticklegs or Blue-Eyes like some others of the border patrol. Of course, he would have preferred to be called by his birth name, but one did not dictate terms to a dragon. Their race was far older, wiser, and mightier than mankind, and deserving of awe and respect. On the other hand, Chuneh was a seasoned warrior, deserving of respect as well, and he had flown enough seasons with She Who Is Sister to the Sun to feel comfortable with a less formal and much shorter term of address for her.

"A good morn to you, Sunni," he said, bowing slightly from the waist.

Fangs as long and as sharp as broadswords gleamed milk-white in blue-black gums as the great golden she-dragon let her mouth gape in an approximation of a human grin. She rose slightly and sank again, cupping the air in vast, leathery pinions, translucent in the sunlight. "I can hover no longer, small brother. Do you stand idle in the face of your duty or do you come with me?"

"With you, my queen," Chuneh answered. His thigh-length kilt of molted dragon scales chimed musically as he sprang high and alit just behind Sunni's mane of black-and-turquoise-banded quills. Sure-footed on the ridged neck, he made his way to the tall saddle in front of the vast wings. Knowing her rider's skills, the dragon took to the air as soon as he sat down. As Sunni gained altitude, Chuneh calmly buckled himself into the harness of wide leather straps and slipped his feet into the sling stirrups. He stroked his palm over the haft of his pike, reassuring himself by touch that the long weapon was close at hand in its bull-hide holster. Eight spans in length and tipped with a bronze spearhead, it was his middle-distance weapon. He much preferred his recurved bow, which allowed him to strike from much farther away. If it came to it, he had the broad-bladed dagger for infighting, but it suited him fine to keep his enemies at a distance. Chuneh wasn't faint of heart—there were no cowards on border patrol—but neither was he eager to die.

His inventory ended as they gained the air above the peaks, and the sun appeared to leap forth suddenly, burnishing the world with a patina of coppery rose. In the blush light, the stylized dragon wings tattooed across Chuneh's chest and shoulders looked as red as fresh blood, and the wings of the dragon he bestrode took on the glowing ruddy hue of metal in the forge. The snows of the highest peaks and the snowy blossoms of the lee valleys were the lustrous pink of shells from the Southerly Sea. Chuneh's shaggy mane was glossy as a seal's pelt as he threw back his head and sang out his own welcome to the new day, a day full of limitless possibilities. Everything was fresh; everything was beautiful. On a day such as this, with the cold and the spirit-dampening shortness of the days behind them, basking in Her warmth and light, one could believe that even the longest-held dreams might come true.

The dragon curved her neck to regard her partner with an eye like an apple-sized opal. "Perhaps this Day of Rebirth will be the one on which you find what you have long sought," she said.

"I was thinking that."

"Yes, you were," the dragon agreed.

"It is not that I am displeased with your company, Sister to the Sun, but you know how I long for a companion."

"Yes."

"I do not understand why my soul's mate has never come to me in all these years," Chuneh sighed, as the dragon banked and turned, headed for the eastern border and the first leg of their patrol. "I am thirty-five on the Harvestake. All around me, those I trained with and knew as children have found their mates and handfasted them. They are raising families, sons and daughters that enrich our clan."

"You have done your duty with honor, always."

Chuneh accepted this as the accolade that it was, bowing his head. "You honor me," he said. After a long moment of silence, he continued, "But I think I would serve our people better if I had my other half."

"Instead of partnering dragons who have lost theirs."

"I did not say that."

"When have you ever needed to say a thing aloud to me?" Chuneh stretched out his hand and scratched the soft skin where the scales ended and the quills sprouted like the petals of a chrysanthemum. The dragon arched her neck and rumbled her pleasure. "Except for my lost comrade, you are the best human I have known."

"That does not speak well of humans," Chuneh teased, hoping to divert her from the constant sorrow of losing both her mate and her comrade-in-arms in the same battle. They were a pair, right enough, both of them freighted with melancholy and yearning for something that could not be bought or won by strength of arms or cunning. The thing they desired with all their hearts and souls came in its own time, or not at all.

"I am of dragonkind; I speak the truth only."

"You know," Chuneh said casually, "I think it is merely a legend that dragons cannot lie."

Abruptly, he was clinging to the double horns of the pommel as Sunni heeled over in a diving roll down the face of a roaring waterfall, close enough to feel the mist. She pulled out just above the churning water at the base of the falls and rocketed skyward, the straps of the harness pulling tight across Chuneh's smooth chest. "But it's certain that they have no sense of humor," he said when he was upright in the saddle.

Chuneh was about to make a joke about the prickly pride of dragonkind when Sunni dove again without warning, taking him completely off guard. Folding her wings in tight, she plummeted headfirst, snapping out of the dive at tree-top level, skimming the canopy as flocks of panicked birds flew up like chaff before the gleaner. Ever-hungry, Sunni absently snapped up a few of the plumper ones, swallowing them whole to be instantly digested by highly corrosive bile. Belched forth, the liquid could reduce a pig to polished bone in minutes; a man in metal armor took a bit longer, but it was not pleasant to wear the armor as it melted. Stalwart indeed was the warrior that did not divest himself of the liquefying metal as quickly as possible.

Chuneh threw his arms wide, grinning out of sheer exhilaration to be astride such a creature. Excellent reflexes saved him being hit in the face by the carcass the dragon tossed back to him like a man throwing a bone to a hound. Wiping the blood from his chin, he grinned at Sunni's notion of a joke and filled his lungs to let another song pour out. The words died on his tongue when she spoke in her deepest register.

"Keep silent," she said as she pivoted on one wing in a tight spiral, riding a rising column of air. Higher and higher they climbed, bearing ever eastward, seeking a broader overview of the terrain.

Chuneh did his best to keep his mind blank, focusing his eyes on the landscape spinning slowly beneath him as the dragon quested with senses beyond his. Anxiously, he noted that they were at the limit of their sentry flight and would pass over the border very soon if Sunni didn't alter her course. Chuneh peered intently down, but the thick forests were impenetrable to his gaze and the foothills that poked knobby knees through the green blanket were riddled with caves and gorges where the sun did not venture. There was no obvious blight on the land, but he felt a profound loathing at the thought of setting foot there. It was from these tangled woodlands that the threats to the peace of his clan always seemed to come. Not only from outlaws and raiding soldiers, but beasts as well. Beasts that had in ages past been twisted by sorcery into fearsome shapes and given intelligence beyond that of other animals. They were cunning and killed for sheer sport. Chuneh said a brief but fervent prayer that they were not about to face such a monster.

"Do you feel it?" the dragon asked.

"I feel as though I am being stretched between two poles."

"Yes, that is the feeling. Is it not stronger to the east?"

Chuneh nodded, and then answered aloud. "Aye, to the east. What is it?"

"A young male is rising."

Chuneh quickly reined back the excitement that wanted to run away with him. "A Singulary?" he asked calmly.

"Did I not say he was in Ascension?" Sunni was not fooled by her comrade's cool tone, and she, too, was excited by the presence of an unfamiliar dragon. If Chuneh could claim the Singulary first, they might form a complete bond and half his dream would come true. Sunni felt no jealousy at the prospect, only joy, but there was something vaguely troubling about the presence she sensed. She could feel the bubbling lava restlessness of one of her kin ready to take to the air for the first time, but she could not catch any of the youngling's thoughts, nor could she pinpoint his location.

"Where?" Chuneh asked tersely, sensing the dragon's frustration. As he opened his mouth to speak again, he was pierced from crown to soles by a bolt of sheer bliss as intense as a lightning strike. As it began to fade, every part of him yearned toward the source of the jubilant flare.

"Farther east," he gasped.

"Yes," Sunni said, her vast wings beat at the air, rowing forward at an ever-increasing speed. "We will be there for his Ascension."

"And if he rises Rampant?"

"Then we will do our duty."

"Of course," Chuneh said, putting his hand on the pike. He hoped with all his heart that the young male did not come into his wings in a surge of mad recklessness. In times past, when more young had been produced, dragonets exultant had sometimes risen in isolation without the guidance of their kin, laying waste to farmland and villages in the exhilaration of their first flight. The destruction was not malicious, but it was costly in land and lives, and there had been tragic cases in which the fledgling dragons had to be destroyed in order to save lives. These were times of great mourning for Chuneh's clan, as well as for the dragons. His people revered and loved the great and ancient creatures as the foster parents of mankind. However, he would do his duty, as would Sister to the Sun.

Chuneh's thoughts were disrupted as another flash of unbridled joy lit him up as though he'd swallowed the sun.

"There," the dragon said, her neck outstretched as straight as an arrow. Chuneh saw light wink in the near distance, where a single peak stood marooned from the rest of the range. "His wings have unfurled."

"Is something amiss?" Chuneh asked when their speed decreased drastically.

"I am not sure."

Chuneh had never heard a dragon sound uncertain about anything, and a chill roughened his skin. "Is he aware of you?"

"I cannot say."

"How can that be?"

"This is a thing outside of memory," the golden dragon said as they drew steadily nearer the pile of rock.

Chuneh's curiosity far outstripped his apprehension—a trait that made him a natural scout—but Sunni's words made him cautious. Each dragon shared the memories of every other dragon that had ever lived, and the fact that Sunni could find no recollection of a similar event was fascinating, but deeply disturbing. "Perhaps we should call on—"

"I have tried," Sunni interrupted. "My voice will not reach the keep."

"Turn around." Chuneh made a sudden decision.

"That would be wise," the dragon said. However, she continued to fly straight toward the column of cold fire that shot from a formation of boulders at the base of the mountain. *Instar...* The play of metallic light called instar was the harbinger of the passage of a dragonet from nymph to adult, and it climbed high before it spread at the top, like a parasol. In moments, the luminous cloud began to dissipate into tiny, twinkling points of radiance that rained harmlessly down on the land. Chuneh and Sunni watched with dazzled eyes, mesmerized by the breathtaking display. Neither saw the attack coming.

Chuneh and Sunni felt the displacement of air caused by something large, and she instinctively rose higher, avoiding a collision by a hairsbreadth. Chuneh caught a glimpse of dark scales that gleamed like obsidian and smelled of hot, wet iron as a young dragon hurtled by, filling Chuneh's vision. The attacker rolled as he skimmed past, dealing Sister to the Sun a stunning blow with his tail. The prehensile length coiled around the she-dragon's neck like a whip, and a half-second later she was yanked violently downward. Chuneh hefted his pike, and then the world was spinning around him as Sunni plunged headfirst toward the rocks. The wind of their descent tore water from Chuneh's eyes, blurring his vision as he tried to find a target for his weapon.

"Sunni!" he shouted. There was no answer. The golden dragon continued to plummet like a stooping falcon. In desperation, he reached out with his mind, but he sensed nothing, not even the weak connection he could sometimes achieve. It was as though Sunni no longer existed. Even as he had the thought, she vanished, and he was falling alone. A shadow fell over him as the pike was torn from his hand. Looking up, he gazed into a large liquid eye and saw himself reflected there. It was the last thing he remembered seeing when he woke several hours later.

CHUNEH sat up with a groan, clutching at his pounding head. His entire body ached as well, and he cursed himself for being so foolish as to fall asleep on the floor. There must have been some sort of celebration last night, because he had the mother of all hangovers. He passed a hand over his eyes, rubbing away the remnants of slumber, and wondered why his cave looked so odd. He'd experienced double vision before, but drinking had never altered the actual appearance of anything the way some drugs were said to do. Where was the folding screen he usually pulled across the cave mouth at night? And why he could hear the sound of water that was several leagues off? What time was it? How long before Sunni showed up for patrol duty?

We were attacked.

Chuneh relived the moment of near impact, the subsequent fall, and Sunni's disappearance. Despite the pain it cost him, he jumped to his feet and made a rapid visual search of his surroundings. There was no sign of Sister to the Sun in the enclosed space. This cavern had a much higher ceiling than the one Chuneh dwelt in, and was part of a series of large chambers that he could see through an opening to his right. The space he stood in seemed to be the end of a chain of bubbles in the rock. Almost at his feet was a vast pool that took up most of the floor, glistening like polished jet in the silvery green radiance. The wide body of water lay between Chuneh and the entrance to the next chamber, the only exit that he could see. Fearless in the air, he had a dread of water that was as strong as it was unreasoning. He looked at the lake for a long moment before concern for Sunni drove him to brave it. Resolutely, he strode the few steps to the edge and put a foot in the darkling waters. When nothing untoward happened, he began wading. As he got farther from the stone shore behind him, he was relieved to find that, while the water was cold, it remained shallow, never rising above his thighs. Fixing his eyes on the distant opening, he slogged doggedly forward.

Chuneh lost track of time in the gloom and silence. Though he felt as if he'd been walking for an hour, the far shore seemed to grow no nearer, and he was encountering obstacles that hadn't been visible when he started out. The rocks that jutted through the still surface were smooth and oddly shaped and were often surrounded by thickets of smaller rocks below the waterline. Chuneh soon learned to steer clear to avoid scraped shins and tripping hazards, sparing them a glance of wonder for their melted candle appearance as he passed by.

Near what he judged to be the center of the underground lake, a small island rose above the still surface, and he headed toward it. The opportunity to see his surroundings from a higher vantage outweighed the trouble of navigating the underwater maze. After a long, hazardous time, he finally stood on a shelf of dry rock, a blessed respite from marching through the resistance of the lake water. He took a few moments to catch his breath and began clambering over the miniature spires of stone that formed a wall around the island.

On the other side of the wall it was more and more obvious that forces other than the elements had shaped the landscape. The living rock had been carved into miniature representations of palaces, castles, and temples in perfect detail. Among them, Chuneh instantly recognized the notched tops of the turrets of Westkeep, the chief fortress of his nation and his home. With the slow, slurred steps of a sleepwalker, he began to move toward the model of Westkeep, but it was as difficult to keep in sight as one tree in a forest. As he cleared the last peak of a very lifelike mountain range twice his height, he reckoned that he should be within sight of his goal, but the ornate model of an ancient temple obscured the view. Absently running a hand over one of the mouse-sized dragon statues as he passed, Chuneh slipped around the side of the doll-sized building and stopped in his tracks.

The soft light emanating from the temple's many small lamps illuminated a scene from one of Chuneh's fondest dreams. Frozen in wonder, all other thought fled Chuneh's mind as he gazed raptly at the beautiful warrior sleeping on a bed of sand. His armor and weapons arrayed beside him, he was curled on his side, as naked as a babe. His limbs were long and well-shaped and his smooth, pale skin glowed in the witch-light. Long white-gold hair veiled his face and fanned around his head like the rays of the Sun Herself. Chuneh was smitten with lust before ever he saw the young man's face, but when he did, his heart followed his loins. The sleeper rolled gently onto his back, and Chuneh was spellbound. Never had he seen a visage so sweet and yet so savage, tender and fierce at once, blending grace and strength and all that was best of man and woman in a third gender that Chuneh had no name for. In his clan, when a man loved a man, or a woman chose to partner a woman, as often happened, there was a word for it. This was something else; something akin to it, perhaps, but not the same.

The young man sighed and shifted, and Chuneh needed all his willpower to keep from kneeling beside the sleeper to run his fingers over the contours of that perfect form. Every line, every curve and hollow was a delight to his eye: the arch of the brows, the winged curves of the upper lip, the willowy camber of the well-defined musculature. Chuneh let his eyes rest on the oval nipples that topped the hard planes of the warrior's pectorals. Under his kilt, Chuneh's unfettered cock began to curve upward. Slowly, as though fearing the young man would feel the intensity of his stare, Chuneh's gaze wandered downward to the juncture of his thighs. Resting against a sack like a fine suede pouch, the sleeper's manhood was a handsome column of dusky rose emerging from a pelt of crisp curls, giving witness that he was no lad despite his youthful appearance. The need to possess this most desirable of all creatures grew in Chuneh until he trembled with the strain of controlling himself. Sunni, the attack, his duty, the world beyond this cave no longer existed. There was only this suspended moment of terrible strain and eager anticipation as he hovered in the space between thought and action.

The sleeper opened his eyes. They were liquid turquoise, pulling in light like magnets, glowing like the moon in the dimness. "You do not look injured," he said in a cool, husky voice that was like frost forming on a windowpane. "Are you well?"

Chuneh blinked. "I… I am well."

The young man stood, swaying awkwardly with arms held out from his sides like an acrobat walking a rope. He quickly gained his balance and lowered his hands to his sides. "It feels so strange," he said under his breath as he took a step toward Chuneh. "This must feel strange to you also."

"Where is this? And who are you?"

"I am called Sadorey," the stranger said, concentrating on taking a few more tottering steps.

"Born of Fire," Chuneh translated automatically. His eyes widened as something struck him. Sadorey was talking in a language that was no longer used except in the sacred ceremonies. "You speak the Firstling Tongue?"

"If that is what you call it."

Sadorey stumbled over the wall of the miniature temple and put out his hands to break his fall. Chuneh sprang forward, grabbing the young man by his upper arms and steadying him. As his hands touched Sadorey's skin, he felt an upwelling of joy so vast that he couldn't contain it, and an aura blazed to life that cocooned them in shimmering light. For a moment, the brilliant flare of iridescent radiance eliminated every shadow in the large cavern, and then it dimmed to a halo around the two men.

"My own," Sadorey said, his voice resonating in Chuneh's head like the shivering summons of a great golden gong.

Chuneh didn't question the impulse to pull Sadorey close and hold him as though fearing he might be taken away at any moment. "What is happening?" he asked calmly.

"I called and you came. I am yours and you are mine." Sadorey raised his face to look into Chuneh's eyes. "Do you not feel the truth of it in your soul?"

Chuneh nodded. He did feel the undeniable sense that he and Sadorey belonged together, but there was something he needed to remember, a task he needed to finish.

"Do you not wish for someone to share your life with?" Sadorey's voice drove the vague, nagging thoughts from Chuneh's head.

"I have hoped so long for a mate," Chuneh said. "I thought I was destined to be alone."

"No, truly you are not. The Goddess made you for me and sent you when you were most needed. I am sorry you have had to wait so long." Sadorey brought his face close to Chuneh's and touched their lips together in a sweet kiss full of infinite promise.

Every cell in Chuneh's body clamored at him to respond in kind, to sink to the ground with the silk-skinned dream in his arms, to make all his fantasies come true. And they would come true; the surety of it washed through him with the pulsing of blood in his veins. This was his mate. Here is where he belonged.

"Where are we?" Chuneh whispered.

"In a sanctuary." Sadorey's smile faltered. "Forgive me. You must be tired and I have kept you standing. Come and sit and be at ease."

Chuneh followed Sadorey's gesture of invitation to a low couch strewn with soft pillows. His steps were muffled by a thick carpet made of the pelt of some large, dappled creature. The filigree metal lamps cast lacy shadows over the velvets and brocades that draped the chamber. For a second, Chuneh wondered how he had come here, and then Sadorey sat beside him, filling Chuneh's world until there was no room for anything else.

"You had a long journey, beloved," Sadorey said, smoothing the hair back from Chuneh's brow.

Chuneh felt the truth of the words, but his instincts whispered that something was askew. Though he felt as though he belonged here, it seemed too good to be true. It was more like a fantasy made flesh: the opulent furnishings, the handsome naked warrior, the feeling of returning home.

Where did I return from? Chuneh tried to remember where he had been before he sat down on the couch. As hard as he tried, he could recall nothing beyond a hazy memory of wading through cold, dark water.

"What troubles you?" Sadorey asked when Chuneh looked at him with panicked eyes.

"Why can't I remember anything?"

"You were injured."

"How?"

"Be calm," Sadorey said soothingly. "You are just risen from your sickbed."

"What happened to me?"

"Robbers attacked you on the road. You were hit in the head, but somehow you made it home." Sadorey stroked Chuneh's cheek. "You almost died."

"I do not remember."

"I know. But someday you will. Until then, I will care for you." Sadorey leaned close and his scent beguiled Chuneh back to into a tranquil state.

"You smell of cloves," Chuneh murmured.

"I chew them to sweeten my breath." Sadorey came closer yet, his lips almost touching Chuneh's. "I hope that pleases you."

"Yes, it is very pleasant."

"I missed you so much while you were not here." Sadorey's breath mingled with Chuneh's. "Do you feel well enough to join with me?"

"I feel fine. I just wish I could remember—"

Chuneh's words were cut off as Sadorey brought their mouths together. Sadorey's lips were soft and insistent, moving against Chuneh's lips until Chuneh returned the gentle pressure. He couldn't deny that he wanted to make love with Sadorey; the proof was stirring under his kilt, and it wouldn't be the first time he'd done this. He had taken comfort with certain of his comrades when the loneliness of sentry duty became too much and the need to feel human warmth was nigh unbearable.

Several vivid scenes flashed briefly in Chuneh's mind like heat lighting among the clouds. *Muscles bunching as brawny arms clasped in a crushing embrace. Sweat-slick flesh gleaming in the light of a guardhouse torch. Callused fingertips digging into a broad back. Grimaces. Stifled groans. White teeth. Sinking deep. A push. A spurt.*

"Yes," Sadorey whispered into Chuneh's mouth. "That is what I wish. Be one with me." Curling a hand around the back of Chuneh's neck, Sadorey drew him along as he reclined on the nest of pillows. "Fill me. Complete me."

Chuneh looked into Sadorey's dark, yearning eyes and his reservations were set at naught by one unassailable fact. This was his mate, and it was right that he should catch fire at his touch. Gripping Sadorey's upper arms, Chuneh leaned into him and took his mouth in a kiss that clearly conveyed his desire to join with Sadorey, body, mind, and soul. He could find no reason not to take what was offered and put himself in Sadorey's hands.

Sadorey rolled so that he straddled Chuneh and reached for the dragon rider's arousal. Crouching over Chuneh's hips, Sadorey guided Chuneh's hard flesh to his lower opening. Chuneh drew breath to suggest that there were other pleasures they could enjoy before this one, but Sadorey flattened a hand against his chest and urged him to lie back. To Chuneh's wonder, and without benefit of oil or preparation, Sadorey sank easily onto his cock, like a sheath enveloping the blade it was made for.

Chuneh had taken his pleasure with men and women, but it had always been a mere physical function, a lessening of the strain, a surcease of the crushing knowledge that he was alone in the world. Those acts of swift and oftimes rough passion had done nothing to prepare him for the emotion that usurped his senses, overwhelming him and changing him forever, as he entered Sadorey. It was more than a simple matter of penetration. He truly felt as though they had become one in spirit, sharing the same desires, greater than the sum of their parts. It was the full expression of something he'd caught the edges of when he soared the skies with Sunni.

Sunni. Golden dragon.

Chuneh frowned, and Sadorey dipped his head in a swift kiss that branded Chuneh's mouth with fire, burning away everything but the need to mate. Placing both palms flat against the tattoos on Chuneh's chest, Sadorey caught Chuneh's eyes and held them as he levered himself off the upstanding rod, and then lowered himself again. Chuneh let out a long groan of pleasure as heat and friction caressed his most sensitive flesh, sending echoes of his joy to every part of him. He wrapped his hands around Sadorey's waist as he lifted his pelvis, meeting his partner halfway on the next stroke. Sadorey's lips curved upward, the needy pout becoming a sultry grin at the speed of flowing honey.

"As one," Sadorey murmured.

Flexing the long, lean muscles of his thighs, he rode Chuneh's cock, setting a pace that was both languid and urgent. Chuneh's hands drifted down to knead the young man's clenching ass cheeks as he fell into Sadorey's rhythm. They moved in perfect harmony, each thrust igniting a stronger burst of pleasure. The coupling was so powerful, so exciting, so good that Chuneh was on the verge of climax long before he was ready for it. Taking hold of Sadorey's arousal, he pumped his fist, willing his partner to join him on the crest. Sadorey undulated in a sensually supple move that took Chuneh's breath away. Sadorey repeated the action, and Chuneh felt his entire being gather itself just before the world exploded in a whirlwind of sparks. His release flooded his farthest shores, and then burst through those boundaries to mingle with the ripples of intense emotion flowing from Sadorey. Sadorey's seed ran hot over Chuneh's fingers as Sadorey doubled over to take Chuneh's mouth in a deep, molten kiss. Welded together at lips and groin, they completed a circuit, and joy ran rampant through both in an unbroken loop, feeding on itself, growing in power. Chuneh had no idea how long they stayed like that; it could have been seconds or days before Sadorey raised his head. His smile echoed the contentment that was stealing through Chuneh, cell by cell.

"Forgive my lack of grace," Sadorey said. "Next time we join, I hope it will not be in haste."

Chuneh lifted his hand to his mouth and licked Sadorey's essence from his scarred knuckles. He had tasted no sweeter wine and opened his mouth to say so, when Sadorey placed a finger over his lips. The young man turned his head in a supple play of neck muscles, and he stared hard at the entrance to the cave. Chuneh didn't move except to breathe, his sated cock pulsing in Sadorey's passage.

"He is here," Sadorey said as he twisted his hips and rolled away from Chuneh.

"Who?" Chuneh sat up, pulling down on the hem of his kilt. He could hear the sound of footsteps on stone, but he couldn't tell from which direction they came.

"He is Aqrey." *Cold Fire.*

"Who is he? Why does he make you frown so?"

Sadorey's eyes were on the iron-banded wood of the door as he snatched up a length of silk to wrap around his waist. "He is my captor."

"I do not understand." Chuneh got to his feet. "You are a captive here?"

"I am sorry," Sadorey said as the footsteps stopped outside the door. "I should not have called you. I had forgotten how powerful he is."

"Is the door locked?"

"That will not stop him."

"Is he a magic wielder?"

Sadorey nodded. "And the great enemy of my family."

"Then he is my enemy too."

"But one beyond your strength. I should not have brought you here." Sadorey shook his head, pale hair sliding over his shoulders. "I thought that if we joined…." He stopped speaking as the door, along with the wall, dissipated into mist.

A tall figure strode through the wreaths of fog and they blew away to reveal a barren island of rock. Chuneh didn't blink as the luxurious chamber disappeared. He kept a wary eye as the stranger walked forward. Aqrey moved with the confidence of a conqueror, the golden threads of his purple tunic and the silver hairs in his dark beard catching the light. "My prince," he said, in a resonant voice as he bowed to Sadorey.

"I am not *your* prince," Sadorey replied.

"You are a charming though ineffectual liar. I call you *my* prince because you belong to me and you know this well."

Chuneh could not let this speech go uncontested. "I do not know you," he said to Aqrey, "but I know that Sadorey does not belong to you. He is mine."

The wizard deigned to notice Chuneh. "To think I actually felt the slightest tremor of fear at the thought of your advent. Now that I see you, I am tempted to laugh. What sort of champion are you? Flesh-poor. Scarred. Past your youth. No, you have not much to recommend you, do you?" Aqrey tilted his head to one side in an elegant gesture as his gaze measured Chuneh's length again. "You do not have one drop of magic in you. You are no threat to me."

"If I am no threat, it will do no harm if you tell me by what right you claim this man." Chuneh glanced at Sadorey.

"I stole him from the royal nursery of Castle Rannois when he was an infant. After I transformed him into the seeming of a dragonet, I encased him in an alabaster chrysalis and left him on this hidden isle to await the time when I would have need of him."

"Why would you do such a thing? You have robbed Sadorey and his family of his childhood."

"The prince has no family. They died in a terrible fire the same night that I took him. All these years, it has been presumed that he died in the fire as well." Aqrey made a face of mock sorrow. "For over two decades, the Roiany throne has stood empty of a true king. The royal line has died out, save for a few cousins of diluted blood with just enough wit to know their heads are safer without crowns. Every season a new warlord arises and seizes power before a few of the others band against him and start yet another civil war. Cities have been destroyed. Crops rot in the fields. A generation of young men lies under the ground. The people cry out for a leader to restore peace."

Aqrey made a flickering gesture with the fingers of his left hand and Sadorey cried out in pain. Chuneh started forward, only to stop in his tracks, bent double over the gnawing agony in his guts. "I can give pain or pleasure at my whim," Aqrey said as Chuneh dropped to his knees.

"Leave him alone, traitor!" Sadorey shouted.

"Silence," Aqrey said. "Unless you enjoy watching this man suffer."

Sadorey closed his mouth on whatever he would have said next.

"Splendid." Aqrey waved his hand dismissively and Chuneh's racking cramps faded, leaving him limp and gasping for breath. The scout remained on the floor as the wizard spoke to the prince. "You may as well become used to taking orders from me, Your Highness. When I removed your family from the field of play, I only kept you to be my figurehead. Thank the gods your face is a veritable copy of your late mother's. None of the nobility will contest your claim; we need only hold the crown once we claim it. With my skills to back you, you will have all the power you need to vanquish any who would oppose your right to rule. When you are securely on the throne, we will reunite the Forest Clans and rule all of Roias. In time, we will raise and train armies to conquer the lands around us." Aqrey paused. "But that is far in the future. You may speak now if you wish."

"Was it you who woke me?" Sadorey asked.

"Aye, I triggered the spell to release you. The realm is ripe for picking and you are of an age not to be dismissed as a boy. I saw no need to wait any longer. After twenty years of patience, I was hasty. If I had taken but a few moments to read the omens, I would have left you in your shell until I arrived. " The wizard turned a sour gaze on Chuneh. "I did not foresee that a Dragon Clan scout would stray into Forest territory as I was invoking the counterspell. Though it is Sadorey's right as prince to name a champion, I would never have predicted his call would summon a warrior from among our ancient enemies. And of course, it was not in my plan that Sadorey would sense the dragon you were no doubt mounted upon and rise to challenge."

"You are a foolish man if you believe that he appeared by chance," Sadorey said.

"You have named me traitor and now you call me foolish. Why is it so hard for you to guard your tongue when you know the consequences of disrespecting me?"

"You do not understand what you have done," Sadorey said as though Aqrey hadn't spoken.

"How tiresome," the wizard sighed. "I know exactly what I am doing. I have been in your thoughts since I woke you. You have no secrets from me." Aqrey smiled. "You will do as I say, prince, because as long you do my bidding, I will not kill this man. He will remain here—alive—and you may visit him whenever you wish. As long as you understand that it is your obedience alone that buys his safety, we will deal well together."

"It is strange that you would expect me to take your word," Sadorey said. "But I cannot deceive you. I will not help you at any price."

"Sadorey," Chuneh said hoarsely. "I do not understand all that is passing between you and the wizard, but I will not be his hostage for your parole."

Sadorey met Chuneh's eyes. "No, you will not," he agreed. "I cannot allow it."

"I did not misread your thoughts," Aqrey said. "You cannot tell me you do not care what happens to this warrior of the Dragon Clan."

"I care," Sadorey answered. "More than someone like you could ever understand. But I will not let you use him to command me. It is precisely because I care so much for him that I will not let him be the cause of a nation's enslavement. I do not think a heart like his could bear the burden of knowing the price of his life. He would not thank me for making such a bargain, and he would no longer respect me. Without respect, where is love?"

Aqrey's dark eyes narrowed in irritation. "That little speech is exactly the sort of thing that made your family extinct," he said. "They were too soft. Roias needs a strong leader and I am going to provide one. Say farewell to your lover."

"Wait." Chuneh dragged himself to his feet, concealing the dagger he'd drawn from his boot. "You have had your say. Now it is my turn." He brought up his hand as though asking leave to speak and threw the knife in the same motion.

Aqrey flung up a hand and blue-white fire flared from his fingertips. The lightning enveloped the dagger, liquefying the metal before it reached its target. The wizard spoke a word that grated on the ear, and Chuneh went to his hands and knees again. "I like you better that way," Aqrey said. "The only reason you still draw breath is that you are useful to me. However, if you try to kill me again, I will destroy you and find another way to control the prince."

"Tell me what to do, Sadorey," Chuneh said in a strained voice.

"Do you trust me?"

Chuneh no longer knew if what was happening was real, hallucination, or a fever dream. The only thing he could be sure of was how he felt about Sadorey. "I trust you with my life."

"That is what I am asking you for." Sadorey held out his hands in supplication. "Free me."

"Tell me how."

Sadorey's lips moved, and though no sound came out, Chuneh read the words *kill him*. There was no doubt in Chuneh's mind about who had to die. Without a second thought, Chuneh threw his body and all his considerable will, developed in thrice-ten years of dealing with dragons, against the sorcerer. He surged up from the floor and Aqrey stepped back, moving his hand in a complicated series of gestures. Chuneh felt as though his heart was being squeezed in an armored fist, but he ignored the crippling agony and reached for Aqrey's throat. Once again, Aqrey kindled the silver-blue lightning and aimed it at Chuneh. The ravening energy leaped toward the dragon warrior, but it did not strike him. With a speed that made him near invisible, Sadorey moved in front of Chuneh.

Chuneh cried out as Sadorey's wheat-colored hair burst into flames with a smell like singed feathers. The young man's skin was smoking under the onslaught of cold fire, as though he were made of something other than flesh and blood. He burned like a votive statue of a young god carved from an amber chunk of frankincense. Horrified, Chuneh tried to smother the flames with his body.

"Stop. I do not want you to be hurt," Sadorey pushed against Chuneh's chest, shoving him away from danger. "You said you would trust me."

"With my life, not yours."

Sadorey's smile broke Chuneh's heart in two pieces, and the young man took one half with him as the sorcerous blaze flared hot and bright, consuming him completely. Tears flowed down Chuneh's scarred face as he turned to face the wizard. He knew this was a fight he had no hope of winning, but he would do what damage he could to the one who had slain his mate. He did not question the depth of his sorrow or the enormity of his rage. He only knew that Aqrey had robbed him of what was most precious, and Aqrey must die.

"You have ruined everything," the wizard said, as Chuneh balled his hands into fists. "I shall take great pleasure in killing you by inches."

Chuneh had nothing to say as he advanced on Aqrey.

"You are truly pathetic. I could burn you to a cinder where you stand, but that would be over too quickly. You are going to suffer for days."

When Chuneh was two steps away, Aqrey spoke a word and froze him in place. It took a great deal of the wizard's energy to hold the warrior immobile, but Aqrey was willing to spend it. He leaned forward slightly, looking into Chuneh's furious gaze.

"I think I shall start by shattering all your bones so the splinters will—"

Aqrey's voice choked off and his eyes bulged from their sockets. He lurched forward, knocking Chuneh off his feet. Chuneh's paralysis broke as Aqrey rose several feet into the air, his legs jerking as though he were trying to run. Chuneh's gaze traveled upward as the gleaming tips of five huge talons appeared through the cloth of Aqrey's amethyst velvet robe. Looming over him was a dark bronze dragon with a mane of ivory quills. Chuneh crouched on the floor and watched as the sleek young male yanked out most of Aqrey's internal organs, along with his spine. The wizard's lifeless body slumped in the great claw and the dragon tossed it away. Chuneh's eyes followed the corpse as it slid down the side of a boulder like a pile of soiled laundry. He saw no need to make sure the man was dead. Rising to his feet, he stood calmly as the bronze fledgling lowered his head.

"Sadorey?" Chuneh said, as the dragon regarded him with his lover's turquoise eyes.

"Yes, my own?"

Chuneh heard the cool, crystalline voice in his head in exactly the way he'd always imagined he would hear his soul's mate. The link between them was so broad and so clear it was as though no barrier existed at all. He remembered who he was and all that had occurred, but he still did not understand it. "What happened here? Where is Sunni?"

"Come outside and feel the wind, and I will tell you, dearest of men." When Chuneh hesitated, Sadorey put his great head all the way on the ground. "Trust me one more time."

"I remember what happened the last time." Chuneh wanted to reach out and stroke the polished scales of the dragon's eye ridge, but he kept his hands at his sides. "You burned up."

"But I returned to you."

"And until you did, my heart was a dead coal in my chest. I had no future and all I wanted was to die… after I killed Aqrey."

"I apologize for bringing grief to you." Sadorey's mane lay flat against his neck.

"You did come back, though."

"Then am I forgiven?"

At last, Chuneh gave in to the urge to run a hand down the occipital ridge that crested the dragon's narrow skull. "If you promise to never do that again."

"You have my word. Now will you come with me out of this dark place?"

Chuneh nodded and stood his ground when the dragon reached for him. Sadorey gently wrapped a talon around Chuneh's waist, and the man prepared to be lifted to the dragon's back. Instead, he felt a wave of dizziness and his vision went snow-blind, and then his ears popped, and he opened his eyes on a place he knew. Sadorey had set him down in a meadow of the barrier range that marked the inner border of Dragon Clan lands.

"How did we get here?" Chuneh asked as he watched the dragon fastidiously wipe off the last of Aqrey in the grass.

"I chose this place from your memories."

"I understand, but… how? How did you bring us here? We are leagues from the cavern." Chuneh looked up at Sadorey. "Are we not?"

"We are, but it would not be possible for me to make you understand even if I had the words to explain. I simply imagine it and it happens."

"You are the only dragon I know that can do this."

"I am not like other dragons."

"No, I suppose you are not." Chuneh thought a moment before he spoke again. "Are you always going to look like this now?"

"Do I sense disappointment?" Sadorey cocked his head to one side. "Am I not pleasing to your eyes as a dragon?"

"You are pleasing to my eyes as either man or dragon."

"But if you had to choose?"

Chuneh leaned against the sun-warm side of the great creature. "I love you in both forms," he said at last, feeling the truth of the words. "I cannot choose."

"Then you shall not." Sadorey curved his neck around Chuneh's back, rubbing his snout against the man's hair.

"You are not thinking of dying again to come back as a man, are you?"

Sadorey made the hissing noise that served dragons as laughter. "No, darling man. I mean you do not have to choose; I can be either man or dragon. Aqrey was a clever wizard, strong in magic, but he did not pay enough attention to details. If he had bothered to gather knowledge of my bloodline a bit farther back, he might have altered his scheme. My most ancient ancestors were of the Wolf Clan, who migrated from the far west with the great herds of gray deer. They were the most successful hunters because they were shape-shifters, but that was centuries ago, and they gave up the practice as they intermarried with eastern tribes and became civilized. However, as Aqrey would have known if he'd tested me, the talent was lying dormant in my blood. He thought his spell gave me the mere seeming of a dragon's child, but indeed, it triggered the seeds of shape-shifting in me. He had no idea of the power he was giving me when he bound me. All I needed to claim the gift was my freedom, which Aqrey gave me, and the will, which you gave me. Without you, beloved, I could never have defeated him."

"Wait a moment." Chuneh moved to where he could see Sadorey's cracked-sky eyes. "Are you telling me you can appear as a man or a dragon at will?"

"In simplest terms… yes."

Chuneh swallowed hard. "And you meant what you said in the cave? You are mine?"

"You are my true companion," Sadorey said. "Do you doubt it? Search your heart."

"I know how *I* feel," Chuneh said. "I just need to be sure of you."

"Can you not feel my heart beating in time with yours?"

"Yes." Chuneh ducked his head. "I guess it is hard for me to believe that my waiting is finally over, that I have a mate."

"Believe it." Sadorey rubbed his cheek against Chuneh's ribs. "I am sorry for the deception in the cave. I needed to bond with you as quickly as possible. I thought if I could convince you that we had been together for years that it would be easier to seduce you."

Chuneh laughed softly. "As if you needed to seduce me. I wanted you the moment my eyes beheld you." He put his arm around the sinuous neck that looped around his waist. The palm of his hand fit perfectly in the hollow between the dragon's eye ridges, and he rubbed absently at the smooth hide. "I am yours," he said, leaning back against the curved sternum of the broad, warm chest. "I wish that Sister to the Sun could see what a fine companion I have gained."

"Then she shall."

"What happened to her when—"

"When I recognized you as my soul's mate, I… transported your comrade to her home. If you are ready, we will go there now."

"That would make me very happy," Chuneh said.

"That is my only wish."

Again Chuneh experienced the odd disorientation he'd felt when Sadorey brought them out of the cave. When once again the world sharpened into focus, he was standing upon the highest parapet of the Westkeep garrison, with Sadorey perched next to him. From this vantage he could see the entire force of Blue Wing assembled, every dragon and rider poised to take flight.

"Greetings, Greatheart," She Who Is Sister to the Sun said, as she rose above the level of the fortress wall below Chuneh.

"Sunni!" Chuneh grinned. "I am glad to see you. You look well."

"I can fly."

"What is happening?" Chuneh asked. "Is the fortress under threat?"

Sunni hissed her amusement. "We are mounting a search for you."

Chuneh was beyond shock by now. "It is nice to know I am so highly thought of," he answered.

"There was also the news of a dragonet in Ascension." Sunni's opalescent gaze slid subtly toward Sadorey.

"Have you nothing to say to my companion?" Chuneh asked.

"I wish very much to speak with him. I am waiting for him to speak first. Out of respect."

"Greetings, Sister to the Sun," Sadorey said. "May I enter your Keep?"

"It would be an honor," Sunni answered. "Welcome home."

THE story of Chuneh's bonding with Sadorey went 'round and a holiday was declared to celebrate the addition of a new dragon to the fold. Late that night, with the torches still burning brightly in the central square, Chuneh and Sadorey left the revels for a more formal introduction. Chuneh was both amused and awed when every dragon in the mews bowed deeply to Sadorey. The young bronze arched his neck like a swan and regarded the others silently for a long moment.

"I wish to call you brothers and sisters," he said at last. "May I join the wedge?"

"We would be proud to have you take your place at the point of our flight pattern, Born of Fire," Sunni answered.

"Why are you all treating Sadorey like a king?" Chuneh asked.

"Born of Fire *is* a king," the golden she-dragon said. "It has been many hundreds of years since the last great ruler of men took to the sky on wild wings. In the earliest days of our long partnership, certain men were chosen to live as a dragon for a term so they might gain wisdom beyond their fellows. Men had not yet built great cities, roaming in tribes as they followed the herds. They lived closer to the earth, in rhythm with the seasons, sharing a kinship with the beasts. There is no longer a place in the world for shape-shifters, but Born of Fire is welcome among us, and we will teach him all of our knowledge."

Sadorey unfurled his wings in a display of joy. "I could not wish for better fortune," he said. "For I do not wish to be parted from this man, and he has sworn oaths of fealty to this clan."

"In time, both our races will count this day and this bond as great fortune," Sunni said. "For, one day, you will take your place as ruler of your people and of all mankind, and you will bring peace to this world."

The bronze dragon lowered his head as he listened to the prediction. "It seems I have much to do, but right now, I am very tired."

"Then all that is left is to settle the question of where you will sleep," Sunni said. "You are welcome in the mews, but would be as at home in a royal bedchamber or in the wild."

"I would prefer to sleep wherever Chuneh does."

"I might have made the man wait a bit longer for that answer," the she-dragon smiled.

"I have not the patience of a dragon who has lived for centuries," Sadorey said. "And I desire nothing more than to share his hearth and bed this night and every night hereafter."

"My heart soars to see my comrade so well partnered." Sunni dipped her head to nudge gently at Chuneh's shoulder, her vaporous breath stirring his unbound hair, imbuing him with the scent of cinnamon. "I share your joy, small brother."

"My joy is large enough for the entire keep," Chuneh answered, tickling the barbels of her chin.

"I am curious," Sunni said to Sadorey. "May I see you in your nymph form?"

The air around Sadorey shimmered like sunlight on windswept water, like the moon on the scales of a leaping fish, and the sleek young dragon was gone. In his place stood the human prince, no less sleek, as naked as the day he was born. Without a trace of self-consciousness, he pivoted on one heel, spinning slowly so the dragons could see every angle of his two-legged form. He accepted their voiceless and somewhat bemused approval of his shape with a sweeping bow. After bidding his new comrades good night, Sadorey took Chuneh's hand and walked from the mews.

"You are very comely," Chuneh broke the silence as they strode along the torch-lined hall.

"I could say the same of you, and mean it."

"Thank you." Chuneh cleared his throat. "You will probably want to start wearing clothing when you are in human form."

Sadorey's laugh echoed in the high-arched ceiling. "I suppose I have much to learn about living among people. I am glad I have you to teach me."

"I think we have much to teach one another," Chuneh said. "Would you like to go back to the feast, or shall I show you where I take my rest?"

"I want to see where you sleep, but only if you are not tired."

"How could I be tired when my true companion waits?" Chuneh said. "Whenever you call, I will answer, even if I must run for a thousand leagues to reach you."

Sadorey shook his head, as he put his hand against Chuneh's cheek. "You shall not run," he said softly. "You shall soar on the wings of one who loves you."

Chuneh leaned forward and touched his lips to Sadorey's in a kiss to seal their spontaneous vows. Sadorey responded ardently, pulling Chuneh closer as the kiss rose in temperature. It was several moments before Chuneh remembered that they were still in a public area and Sadorey was naked. He ended the kiss, drawing back a bit to look into Sadorey's eyes. "It is so strange and wondrous," he said, stroking Sadorey's pale, silky hair. "I know that I love you with all that I am, but I do not know if you would like butter or jam on your toasted bread in the morning. I do not know what your favorite flower is or the names of your—"

Sadorey stopped Chuneh's words with another kiss. "We have a lifetime to learn all the little things," he said. "Now take me home. I cannot wait to start our life together."

CONNIE BAILEY is a Luddite who can't live without her computer. She's an acrophobic who loves to fly, a fault-finding pessimist who, nonetheless, is always surprised when something bad happens, and an antisocialite who loves her friends like family. She's held a number of jobs in many disparate arenas to put food on the table, but writing is the occupation that feeds her soul.

Connie lives with her ultralight designer husband at a small grass-strip airfield halfway between Disney World and Busch Gardens. Logic and reality have had little to do with her life, and she likes it that way.

Visit her Web site at http://www.conniebailey.com/ and her blog at http://baileymoyes.livejournal.com/.

The Sower and the Reaper

Helen Madden

THE boy came in through the swinging doors of the bar, his eyes darting around the dimly lit room. They were dark eyes, hollow and hungry, desperately searching for a spark of hope. Ozzie knew right away who the boy was looking for, and he drew back into the shadows, hoping to stay hidden. He wasn't up to performing miracles today, certainly not at this hour of the morning.

But the boy was obviously determined and on a hunt. He took a few steps into the smoky room, straightened his shoulders, and called out.

"My name is Hosa, from the Red Sky clan. I'm looking for a God. Is there one in here?"

A few of the patrons in the bar muttered to themselves. Those nearest to Ozzie glanced in his direction, but said nothing. The boy waited, then spoke again.

"I said I'm looking for God. I'm on a holy mission. My people need him. Is he here?

Ozzie winced. Holy mission. He hated those words. It always meant the same thing to him—work.

"Which God you lookin' for?" a grizzled old drunk called out. That was Saul, who almost never cracked open his lips when he was drinking unless it was to pour more rotgut down his throat. He and Ozzie went way back, almost to the beginning of the colony. That meant Saul knew the rules just about as well as Ozzie did, and he expected them to be followed.

The boy's eyes locked onto the old man. "The Sower. The Green Man. The One Who Provides."

Saul shot a bleary look toward the corner where Ozzie hid. "He's over there," the old man grumbled.

Ozzie blew out a heavy sigh and leaned forward, finally showing his face. As the boy marched over to him, Ozzie raised a hand to Brewster, the barkeep, who nodded and poured a couple of beers.

"Are you a God?" the boy asked, coming to a halt before the scarred table where Ozzie sat.

"And a fine good morning to you too, young man. What'd you say your name was? Whosit?"

"Hosa." The boy glared at Ozzie, taking in his rumpled appearance and stubbly chin. "You don't look like a God."

Ozzie shrugged. "You don't look like a little raven, but that's what you're called."

Brewster showed up with two beers. He set them on the table in front of Ozzie.

"Yours is on the house," he told him. Then he pointed to the boy. "But this one's got to pay."

"I'm on a holy mission," the boy said with a sneer. "No food, no drink. Certainly not this piss-water."

Brewster cracked his knuckles. "I don't give a damn what kind of mission you're on, boy. You show some respect here, to me *and* to him." He hooked a thumb at Ozzie. "Most especially to him."

"Brewster." Ozzie held up a hand. "It's okay. Like the kid said, he's on a holy mission. No food, no drink for how many days? Bound to make him cranky."

"Don't give a damn. You don't come in here looking for a God and then piss in his face," Brewster muttered, but he walked away when Ozzie waved him off.

Ozzie picked up his beer and leaned back. He pushed out the chair opposite him with his foot.

"Take a load off, kid. Tell me about this holy mission of yours."

"Don't you know?" the boy said, sneering. "You're a God, right? You're supposed to know everything that goes on."

"I've been pretty busy lately. Enlighten me."

Hosa grimaced. "My people are the Red Sky clan. Our settlement's about three days' hike from here. We got hit by that big meteor storm a couple weeks back. Wiped out all our crops. If we don't get a miracle quick, we're gonna starve this winter."

Ozzie took a long, hard look at the boy. His eyes weren't the only thing that looked hollow and desperate, he realized. The boy's long, dark hair framed a face that was too thin for one so young. And his clothing—a worn farmer's shirt and dull grey breeches—hung on his narrow frame, turning him into a scarecrow. Ritual fasting hadn't made him that skinny. Not in the last few days, anyway.

"Looks to me like your people might have been starving already," Ozzie said, taking a sip of his beer.

The boy looked away. "Harvest hasn't been good the last few years. Drought, disease, early frost...."

"Plus I hear your chief blew more than half your clan's allotment of seed at a poker game last season. That certainly couldn't have helped matters."

A storm of anger clouded over the boy's face. "He was stupid. He gambled with what wasn't his to give. Now we're all paying for it."

"You especially," Ozzie replied. "You know my services don't come free."

"I don't have any money—" the boy began.

"Don't play stupid with me, kid. I'm a God, remember. I get my drinks for free. You really gonna pretend I'm talking about money?"

The answer to that was a long time coming. The boy sat and stared at the scarred surface of the table. Ozzie finished off his beer and stared at the remaining untouched drink. He was about to reach for it and polish that off too, when the boy finally spoke.

"I heard the rumors."

"Not rumors. Gospel. Truth. You want something from me? I need something from you. Assuming you're of age. The rules are very clear on that point. I wouldn't want you to gamble away what isn't *yours* to give, namely consent."

"Of course I'm of age!" the boy shot back. "I told you, I'm on a holy mission! I'm a warrior for my people."

Ozzie snorted. "You mean you're on a dream quest?" He sighed and rubbed his face. "I should've known. Coming of age ritual. That puts you right at the line of legal. I guess you're old enough then. But I should warn you. You ain't gonna get much sleep on this dream quest of yours. A God needs worship and prayers to make miracles happen. And given the state I'm in right now, I'm gonna need every bit of worship you can give."

A crimson flush crept up the boy's neck and spread right up to his hairline.

"So... when... I mean, how...?"

"Relax, kid. We're not gonna do it here in the bar. We'll work out the details on the way back to your clan."

Ozzie picked up the second beer and drained it in one long swallow.

"Brewster? Get us a meal, and then pack up some provisions for a three-day hike. Enough for three."

"Three?" Hosa exclaimed. "Who else is coming?"

"Me," Saul said. He stood up slowly, his aged joints popping with the effort. "I'm coming too."

"What the hell for?" Hosa demanded with a sneer. "You a God too, old man?"

"Nope. I'm his high priest." Saul wiped his mouth on his sleeve and pointed at Ozzie. "Wherever he goes, I go. It's the rules."

Hosa looked back at Ozzie, who shrugged. Saul knew the rules, all right. He'd been around long enough.

THE sky overhead was a sallow shade of grey, the kind of color you only see on the faces of the dead and the dying. The road they followed wasn't much better to look at. Ragged clouds spat out a freezing drizzle that mingled with a thick layer of ash lingering in the air. The murky mixture collected in curdled pools on the ground. Ozzie stepped into a puddle of filth and scowled. The wet weather had started out as a blessing, since it had helped to put out the wildfires caused by the meteor storm. But now it felt like a damned curse. Especially with the ash mixed in. The sooty mixture stained everything black until the whole world looked like it was dressed in funeral garb. Ozzie hated it. A God like him wanted sunshine, and plenty of it. But he hadn't seen the sun in almost two weeks now, and it was starting to wear thin. No sunshine just made his job that much harder.

"How come you didn't come?" Hosa asked, hefting the pack on his back.

"Hmm?" Ozzie looked up, distracted from his morbid ruminations by the question.

"How come you didn't come to help us?" the boy demanded. "You're a God. You're supposed to help people. So how come you didn't come help the Red Sky Clan when the meteor storm hit our village? How come I had to come find you?"

"Hosa, do you know how big that storm was? About a dozen clans lost everything they had. And then there were the wildfires. Shit, the whole world's been going to hell the last few weeks. Your people aren't the only ones who need miracles."

"Oh."

"Yeah. Oh"

Ozzie kept walking. He kept his head down and started counting his paces. After five paces, Hosa cleared his throat.

"Now what?" Ozzie said.

"The old man. He really a priest?" The boy looked back over his shoulder at Saul, who trailed behind them.

"Yep," Ozzie said. "Been one just about as long as I've been a God."

"How's a drunk like him get to be a priest? For that matter, how's a bum like you get to be a God?"

Ozzie snorted. "Jesus, kid! You think we've always been like this? Saul and me, we been around a while."

"How long?"

"Dunno. Lost count of the seasons a while back. Let's just say I can remember when Saul used to be as young and beautiful as you are now and leave it at that."

Hosa took another look at the old drunk shuffling along behind them and screwed up his mouth in a grimace. "Hope to hell I don't end up like him some day."

"You could do worse, kid. A lot worse. Trust me."

They trudged on through the rain and the falling ash. Ozzie kept his mind blank, trying not to think about where he was going or why. But he could feel Hosa beside him, a taut bundle of nervous energy practically bursting with curiosity. The God counted out another twenty paces before the next question sprang from the boy's lips.

"Why are we walking back? Why not take a vehicle?"

"Because I don't own a vehicle," Ozzie said.

"What about somebody else? Maybe that guy from the bar, Brewster—maybe he has an ATV. He's got to have something, right? To get supplies in every month? He'd probably loan it to you."

"Brewster's ATV is down for repairs. Filters are all clogged with ash."

"What about somebody else then? Someone back in town's got to have a working vehicle. I mean, come on, we're in a hurry!"

"Maybe you're in a hurry, kid. Not me. You walked here. We'll walk back. We're gonna need a few days together anyway. Might as well do what we need to do on our way to your village. More privacy that way. That is, unless you want to wait until we get there. If we wait, we can have the full-blown ceremony, let the women set up the conjugal tent, and have your chief perform a blessing on our union. I don't mind going through the rituals if that's what you want."

"Shut up!"

"I'll take that as a no, then. In which case, keep walking."

Hosa stayed quiet after that, though a cloud of tension and anxiety remained about him. Ozzie kept his head down and counted his steps. Saul splashed along behind them. They kept going, through the mud and ash and rain, until Ozzie came to a halt.

"What is it?" Hosa asked.

"We're stopping for the night. Sun's going down."

Hosa looked up at the dull, grey sky. "How the hell can you tell?"

"He can tell, kid," Saul said, ambling up behind them. "He's a God, remember? He's tuned in to that sort of thing. You want me to set up your tent, Oz?"

"I got it, Saul. Take care of yourself for now."

"Right."

The old man pushed past them, abandoning the road for the tree line. Ozzie followed.

"It's still light out!" Hosa called after him. "We could keep going at least another hour."

"And set up our tents in the dark? Don't think so," Ozzie called back. "Besides, you and me got a date tonight. Or have you forgotten?"

"Fuck you!"

"That's the general idea."

A string of curses followed Ozzie into the woods. He ignored them and kept hiking until he came to a clearing. Saul's tent, a single-man pop-up, was already up and staked to the ground.

"You sure you don't want me to set yours up?" Saul asked.

"Nah. Kid'll do it for me."

Saul cocked his ear and listened to the swearing that continued beyond the edge of the clearing. "He will, huh?"

"He's gonna have to, Saul. I told Brewster to only pack two tents. One for you...."

"And one for you, with him as your guest. Kid's not gonna like that. He's already madder than a wet hen at you."

"Maybe. Or maybe he's just putting on a show. The reluctant virgin and all that crap."

"You think so?"

Ozzie sighed. "He came looking for a God, Saul, not a Goddess."

"Maybe that's just because you were closest."

"Don't think so. Corn Woman's been buzzing around these parts. He could have dug her up." Ozzie put his pack on the ground and settled on it. "Anyway, kid wants it. I can tell."

"Bullshit."

"No, seriously. I'm a God, remember? I'm tuned in to these sorts of things."

"You're a fucking pervert," Saul replied, but not without a grin.

"God. Pervert. Same thing."

The old man gave a laugh and turned back to his tent. Hosa came tramping into the clearing a few moments later. He dumped his pack at Ozzie's feet.

"Now what?" he snarled.

"Set up our tent, kid."

"*Our* tent?" Hosa's eyes went wide.

"Unless you plan to sleep in the rain tonight. Oh, and make sure you do it right. Entrance should face east. Prayer flags run north to south. And stake it down good. We don't want to accidentally knock it over in the middle of the night when we get busy."

Hosa started swearing again. Ozzie laughed. Sometimes it was good to be a God.

IT TOOK Hosa several tries to get the tent set up properly. Unlike Saul's tent, the God tent was a more complicated affair, with poles to erect and lines to string, plus several strings of prayer flags and heavy canvas panels printed with the story of Ozzie's godhood.

"Why the fuck does he need this fancy bullshit?" Hosa muttered as he struggled to stand the center pole upright in the muddy ground.

"It's his temple," Saul replied. The rain had plastered his thin hair to his scalp. "This is his house of worship. When Ozzie goes on the road, he's got to have a place to gather with his followers. Straighten that pole out. You've got it crooked again. It's gonna fall over."

"God dammit!" Hosa wrestled with the pole and slipped in the mud. "Fine, he needs a temple he can take with him. But why's it got to be so damned difficult to set up?"

"Think of it as a test. You want a God to perform a miracle, so you've got to welcome him, provide him with a place to stay. The more difficult it is to set up, the harder you have to work. The harder you work, the more he sees your devotion."

"I thought he was supposed to see my so-called devotion later tonight!" Hosa snapped. He stepped back from the pole. It swayed, and then toppled over into the mud.

"Fuck!"

Saul stepped in and picked up the pole. "I keep telling you, you've got to plant it deeper into the ground."

Hosa took the pole from him, defeated. "I can't do it."

"Can't do what? Set up this tent? Or show Ozzie your so-called devotion later tonight?"

The kid didn't answer. He looked up into the rain. Heavy drops splashed on his face and spilled over his cheeks.

"Fine. I'll help you set up the tent," Saul said. "Otherwise we're gonna be out here until midnight getting soaked."

He took back the tent pole and stabbed it firmly into the ground.

THE rain turned to a downpour just as Hosa and Saul finished with the tent. Ozzie came out of Saul's pop-up, where he'd been resting, and cast an appraising eye over their work.

"Good. Looks real good."

"It should," Hosa grumbled. "We only spent three hours setting the damn thing up."

Saul cuffed the back of his head. "Wrong attitude, kid. This is a God you're talking to, remember? Your God. You're the one asking him to perform a miracle, after all."

Hosa winced. "Sorry. Sorry, sir."

"Forget the 'sir' shit," Ozzie said, taking Hosa by the arm. "Let's just get inside and get you dried off. You're soaked. Saul, you shut the door behind us?"

"Like always."

Ozzie pulled a dripping-wet Hosa into the tent. They heard Saul outside, chanting as he tied up the front flaps behind them.

"What's he gonna do while we're in here?" Hosa asked.

"Say prayers. Keep watch. Make sure nothing disturbs us. Come on, take off your clothes. You're dripping water all over the place."

Ozzie turned away, giving the kid a modicum of privacy while he dug through his pack for a small towel. When he found it, he tossed it over his shoulder, not looking to see if Hosa caught it. Now that they were in the temple, Ozzie knew it was time to quit acting like a jerk and actually start playing God.

"You dry?" he asked a few minutes later.

"Dry as I'm gonna get," Hosa said after a long pause.

"Here. Take a blanket and cover up," Ozzie said, shoving a striped bundle of cloth behind him. "Then we'll talk."

Ozzie didn't turn around until Hosa let him know he was ready. When he did, he saw he wasn't the only one who realized it was time to drop the act. The kid had transformed, shedding his cocky attitude along with his wet clothes. Now Ozzie saw the real Hosa: a young man, naked, vulnerable, and a little afraid of what he was about to do.

"Okay," Ozzie said, settling down in a pile of pillows and blankets across from the kid. "This is how this works. You need a miracle. I need power to make one happen. A God's power comes from worship and adulation. The more enthusiastic the worship, the more power I get. The more power I get...."

"The bigger the miracle," Hosa whispered.

"Exactly. Now I can't make you do anything you don't want, and I don't even want to try. That would just defeat the purpose. So it's up to you how this proceeds. You can spend all night sitting up, chanting prayers to me, if that's what you want to do. That does work, believe it or not, and Saul will even come in here and chant right along with you to help you out. But it takes longer, and it doesn't produce the same results."

"How's it different?" Hosa asked.

Ozzie looked away, into the shadows at the edge of the tent. "Let's just say you'll get your basic miracle, but there won't be anything else beyond that."

"What else more could I want?"

"You tell me," Ozzie replied. "Maybe you want to ward off drought to ensure future harvests will be good. Maybe you want to heal everyone who's sick in your village. And maybe, just maybe, you want something for yourself."

Hosa shivered and drew the blanket around him tighter. "There's nothing I want for me."

"Nothing? Nothing at all? Not even redemption?"

"What are you talking about?"

Ozzie leaned back in the pillows until he rested on one elbow. "I've been around a long time, Hosa. Since the beginning, when people first came to this world. I'm one of the original Gods, one of the first the scientists made. So I know what it's like to have to clean up after somebody else's mess. You know about the First Cataclysm?"

Hosa looked at him, wide-eyed. "You're that old?"

"Yeah, that's me. Old as dirt." Ozzie chuckled, and then turned serious. "Anyway, I know what it's like to pay for someone else's mistake, because I did it way back then. And I'm thinking now you're paying for your dad's mistake, because he's the fool who gambled away your clan's seed allotment."

Hosa shifted beneath his blanket. "He was so stupid. I told him not to, but he was drunk and he never would listen to me. And then afterward... I did everything I could to make it up to our clan. I worked in the fields, I hunted, I even paid for more seed with what little money I had. But then the drought hit, and the blight after that. And all anybody could ever remember is that my dad is the one who fucked everything up."

"Why didn't your people come find a God sooner?" Ozzie asked. "Why wait until things got so bad that everyone was half-starved?"

"Dad wouldn't do it. He's clan chief, so it was supposed to be his job to ask for help, but he wasn't about to admit he'd messed up. And nobody else would go. It's been so long since we've needed a God, nobody believes the stories anymore. So I waited until I came of age, and I struck out on my own. I'm the clan chief's son. If he won't fix things, I have to. Otherwise, how can I live with my clan?"

Ozzie rolled back onto the pillows and looked up at the constellations painted on the ceiling of his tent. "Hosa, you put your people first, even though they treated you like a pariah. When this is over, you'll be a hero. The Red Sky Clan will know you did what was necessary to help them, even though they made you an outcast. And they'll know you're sacred to a God. You'll know it too."

"Sacred?" Hosa asked.

"Very sacred. I know I made a lot of jokes on the way here, but I'm not joking about that. A God needs devoted worshippers. Otherwise, he's nothing."

Hosa thought for a moment then nodded. "Devoted. Okay. So how do we start?"

Ozzie held out a hand to Hosa. "We start slow and easy and that's how we keep going until you say otherwise."

Hosa accepted Ozzie's hand and crawled into the pile of pillows next to his God. "Slow and easy," he whispered, resting his head on Ozzie's shoulder.

"Very slow. Very easy."

Ozzie planted a kiss on Hosa's forehead. The boy smelled of sweat, wet leaves, and ashes. His skin was chill to the touch in spite of the blanket wrapped around him. Ozzie brushed a damp strand of hair from his face.

"We need to warm you up. You're like a block of ice."

"So warm me up already."

"Jesus, you're a pushy one. Okay, kid, you know how to make a fire?"

"How?"

Ozzie eased his breeches open. "You gotta rub the sticks together...."

His cock slid out, thick and heavy, to rest on Hosa's blanketed thigh. The boy hesitated for a moment, and then twitched apart the fabric. He moved closer until his hips pressed against Ozzie's.

"Now that's what I'm talking about," the God sighed as he felt Hosa's erection rub against his own.

Ozzie slipped an arm around Hosa's waist, pulling him the rest of the way out of his blanket. They moved together, slowly grinding against each other until the chill evaporated from Hosa's skin and he moaned into Ozzie's neck.

"This is worship?" he gasped when Ozzie pushed him back on the pillows. "I thought it would be harder."

"Give it a few minutes," Ozzie answered as he kissed his way down Hosa's naked torso. "It'll get harder. And bigger. I promise."

He stopped just above Hosa's groin and lingered there, nuzzling the boy's flat belly. He slid a hand between Hosa's legs, easing them apart. His fingers glided up and down the boy's thighs. Hosa groaned and arched his back.

"Please," he groaned. "Please...."

"Say my name," Ozzie ordered. His hand moved further up Hosa's thigh.

"Ozzie... Ozzie...."

"No. My full name. Say the name of your God."

He closed his hand around Hosa's scrotum, gently pulling on it. The boy cried out.

"Osiris! My God, Osiris!"

Ozzie squeezed again, forcing Hosa's hips up off the blankets. The boy's cock stood up, rigid, like the center pole of the tent. Ozzie slid his lips over it and began to suck. Hosa shouted his name again.

"Osiris!"

That cry became Hosa's first prayer. Ozzie felt it inside him, where it triggered certain chemical reactions in his body. A flush of energy pervaded him. He sucked harder on Hosa's cock. The boy screamed his name over and over while Osiris slid his tongue and lips over his erection until he finally came in his God's mouth.

"Oh, God! Osiris! Please!"

Ozzie swallowed and came up for air. He reached for Hosa.

"You okay, kid?"

Hosa nodded, then burst into tears. Ozzie cradled him in his arms.

"It's okay. You're gonna be okay."

He murmured the words over and over to the weeping boy until they both fell asleep.

TWO nights later, Ozzie and Hosa lay in the God's tent, on the border of Red Sky Clan territory. The rain had stopped the day before, but the sun had still not come out. Ozzie yearned for its warmth and light, especially now, but there was nothing to be done about it. If he wanted warmth, he would have to rely on Hosa to provide it instead. As for light....

Well, that was Saul's job, wasn't it?

The old man's voice rose and fell outside the tent in an endless looping chant that sent shivers along Ozzie's spine.

"What's he singing?" Hosa asked. His fingers trailed down Ozzie's abdomen and slid beneath the blanket. The God sucked in a sharp breath when they reached his cock.

"It's... a song... about the long night... and the morning that comes after...."

He groaned and rolled toward Hosa, pushing him back into the blankets. In the last couple of nights, the boy had gone from frightened supplicant to eager worshipper. He ground against Ozzie, buried his face into the God's neck, and bit down hard.

"Ow! Dammit, kid, you're supposed to love me, not eat me."

"But I thought you liked it when I ate you." Hosa pushed back and rolled on top of Ozzie. He nuzzled his way down to Ozzie's hips and lavished attention on the God's cock with his tongue. Ozzie wound his fingers in Hosa's hair and held the boy's head steady while he thrust into his warm, wet mouth.

"You dirty boy," he whispered. "You beautiful, filthy, dirty boy...."

Hosa responded by sucking harder. The heat of his mouth, the passion of his worship, set off all kinds of reactions in Ozzie's body, not just an orgasm.

When they were done, Hosa made his way back up Ozzie's body, planting gentle kisses along the way. Ozzie gasped for breath, his heart pounding so hard he thought it might burst.

"You okay?" Hosa asked. He leaned over Ozzie, his long dark hair falling in a curtain to either side of his face.

"Yeah... yeah, fine." Ozzie gasped again. A sharp pain lanced through him. Even though he had been expecting it, it still caught him by surprise. Ozzie rolled over, clutching his side.

"Ozzie!"

"Get Saul," he gasped. "Tell him it's almost time."

"Time for what?" Hosa demanded. "What's wrong with you?"

"Nothing's... wrong... Hosa." Ozzie forced the words out with great effort. "Now get Saul!"

Hosa scrambled to his feet and rushed to the tent's front flaps. His scent lingered behind, rising from the nest of blankets to fill Ozzie's nostrils. It smelled like sweet summer grass baking in the sun.

"Saul!" he heard Hosa cry out. "Saul, he's sick! Ozzie's sick!"

The muffled sound of swearing followed by heavy canvas being pushed aside reached Ozzie's ears. Saul tramped into the tent with Hosa on his heels.

"He just... he just got pale all of a sudden," Hosa babbled. "And he acts like he's hurt."

"Ozzie?" Saul knelt down beside the god.

"It's time," Ozzie groaned. "Get me to the village."

"You told me this morning we had one more day," Saul said.

"I guess I underestimated... the power... of his devotion."

Ozzie managed to roll over and give Hosa a smile. "Don't worry, kid. This is... supposed to happen... aaah!"

"Shit." Saul rubbed his grizzled face. He turned to Hosa. "You. Get dressed. We got to carry him to the village now."

"Why? What's happening?"

"Don't ask questions, kid. Just get dressed!"

Hosa opened his mouth to argue, but bit his lip when he took another look at Ozzie. Without a word, he grabbed his clothes and pulled them on.

THEY carried Ozzie through the night, slung between them in a blanket, Hosa at his feet, Saul at his head.

"How... much... farther...?" Ozzie gasped.

"Not long," Saul panted. "Kid said another hour."

"Has... to be... before... sunrise...."

"I know, Ozzie. Trust me, I know. You'll get there."

They stumbled on. Ozzie kept his eyes on the stars above him. The clouds had cleared. The sun would finally be out tomorrow. But he wouldn't be there to see it.

Damn.

"We're here!" Hosa shouted. "We're here!"

People came. Ozzie could hear them, but couldn't lift his head out of the makeshift sling to see them.

"Hosa!" he heard someone cry out. "Where have you been?"

"Who is this? Is this man dying?"

"No!" Hosa shouted back. "He's a God. I brought him to save us."

"Shit, kid. That one's not saving anything."

"Shut it! All of you!"

That last was Saul. He and Hosa set Ozzie gently on the ground.

"Shut up and listen to me!" he bellowed again. The crowd fell into an uneasy silence. "I'm Saul," the old man rumbled. "High Priest for Osiris, the Sower, the Green Man. He Who Provides! Your boy Hosa came to him seeking help, and the God agreed to give it. The appropriate prayers have been made. Hosa has worshipped and loved this God, and in return, the God will perform a miracle for the Red Sky Clan. Now somebody bring me a shovel. We've got some digging to do. Move it, you bastards!"

He heard the sound of scrambling feet, people tripping over themselves to obey an old drunk suddenly become High Priest. A dark shape hovered over Ozzie, blocking out the stars.

"Ozzie? Ozzie, wake up." Hosa wept. The tears fell like rain on Ozzie's face and made the changes taking place inside him go that much faster.

"Ease up, kid." Saul pulled him back. "You're gonna get him done before he's ready."

"I don't understand," Hosa cried. "What's happening to him? What are we doing?"

"We're digging a hole," Saul explained. "And then we're going to put him in it and cover him with dirt."

"No! No, no, no, no, noooooooooo! Osiris, no!"

Hosa's final prayer swept Ozzie into the long, deep dark of night.

DIRT. Earth smell. Pressing down on him, getting inside his nostrils, his ears, his eyes. Ozzie opened his mouth to scream. More dirt came pouring in.

This was the part he hated; the long, deep dark, the sacrifice that came before the miracle. He wished he'd listened more when the scientists had explained this to him. He wished he'd understood.

Because if he'd known he'd be awake through it all, he never would have volunteered, no matter how desperate he'd been to make things right.

Ozzie was awake. He was awake and dying—or changing, which pretty much amounted to the same thing. His body decomposed at a rate much faster than a mortal body would, yet his mind, his immortal God mind, stayed intact. It watched the bits and pieces of his decaying matter take on a life of their own and disperse, into the soil. Burrowing, tunneling, looking.

Searching for a miracle.

The crops were dead. The parts of him that tunneled upward to the soil surface found the brittle roots. Corn stalks and wheat cut down before their prime, slaughtered by the slings and arrows of outrageous fortune from outer space. Dead, dead, dead, and too late in the season to plant new. He would have to revive them, wake them from the cold, deep dark and bring them back into the light, then feed them with his own decaying matter. His body broke down even further and entered into the roots.

Why am I doing this? He wondered as he spread through the dead stalks, moving from one cell to the next, assessing the damage. *Why did I agree to be a God and solve everybody's problems? Why didn't the scientists stay and do this instead? They had all the knowledge and the power. They would have known exactly what to do!*

But they didn't, a tiny voice inside him said. *Remember? They made their mistakes too. That's why they asked you to become a God.*

We need you to be our tool, another voice said. A scientist's voice. Which one? Dr. Lazarus? Yes, that one. Ozzie remembered him: tall, dark hair, brown eyes, a kind smile and gentle hands. Years ago, Ozzie had worshipped the ground he walked on. He would have done anything for Dr. Lazarus.

What kind of tool? Ozzie remembered asking. The conversation was centuries old, but the memories were as fresh as new spring grass.

We need people who have a special connection with this planet. People who will understand it, not just the way scientists do, but in their blood and in their bones.

Why?

Because when something goes wrong, these people will be able to fix things, Dr. Lazarus said.

Why can't you fix things when they go wrong?

We tried, Ozzie, but we just made things worse. We thought we could remake this planet however we wanted, but the planet had other ideas, and now it's killing people like they're some kind of foreign virus invading its body. And the sad thing is, we didn't do it to just this world, we did it to others too. There are millions upon millions of people out there, and they're all struggling to survive what we've done. So we need your help.

What is it you want me to do?

We want to make some changes to you, big changes. When we're done, you'll be a living, breathing conduit between the colonists and this planet. They'll be able to ask you for things, and you'll be able to talk to the planet and make it happen. It won't be easy, but if the people take care of you, you'll be able to take care of them.

These changes. Will they hurt?

...Sometimes. And you'll be lonely sometimes, too, because these changes are going to make you different, very different from the others. But we need you to do this, Ozzie. Your people need you....

They need me, Ozzie thought as he flowed through the dead corn. *They need me to make food so they don't starve. I made a promise, to*

Hosa and Dr. Lazarus and Saul. I promised to help, no matter what.

Saul's song, the one he sang on Ozzie's last night with Hosa, echoed in his ears. He latched onto that song and echoed it, sent it thrumming through the dead plant. Sunlight and soil, dark and light. Death and life. Ozzie surged through the ruined stalk, infusing it with all the energy he'd garnered from Hosa's worship. He was God, Osiris, the Green Man, the Sower, He Who Provides. He lit up the corn stalk and made it burst into living green leaves. And then he did the same to the next one, and the one after that. The entire crop, cut down to its roots, came springing back up out of the soil, out of the long, deep dark, and Ozzie came with it, finally feeling the sunlight cascading over his face.

TIME. Green and growing. Golden hours, swaying in the summer breeze.

Sometimes it was good to be a God.

In the morning, he felt Hosa walk through the rows of corn, heard him sing his praises, tasted the salty tears of joy and sorrow that fell upon the earth, and it was good.

In the afternoon, children ran through the rows, laughing and chasing each other among the healthy, vibrant stalks of corn.

"Osiris! Osiris!" they cried out, clapping their hands, and the God bowed his leafy head and smiled.

In the evening, he heard Saul on the nearby hill, singing his heart out, calling to him, summoning him back from the earth. Ozzie withdrew slowly, reluctantly. His scattered bits and pieces flowed back down into the ground, exhausted now. They burrowed through the soil and made their way to the hilltop. Saul sang of sunlight, of the morning after the long, deep dark. Ozzie reassembled himself beneath the sod and burst forth, choking and sputtering.

"Jesus, Ozzie. You look like shit."

"Yeah?" Ozzie coughed and spat out a mouthful of dirt. "You try coming back from the dead like this all the time. See how you like it."

"Not my job," the old man said. "When I finally go into the ground, I'm staying put."

"Yeah, maybe one day I'll stay put too."

"Not on my watch," Saul said. "Not while I got breath left to sing. And not on his watch either."

He pointed to the hillside. Climbing through the tall grass, silhouetted against the setting sun, was the lean figure of a young man with long, dark hair.

"No...." Ozzie groaned. "Tell me you didn't recruit him, Saul. Please say you didn't."

"I didn't. He volunteered. Said after seeing what you'd done, there was no way he was ever going to let you walk alone. Let's face it, Ozzie. You need a high priest, and I ain't always gonna be around."

"He'll grow old, just like you did."

"And he'll love you, just like I still do. Now quit your damn whining and get out of the fucking dirt." He held out his hand and pulled Ozzie to his feet. "It's three days' walk back to Brewster's, and I'm parched."

"Me too, Saul. Me too."

They waited on the hilltop for Hosa to join them, and then all three walked back through the night together.

HELEN E. H. MADDEN is a writer and graphic artist who quit her lucrative day job years ago to tell dirty stories for fun and profit. In the last three years, she has written at least one erotic short story a week. That's a lot of smut! Helen's mother often introduces her as "her daughter who writes porn." She introduces Helen's sister as "the actress." Helen's mom says Helen can write whatever she wants, so long as her sister doesn't star in it.

Not content to simply write erotica, Helen also records her work for audio podcasts and does readings where she frequently proves to her audiences that she has no shame whatsoever. In her spare time, Helen draws dirty pictures. When she's not writing or drawing, Helen thinks about sex. A lot.

Visit Helen's web sites at http://www.cynicalwoman.com and http://www.heatflash.libsyn.com.

The One

Ariel Tachna

RYLAN limped toward home, cursing the injury that had forced him out of his faster form and left him naked and vulnerable to anyone who happened across him. He only hoped he'd managed to outpace the hunters whose arrow had scored his flank before he was forced to change. He knew their kind. He'd be in a cage before he could blink if they caught him, and that would kill the wild heart within him—a death sentence for sure. He could survive quite well in either form for extended periods of time, but he needed the freedom to run, as man or beast.

He stumbled, his injured leg giving out on him, the fall leaving scrapes on bare skin. He cursed again, wishing he could shift. Four legs would be far steadier than two.

"Are you all right?"

The sound of a voice in this usually deserted corner of the forest surprised Rylan. He tried to push himself to his feet, but his leg gave out again. "No," he admitted, studying the man who stood a few feet away in the woods. He was tall and broad through the shoulders, but lean at the waist and hips, with long, long legs, perfect for gripping the back of a horse—or a lover's body. Pitch-black hair topped olive-colored skin, the equally dark eyes warm with the offer of aid. Usually skittish around strangers, Rylan could sense no ill intent, nor did the beast inside him stir as it was wont to do in the presence of a threat. "I've hurt my leg."

The man stepped closer. "May I look at it? I've some skill with healing."

Rylan had no idea what a human's tricks could do for him, but he did not see any harm in finding out. Even if all he got was a bandage around his thigh and a hand to keep going until he could get home, it was more than he had now. Carefully, he rolled to his side, showing his benefactor the long gash on the back of his leg.

"You didn't do that yourself," the man said immediately. "You were shot."

"It's clean," Rylan told the healer. "The arrow merely grazed me rather than penetrating."

"It *was* clean," the healer corrected. "It's caked in mud now. We need to get you to shelter so I can clean and dress it properly. I'm Thorin, by the way. If you'll lean on me, I have a horse not far from here. She can carry you to my cabin, where I can get you patched up and on your way."

Rylan shook his head, for as delightful as it sounded not to have to walk, he knew what would happen if he tried to mount the animal. He'd been thrown before. Horses didn't need to see his other form to know he wasn't fully human. Their equine senses recognized him immediately and refused to let his human form mount them any more than if he'd been in his true form. "She won't carry me. Thank you for the offer, though. I'm Rylan."

"How do you know?" Thorin asked, confused. "You haven't even seen her yet."

Rylan shook his head. "I've yet to meet a horse that will let me on its back for more than the few seconds it takes to throw me. If you'll help me to my feet, I'll be on my way again. My own home is not far."

Thorin approached and offered Rylan a hand. Rylan managed to get to his feet, but his leg held him for only another few steps. With a muttered curse, he looked up at Thorin. "Perhaps I am more in need of assistance than I realized."

Rylan was right about the horse, but he had not counted on Thorin's determination. The mare would not bear him, but Thorin did not give up, loading the entirety of his pack onto his horse's back instead so he could put his shoulder beneath Rylan's arm and his arm around Rylan's waist, taking the bulk of Rylan's weight on himself. They moved slowly, but they made progress, and an hour before dark, they reached a little dwelling nestled in the woods.

Rylan's sense of direction told him they were far closer to his own home than he would have expected, for he thought he knew the woods and its inhabitants well. "Have you lived here long?"

Thorin shrugged. "For three seasons now. When winter gives way to spring, I will have been here a year." He helped Rylan inside, the beast within Rylan growing restless at being confined in the unfamiliar space. Rylan soothed it with the reminder that he needed help and that Thorin had been nothing but considerate.

"I'm surprised we have not met before," Rylan murmured, breathing a sigh of relief as he was able to sit and take the weight completely off his wounded thigh.

"I don't go out much," Thorin said as he opened a cabinet and began taking out herbs and tinctures to tend Rylan's wound.

"Why not?" Rylan asked, surprised. "If you have the skill you say you have, I would think you would be in high demand."

"That was the problem," Thorin muttered, so softly Rylan would not have heard him without his acute senses. Deciding it best not to reveal the abilities brought about by his dual nature, Rylan let the comment go, waiting until Thorin gave a louder answer. "My skills are mine to use as I see fit."

"Then I shall say thank you for using them on me," Rylan said as Thorin approached.

"We'll see if you still say that after I've dunked you and dosed you," Thorin said with a laugh. "My medicines will do no good on a dirty wound."

AS THE sun dropped below the horizon, Rylan settled on a pallet in front of Thorin's fire, amazed at how much better his leg felt already. The healer had washed his wound carefully, making sure it was completely free of dirt and debris before covering it in a thick paste the color of the sunset. Rylan had no idea what was in the paste, but he could practically feel his leg healing as he lay there.

In the dim light of the fire, Rylan could see little detail of Thorin's home, naught but the table set into shadows, yet the place felt safe. Rylan's beast was as relaxed as he was, a surprise in itself because of the wound that kept him from changing. Usually, when he was hurt, he had to fight to keep the animal inside him under control. The pain kept him in human form, but the inability to shift left his mind in turmoil. Thorin seemed to have a calming effect, making Rylan wonder what magic besides healing the man possessed. In his other form, perhaps he could have identified the source, his beast able to sense far more about a person than Rylan could do in human form. Given his current inability to change, he would simply have to accept the situation at face value.

The exterior door opened, allowing a gust of wind to enter, chilling Rylan even beneath the thick blanket Thorin had provided him. "Are the animals settled?"

Thorin nodded, turning his back to Rylan and stripping off his shirt. Rylan barely smothered a gasp at the sight of the scars crisscrossing Thorin's back. They appeared healed, but it was obvious someone had taken great pains to whip the man badly in the not terribly distant past. Rylan's beast screamed in protest at the thought, surprising the man with its ferocity. Then Thorin turned, and Rylan caught a glimpse of a much more foreboding mark. Thorin had an M branded into his shoulder. M for murderer.

The rational part, the human part of Rylan's brain urged him to flee, but he was not strong enough to get far. Even more importantly, the animal inside him felt no fear. Thorin might be many things. He might even be a murderer, but he was no threat to Rylan. Of that much he was sure.

"Who died?"

Thorin's head whipped around, his hand covering his shoulder automatically. "You… you can see my mark?"

Rylan cursed silently. He should have realized Thorin would never have undressed if he thought Rylan could see him. "I've always seen well at night. You didn't answer my question."

"The local lord's son," Thorin said, his voice tight as he pulled a clean shirt on over his head. "I tried to help him, but he was too far gone by the time I got there. I tried explaining that, but the man was crazy with his grief. He insisted I had killed his son. They tried me and branded me. They were going to hang me, but I escaped."

"Three seasons ago."

Thorin nodded. "I won't go back. I don't want to hurt you, but if you try to turn me in, I will find a way to stop you."

"Don't worry," Rylan said, though he knew Thorin had no reason to trust him. "I have my own reasons for wanting to stay as far away from the nobility as possible."

"Why aren't you afraid of me? Everyone else who has ever seen it has run away in fear."

"Because I know you don't mean me any harm," Rylan replied honestly.

"How?"

"You aren't the only one with secrets, Thorin," Rylan said, evading the question. "So they accused you of murder and you ran here to hide."

"They say a terrible beast lives in these woods," Thorin explained. "The people from the village won't come here."

"And if the beast finds you?"

"I'll take my chances," Thorin said.

Rylan hid a smile. He already knew what the beast's reaction to Thorin would be. "If you see the beast, just remember that it can read your intentions. It will never hurt someone with a pure heart."

"How do you know?" Thorin asked, coming to sit at Rylan's side, his eyes alight with excitement.

"You aren't the only one who lives in these woods," Rylan reminded him, though it was no real answer. He could hardly tell Thorin that *he* was the beast. For one thing, Thorin would never believe him, and he couldn't change in his current state to convince the man.

"You've seen it? What does it look like?"

"It looks like a horse, with a few minor exceptions," Rylan answered honestly, having seen his reflection in the pond as he drank. "It has a horn that sprouts from its forehead and extends nearly the length of your arm. Its coat is black as night during the day and white as the moon at night. It is a peaceful creature, as long as it isn't threatened, but if it fears you, it can use its horn with all the dexterity of a sword. I have seen more than one man spitted through by its sharp point."

"It sounds fearsome," Thorin said. "I will do my best to avoid coming to its attention."

Rylan could have told Thorin he had nothing to fear, but then he would have to give an explanation he was not ready to offer. The few people in the past he had told had reacted badly. In one instance, he had barely escaped with his life. No, it was far better to keep his secret for the time he was here and leave Thorin in his ignorance.

THREE days later, the wound on Rylan's thigh had closed completely. Although it was still stiff and sore, Rylan could move his leg and even put his weight on it for short periods of time. With the freedom from debilitating pain came the need to shift, something he could not do in Thorin's company or in his home. Even if the man could accept it, Rylan's animal would not. In his other form, he could not bear any kind of confinement.

When Thorin went out to check on his animals, Rylan disrobed so he would not damage the clothes Thorin had lent him and slipped out into the woods. As soon as he could no longer hear the cackling of the hens the healer kept in a pen behind his house, Rylan changed, his body stretching and reforming to become the black unicorn that struck fear into the hearts of the villagers in the surrounding towns. He shook his head, ruffling his mane, the movement working its way down his body until he had stretched every muscle.

Taking a few tentative steps, he tested his injured leg, finding the muscle as sore in animal form as in human form, but not so much that he could not walk. His animal mind resented not being able to run, but even in equine form, he retained enough of his humanity to control the urge to ignore the pain and gallop through the woods toward home. He knew he should go back to Thorin's and take his leave properly, but the desire to find the solace of his own abode was nearly overwhelming. He turned his head back toward Thorin's cabin, and then regretfully began the long walk home.

An hour later, he was regretting his decision. His leg was throbbing, making it harder and harder to walk, and he still had some distance to travel. Furthermore, he could hear someone approaching. When he was well, he feared no one, but in his current state, he did not have the speed to defend himself should the need arise. There was nothing for it, though. He would have to face his tracker and hope for the best. Lowering his horn threateningly, he turned back and waited.

Thorin walked into the clearing where he stood.

The sight of his benefactor took Rylan's breath away. In his human form, he had come to know the man over the past few days, appreciating Thorin's gentle hands, his sharp wit, and his handsome face, but now, as a unicorn, he could sense so much more. He could sense the basic goodness at the heart of the man and the untouched innocence, which lured the unicorn like nothing else. He was not repelled by the sexual experience of those around him, but the unicorn inside him still felt the lure of the virgin. Especially when he already knew and cared about the virgin.

Slowly Rylan lifted his head so his horn pointed toward the sky rather than toward Thorin's chest, and waited to see what the man would do. Even with the distance between them, Rylan could hear Thorin's heart pounding in his chest, another advantage of his shifted form, but the man did not back away.

"Rylan was right about you," Thorin said. "He told me you were peaceful as long as I didn't have any ill intent." He took a step forward.

Rylan's muscles quivered, but he stayed where he was. His human mind knew he should leave before Thorin saw the wound on his thigh, so comparable to the one the man had been treating, but the unicorn's desire was stronger, the need to feel Thorin's hands on his neck, his shoulder, his flank too great to overrule. Angling his body so Thorin would approach his good side, he let the man draw near, blowing hard to ruffle his black hair.

Thorin laughed and stroked his long nose gently. "I can't believe you're letting me touch you."

Rylan couldn't believe he had gone this long *without* Thorin touching him. His entire body vibrated with the sense of rightness at each stroke of tender hands over his hide, his heart crying out in joy at the nearness of an innocent, someone who could be his One. He nickered softly, trying to convey without words how much he enjoyed the caresses, how much he wanted them to continue.

Thorin laughed again, a sound Rylan had heard too rarely in the days they had spent together. The fear of discovery kept Thorin somber more often than not, but it seemed Rylan's unicorn form brought out the lighter side of his personality.

"What is this?" Thorin said suddenly. "You're hurt!"

Rylan did not stop to think. He fled.

He could not let Thorin discover the truth. That reality had been driven into him since he was a child and had first learned to change. He could not let anyone realize his dual nature, at the risk of being captured or even killed, and experience had only reinforced that lesson. He ran as far as his injured leg would carry him, collapsing to the ground in human form when the pain became too much.

He cursed under his breath at finding himself back in the same position as when he and Thorin had first met. His leg was in better shape now than it had been then, even after his reckless run, but the weather was far worse. The wind whistled threateningly in the trees above his head, bringing with it the heavy smell of impending rain. Lightning crackled between the low-hanging clouds, the acrid smell of ozone making him realize how close the storm really was. He pushed to his feet, limping as he tried to continue toward his home.

"Rylan!"

Shoulders slumping, Rylan turned to face Thorin. "We have to stop meeting like this," he joked, but Thorin's face remained stern.

"What are you doing out here with a storm brewing and no clothes on?" Thorin scolded.

"It's a long story," Rylan said with a sigh as the first fat raindrops hit the canopy of leaves. "My home is not far. If you will help me there, I'll try to explain."

Thorin nodded and slid his shoulder beneath Rylan's arm, supporting his weight as he had done the day they met. "Which way?"

Rylan guided them through the woods to his home, the stone dwelling built into the cliff face next to a small waterfall that fed a normally placid pond. The wind and driving rain stirred the surface, leaving it choppy with white-capped waves. They stumbled to the door, Rylan working the locking mechanism to allow them entrance. Heart pounding, he stepped over the threshold, Thorin at his side, the first man to ever enter Rylan's domain.

"You should dry off," Rylan said, avoiding Thorin's eyes. "There is a towel by the sink. I will find something dry for you to wear, even if it's only a blanket."

"Take the time to dry off and dress as well," Thorin urged. "I will start a fire for us."

Rylan nodded and retreated into his bedroom, shutting the door behind him and leaning back against it for a moment. He had invited a man into his home. He wasn't a monk. Thorin would not be his first lover—he had no illusions they would end up anywhere but in Rylan's bed—but Thorin would be the first man Rylan had welcomed into *his* bed. The first man his unicorn had ever acknowledged. The One, the virgin he would bind to forever.

Taking a deep breath, Rylan found a towel and dried off, dressing in his own clothes again for the first time in three days. He rummaged through the armoire, looking for something that would fit Thorin, but the man was too big. Rylan settled for pulling the blanket from his bed. Stepping back into the main room, he paused for a moment to appreciate the vision of Thorin in only a towel, kneeling in front of the fireplace, his body limned in gold from the light of the burgeoning flames.

"You must be cold," Rylan said, struggling to keep his voice even as he draped the blanket around Thorin's shoulders. "What were you doing out in the woods?"

"I could ask you the same question," Thorin replied, rising from his crouch to face Rylan.

"I was coming home," Rylan replied honestly. "I'd imposed on your generosity long enough."

"Then why run away like a thief in the night?" Thorin asked. "You could have asked me to come with you, if only to make sure you got here safely. You didn't need to sneak out of the house—naked, no less—while I was outside."

"I told you that first night you were not the only one with secrets," Rylan said defensively. "I didn't mean to discover yours, but that doesn't mean I'm ready to share mine."

Thorin wrapped the blanket more securely around his shoulders. "So you ran away instead."

Rylan shrugged. "That's why I was in the woods. What's your excuse?"

"I was looking for you," Thorin replied slowly, his eyes searching Rylan's face as if he could find answers to some silent question there. "I found far more than I expected."

Heart pounding so loud he was sure Thorin could hear it, Rylan struggled to keep his voice steady and his face blank. "Really?"

"I met the beast you told me about," Thorin said. "He isn't a monster at all. He's beautiful."

Rylan shrugged silently.

Thorin frowned, but went on. "But I noticed something odd. He had a scar on his left hind leg that matches the wound on your thigh perfectly."

"That is odd," Rylan agreed, his voice sounding strangled to his own ears.

"Why didn't you tell me you were a shifter?"

"For the same reason you didn't tell me about the brand on your arm," Rylan snapped. "It's a good way to get myself killed."

Thorin's hands landed hot and heavy on Rylan's shoulders. "You know better than that. If I had any intention of harming you, I would have done it already."

"But that was before you knew what I am," Rylan reminded him. "Unicorns have been killed for their horns. Surely you know that."

"I do," Thorin agreed, "but I also know they're less likely to be killed than a man with the mark of a murderer on his arm. Unicorn or not, I mean you no harm. For the first time in three seasons, I have had the company of another person for more than a swift business transaction. You saw the brand on my arm, but you never once condemned me. You asked me who died, not who I had killed. I think I fell in love with you from those words alone."

Rylan started to shake his head, but Thorin's lips brushed his, stilling the movement and winning a gasp of surprise from Rylan's lips. The kiss was awkward in its innocence, Thorin clearly having no idea what he was doing, but Rylan could not have cared less. His innocent, his virgin, his One, was kissing him of his own volition, and nothing had ever felt so right.

"I need you to hear me," Rylan said, breaking the kiss with difficulty. "Right now, my beast desires you, and if you choose to leave, it will fight to go after you, but I will win because I am not my beast. If you stay, if you let me have you, you will be mine, my One, and no power in the world will be enough to keep me from coming after you if you try to leave. If you are not completely sure you can love me in both my forms, you need to leave now, because I won't be able to offer a second time. The lure of the virgin is nearly overwhelming for a unicorn, and my own attraction to you only adds to that." He took a breath to slow the rush of words, steeling himself for Thorin's rejection. "You need to decide now."

"There is nothing to decide," Thorin replied, renewing the kiss. "You are all I stopped letting myself dream of the moment they put this brand on my arm."

Rylan wanted to ask if he was certain, but he could only fight the unicorn within him for so long in the face of such provocative temptation.

"You are mine now," he swore, pushing the blanket aside and turning Thorin toward the bedroom.

Thorin made no protest as they moved into the other room, though Rylan could sense his nervousness. He turned Thorin back around, kissing him tenderly, the emotion in the gesture, the interest his beast showed for the first time in his intimate life, making it easy to go slow and give Thorin a moment to adjust to their intimacy. Rylan had fucked many men in his life, but never before had he made love. Never before had he taken a man to his bed with the full acceptance of his unicorn nature. Never before had he claimed a man.

His hands wandered carefully, gentling Thorin as earlier Thorin had gentled the unicorn. Their lips stayed pressed together, moving against each other, parting for a quick breath, then joining again. Rylan could swear he felt their souls touching in that contact. He waited for Thorin to touch him in return, but his virgin was too shy for that, apparently. Rylan looked forward to teaching him confidence, but that could wait for later, when Thorin trusted the depth and permanence of Rylan's love. For now, Rylan would take charge and claim his virgin, his mate. His One.

He had always known his other half would fixate on someone someday, and that when that happened, he would be bound to that person for life, but knowing and experiencing were two completely different things. The reverence that imbued his touch as he discovered every plane and hollow of Thorin's body had never before been present in his bed sport. His own pleasure had no importance in the face of Thorin's need. And when their bodies finally joined, the tender indignities of flesh piercing flesh faded to nothing compared to the knowledge of soul mating with soul.

Time stretched and slowed as their breathing returned, finally, to normal and their pulses steadied again. Rylan rolled to one side, keeping Thorin tightly in his embrace so his virgin—even if Thorin was considerably less virginal than an hour ago—would not feel rejected.

"So what happens now?" Thorin asked after a few minutes. "You called me yours, but I don't know what that means. In practical terms."

Rylan pushed up on one elbow. "Unicorns are fascinated by innocents, virgins. I'm not sure you could have approached me in animal form earlier tonight if you hadn't been untouched. I wouldn't have hurt you, because I knew you meant me no harm, but I'm not sure I could have stayed still while you petted me like you did. In my human form, it isn't simply an abstract fascination. It's a mating instinct. I've always known that, someday, my unicorn would find a virgin who would be my virgin, my One."

"Except I'm not a virgin anymore," Thorin pointed out.

"No." Rylan had to agree, since he had taken part in the deflowering. "But *I* caused that, and so instead of my unicorn seeing you as tainted, it sees you as mine. Nothing we ever do together in love will tarnish your innocence in the eyes of my beast. How is it that you have reached an age and a maturity to be my One without ever having taken a lover?"

"I never met a man I respected enough to take to my bed," Thorin replied. "Apparently I needed a unicorn instead."

The answer was, perhaps, simplistic, but Rylan accepted it for now. He would have time to learn more of his mate's past as they built their future. The details could wait.

WINTER had given way to spring finally, and both Rylan and Thorin were ready for the freedom the warmer weather allowed. The snow had been uncommonly heavy, making it hard for Rylan to run in unicorn form. He had changed frequently, his unicorn as possessive of Thorin as Rylan was, but while he had reveled in letting Thorin brush him and stroke him, they had not been able to go for many rides. Now that the snow had finally melted everywhere but under the densest stands of trees, Rylan wanted to take his mate on his back and run.

Over the winter, they had worked toward Thorin being able to ride Rylan in unicorn form. Even with Thorin, his One whom he trusted implicitly, Rylan's unicorn had been nervous at first about accepting a rider. It had taken all of Rylan's will and all of Thorin's persuasiveness to convince the animal to let Thorin first lean and later sit on its back. Finally, though, they had reached the point where Thorin could take a short ride around the protected yard. The sensation of having Thorin's long, long legs stretching across his back and down his sides, gripping him tightly for even that distance, had been enough to result in a frenzied session of lovemaking. Rylan could only imagine—and anticipate—the results of a real run.

"Are you ready?" he called impatiently to Thorin, who was still in the house.

"Hold your horses," Thorin joked, coming out of the house.

"Who are you calling a horse?" Rylan retorted, a grin forming at the easy teasing.

"Not you," Thorin said immediately. "I want my ride today, and I know what will happen if I insult you."

"What will happen?" Rylan asked, drawing Thorin into his arms. He stroked the strong arms bared by the sleeveless shirt Thorin wore, thrilled that the man no longer felt the need to hide the brand from Rylan's eyes.

"You'll pout, and the unicorn won't let me mount," Thorin said. "And that would ruin the rest of my plans."

"And what are the rest of your plans?" Rylan asked, though he thought he knew.

Thorin grinned mischievously. "Finding a secluded spot and convincing you to switch back to human form so you can ravish me thoroughly."

That coincided exactly with Rylan's plans. "What makes you think I have any intention of ravishing you?"

Thorin held up the small vial he had found tucked among his clothes that morning. "The fact that you left this for me, since you can't carry anything when you're in unicorn form. Come on, change already, so we can go."

Rylan stripped, shivering a little as the breeze picked up, his human flesh far more sensitive to temperature than his equine body. Usually, Thorin's hands would have been all over him as he bared himself for the change, but today it seemed the man was as eager as Rylan was. With a stretch and a shake, he shifted, turning to nudge Thorin with his horn. Thorin approached the animal cautiously, because even after their practice rides, the unicorn remained skittish at first, but Rylan's eagerness overcame the beast's fears and Thorin mounted with ease. Rylan took a deep breath, calming his unicorn's nerves and reining in his own anticipation. Thorin's pat on his neck gave him the sign he needed that his One was settled and ready to go.

The unicorn began at an easy walk, growing accustomed to the extra weight on his back, to the way it moved and shifted with and against him. Thorin made no move to guide Rylan, content to let the unicorn explore on his own, much to Rylan's relief. He was not sure the animal inside him would have taken such direction.

When he was comfortable, he picked up the pace a little, alert for any sign of discomfort or distress on Thorin's part. Despite his intention of being careful, their lovemaking the night before had degenerated into a pounding, Thorin demanding more and more until Rylan's reserves broke. The body on his back moved with him easily, though, nothing in the hands resting lightly on Rylan's mane or the legs wrapped firmly around his girth suggesting anything more than pure enjoyment of the day and the sunshine and the ride.

The need to run became overwhelming finally, and Rylan gave in to it, his hooves pounding the uneven ground as he raced along the narrow track between the trees. Thorin moved with him as if they were one body, making Rylan long for them to be joined in another way.

Turning toward the hot springs that bubbled up from the base of a nearby mountain, he raced in that direction, already anticipating making love to his One in the bubbly water.

Thorin dismounted when Rylan stopped near the springs. The unicorn gave a restless shake of its head and transformed back into the man. The very aroused man.

"It looks like you enjoyed our ride nearly as much as I did," Thorin said with a grin, pulling Rylan toward him.

"I don't know," Rylan teased, moving into Thorin's arms. "You still have clothes on."

Laughing, Thorin pulled the shirt over his head and started undoing the laces on his trousers. Rylan moved to help when a noise caught his attention. "Someone's coming," he said tersely. "It sounds like a group."

Thorin nodded, his face sober as he refastened his pants and reached for his shirt. "Change. We can always come back later."

Rylan stretched, his body transforming as Thorin pulled his shirt over his head. Before Thorin could mount, though, five men broke free of the woods. Everyone froze for a moment before one of the men shouted Thorin's name. The others took up the cry, rushing toward the man, heedless of Rylan at his side.

The fell intent in their hearts spurred Rylan forward, his body blocking Thorin's from the oncoming crowd. They did not appear to have bows with them, fortunately, but Rylan would have fought them even then. No one threatened his One. No one. He lowered his horn, charging the group. He hoped his aggression would frighten them into retreat, but he had not counted on their greed. The emotion he could feel roiling from them made no sense until one of the men shouted about the price on Thorin's head. That only added to Rylan's anger. These men would steal his heart from him for money? They could think again.

Rylan reared high, his hooves thrashing just above the head of the nearest man. When the man's response was to draw his sword, Rylan lowered his head and skewered the man without regret. He tossed his head, the man's body flying through the air to land lifelessly at the feet of a nearby tree. The other four hesitated after that, not sure they wanted to face Rylan's horn, but the lure of the bounty was great.

Before Rylan could lunge again, he felt tender hands on his side and a leg over his back. "Go," Thorin said. "Don't sink to their level when their only crime is greed. They can't follow us. Run."

Rylan was tempted to ignore the admonition, but his One ruled his actions as surely as his heart. Springing forward, he reached the track the men had taken to arrive, hoping to throw them off his trail by not returning directly home. His hooves thundered hard on the forest floor as he raced away from those who would have hurt Thorin. He could feel Thorin clinging to him, bent over his neck, hands tangled in his mane. All the pleasure of the earlier ride had disappeared in the face of the villagers' violence, and not even Thorin's legs squeezing tightly around Rylan's belly could restore it. Not until he knew Thorin was safe.

Arriving at a stream, he splashed into the bed, traveling downstream for some miles so the water would hide his tracks before leaving the watercourse and turning toward home. His subterfuge would slow their pursuers, but the villagers knew Thorin was in the woods now, in the company of the beast. They would be back, and in greater numbers. When they entered the yard, Thorin slid from Rylan's back.

"You defended me," Thorin said as Rylan shimmered back into human form.

"Gather everything of value," Rylan said. "We must leave as soon as we can load the pack horse. It will take them time to find us, but they will not give up."

Thorin caught Rylan's arm as he started toward the house. "You defended me."

The repetition caught Rylan's attention. "I'll always defend you. You are my One."

ARIEL TACHNA lives in southwestern Ohio with her husband, her daughter and son, and their cat. A native of the region, she has nonetheless lived all over the world, having fallen in love with both France, where she found her career and her husband, and India, where she dreams of retiring some day. She started writing when she was twelve and hasn't looked back since. A connoisseur of wine and horses, she's as comfortable on a farm as she is in the big cities of the world.

Visit Ariel's web site at http://www.arieltachna.com/ and her blog at http://arieltachna.livejournal.com/.

Of Genies and Sea Monsters

scarlet blackwell

I

ONCE upon a time there was a man named Ephram. Ephram was a seller of all that glittered—gold, diamonds, rubies, and emeralds—in a place far, far away. He earned a good living at his trade and he lived well, but it had not always been so.

Ephram had once lived with his soulmate, a man named Eber. The two had lived in poverty and despair until Ephram left on a ship bound for the east to seek his fortune. Their parting had been tearful. Eber wanted Ephram to stay. Ephram told him it was for the best, that he would bring home vast purses full of gold and they would live in happiness until the end of their days. Eber pointed out that he already lived in happiness, that Ephram was all he needed.

Ephram only realized this was true when he was without Eber. The money he earned did not fill the chasm within him that leaving Eber had opened.

Ephram loved Eber to the bottom of his soul, but he vowed that only when he had enough money would he return to his love. So the time dragged on, and despite the beautiful men and the beautiful women surrounding him in the fair Land of Plenty, none of them caught Ephram's interest in any way. Only when his lover's birthday loomed did Ephram begin to mourn with desperation.

His heart bled for Eber. His lips yearned for his kiss. His soul ached for the other half of him. He gave notice on his sumptuous lodgings and packed up all his things. He went down to the harbor and there enquired about passage across the world to the Land Beyond the Sea.

The first man he approached shook his head, his turban glittering with jewels in the sun. He told Ephram that no one was traversing that body of water anymore because many ships had been wrecked there by a foul monster of the deep which swallowed ships whole.

Ephram scoffed, because although he believed in monsters, he did not believe that one could swallow a ship. He moved along the dock to the captain of a large schooner, asking him when he was sailing to the Land Beyond the Sea.

The man, a crusty old sea dog with one leg and an eye patch, cackled, showing blackened teeth. "No one sails that way anymore. You would be wise to remain where it is safe, pretty one."

Ephram glowered at him. "*Someone* must be going that way."

"There is no one who would dare. Be thankful for your life here and accept it."

Ephram walked up and down the bustling dock for an hour, quizzing every sailor, but to no avail. Apparently everyone lived in fear of the sea monster. He returned downhearted to his lodgings and knocked timidly on the door of his landlord, a crazy man with birds'-nest hair named Arteus.

Arteus wore a long, flowing, purple robe and long, black beads which swayed and caught up everything in their path. He bade Ephram enter and continued a conversation with his cat, Tiger, as though Ephram hadn't interrupted them. Turning away from the door, his beads caught around the handle and almost garroted him.

Ephram helped untangle him and Arteus smiled absently, returning to his silken cushions on the floor and picking up a discarded pipe, puffing thoughtfully and asking the cat what it thought of the town's plans to extend the grand bazaar's opening times.

"Sir," Ephram said, because Arteus was a magician and he was fearful that upsetting him might result in his turning Ephram into a toad. "I was wondering if I might take my notice back. It seems I may not be leaving for the foreseeable future."

Arteus regarded him with heavy, blue eyes. "The sea monster," he said, to Ephram's surprise. The gem merchant nodded and then sighed, his heart heavy.

"I wanted to be home for my love's birthday," he murmured as the smoke from Arteus's pipe made him feel decidedly discombobulated.

"And who is your love?"

"Eber."

"Eber of the doe eyes." Arteus lay down against the cushions, his eyes half-closed.

Ephram's mouth fell open. "How do you know that? Have you been in my room?" There was an etching of Eber by his bed, an etching he spoke to every night before he went to sleep.

"No," Arteus said, looking offended.

"Then how…." Ephram was uneasy and unsettled.

"Careful of what you accuse me," Arteus warned. "Or I shall not furnish you with the means to get home."

Ephram stared.

Arteus smirked. He offered the pipe to Ephram, who declined. "You are a model tenant, Ephram. Maybe I can give you something to ease your pain and your loneliness."

The sometime magician crawled ungracefully to his feet, stumbling over his robe and getting the beads caught in the bars of a birdcage, so that the cockatoo within pecked at them eagerly and Arteus almost dragged the cage from its pedestal.

He went to a carved wooden chest in the corner, and from there he withdrew a tarnished golden lamp and turned around, holding it out to Ephram.

Ephram regarded it, nonplussed.

"Listen to me well," Arteus said, his tone and face for once serious. "If you seek a solution to your problems, then polish the lamp and restore it to its former beauty. But only do so if you are prepared to deal with the consequences. And remember this. Watch for the wolf in sheep's clothing. Do not trust him, even when he offers you the earth."

"What?" Ephram asked. "Who?" He was confused; one moment they were talking about a lamp and now they appeared to be talking about a man.

Arteus smiled benevolently. "You shall see. Now excuse me."

Ephram took the lamp and made his exit. He hurried up to his room and threw himself on the bed, letting the unwanted gift fall heavily to the ground.

"Ouch," came a loud voice. "Why don't you be more careful? I'm delicate and I bruise easily."

Ephram leapt upright on the bed in horror, reaching for the dagger he kept under his pillow, grasping its jeweled handle and holding it before him as he surveyed the huge man in his room.

II

HE WAS enormous: A giant of a man wearing a white linen shirt which virtually strained at the seams, and silver pants caught up with a wide, golden belt that sparkled with gemstones the likes of which Ephram had never seen before.

Beneath these cropped pants, his ankles were incongruously skinny, and on his feet he wore golden, curly shoes in the tradition of the country.

Ephram gaped at this apparition. The man didn't wear a hat and his hair was dark and closely cropped, his face pale for one from the area, and his features fine and regular. His eyes were rather stunning, reminding Ephram of the smoky quartz he carried in his display case, but with flashes of emerald and gold.

The stranger grinned at the expression on the merchant's face, his teeth shockingly white and perfect. "Like what you see, Ephram?"

"Who are you?" Ephram jumped off the bed, brandishing his dagger at the interloper. "How in God's name did you get in here and how do you know my name?"

The man continued to look amused. "Answering your questions in order, I am Drakon. You brought me here, and I know your name because I know everything. There is nothing I don't know." He smirked, arms folded.

"Oh yes?" Ephram snapped. "Who was the first pharaoh of the second dynasty?"

Drakon smiled. "Hotepsekhemwy."

"When did he rule from?"

"2890 BC. I knew him."

"What?"

Drakon smiled beatifically and said nothing further.

"Is Arteus a magician?"

"Certainly. But hardly in my league."

"You're a magician?"

"You're a quick one, Ephram."

"What do you want?"

"What do *you* want?" Drakon shot back at him. "*You* summoned *me*."

"I didn't!"

"You did. You dropped me on the floor."

Ephram looked down. "What? You came from the lamp?"

Drakon clicked his tongue. He started to walk around the room, yawning and stopping to look at trinkets. "Do I need to speak slowly and use words of one syllable?"

Ephram glared at him, drawing himself up to his full height and puffing out his chest. "Get out of my room."

Drakon quirked one eyebrow, his gaze straying to the bedside table. "Who's this?"

"Put him down." Ephram tried to snatch the etching away.

Drakon put the palm of his hand square into Ephram's face and shoved him onto the bed. "I can't leave, simple one. You've made a contract with me by summoning me from the lamp. Now tell me what you want."

"Oh, God, this is some horrible nightmare," Ephram said, pulling at his hair.

Drakon put the picture back and regarded Ephram. "You're tiresome. Tell me what you want or I'll beat it out of you." He smiled horribly.

"Oh, God, I want to go home! Now leave me alone, foul demon!" Ephram threw himself face down on the bed and told himself that when he opened his eyes, the interloper would be gone.

"I'm sorry?" came an icy voice. "*Foul*? I've been voted most beautiful creature in the world five years running by the Monsters, Ghouls, and Associated Beings society! How dare you!"

Ephram put his hands over his ears and tried to count to ten.

"You offend me greatly. Why should I even grant you your wish?"

Ephram removed the hands from his ears. He sat up and turned around so fast that he hurt his neck. "What? You can send me home?"

Drakon sniffed disdainfully, nose in the air. "Certainly."

Ephram's jaw dropped. He threw himself to the ground, hands around the skinny ankles, lips lowered to one curly shoe.

"Get off." Drakon lifted his other foot and kicked at Ephram. "Do you know how much these shoes cost?"

Ephram scrambled to his feet. "Did you mean it? You can help me get home?"

"I said yes, didn't I?" Drakon smiled and a sly little light came into those golden eyes. "However, I would like a small favor in return."

"Name it!" Ephram burst out. "Anything!"

Drakon lifted one eyebrow. "Anything?"

Ephram reddened. "Not quite anything."

Drakon laughed. "You think I would ask you for *that*, Ephram?"

"No."

"Then you don't know me at all, because I would, actually," Drakon cackled. "I would ask you to please me with your mouth, and more. I'm a villain that way."

Ephram looked at him in horror.

Drakon smirked. "But you are in luck, because I am promised to another. He holds my heart, and there is the favor I wish you to grant me. I wish you to make this man fall in love with me. Failing that, I at least need you to subdue him long enough for me to do unspeakably bad things to him with my tongue. And then I will send you home."

Ephram stared. "Does he feel favorably toward you?"

"Oh no," Drakon replied airily and reached to the table, popping a Turkish delight in his mouth and chewing. "He hates me with a passion."

III

EPHRAM took a deep breath. He moved out of the bedroom to the living quarters, going to a crystal decanter and pouring himself and the genie of the lamp a shot of the local liqueur. Drakon took his glass and tossed it back, smacking his lips with pleasure, while Ephram sipped his more sedately.

"So you want me, who has no magical powers, to make this man, who despises you, fall in love with you or at least allow you to place your tongue in an unspeakable place?" he asked the genie.

"Just so." Drakon helped himself to another drink, a larger measure this time, which he threw back just as fast. It was said that the local drink gave one hallucinations, and three small drinks were enough to intoxicate the strongest man, but the genie seemed untouched.

"And how would you like me to do that?" Ephram's heart sank more and more in dismay.

Drakon shrugged his powerful shoulders.

Ephram clenched his teeth. "Is he a magician too?"

"Not that I know of. Or maybe he is, to be immune to my obvious charms." Drakon smirked.

Ephram rolled his eyes. "His name?"

"Darack."

"Where does Darack live?"

"The other side of the harbor from here."

"And he knows you?"

"Of course he knows me. Formerly, before I was put in the lamp, I made myself very well known to him." Drakon coughed.

"What have you done? Harassed him?"

"That's a strong word." Drakon returned his attention to the decanter.

"So you have. Why does he hate you exactly?"

Drakon sighed. "He says I am stubborn, prideful, thoughtless, arrogant, callous, and cold. In short, I have no redeeming features whatsoever. Well, apart from my beauty."

"It sounds like love," Ephram responded dryly.

Drakon laughed loudly. "I like you, Ephram." He tossed his drink back like water.

Ephram eyed him uneasily, because Drakon was on his third drink and he didn't want the genie vomiting on his Turkish rugs. "And how do I sell you to Darack when, clearly, he knows you very well?"

"Possibly you will have to seek the services of another magician."

Ephram sighed. "Come on. A magician gives me the lamp. Another magician comes out of it and promises me my dream but only if I seek *another* magician to make his dream come true! This is foolish."

Drakon's eyes narrowed like a cat's. "Would you prefer me to go back into the lamp? And leave you here again for a second year?"

"No, no," Ephram said hastily, even though, in the back of his mind, he was sure that Drakon was supposed to be grateful to *him* for releasing him from the lamp. He wasn't sure how the genie was walking all over him, but he was. "Furnish me with this man's address and I shall make enquiries."

Drakon smiled. "I shall stay here and…." He indicated the decanter of alcohol.

Ephram sighed, reached for his coat, and listened to the directions to the house of Darack, this man who seemed to have Drakon's character down just fine.

IV

DARACK lived in a small house overlooking the harbor, with a very pretty front garden, scarlet and violet flowers spilling over the wall, and blooms the color of sunshine curling around the door. The sun beat down on its white walls, making it gleam with virtual iridescence. Although it was modest compared to Ephram's own dwellings, it was prettier and more homely. Ephram was starting to realize more and more that money was not so important after all. He knocked and waited nervously on the step.

The man who opened the door was stunning—which wasn't so much of a surprise when one looked at the man who wanted him. He had dark locks flowing over his shoulders in a shining, glossy wave like the mane of a horse, and his eyes glowed a pale turquoise. His body was encased in black clothes which hugged his muscles favorably. Ephram was entranced.

"Yes?" the man asked when he stared too long.

Ephram regained a grip on himself. "I'm looking for Darack."

"I am he," the vision of loveliness said. "What can I do for you?"

"My name is Ephram. I come on behalf of Drakon…."

Darack groaned before he could get any further. "Please, sir, leave at once." He tried to shut the door, so Ephram had no choice but to stick his foot in it, grimacing as his toes were squashed.

"Please," he said urgently. "Listen to what I have to say. I beg you."

The man regarded him irritably before he opened the door and beckoned Ephram in. Inside, the house was immaculate, light and airy and painted in pale colors. Darack bade Ephram sit in the living room and brought a tray of apple tea, pouring Ephram a glass and placing it on a saucer with a sugar lump before pushing it toward him. Ephram took it with thanks and sipped.

"I thought I had heard the last of him." Darack sat back in his chair, cradling his glass.

Ephram shook his head. "He has been… abroad," he said, because Drakon had told him a wicked magician had imprisoned him in the lamp six months ago. Arteus had purchased him and his new home for a bag of figs and a kiss from a seller in the grand bazaar some two weeks ago.

"And now he has persuaded you to carry out his dirty business for him," Darack said dryly.

Ephram sighed. "Have you no regard at all for him?"

Darack glared. "He is stubborn, prideful, thoughtless, arrogant, callous, and cold. In short, he has no redeeming features whatsoever. Not even beauty."

"Actually, he said you thought he was beautiful."

Darack's lip curled. "I've had better."

Ephram resisted the urge to pull at his hair. "How did Drakon court you?"

Darack sipped his tea. "I met him one day at the harbor, where he was hanging around looking at sailors in tight pants and generally making a nuisance of himself. He had been chased away by a group with sticks when he saw me walking past. He followed me home, his tongue hanging out, begging me for my affections. I was not impressed. I slammed the door in his face and he stayed outside all night, shouting up at the window the filthiest words I've ever heard about what he wanted to do to me."

Ephram coughed and averted his eyes.

Darack, it seemed, wished to expand. "He described in great detail which parts of his anatomy he wished to put into which parts of my body."

Ephram smothered a gulp and shifted in his seat. After a year of celibacy, he didn't need images of the huge genie satisfying Darack.

"He spoke of fingers and tongues and how he wanted to taste and swallow me. How he wanted me on his face...."

Ephram crossed his legs, putting his hands over his crotch. He tried to speak, but his throat was dry.

"He told me about all the positions he wanted me in, and how he wanted to cover my naked, glistening body with fruit and cream and lick it off, dipping his tongue into every crevice and savoring the taste of my sensual, beautiful skin."

"Stop..." Ephram whimpered, but Darack paid no attention.

"He spoke of how he would have me on all fours, with my hand around myself, shouting as he spread me open and slid into my velvety depths."

Ephram bit his lip hard as a groan threatened to spill out. Something wet his undergarments.

Darack put his tea down and stared hard at Ephram. "Filth is not the way to win my affections, Ephram."

Ephram's head lolled back against his chair. "Of course not," he said in a slurred voice which sounded like he'd had a stroke.

"I demand love and respect, not tongues in unspeakable places."

"Yes," Ephram said, "oh, yes."

"We understand each other?"

"Without doubt." Ephram stifled a yawn. He wanted to curl up on the chair and snooze awhile.

"Good." Darack stood. "Then I'll let you take that message back to your friend."

Ephram staggered weakly to his feet. "He's no friend of mine, sir," he muttered as Darack all but shoved him out the door.

He stood there a moment on the step before thinking to knock on the door again. When Darack answered it, crossly, Ephram said, "Is there someone else? If there was, I could tell Drakon and he might give it up as a lost cause."

Darack nodded curtly. "There is. His name is Xan."

Ephram smiled eagerly. "And you love Xan?"

Darack shrugged. "Not really. He's just something to pass the time."

Ephram frowned. "But I thought you believed in love and respect."

"I do. Which is why I'm still looking." He slammed the door.

EPHRAM found the genie, facedown and unconscious, on one of his Turkish rugs, the empty crystal decanter upturned by his side. He gripped Drakon under the arms and dragged him with great difficulty into the center of his nest of silken cushions, where Ephram let him drop unceremoniously, before retreating to make himself some tea.

Ephram spent some hours watching the genie snore ungracefully before Drakon awoke, groaning and holding his head, turning a baleful eye on Ephram as though he held him personally responsible for his own lack of control.

"Darack," he growled.

"He demands love and respect, not tongues in unspeakable places," Ephram stated.

Drakon snorted in derision, rolling to a sitting position. "Once he has my tongue in there, he will forget everything else. He will beg and plead with me for something more..." he thrust his groin crudely, "...*substantial* to fill him."

"You need to leave," Ephram said in a choked voice.

Drakon raised an eyebrow. "And where would you like me to go? Seeing as you raised me from my home and now I have none. Would you see me out on the streets?"

Ephram sighed. "No. Stay out here. I need some... private time." He hurried into his bedroom and closed the door.

V

"DARACK has another," Ephram said at breakfast while the genie sat devouring half a watermelon held in his huge hands, spitting out the pips into a bowl.

Drakon lifted his head, juice dripping from his chin, and scowled. "What?"

"Darack has another. A man named Xan, which is why he'll never be yours. It would be wise for you to transfer your affections to one more available."

Drakon's face was black as thunder. He stood up and hurled the watermelon down. Then he grabbed Ephram by the throat. "It has been said that I have all the malice and rage of a stampeding rhinoceros when I am roused. You would be wise not to rouse me, Ephram." He pushed him away. "Now get me Darack, and not only do you get to keep your life, but you get to go home too." He smiled sweetly.

ARTEUS looked dazed when he opened the door and Ephram stumbled inside. "You have to help me," he cried. "What have you done? You've sent me a genie with a split personality! He's alternately lascivious and psychotic! He has me harassing some poor man who cares nothing for him, and he tells me if I don't win this man for him, he'll kill me! What am I going to do? I just want to go home!"

"Hush now, my child," Arteus said soothingly, curling an arm around Ephram's shoulders and guiding him into the living room, where he had been puffing on the omnipresent pipe. "Sit down there with my pipe and rest awhile. We will deal with Drakon in due course." He smiled sweetly.

EPHRAM was considerably more relaxed an hour later, after several puffs on the pipe and a few ribald stories.

"Now," Arteus said. "Evidently the only way you're going to get home is to win Darack. So we'll have to try another magician."

Ephram sighed. "Maybe someone a little more mentally stable than Drakon?"

Arteus shook his head. "That's a contradiction in terms. You have to have a few bats loose in the belfry to be a magician. The crazier you are, the better the magic."

Ephram closed his eyes. "Send me to him. And if this doesn't work, then so help me, I will swim across the ocean myself to my love, sea monster be damned."

Arteus cackled. "You are brave, Ephram, but you're an idiot."

EPHRAM sat on a plush sofa across from a short man wearing a bright green robe edged with silver and a ridiculous red fez that was too small for his head. The hat seemed to perch precariously on the very back of his crown, as though it would tumble off at any moment, so Ephram's eyes roamed to it constantly, fascinated.

"So," Magician X said, for that was how he was known. "Who sent you?"

"Arteus."

"Ah, that cretin," Magician X said, almost fondly. "And what do you want?"

"For you to put a spell on a man named Darack and make him fall in love with, ah, a friend of mine." Ephram almost choked on the word.

Magician X regarded him suspiciously. "Who?"

Ephram stammered. "Drakon."

"I see." Magician X's face went cold as stone and Ephram's heart sank.

"I can pay you," he said quickly. "*Anything*. I beg you. Drakon will only grant me my wish if I make Darack fall in love with him."

Magician X looked disgusted. "How surprising. That man never did anything out of the goodness of his heart. He never did anything for a fellow man without it having strings attached to it. He is incapable of loving another."

Ephram said nothing, heart sinking further and further, right into his very shoes.

"What is your wish?"

"That Drakon send me home across the ocean to my love."

Magician X studied him a moment with dark, thoughtful eyes. "My mother always said I should do one good deed a day, and as much as I hesitate making an innocent man fall in love with that villain, I would like to help you get your wish."

Ephram nodded with a grateful lump in his throat.

"But I, of course, require a wish of my own."

It was all Ephram could do not to slam his head against the nearest wall.

"My terms are simple." Magician X smiled serenely. "Tell Drakon that I require a kiss. Ask him to present himself this very day. On delivery of the goods, we shall advance to this man Darack's home and put him under the sweetest love spell." He leaned back in his seat with a satisfied smirk, almost smacking his lips like a cat in anticipation of the finest cream.

"YOU'VE been to see him?" Drakon demanded. He had been found with his face in the other half of the watermelon, juice soaking the front of his shirt and dripping onto the floor.

"You have history."

Drakon glared. "We do."

"What?"

"None of your deuced business," Drakon growled. "*Big* boys' business. I presume he has demanded a fee of you."

"Of course," Ephram said sullenly. "A kiss from you."

Drakon lifted an eyebrow. "A kiss? Oh, he'll be getting much more than that. Let's go." He tossed the watermelon away, wiped the back of his hand over his mouth and wrenched the door almost off its hinges.

DRAKON didn't spend time on pleasantries when they reached the magician's house. He merely gripped Magician X by the neck and shoved him backward, hard, following him inside, lips fixed to his. Ephram, lingering in shock on the doorstep, heard crashing and banging and a few angry yells from within.

God, what if Drakon was actually killing Magician X? He would never get home. He stepped inside, moving to the living room door, freezing in place as he saw the scene within.

Drakon had the magician on his back on the Turkish rug, kneeling above him. He reached out and ripped his robe open clean down the middle, exposing Magician X's muscular body, the man naked and erect beneath.

Drakon growled in delight, leaning over him. "And you can take the stupid hat off too, X," he said, wrenching the fez from his head and tossing it across the room.

Drakon tossed his jeweled belt aside and pulled down his silver pants. Then he gripped Magician X beneath the knees and hoisted his legs over his shoulders.

Ephram drew away from the door, leaning against the wall. He needed to go home and spend some private time with the etching of Eber. He stood a little way away and tried not to listen to the yelling in some strange, arcane language coming from inside the house.

Finally, he heard a hand slap flesh and Drakon say, "I hope you'll grant me my favor now, X."

"Anything," came an exhausted sigh. "Anything."

"Good boy."

VI

"DID that get you off?" Drakon asked with a vicious smirk as he came out of the living room, still fastening his belt.

Ephram mumbled something, averting his eyes. Drakon shot out a hand and groped his groin roughly. "Not yet, I see," he cackled as Ephram stumbled back in outrage, going tomato red. "Now get you to Darack's house. I've held up my *end* of the bargain." He left the house, whistling.

A moment later, the magician appeared, looking flushed and disheveled, the fez at an even more ridiculous angle than usual. "Let's go."

DARACK groaned when he opened the door to them. But no sooner had he done so than Magician X sprang forward, placing the flat of his hand on Darack's forehead, forcing him backward into the house while chanting loudly in the arcane language he had used during his tussle with Drakon.

Darack stumbled back, Magician X advancing on him, Ephram following, with reservation, into the house. The three made their way into the living room, Magician X's chanting growing louder and the fez bobbing crazily on his head.

"He's strong, his mind resists me!" Magician X cried over his shoulder as Ephram stood frozen in place.

"What in the name of the devil's briefcase do you think you're doing?"

The three of them turned toward the voice, finding a thin man with dark hair in a white robe standing on the far side of the room. Magician X's hand fell from Darack's forehead and he gaped at him. The short man's dark eyes moved to his, and he did the same.

Darack gasped a little, doubling over and rubbing at his head. He tried to speak and could not.

Ephram presumed the thin man was Xan, Darack's lover. Something strange seemed to be happening. He and the magician could not take their eyes off each other.

"My God," Magician X breathed, "if you aren't the most divine creature I have ever seen in my life."

Xan reddened, smiling.

As Darack watched helplessly, the two stepped forward and Magician X swept Xan off his feet and into his arms, their lips meeting in a passionate kiss.

Ephram's mouth dropped open. Xan and Magician X spun around in a circle, frantically lip-locked, until a plume of glittering smoke arose from the floor and, a moment later, the two vanished.

"That's wonderful," Darack said. "The perfect end to a perfect day. Thank you, Ephram. Tell me, what other methods shall I expect you to employ? Why don't you just kidnap me, tie me up, and let him use me as his sex slave?"

Ephram shook his head in regret. "I'm sorry," he said and fled the house.

But the nightmare wasn't over yet, because there, rounding the curve of the harbor and walking up the street, was Drakon. The genie was wearing fresh clothes, his hair gleaming as brightly as his curly shoes, and in his hands he clasped a bunch of freshly picked blood-red roses. He had come to woo Darack, and Ephram almost smiled at the earnestness on his face.

Drakon's expression fell when he saw Ephram looking so harassed.

"Drakon." Ephram stopped him with a hand on his arm. "Something has gone terribly wrong."

"What?"

"Magician X ran away with Darack's lover."

Drakon stared at him a moment; then he straightened his shoulders and set his jaw. "No matter. I can still do this alone. You shall see."

"Oh, God!" Darack cried when he opened the door, and he tried to slam it again on the genie.

Drakon stuck a curly shoe in the gap and leaned forward. "Hear me out. I come to declare my love."

Darack's hand slammed into the genie's chest and knocked him backward off the step. "I don't love you. I will *never* love you, not even if you were the last man on earth!"

Drakon's expression darkened, blood suffusing his cheeks. "I bring you flowers," he said in a hurt, almost childish tone of voice, holding them out.

"Take a look around you." Darack gestured to the blooms around his door, rolling through his beautiful garden. "I have no need for flowers, least of all blooms that you stole from someone's garden on the way here. I *detest* you."

Drakon trembled with rage. His large hand curled around the stems of the roses until blood started to run down his wrist, soaking into the sleeve of his pristine white shirt. He dropped the flowers to the ground and reached out, slapping his hand against Darack's cheek, where he dragged his fingers down his face to his neck, leaving the pale skin smeared in blood.

"I bleed for you, Darack," he hissed, eyes dancing wildly. "I bleed for you!"

Ephram staggered back as Drakon turned around, almost knocking him over. He stood on the path, watching, as Drakon stalked down the street.

VII

EPHRAM was in for a terrible surprise when he got home. The front door was hanging off its frame and smashing sounded down the street. With his heart in his mouth, he climbed the stairs and peered within. Drakon was sitting in a corner of the destroyed living room with his knees drawn up to his chest. Everything Ephram owned was in pieces—glass and broken furniture strewn across the floor, pictures ripped from the walls, and his display case of precious gems scattered over his Turkish rugs. On the pale walls was Drakon's blood, handprints littering it in a grotesque pattern.

"What have you done?"

Drakon lifted his head. "Oh, shut up," he said scornfully. "It can be fixed."

Ephram stared at him. He virtually quivered in rage. "*Fixed*?" He let out a yell of rage and stormed forward. He grabbed Drakon by the throat with both hands and dragged him off the floor with a strength he never knew he had.

"Arteus was right about you! He said you were not to be trusted, and Magician X said you've never helped another man in your life, and I come back here and you have destroyed my house!" He dragged the shocked Drakon to the door, almost bouncing him off the walls.

"I never want to see you again as long as I live!" Ephram shoved Drakon from the top step.

Instead of having the satisfaction of seeing the genie tumble to the street below, though, Drakon merely disappeared in a puff of smoke. Ephram screamed in thwarted frustration and slammed his broken door literally off its hinges, so it fell pathetically down the steps into the street, leaving his wrecked house exposed to any nosy passerby who wanted to see. Then he sank down amongst the glass and the blood and cried.

HE AWOKE the next day in a strange bed, after his landlord had climbed the stairs cautiously and picked him up from the floor, taking him home and plying him with the pipe and the deadly local drink until he had to carry him to bed.

Ephram climbed out of bed and pulled on a robe, making his way to the kitchen, where Arteus sat at the table, drinking mint tea and eating bread and fruit.

"Sit down, my friend." Arteus pushed a glass toward him.

Ephram did so, taking the tea gratefully, his head pounding. "I wish you'd never given me the lamp."

"I'm sorry. Drakon does tend to cause havoc everywhere he goes."

Ephram lowered his head and let the steam from his tea heat his face. He shook his head sadly. "I will go down to the harbor again and seek passage across the ocean. If no one will take me, I will hire a boat myself and take my chances with the sea monster."

"No, Ephram."

"I must. I can't bear to spend one more minute away from my love."

DOWN at the harbor, the salty sea dogs laughed at him and sent him up and down the vast array of boats, seemingly all in cahoots for amusement at his expense. When he asked to hire a boat, they cackled uproariously and asked how they would get it back when the only way to do so would be to cut it from the belly of the sea monster. Ephram blanched at this, but was firm in his determination, spending most of the day arguing, cajoling, and finally begging until he returned, sunburned and weary, having promised his entire fortune to one man.

He dragged his feet home. Every single penny he had made to take home to Eber had been spent on buying the boat. A year away from his love had been totally in vain. How would he ever face Eber and see the disappointment on his face at Ephram's foolishness? He cried all the way home for the way he had ruined everything and the time he had pointlessly frittered away.

Then he stopped on the street when he saw his front door was attached once more. With confusion and trepidation coursing through him, he ascended the steps and went into his house.

Drakon sat sprawled amongst the silken cushions, wearing black pants with silver embroidery and silver shoes. His shirt was open to the waist, showing his impressive body. Ephram looked around him.

His house was exactly the same as it had been prior to Drakon destroying it, as though it had all been a dream. There was nothing smashed, there was no blood on the walls, there were only Ephram's expensive furnishings and beautiful rugs.

"How did you…." Ephram started to ask and then stopped, because Drakon was a magician and he kept forgetting that.

"I humbly beg your forgiveness," Drakon said contritely. "Everything you say about me is correct. I will send you home and I ask for nothing in return."

Ephram gaped. "What about Darack?"

"Darack will never love me. What is there about me to love?"

Ephram stood looking down at him a moment. Then he turned to the crystal decanter, which had magically replenished itself. "Let's have a drink," he said softly, because the genie was so downcast that he could not bear to leave him this way, despite everything.

EPHRAM woke with another hangover the next day. He crawled from his bed and splashed some water on his face. As he left his room, he stopped in his tracks as he heard singing coming from his bathroom.

Amid the sounds of splashing was a soft but powerful voice, singing beautiful words in some unfathomable language. Ephram stared, one ear pressed to the door, unable to believe what he was hearing. He listened for a while and then tiptoed away. He was making tea when Drakon appeared in the kitchen with nothing but a towel to preserve his modesty, and the smallest towel Ephram owned at that. Ephram averted his eyes, aware of the outrageously luscious curve of the genie's backside and the heavy swing of the equipment between his legs. For sure, Darack would be a lucky man—physically, if not mentally.

Drakon smiled a little sadly and sat down at the table. "No watermelon?"

Ephram shook his head, and the genie swept his arm across the table, muttering something, before a huge watermelon appeared, already cut open. Drakon immediately took up one half and glued it to his face.

"That stuff is the devil's drink, Ephram," he told him around bites and dribbles.

Ephram nodded, which hurt his head. "I heard you singing."

Drakon looked a little embarrassed.

"Your voice is beautiful. I think we should make one last attempt with Darack. I shall play the zither while you serenade him at his window."

Drakon gaped at him, juice falling from his chin. "Are you serious?"

"Deeply," Ephram said. "You win him this evening by hook or by crook, and I go back to Eber tomorrow."

VIII

IT WAS pitch black, ornate street lamps lighting the harbor, the gentle swell of waves knocking the boats gently on their moorings. Ephram carried his zither under his arm, while Drakon, dressed to the nines and covered in jewels and perfume, walked quietly by his side.

Ephram was nervous. He was going home regardless of whether Drakon won Darack tonight or not, but this adventure nonetheless mattered to him, more than he could say. They stopped on the path, amongst the flowers, the scent of the blooms filling the night. A candle flickered behind the voile curtains at the open upstairs window, the breeze gently stirring the panels, no sound coming from within.

Drakon held a single red rose in one hand, despite the horror of his last attempt at flowers. He considered it romantic and would not be dissuaded, promising Ephram that there would be no blood involved and no mention of tongues in unspeakable places.

Ephram, standing in the shadows, tuned his zither as lightly and discreetly as he could and then he looked at Drakon, fingers poised over the strings, awaiting his cue. Drakon looked nervously across at him.

"Are you ready? One, two, three."

Drakon started to sing, and with his voice echoing through the balmy night, it sounded even more beautiful than it had during their many rehearsals earlier that day. He stood with the rose clutched in his hand, looking up at Darack's window as he sang his heart out like the most eloquent of songbirds.

The curtain drew back and Darack appeared at the window, dressed for bed. "What in God's name are you doing?"

Drakon didn't stop; he only sang louder and more passionately, his voice soaring to the very heavens, his eyes fixed on Darack in desperation.

And Darack fell silent. He stared down at Drakon motionlessly, his hands braced on the windowsill.

It soon became apparent that the object of Drakon's affections was crying. Drakon moved closer to the house, some of his words trembling with emotion.

Ephram had a lump in his throat. He wondered if Drakon had stolen this song the way he had stolen roses from someone's garden, or if he had written it himself.

The silence in the evening air was crushing once Ephram's zither died away. Drakon was holding his breath, looking up at the window.

It seemed like hours before Darack responded. Without speaking, he held his hand out, palm upward.

Drakon gaped a moment in disbelief before he dropped his rose to the ground and scrambled forward in almost comical haste, as though Darack would change his mind. Gripping handfuls of the vines growing up the walls, he climbed up the house with surprising skill despite his size. Ephram wondered if he could have magicked himself up there but preferred to show off his athleticism to Darack.

Drakon made it to the top of the window, and there his hand grasped Darack's. Darack's arm went around the genie's neck, and their lips met.

Ephram stared as they kissed for some seconds before Darack moved back and Drakon put one leg over the windowsill. Before he disappeared into the room, he turned back and winked at Ephram. A moment later, the curtains were pulled across.

Ephram, left outside, felt his pangs for Eber ever stronger. He had tears in his eyes. He plucked the fallen rose from the path and held it a moment to his nose. Then he took his zither and headed home.

IX

DRAKON returned some time after midday, while Ephram danced on eggshells and almost tore his hair out, thinking he would never manage to pry the genie from Darack's bed. He had all his belongings packed up in a pile in the center of the room, ready to return to his love, and he received Drakon eagerly as the genie walked in the door, looking like the cat that had got the cream.

"It went well?"

"Oh, yes." Drakon was flushed and disheveled, his hair standing on end, his clothes crumpled. "He would barely let me out of his bed this morning. He ravaged me senseless, forcing himself onto my face, begging me repeatedly to put my tongue in unspeakable places."

Ephram rolled his eyes. "I'm sure." He gestured to the room. "I'm ready to go."

Drakon nodded, looking thoughtful. "We will have to… condense your items somewhat. There will be no room."

Ephram frowned. "Is the boat not so big?"

Drakon grinned, teeth gleaming. "Boat? Who mentioned a boat? You go by magic carpet, boy!"

Ephram's mouth fell open. "But… I'm afraid of heights," he said in a small voice.

Drakon lifted a sarcastic eyebrow. "Is that so? No matter." And he put out a hand and pressed his palm to Ephram's forehead, muttering some words under his breath. "Now you're not."

He turned his attention to the pile of suitcases and other items in the center of the room. He passed his hand through the air several times with eyes closed, chanting softly in the same arcane language Magician X had used. A plume of smoke rose from the floor and engulfed Ephram's belongings.

Ephram stood back, coughing, eyes wide with fear that Drakon was incinerating all his worldly possessions. There was a loud bang, which startled him, and then the smoke cleared and everything he owned had vanished. All, that was, apart from a small, golden box the size of his palm.

Drakon stooped and picked it up, holding it out to Ephram. "There. Now you can take everything with you in your pocket. When you get home, utter the words *gazuum gazee,* and all your possessions will be returned to you. Whatever you do, don't say the words while you are flying home, or you shall crash into the ocean and be eaten by the sea monster." He smirked and winked as Ephram paled.

"That's not to say that the sea monster can't get you from the sky," Drakon added.

"What?"

Drakon shrugged. "He has been said to pluck travelers from their carpets. It may just be a rumor."

Ephram turned cold all over. "What will I do?"

Drakon looked thoughtful. "Do you have any watermelon?"

Ephram sighed. "No."

Drakon reached out his hands and a huge fruit appeared between them immediately. He held it out to Ephram. "Placate Caden with this."

"I'm sorry? Caden? The sea monster is a man?"

"Just so. If you make him a gift of watermelon, he will let you pass unmolested."

Ephram thought it was the most ridiculous thing he had ever heard. "How do you know this?"

"Because when he and I were lovers, he ate nothing but watermelon."

Ephram gaped. "You were lovers with a sea monster? Did you live in the sea?"

"For a time," Drakon replied casually. "But it was too wet. It wasn't good for my skin."

Ephram was sure he was about to wake up at any moment and find himself lying dazed on Arteus's floor, holding the magician's special pipe.

"Come." Drakon gestured. "Let's go."

Ephram put the golden box into his pocket and took one last look around his home. He followed Drakon outside and then handed the genie the watermelon and asked him to wait while he went downstairs to his landlord. Arteus answered with his pipe in hand.

"I'm going," Ephram said. "Drakon is sending me back to the Land Beyond the Sea."

Arteus nodded and exhaled a cloud of smoke. He held out a small bit of paper. "Here is my card, should you be in need of any magic in the future."

Ephram pocketed it. Arteus put an arm around him and squeezed him tightly. "Good-bye, Ephram. You were a model tenant. Have a safe journey."

"'Bye, Arteus."

Ephram went down to the street. On the path lay a large Turkish rug in vibrant shades of red and yellow. Drakon motioned to Ephram to get on it. Feeling foolish, Ephram went to stand in the middle of it, taking possession of the watermelon.

"I would sit down if I were you," Drakon said. "It will be more comfortable."

Ephram did as he was told, sitting cross-legged in the center of the carpet with the fruit between his knees.

Drakon lifted an arm, fingers pointing to the sky. "Are you ready?"

Ephram nodded, his stomach churning with anxiety.

Drakon shrieked some words in an unearthly wail that made Ephram's ears hurt. The carpet rose five feet off the ground, to the level of Drakon's chest.

Ephram tried to cling onto something as he rocked gently against the material.

"Relax," Drakon said with a smile.

"How long will it take?"

Drakon shrugged. "Three or four days."

Ephram's heart sank. It was only two days to Eber's birthday. "I can't make it go any faster?"

"It may take less time. I can't make any promises."

Ephram nodded sadly. "What will I do for food and water?"

"Anything at all that you want, just picture it in your mind and utter the words *brolam brolee,* and it shall be yours. Only, don't make it too heavy or you shall crash into the ocean and be eaten by the sea monster." He smirked. "Although I can think of worse ways to go. You may have to eat *him*. Caden always liked a tongue in unspeakable places."

Ephram rolled his eyes. "Thank you, Drakon." He held out his hand.

"No, thank *you,* Ephram. Without you I would still be in the lamp, dreaming about one day putting my tongue—"

"Yes, yes," Ephram said hurriedly. "Just know that my debt to you is worth all the gold in the world." He leaned over and hugged Drakon awkwardly around the waist.

The genie actually blushed. He lifted his hand and the carpet rose slowly through the air.

Ephram waved as he got higher and higher into the air, until Drakon was just a shiny dot beneath him. As the carpet turned itself toward the city limits, he watched Drakon start to walk away, heading toward the harbor and Darack's house.

The carpet travelled over the glittering spires and walls of the city until land was left behind, and suddenly Ephram was over the vast, sapphire-blue ocean. Looking down, he was relieved that Drakon had indeed cured him of his acrophobia, but he was nonetheless anxious. How did the carpet know where it was going? What if the sea monster didn't accept the watermelon as a gift? What if it took him four days to get home and he missed Eber's birthday?

He sighed and lay down gingerly on the carpet, curling up and holding the watermelon between his hands lest it roll away, letting the soft sway of the rug lull him to sleep.

A VIOLENT rocking of the carpet startled him roughly from sleep, and Ephram scrambled to his knees fearfully, lurching back with a cry of shock as he found a face peering over the edge of the rug at him.

The man holding the carpet, chin resting on it, was blond with pale brown eyes. He wore an odd crown on his head that appeared to be made completely of seashells, and he had a similar necklace around his throat, hanging down over his bare chest.

He smiled, and the sinister light in his eyes chilled Ephram to the marrow. "Hello, pretty," he purred, "where are you going?"

"To the Land Beyond the Sea," Ephram said timidly, not taking his eyes off the apparition.

"Do you know who I am?"

"Are you… Caden, the sea monster?"

Caden smirked, preening. "My fame precedes me." His eyes slid to the watermelon. "I see you come bearing gifts."

Ephram nodded quickly and rolled the fruit toward him. Unfortunately, Caden did not put out his hand and the watermelon rolled right off the edge of the carpet, disappearing into the sea, a distant splash sounding as Ephram gaped in horror.

Caden's smile widened. "Oh, dear. Now what?"

"I can get you another!" Ephram babbled. "Wait…." And he closed his eyes tight, trying desperately to think of those words Drakon had told him would bring him anything he wanted. "*Gazuum gazee*! No, I mean…."

But it was too late. There was an awful noise, like thunder, and he realized it was coming from the golden box in his pocket. The box shifted against his leg, vibrating, humming furiously, and Ephram moaned in horror as the rug started to rock beneath him.

A moment later, a flash of light blinded him, just before suitcases and items of furniture started to appear on the carpet. The sea monster laughed at him in glee as the magic carpet plummeted into the ocean, taking Ephram, screaming, with it.

X

EPHRAM came back to consciousness clinging to the edge of the carpet, which was—by some miracle—still floating, as were his belongings, all around him. He shook his wet hair out of his eyes, the sun beating fiercely down on his face, but the water was ice-cold and he looked around fearfully for both sharks and the sea monster.

"Hello," Caden said behind him, so that Ephram turned around in fright.

"Look...."

"No, look *you.*" Caden moved closer, an arm going around Ephram's neck and a tongue coming out to lick obscenely at his ear.

Ephram craned his head away, cringing. "Please! Listen, I can get you a hundred watermelons! *Brolam brolee*!"

Suddenly it was raining watermelons from the sky, the fruit falling into the sea like bombs, one striking Ephram on the head and almost knocking him senseless. He fell beneath the surface of the sea, semiconscious, floating there with eyes open but not seeing, dazed for a good few seconds.

Arms went around his waist and his gaze sharpened as he felt softness brushing his legs, and looked down. Caden had a tail. Ephram struggled, kicking himself to the surface, coming up spluttering.

"You're a merman!"

Caden was still hanging onto him, looking amused. "Your powers of observation are stunning."

"How did you and Drakon...?" Ephram closed his mouth, flushing.

Caden stared at him. "You know Drakon?"

Ephram nodded, biting his lip.

Caden regarded him, smiling slowly. "I see." One arm tightened around Ephram, his hand coming down to cup his buttocks lasciviously. "Drakon had a very talented tongue."

Ephram tried to wriggle out of his grip.

"If you prove yourself equally talented, I may let you go." Caden smirked.

Ephram regarded him in horror. "I'm not going to use my tongue on you! I am promised to another. I am going home to him!"

Caden looked a little vexed. "No, you *think* you're going home."

"Look, please… I brought you watermelons, didn't I?"

"They are all sunk to the bottom of the ocean," Caden said in distaste, glowering.

"And you're half-fish! Swim down and get them!" Ephram's head was aching from being struck by the aforementioned fruit.

Caden was starting to look more and more angry. "I cannot be bribed this way, anyway. Drakon thought it only took a watermelon and his tongue. I have progressed since then."

Ephram clutched the edge of the carpet, still trying to dislodge Caden. "Then what? What can I give you instead?"

Caden looked thoughtful. "Bring me Kepheus and I shall let you go."

"Who's he?" *Please God, not another Darack/Drakon fiasco.*

"A hermit who lives on a desert island fifty miles hence."

"Does he know you?"

Caden shook his head. "I've watched him for a long time. Occasionally he has almost caught sight of me, but I am quick to hide."

"Why haven't you made yourself known?"

"Ephram," Caden said sternly, as though he were backward. "I have a tail instead of legs. He is a man."

Ephram sighed. "Caden, Drakon lived with you here, didn't he? Surely…."

"Drakon is a magician. When he wanted to be intimate with me, he gave me legs."

Ephram flushed. "And are you not yourself a magician, Caden?

Could you not…?"

"My power is limited, or do you not think I would have?"

Ephram's heart sank into his very shoes, because here was a mission even more impossible than wooing Darack— selling a man with a tail to a man with legs.

"How do I get to the island?" he asked wearily.

"I can send you there. Climb onto the carpet."

With great difficulty, Ephram tried to hoist himself onto the rug, his wet clothes weighing him down. His teeth chattered despite the sunshine. He felt Caden's hands on his buttocks, assisting him while copping a nice, long feel.

The sea monster smiled at him when Ephram was sitting on the carpet. "You're beautiful, Ephram. You have eyes like the clearest tropical seas and skin like milk."

"Shall we focus on Kepheus?" Ephram interjected quickly, embarrassed.

Caden started to chant in a low voice and the carpet lurched out of the sea. Ephram tried to hold on, once again, to nothing, watching the sea monster recede from view beneath him.

He sighed as he was taken high into the sky over the azure sea, the sun burning him, his clothes and hair drying. Maybe there was a way to hijack the carpet and go home instead of going back to Caden. He closed his eyes, thought carefully of the words, and then said *brolam brolee* as he thought of going home to Eber.

The carpet rocked insanely, and then started to hurtle toward the sea.

"No! No!" Ephram threw himself onto his face, spreading his arms and legs and bracing himself for the crash. The carpet went at a dizzying speed and he peered over the edge in fright, to see palm trees and rocks looming up below him. Faster and faster he approached, until all he could see was sand and, suddenly, the desert island was upon him.

He yelled as he was tipped headfirst off the carpet, landing face-first on the beach.

"Who in all holy hell are *you*?"

Ephram lifted his sand-encrusted face to see a man wearing nothing but a flimsy piece of silk wrapped around his waist like a sarong, hardly camouflaging what lay beneath.

"Ephram," he said, crawling to his knees and sitting there a moment to reassure himself that nothing was broken.

"Well, Ephram," the man growled, "why don't you tell me why you just crashed onto my island, and it had better be the best reason ever or I'm going to turn you into a toadstool."

"You're a magician?" Ephram didn't know why he was even remotely surprised.

The man he presumed was Kepheus ignored him. "You have ten seconds."

"I'm here to tell you that you have an ardent admirer." Ephram jumped to his feet. "His name is Caden, he's a sea… a merman and he adores you and wants you to be his."

Kepheus looked less than impressed.

"Please, at least just meet with him. He won't let me go unless you do. I want to go home, that's all I want, and I've been through such an ordeal. First a genie from a lamp with a fixation for watermelon…."

Kepheus interrupted him abruptly. "Drakon?"

"You know Drakon?"

Kepheus smiled sourly. "I know Drakon. Good with tongue and even better with dick. I put him in the lamp."

Ephram gaped. "Why?"

"He needed a lesson in humility. Has he learned it?"

"I think he has now."

"Good. So you're going home?"

"Only if Caden lets me go. Please help me."

Kepheus regarded him thoughtfully. "Is he handsome?"

"Yes," Ephram insisted. "He's quite a catch." Then he flushed at his own terrible pun.

Kepheus cackled. "I like fish. I'll meet him. If I don't like him, I'll eat him for my supper with tartar sauce."

Ephram paled. "No, I don't think…." Who would guide the magic carpet if Caden perished?

"Relax," Kepheus said with a wicked grin. "Let's take your carpet back and meet this character."

XI

EPHRAM didn't know who had been in charge of the carpet—whether it was Kepheus, or Caden from afar—but either way, it had just crash-landed in the sea again, leaving the magician's scrap of silk to float away and Ephram feeling mightily fed up.

The two trod water for a few moments, looking around, before something scaly brushed against Ephram's legs and a blond head broke the surface of the ocean.

Caden's eyes fixed on Kepheus, and the magician regarded him in return. "I am charmed to meet you." The sea monster held out his hand.

Kepheus took it, smiling.

"I know I'm probably not what you're used to." Caden seemed to have lost his composure and was babbling, much to Ephram's surprise, his cheeks glowing rather endearingly. "But I can maybe find a spell to get rid of my tail. I understand you might find me unattractive but…."

He was cut off by Kepheus moving over to him, putting an arm around his neck, and kissing him.

Ephram was rooted to the spot, staring. The hermit pulled back after a moment, and then suddenly dived beneath the water. As he did, a long tail, shining green-silver in the sun, flicked up behind him, showering Caden and Ephram with water.

The two were open mouthed when Kepheus broke the surface, his black hair plastered to his head, drops of water on his eyelashes. "I am a powerful magician, am I not?" He put his arm back around Caden's neck. "I've been alone for six months," he said, lips resting against the sea monster's. "You're like water in the desert. You might be the most beautiful creature I've ever seen in my life."

Caden tried to speak, but Kepheus kissed him again, and slowly the two sank beneath the surface of the waves.

IT WAS a while before either emerged. Ephram lay restlessly on the magic carpet, praying Caden's promise had not been a trick and that, eventually, he would reappear and send him home. He tried *brolam brolee,* but the rug did not move. Instead he wished himself some water, a jug of wine, and some sweetmeats. Consuming them all, he lay down in the sun and slept.

He dreamed of Eber, lying beneath the covers in a cold bed, snow on the ground outside, waiting for Ephram to come home, and he cried in his sleep with need and despair.

When he woke, the sea monster was watching him from the edge of the carpet, Kepheus swimming lazily behind him. "You grieve, Ephram," Caden observed in a tone vastly different to his usual. "It is time to go home." He held his hand out and showed Ephram the golden box he had formerly had in his pocket. "All your belongings are back inside."

Ephram nodded gratefully. "Please, can you get me home in two days?"

"Of course." Caden lifted his hand and started to chant.

The carpet shuddered and lifted from the sea. Ephram watched the two mermen recede into the distance before collapsing, exhausted, onto the carpet. *Please God, don't let anything else come between me and Eber,* he begged silently. *Please, just take me home.*

By nightfall, Ephram was frozen, and he magicked himself a thick coat and some hot tea, along with some food.

Afterward, he lay down and watched the stars. His mind drifted to his adventures. He could not help but think of the eccentric genie and hoped he was treating Darack well.

He fell asleep and dreamed of Magician X and his ridiculous fez and that look in his eyes when he had first seen Xan. He dreamed of the sea monster and the hermit, and he dreamed of Drakon climbing creeping vines into Darack's bedroom to put his tongue into unspeakable places.

He woke with a start. He was alone in the silent sky beneath the stars, and Eber was still many miles away.

XII

FOR two days Ephram lay restlessly on the carpet, watching endless sea and sky pass him by. He counted the hours by the rising and the setting of the sun, and by the second sunset, he knew it was almost time.

He wished himself water, a razor, and a mirror, and he shaved carefully and washed. Then he magicked himself a new outfit, a fine, sober suit of black that made his eyes look greener and his skin glow. He studied himself critically in the glass, looking at the fine lines beginning beneath his eyes and wondering if he had aged and if Eber would still think him, as he had once called him, the most beautiful man in the world.

He thought of the golden box in his pocket, which held all his possessions, as he sat cross-legged on the carpet, drinking a little wine to steady his nerves. He imagined Eber's face when he poured out the rubies, diamonds, and emeralds he had brought home with him. He thought of Eber never needing to go out to work again on a bitterly cold winter's morning, instead staying in bed with Ephram, their love keeping them warm.

He hoped Eber still thought of and missed him, and then his thoughts darkened, because a year was a very long time and what if someone had replaced Ephram in Eber's affections? Someone who would be there for him and could give Eber what he needed, physically and emotionally.

He sighed, lying back on the carpet with tears pricking his eyes. Now was not the time for paranoia and regret. Now was the time to prepare himself to take back the love of his life.

Still, his dark thoughts overwhelmed him and he shivered in fear beneath his heavy coat, even as he saw light through the clouds below him. And then the carpet suddenly started to descend.

Ephram's muscles went rigid and nausea clawed at his throat. His eyes strained through the darkness, recognizing the familiar spires and rooftops of the little town. Lower and lower the carpet moved, and he saw the small market where Eber worked six days a week, bringing home the same amount of money in a year that Ephram had made in a day in the Land of Plenty.

He could make out the streets now, the rows of little white houses, the barns with horses stabled for the night, and he saw a thick blanket of snow covering everything, not a soul to be seen, everything as silent as the grave.

And there was his street. And there was his house. A soft moan of fear and need grew in Ephram's throat. The carpet started to hurtle steeply to the ground, because clearly there was no concept of a smooth landing where this method of transport was concerned.

He spread his arms and legs and covered his head, eyes closed as he saw the trees in his garden, the red front door, and with a cry he was tipped headlong into the snow.

He lifted his head, eating and breathing snow, looking around, lying there stunned for a moment, and then he climbed to his feet. Behind him, the carpet lurched up from the ground and disappeared into the night sky.

Ephram brushed the snow from his coat and smoothed his hair back. The house was still and dark. He bent down and retrieved the key from under the pot beside the front door. It was still there; some things hadn't changed. So far, so good.

Just then, a distant chiming split the night silence and Ephram cocked his head, listening and counting to twelve.

It was Eber's birthday.

He slid the key into the lock and turned it, opening the door and stepping into the house. It was as cold and dark within as it was outside, and Ephram sighed in dismay. He kicked off his boots on the doormat. He took the golden box from his pocket and placed it at the foot of the stairs, and then he slid off his coat and hung it over the banister.

With his heart in his mouth he began to climb the stairs.

It was so cold in the house that the window at the top of the stairs had ice on the inside. Never had Ephram hated himself more than in that moment for his abandonment of Eber. He had lived a life of luxury in the Land of Plenty, while at home, the other half of him had lived in squalor and poverty. How was he to ever start to make up for that?

His eyes burned with bitter tears as he reached the bedroom door. Maybe he should turn away now, because he knew he no longer deserved Eber. He should leave him to make his own way in the world, without him. He was no longer worthy to so much as look upon Eber's face, but he resolved now to do that. To look upon his love's face for the last time and then slink away like the dog he was.

With a lump in his throat, he pushed open the door. It was colder in here than the rest of the house, the wind whistling through the room, so that Ephram surmised there must be a window broken, allowing the frigid night air in. He was chilled to the marrow immediately and went quickly to the fire, for the moment ignoring the dark shape under the covers of the bed, because he did not want to deal with the very real possibility that Eber might be lying frozen and dead.

Of course there was no wood by the fire, and Ephram almost sobbed aloud in frustration. He had to warm Eber. Squeezing his eyes shut and begging whoever would listen, he whispered *brolam brolee* and prayed for a roaring fire and a new pane of glass.

There was a sudden *whoosh* within the hearth, a crackling of wood igniting, and a fire rose from the dead embers lying within. Ephram stared for a moment with open mouth and then he turned around.

His hand trailed lovingly over the wooden bedstead as he made his way to the opposite side of the bed. He smiled to himself when he remembered how they had saved for this bed—the one good item of furniture they owned between them—and the loving it had seen. His heart beat in his ears and his palms were damp.

Eber lay facing him, breathing softly in his sleep, the covers tightly swaddled around his body, only his face visible. And what a face it was. Ephram sank slowly to his knees, staring down into that beloved face and committing every detail to memory for one last time.

He reached out and placed his fingertips against one cheek, tracing the curve of it with a touch lighter than a feather. As he felt the velvet skin, he realized it was wet, the tracks of tears drying there.

"Oh, my love," spilled in a whisper, unbidden, from Ephram's lips. "My love."

Eber stirred gradually, as though struggling up through layers of the heaviest sleep. His dusky lashes fluttered for the longest time until they lifted and his beautiful eyes, jet black in the dim light, focused on Ephram.

His mouth opened in a perfect "oh" of shock, and Ephram let out a cry, wrenched back the covers, and threw himself into Eber's arms, sobbing his heart out.

Eber's arms gripped him hard, crushing the breath from him. He was naked, his skin cool and soft, and Ephram's face buried against his neck, mouth dropping compulsive kisses as he cried, hands clutching Eber desperately.

"You're home," Eber moaned softly beneath him, his voice cracking.

Ephram lifted his head and pressed his lips against Eber's, seeing stars as Eber returned the kiss eagerly, his breath hot, his mouth achingly soft.

Ephram pulled away. "I don't deserve for you to take me back this way," he wept. "I left you here. I come back to find you freezing and destitute. What sort of a man am I to have left you this way?"

Eber took his face firmly in his hands and looked into his eyes. "A man who wanted something better for us," he said, his voice steady now with that tone of reason and strength that Ephram had always so admired. The tone that had kept Ephram on the right path in this life for many a year.

Ephram laughed bitterly through his tears. "I bring you riches beyond your wildest dreams my love, but oh God, they were earned at a price. The price of being without you." His head fell against Eber's heart and he sobbed.

"No more." Eber's voice was tender and his hands were soothing on Ephram's head, stroking his hair. "It's my birthday and we are together. All is right again."

Ephram lifted his head to look at him. Swiftly he leaned down and captured Eber's lips again with his own. He undressed with Eber's help, fingers fumbling at buttons desperately.

Naked and skin to skin, their hands explored, remembering hills and valleys of muscle and bone, softness and hardness. Eber's lips followed his hands, pressing Ephram back and moving down his body, licking and kissing, lying between Ephram's legs and taking him inside his mouth.

And Ephram writhed in long-remembered bliss, his throat still hitching with sobs. "Please…." he said desperately to Eber, a hand tangling in his hair. "Take me."

Eber slid above the surface of the covers, looking down into his eyes. He took Ephram's mouth with his own and then he pressed into his lover, so Ephram's hands gripped his back hard.

Ephram arched beneath him as Eber dropped kisses on his throat. Each movement set his body on fire. Each moment drew him further and further out of the darkness of his own making.

He cried and moaned as Eber drew him to the end effortlessly and sent him spiraling into ecstasy.

As they lay there in a tangled heap, they both started to laugh softly, curling together and exchanging kisses.

"So tell me," Eber said softly. "Did you have any trouble getting back here? I heard tell of a foul monster of the deep that wrecks ships and eats men alive."

Ephram smiled indulgently. "He was a pussycat. He didn't give me any trouble."

He pressed his lips to Eber's and he thought of the genie in his golden curly shoes; of Darack, the poor man who would now be going through life with Drakon's face attached to his backside; of Magician X and his ridiculous fez and Xan, his love at first sight. He thought of the sea monster and the hermit making love beneath the deep.

And he smiled to himself in satisfaction, because while he still believed he had let Eber down and would spend the rest of his life making that up to him, he knew he had made six people very happy in the process of coming back to make amends to Eber, and for that, he felt at peace.

"I love you," he told Eber before he closed his eyes and slept with great relief, dreaming of opening the golden box in the morning and seeing the expression on his soulmate's face.

AND Ephram and Eber lived happily ever after.

Of course, reader, there is a postscript to this tale. Once Ephram and Eber were ensconced in their new house on the other side of town, Ephram set up a matchmaking agency, promising to find the lonely a mate for life. He charged no money for this, only one ripe watermelon per customer.

The posters tacked up around town advertising his services stated: *Only monsters, ghouls, and associated beings need apply.*

SCARLET BLACKWELL has loved books all her life. She would love to own a second-hand book shop and sit behind the counter reading her wares and writing her own all day.

She has been writing since age thirteen and her stories always feature two soulmates finding the other. She loves cats, rock music, and American TV shows. She lives in the United Kingdom.

The Wild Hunt

cari z.

DAVID Evans first witnessed the wild hunt when he was five years old. It was Halloween night, and his mother was dressing him up as a pumpkin. David would much rather have been dressed as a Ninja Turtle, Donatello by preference, but his pleas fell on deaf ears. Cuteness won out over being cool, and early that evening, a saggy orange ball protecting his body from the cold Colorado air and a green woolen cap tied tightly to his head, he and his older cousins headed out to make the rounds in their sleepy mountain town.

The sky had already darkened by the time they left the house, and the wind, which tended to be fierce at that time of year, had picked up speed. It buffeted his ungainly little body and almost made him lose his empty pillowcase. The twins had sighed and begged their sister Megan to stay with "the baby," and given permission, they ran happily ahead. Megan held David's hand and helped him down Main Street, promising him that soon they would be back indoors and he'd have all the candy he could eat.

The wind howled down the street like a living thing, picking up fallen leaves and pine needles and throwing them through the air like darts. Thunder rumbled in the sky and tremendous clouds rolled by overhead, followed by a quickly creeping white mist. In the distance, David heard snarls and growls and he stopped in his tracks, eyes wide.

"What?" Megan asked him. She was fourteen and feeling kind of embarrassed about trick-or-treating at such an advanced age, so having David to look after wasn't hard on her. She knelt down beside him. "What is it?"

"Hear it?"

"Hear what?" Megan asked. "The wind?"

"No," David said, bright blue eyes staring straight ahead. "The dogs."

"Dogs?" Megan turned and looked down the road. Apart from the fast-incoming storm and a few other determined trick-or-treaters, there was nothing there. "What dogs?"

David raised his free, orange-mittened hand and pointed down the road. "*Those dogs*."

How could anyone not see it? David saw them plain as day—sleek, tremendous hounds that raced faster than the wind, hounds with shining black bodies and luminous, shimmering eyes. They howled out fierce, joyous cries, warning the living and the dead that there was no escape. The dead were listening too. David saw them as well, ghostly apparitions streaming in on the mist, faces ecstatic with the fury of the hunt. The dogs roared by and the dead followed them, and *he* was there as well, shepherding the frenzied procession.

He rode a massive stallion, as white as the mist beneath its hooves. His body was covered with armor, ever-shifting, first like metal, then leather, then bone. The top half of his face was covered by a helmet, his eyes glowing white through a narrow slit. From the crest of the helmet, two tremendous antlers extended into the sky. Pale blond hair flew wildly in the wind, partially covering his face. David could see him smile, though.

The hunter stopped his great horse for a moment and looked down at David and Megan. "Small prey," he said, and his voice was an eagle's scream, fierce and proud. "Too small yet to take, and too rare to waste. Run home to your mother, child, and go no more this night." His white horse reared, dagger-like hooves flashing in the flickering light, and then he was off again, the spirits of the dead following helplessly in his wake. For a moment David thought he saw regular people too, wild-eyed and panting, but then the hunt had passed.

"Whoa!" Megan exclaimed, pulling her witch's cloak tighter around her body. She took in her little cousin's stunned, blank expression and shook her head. "That's it, we're going home." It was too blustery and cold for David to be out tonight. "C'mon, Davey." He didn't move when she tugged on his hand. "Davey?"

"He had a horse."

"Who did?"

"And dogs. And he had antlers."

"What, like a costume?" Megan looked around briefly. "There's no one else here, Davey. Let's go home, okay?" She pulled again and this time he came, still silent but at least walking in the right direction.

"That was fast," David's mother remarked as they reentered the family's small cabin.

"Yeah, it was too windy out," Megan explained, untying her cloak and throwing it over a chair. "I thought Davey was gonna get blown away. And he got weird on the road, Aunt Claire."

"Weird?" Claire knelt before her silent son and started to deconstruct his costume. "How weird? What happened, honey?" David still wasn't talking. "David?"

"He had dogs, Mommy."

"Who had dogs?"

"And a horse, and antlers, and ghosts."

Claire looked at her niece in confusion. "What's he talking about?"

"I don't know. The wind picked up and he wouldn't move a muscle down the sidewalk. He just stared out at the road. He told me he saw someone like that, but there was no one there."

"Huh." Claire got her son's mittens off, then started in on the pumpkin part. "You okay, baby?"

"Yes, Mommy." David looked down at himself. "He said I was too small to take."

A chill suddenly gripped Claire's heart. "Who wanted to take you?"

"The hunter, Mommy. With the antlers. He told me I was small prey." David frowned, confused. "What's prey?"

Claire didn't answer her son. She turned and stood and grabbed Megan's shoulders, clasping them tight. "Are you sure you didn't see anyone?"

"No, Aunt Claire," Megan replied, a little frightened by the stark intensity in her aunt's gaze. "No one, I promise."

"I believe you." She let go of her niece and picked David up, still enclosed in his puffy orange suit. "Let's go have some hot chocolate, huh, baby?"

"'kay, Mommy."

An hour and two cups of hot chocolate later, Claire was settling her son in his bed, stroking golden hair away from his face and trying to reassure herself. He could have learned that word anywhere—from his cousins, from the television. One of his cartoons. Surely it meant nothing. In the end, though, no amount of reassurance was enough, and she climbed into her son's small bed and hugged him close, making a shield out of her love. They slept through the night that way.

David realized pretty quickly that no one believed he'd actually seen what he'd seen. Megan attributed it all to the wind and the mist, his mother thought he must have been tired, and his aunt and the twins thought he was making it up to get attention. Simon and Harry, both twelve, got a kick out of teasing him about it, barking at him like dogs whenever his mother wasn't around. Megan glared, but his Aunt Anne ignored them. Their refusal to believe didn't faze him, although David did become more circumspect about talking about it. When his mother asked him tentatively a few days later whether any strangers had been bothering him lately, David knew enough to say no. She had looked relieved and made him peanut butter and jelly with the crusts cut off, and everything was okay.

He dreamed about what he'd seen every now and then. Sometimes he saw the massive dogs, sometimes he saw the wispy, inconstant figures of the ghosts. Most often, though, he dreamed about the hunter on his horse, his hair flying in the wind and his glowing eyes, and his strange, ferocious smile. David tried to draw him, and felt frustrated when he failed.

The next Halloween David escaped being a pumpkin, instead asking his mother if he could be a hunter. She had interpreted this to mean Robin Hood, and so he was decked out in an outfit somewhere between a pointy-toed elf and a minstrel, but at least he had a plastic bow and arrows. Megan was going to a party, so David left the house with Simon and Harry. They ditched him after two blocks, but David didn't mind. He wasn't all that interested in candy anyway. He walked back out to the main street, found approximately the same spot as the year before, and waited.

It took a while, but soon he could discern a change in the air. He quivered with eagerness, feeling the mounting energy around him like lightning in the air. It didn't storm the same as last time, but he still heard the shriek of the wind, heard the baying hounds barreling toward him on spectral limbs. Other children passed him by, curious and staring, but he ignored them all. There… the mist was flowing in now. There were the dogs, sleek and dark like he remembered, howling joyously. The ghosts teemed in the mist, and rising up in the center of it all was *him*. The hunter. What David had really wanted to be. His armor was still amorphous, changing in some new way every second, but his burning eyes were focused on the child staring him down.

He stopped his horse abruptly, the same as before. "Hast sought me then, boy?" His tone was amused, less fierce than before but no less powerful. "Bold prey, to seek me out uncalled. Still too small, though."

"When will I be big enough?" David asked. Big enough for what, he wasn't certain, he just knew he wanted to get there fast.

"When you are ready to join the Hunt, you will know," the apparition replied. "Perhaps there will be more for you than the chase, when the time comes. Until that day, I suggest you strive to make yourself worthy." His horse reared again, screaming its impatience to be off, and the hunter loosened his reins and gave the beast its head. They sped away into the night, melted into the darkness, and the dead raced after him. Again David saw what he thought might have been real people mixed in with them, but they passed by him so fast that he couldn't be sure.

When he got home that night, David told his mother he wanted to start taking karate lessons. She was surprised but amenable, and the next day she signed him up for classes at the local Y. The instructor didn't look anything like the hunter, but David knew he had to start somewhere.

The next Halloween it snowed. It snowed huge amounts of champagne-powder flakes, forming great, piling drifts that reached over five feet high before it finally stopped falling from the sky. Claire told her son, in no uncertain terms, that he wouldn't be trick-or-treating that year. "You'd get lost out there!" she exclaimed. "Besides, I couldn't let you go alone anyway." The twins now considered themselves too old for trick-or-treating, and Megan was sixteen and sulking over not getting to go to a party with her boyfriend, and thus no help at all.

Panic filled David. He knew throwing a tantrum wouldn't help; his mother would just think he was sick and try to baby him. He ate dinner fast, then went to the room he shared with his cousins. They'd decided to play Nintendo in the living room, which usually he begged to be allowed to play with them, but tonight he was glad to be alone. He put on his gi, tied his blue belt tightly around his waist, put on his boots and his heavy down jacket, and unlocked his bedroom window. It slid open with hardly a squeak, and a moment later he was outside, sliding down the drift beside the house and wading awkwardly toward the sidewalk. Not even the snowplows were out yet, so the sidewalk wasn't much help, but a few cars had driven the streets. He struggled into one of their tracks and headed toward Main Street.

The sparse street lamps cast soft, yellow light over the fresh snow, making it sparkle like gold dust. David hugged himself tightly and waited, watching his crystal breath float through the sky. Misty, but not like the mist that came with the hunter, so heavy and roiling it had to be real, probably cool and thick on his skin. He wanted desperately to see that mist. He wanted to hear the hounds. He wanted to see the hunter again. Minutes drifted by, and David began to fear that he had come too late, that his chance had passed. His next breath was blown back into his face with a sudden gust of wind, and despite the stinging coldness of it, David smiled. He knew that wind.

There it came. The darkness, the howling, the wild, terrible beauty of it. It was coming and he was standing in the center of it this time, no way to avoid being overrun by it. Some part of his mind said he should move, that even small prey was better than no prey at all when it threw itself into the hunt's path, but he couldn't. He could only watch the dogs bear down on him and the creeping mist come to roll over him in awed silence.

The rider surged forward at the last moment, passing his hounds, and reached one long arm down to snatch David up from the ground. The shock of impacting the hunter's chest drove the air from David's lungs, and he reached out unthinkingly to clutch at the figure holding him.

"Fool child," the hunter snarled in his ear. The sound was terrible, and David shrank in sudden fear. "Perhaps you *are* merely fodder for the chase, at that." The hunter spoke viciously, but his arm was gentle around David's shoulders, and he relaxed against the larger body. It was strangely warm, despite the frigid air.

The next thing he knew he was outside his house again, and the hunter was setting him down. "Do not tempt fate needlessly, Dafydd ap Evan," the hunter growled, but there were the edges of a smile curving his lips. "You've ample courage, though." Then he was gone, and the raucous clamor of the hunt followed him away. David stood and stared in that direction until he was shivering from the cold, and then climbed back in the window. Unfortunately, his cousins were just coming into the room.

"You were outside?" Harry asked. "Why did you go outside?"

"Snuck outside," Simon corrected with a smirk. "You miss twick-or-tweating, widdle baby? Your mom's gonna let you have it. Aunt Claire!" he yelled. "Davey snuck outside!" Then he turned back to David and shoved his shoulders. "Now you're in trouble."

David decided at that point that it wasn't right for him, witness to a mighty hunt, who the hunter *himself* had said had courage, to shrink before his obnoxious cousin. He stomped one booted foot down on Simon's bare instep. His cousin shrieked and fell over onto his bed.

"David!" Claire ran into the room, disturbed to see her nephew rolling around in pain but more disturbed to see her son in his winter jacket, covered in snow. "What did you do?"

"He kicked me!" Simon yelled.

"He did," Harry said, looking at David strangely.

"Good!" Megan yelled from the living room.

"Megan!" his Aunt Anne exclaimed.

It just got more confusing from there.

The night ended with David apologizing insincerely to Simon for hurting him, Megan mocking her brother the whole time for getting taken out by a kid half his age, and David getting grounded for the next week by his mother, who was more upset by his sneaking out than anything. He didn't mind any of it. David had ridden, just for a moment, with the hunt. Better, he had ridden with the hunter. He swore to himself he would do it again someday. He stayed up late that night drawing a picture of the hunter, and by the time his mother made him turn the light out, it was almost right.

The next Halloween was different from the previous ones. David wasn't in the small town he'd grown up in. He was in Denver with his mother and aunt, and his mother was sick. She had been sick for months, and then she lost her hair, and finally the treatments made it necessary for her to stay in the hospital, and so there they stayed. She wanted him close to her, and he didn't want to leave her side. While his aunt slept in a nearby hotel, David held his mother's hand and stared bitterly out the window toward the mountains.

"I'm sorry, honey," Claire said drowsily from her pillow, her cold fingers rubbing gently at the back of his hand. "I know you wanted to go trick-or-treating."

"I don't care about trick-or-treating," David said honestly. "I want to stay with you." And he did, but… he was going to miss it. Miss him, miss the hunter and his wild, mighty hunt. It made him hurt inside, like he hurt when he looked at his mother while she was sleeping and realized how much she'd changed.

His mother fell asleep, but David kept holding her hand. A nurse came in and offered him a snack, but he turned it down. He stared out the window, out past the highway and toward the dim, distant foothills, and brooded. He was so engaged in brooding he almost didn't notice the sudden rattle of the window as the wind picked up, or see the first streaming edges of shimmering spirit pour toward the street below him. When he realized what he was seeing, David's breath caught in amazement. So many spirits were flooding out of the hospital! Now he could hear the call of the hounds; now he saw the mist, and he saw it burgeon with new souls as it passed them by. There were the dogs, there was the horse, and there! The hunter! He didn't stop, but his antlered head turned toward David. One hand rose in acknowledgement, and David pressed his free hand to the glass, reaching toward something he wanted almost more than he wanted to be with his mother. In another instant the hunt had passed, taking its growing crowd with it, and David sat back in his chair in amazement.

"Davey?" his mother said suddenly, rousing from her shallow sleep. "Are you still here?"

"Yes, Mom."

"Good," she breathed. "I thought for a moment that someone had taken you."

"No," he said. "No one will take me from you." He said it and he meant it, and it both hurt and felt right. He was still small prey, and would stay that way until his mother didn't need him anymore. Someday, though, he would join the hunt. He would join the hunter.

His mother eventually recovered and they moved back up to the mountains. That year, David joined a Boy Scout troop. Not because he was really interested in being a Scout, but he wanted to learn how to live in the wilderness, and it seemed like the best way since none of his family was interested in camping or canoeing or hunting. David made new friends, earned merit badges, and came a little way out of his introverted shell. He kept up with karate, and as soon as he was old enough, started to learn how to wrestle. He liked sports; he liked being strong. He was growing, and every year he was getting closer and closer to being worthy of joining the hunt on his own terms.

He did research. He went to the library and checked out books on mythology, and he looked up the wild hunt. There were so many different versions of it, he wasn't sure which one he was looking for. Maybe some of all of them. He remembered that the hunter had called him "Dafydd ap Evan", and a little more digging told him that that was the Welsh version of his name. That pointed him toward Gwyn ap Nudd, the king of the Tylwyth Teg, the fairies. It fit in more ways than that, too: he collected the souls of the dead and was accompanied by the Cŵn Annwn, the spectral hounds that escorted the souls on their journey to Annwn. Annwn was like a heaven, a paradise, an Otherworld populated by fair folk and the souls of humans lucky enough to believe in it, or pulled in by the hunt. Regular humans could get caught up in the hunt as well, and for a short time rest in Annwn, but they had to return before the sun set on All Saints Day, or die.

There were a thousand variations, but this was the version that David liked best, and so he stuck with it. The next year, he was allowed to go trick-or-treating alone. It was almost warm that evening and he was dressed up like a pirate. The knife on his belt was real, though, a present from Megan for his ninth birthday. Megan totally got him.

The wind picked up, the mist rolled in, and the sharp baying of the hounds set his blood on fire. David watched them draw closer, standing safely to the side this time. He felt the pull of the hunt, though. He felt it stronger than ever. It almost hurt him to see the hunter come into view this time, he was so eager for it. The stallion thundered to a halt, and David matched the hunter's smile with one of his own. "Greetings, Gwyn ap Nudd," he said firmly.

The hunter laughed, and his laughter was joyous and strong and prideful, like a lion's roar. "Clever Dafydd is no longer easy prey," he said. "That is well, boy. You're becoming a hunter yourself."

"Someday I'll hunt with you," David promised.

Something in Gwyn's sharp, fierce smile softened, and even his stallion stopped pawing the ground for a moment. "To that, I hold you." He bared his teeth in a grin again. "Be careful what you promise the Fair Folk, boy. Our memory is forever." Restless energy poured back into him, and with a sudden bunching of massive muscles, his horse leapt forward, driving the crowd that teemed around it on and on. David watched him go, totally ignoring the curious stares he got from other children as they shivered, briefly, before continuing on their quest for candy. David went home instead.

Life continued, for the most part very quietly, in his small mountain town. Megan went to college, moving to Albuquerque to do so. Aunt Anne drove her out in a U-Haul and drove back in a used BMW, a gift from her suddenly acquired boyfriend. Soon she was spending at least half the year in New Mexico, leaving Claire to manage the boys. Simon and Harry were terrors, but at least they had each other, which was a relief to David, since he honestly didn't want anything to do with either of them. When they graduated, when he was eleven, and moved to New Mexico as well, David stood in the doorway, his arm around his mother's waist, and held her while she waved good-bye. Once they were out of sight he brought her back inside, handed her a tissue, and made her some tea. It was one of the best days of his life.

Halloween was officially David's favorite holiday. As he grew older, he convinced his mother to let him stay out later, shrugging when she smiled and asked about parties and girls. Claire worried about him, about her only son who seemed to like being on his own, who would spend days losing himself in the wilderness and who only seemed to have time for his training, his art, and her. David was a talented artist, gifted at drawing the world around him. He left a notebook of his out on the kitchen table one evening, and Claire casually pulled it over to flip through when he left to use the bathroom. It contained sketches in pencil, charcoal, and ink—mostly animals he probably saw while he was out hiking, but also some trees and flowers, and a few gorgeous views of the peaks. She smiled and turned the pages, gazing idly at the scenes of nature until one page drew her up short.

This was nothing out of nature. This must be pure fantasy, something he'd thought up one evening. He had all those mythology books; it must be something from that. Claire gaped at the drawing, unable to pull her eyes away even though looking at the image made her strangely uneasy. At the base of the page were three snarling hounds, their back halves obscured by smoke or mist or something. There were faces in the mist, spectral, moaning faces, and each one was filled with a disconcerting savagery. Behind the hounds was a horse, bearing down on the observer as though it would leap out of the picture. On its back was a man… sort of. A cloak swirled around his shoulders, melding with the mist. Four-point antlers sprouted from his head, and his eyes were obscured by a helmet, and yet… yet she could see them, somehow. Long hair spread out from his shoulders, and his expression could only be described as hungry. Wanting. Claire stared at him and found her hands were trembling.

Long, tanned fingers reached around her and gently closed the sketchbook. Claire turned and looked at her son. "I'm sorry," she said awkwardly, "I didn't mean to… to pry."

"It's okay," David replied.

"It's a very interesting picture, baby."

David shrugged. "Just something I thought up one day."

A memory chimed through Claire's mind. "David… do you remember the first Halloween you went trick-or-treating, when you were five?"

"Yes, Mom."

"Do you remember what you talked about when Megan brought you back that night? You said you'd seen a man with antlers, and dogs. You asked me about…."

"I remember," David said calmly. "It's just a picture, Mom. Don't let it worry you."

"Worry me." Claire rolled her eyes. "Everything worries me. It used to drive your daddy nuts."

"Well, don't worry about me." Her son leaned in and kissed her cheek. "I'm not going anywhere."

Not yet, Claire thought to herself as she got up and started getting things out for dinner. But he would leave someday. She just hoped she understood why in the end.

David wanted to be honest with his mother, but there were some things that just couldn't be explained. He knew he worried her, so he tried to be open with her about the other aspects of his life. When he realized he was gay, he told his mother immediately. Claire didn't argue or point out that he was only fifteen, so how could he possibly know what he wanted. She just pulled him close and hugged him and told him that she loved him unconditionally, and that she'd love whomever he loved. David had almost choked on that, caught somewhere between laughter and tears, but he took his mother's acceptance and loved her even more for it. It wasn't her fault he couldn't tell her everything. It wasn't her fault he was in love with a god.

Ten years of once-annual meetings, the longest of them barely a minute, and yet David's heart was firmly set. He was in love with Gwyn ap Nudd, the King of the Faeries, the Lord of Annwn, the Winter God. Not just in lust, although there was plenty of that too, but genuinely in love. If it weren't for the devotion he felt to his mother, David would have gone with him years ago. Even if he was nothing more than a brief diversion for Gwyn, it would be worth it to be with him… but somehow he knew he was more than that. David wasn't given to inflating his own ego, but he felt he'd come a long way. He'd worked so hard to prepare himself, to make himself strong: a fighter, a hunter. He had black belts in two martial arts; he was a state-champion wrestler; he could track animals and had hunted and killed a deer with his bow last season. He was worthy, or he would work until he was. Good enough for the hunt. Good enough for Gwyn.

He didn't stay celibate. David knew he was fairly attractive; he was certainly in good shape. There were plenty of guys who were interested in him, and he played around enough to know that, yes, the right men made him hard, achingly so. He wanted them, and he had some of them, but they never penetrated deeper than the surface of his affections. Even the most determined lover gave up in the face of such overwhelming casualness, until casual was all that was left, and that was fine with David.

The summer he turned eighteen and graduated from high school, David went to work for a mountain guide company, leading motivated tourists up many of the different peaks that were part of the Continental Divide. Claire was upset by his decision, and asked him repeatedly why he didn't want to go to art school instead. "You're so talented," she said sadly. "You could do such amazing things."

"I like what I'm doing," David replied. His mother knew when to push, and realized that now wasn't one of those times. She consoled herself with the thought that David was still young, and after he had worked for a while he might change his mind. He was so handsome, her son, his hair still golden instead of darkening with age as hers had done. Maybe it was all the time he spent in the sun. He was tanned and healthy and seemed to be happy, and so she had to be content with that.

In the spring of his twentieth year, David's mother got sick again. She had to stop working and restarted treatments, although the prognosis wasn't good. There was a decent hospital closer than Denver now, so they were able to stay in the cabin, but nothing really seemed to help. Aunt Anne came back to live with them, and so did Megan, now twenty-nine, divorced and mother to a four-year-old girl named Wendy. Megan was a genuine help, Anne less so. David's aunt didn't bother to hide the fact that she planned to take the cabin back once Claire passed on, which was sadly only a matter of time now. Her Albuquerque romance had withered half a decade earlier, and she was far too hot in New Mexico anyway.

Claire welcomed their presence, happy to have someone else to relieve the burden on David. David was less sanguine about it, but he didn't object too heavily. He didn't say anything at all when his aunt informed him of her intention to kick him out once his mother was dead. He hadn't planned on staying in any case. Wendy was surprisingly good company, and he drew two portraits of her on her birthday, one of her sitting still and pretty in a chair for her mother, and one for her, with her dressed like a princess and riding a massive dog saddled like a pony. Wendy was delighted, Megan bemused, and Claire, a little worried. Anne never even noticed.

Things were all right until Simon came back to live with them as well. Harry had gone into the Air Force and was a pilot now, but Simon never really found his place. He'd dropped out of college, been kicked out of the Army, and eventually scraped together enough skills to get by as an auto mechanic, slinking from town to town and living with his mother when he didn't have a girlfriend to stay with. He was single now, and his arrival at the beginning of autumn felt like a bad omen to David.

They had to share a room again, which would have been fine if Simon could have kept from smoking in it. He couldn't, and after fighting about his habit and Anne at last making him promise to smoke only in the bedroom with the window down or outdoors where it couldn't affect Claire, David started sleeping on the couch next to his mother's hospital bed in the living room. The smoke filtered through anyway, but Claire did her best to ignore it. Simon smoked and lazed about and Anne drank and watched television, finally moving the set into the bedroom she shared with Megan and Wendy when it kept Claire up too much. Megan worked nights as a pastry chef for the local supermarket, and David restricted his guiding to day or weekend trips, so someone was always available to look after Claire and Wendy.

"You look exhausted," Megan said bluntly one Sunday evening as the two of them washed and put away the dinner dishes. Simon was out on a date and Anne was already settled into her room, watching a rerun of a popular reality show. Wendy was sitting with Claire on her bed, playing with a stuffed unicorn and telling her aunt a story about it. It made Claire smile, which was all David cared about.

"So do you," David returned, wiping off a blue stoneware plate and putting it into the cupboard. "You're working too hard. When do you sleep, Meg?"

"After I drop Wendy at preschool," she shrugged. "Aunt Claire usually sleeps until noon, so that gives me a good five hours. And I catch naps in the evening before I go to work, as you know. But you… you're wearing yourself down to nothing. I swear, if you have any body fat at all, it's in your pinkie toe." She smiled suddenly. "You're pretty enough to be a model, though. Gonna fly away to New York City and set the runway on fire?"

"I'm not going to New York," David replied, blushing slightly.

"But you are thinking of getting away?" she pressed. "Seriously, Davey, you've been stuck in this same small town your whole life. Don't you wonder what's out there? Don't you want to see more of the world?"

"I know what's out there," David said softly. "And I want it. But I can't go yet."

"Promise me you'll go someday," Megan encouraged. "You deserve to be happy, David."

"I am happy," he told her. "But I promise, Meg, I'll go someday. I will."

"Good."

The quivering aspen trees turned golden, then brown, then bare. The change from gentle autumn to winter gales seemed to happen overnight, a few weeks into October. The snow fell heavier and thicker than it had for nearly a decade, and the streets and sidewalks had to be freshly dug out and plowed every morning. David shoveled outside their cabin and the stairs leading to the front door, and made sure Megan's car was accessible and had chains on when she needed them. Halloween turned out to be far too cold for Wendy, now five, to go trick-or-treating, so they all planned a quiet night in.

Simon was supposed to be working at the garage, but when he came home, he stank of tequila and beer. He was smoking too.

"Not inside," Megan said from the kitchen table, where she and Wendy were drawing faces on pumpkins.

"'S cold out."

"Then go smoke in the bedroom."

"'S cold in there too." Simon kicked his boots off and left them in front of the door. "Fucking heating doesn't work in this damn place. That room always feels like a fucking freezer."

"Put a sweater on," David said coldly from where he was sitting with Claire. "But don't smoke around my mother."

"Aunt Claire doesn't mind," Simon whined. "Right?" Claire managed a small sigh, then shook her head minutely.

"See?"

"It's not good for her." David turned back to his mom. "It's not okay for him to smoke around you, Mom. Don't give him an out."

"Your mother doesn't need you to hold her hand all the time. She can tell us if she doesn't want something," Anne yelled her two cents from the bedroom.

"Well, I don't want you smoking around Wendy either," Megan said.

"Then send her to her room."

"Simon!"

David stood up and faced his cousin. "Put it out," he said quietly.

The tension of the past few months was flowing through him now, filling him with dark, tightly wound energy. Every emotion he tried to subsume for his mother's sake, every moment of anger and fear and a deep-seated, barely recognizable longing poured through him like a flood, and it was all he could do to keep from lashing out.

Simon smirked at him. "No."

"I'll give you three seconds."

"Simon," Megan tried, sensing something different about this confrontation. David and Simon had always fought, but it had never been so intense before.

"One."

"No fucking way."

"Two."

"David," Claire said weakly from her bed, "please…."

"Three."

Simon grinned and blew a long plume of smoke into David's face.

A second later the cigarette was torn from Simon's hand. A second after that and his face met David's fist, then his elbow. Two sharp hits and Simon's nose and one of his front teeth were broken, and he swayed into the wall, then slumped to the floor. His incoherent whining was all that broke the stunned silence.

It wasn't enough. The energy was still building inside of him, dark and horrible and wonderful, and there was no way for him to let it out. David looked helplessly around the room. He needed an escape, something, anything….

A curling gust of wind rattled the front door. In the wind, David thought he could hear the baying of hounds. The wild hunt was coming, calling to him, and this time he knew he had to go. He shoved his feet into boots and ran outside, slamming the door shut behind him. He was cold in only a thin T-shirt and sweater, but the rage and desire he felt was like a fire in his blood. He ran into the darkened street, away from his house and his family, his responsibilities. He ran toward the hunt, not as prey but as a willing, eager participant. There… the mist was coming now, tendrils reaching hungrily toward him, and he welcomed them. The ferocity of the hounds matched the feelings inside him, and seeing them was like recognizing his true kin. And then there was the horse, and with it appeared its rider.

Gwyn ap Nudd bore down upon him, and this time it was David who reached out. An instant later he was pulled in front of the Winter God, arms like iron encircling his waist, and the horse leapt beneath them both and carried them along at the forefront of the storm. The tempestuous fury of the moment felt so right, so perfect. David let go, howling with the hounds, screaming with the pure and perfect wildness of the spirits who flocked to the hunt. Gwyn's arms tightened around his waist, and the low, dark laughter that emerged from the Fairy King's lips was approval and sensual promise wrapped together.

They sprang through the night, gathering the souls of the dead that could hear them. Other mortals joined the train, but David paid them no heed. The very air obeyed his commands, followed the direction of his rage, and for the first time since Sir Francis Drake, a mortal led the wild hunt. They spanned continents, oceans, and it felt like minutes and hours and days and yet no time at all. There was no room in David for anything other than the hunt and the fierce satisfaction of feeling Gwyn at his back, holding him tightly to the mighty stallion.

Dawn followed them, chasing them and driving them back. As the troop began to slow, gliding over a terraced mound toward a roofless tower in a cold, green land that David didn't recognize, Gwyn took the reins from his hands. Just before they rode into the tower, he whispered a word. A moment later they were in a different land entirely—still green, but warm and bright. The hunt came to rest in a field full of small white lily-of-the-valley blooms and flowering hawthorn trees. The spectral mist disappeared, and the souls of the dead looked human again, and happy, not driven and desperate.

The living appeared differently. Happy, filled with awe and wonder at where they were, but their bodies were gray, not flushed with warmth and life. David looked down at his hands in amazement. It was the same for him. He realized then that, while he could see the color, and could tell by the expressions of others that there was warmth and fragrance here, he didn't feel it himself. The only warmth he felt was when Gwyn laid a hand on his arm. "Dismount, hunter," he said softly, and David obeyed. The ground was firm and lush beneath his feet. He looked up and saw people approaching the new arrivals, wearing smiles and holding their arms open. The rage had completely dissipated, and those who recognized their loved ones went flying into their arms. Other folk, Fairy or contented dead, welcomed the living visitors.

David and Gwyn were left alone as the crowd dispersed, although many curious glances were thrown their way. "The dead are here to stay," Gwyn said quietly in David's ear. "The living have a choice. They will be offered food and drink—elderberry wine and hawthorn brandy and meat from the white hind. If they choose to partake, their bodies will cross over with their souls, and they will reside in Annwn forever." He turned David to look at him fully, his bright green eyes now visible once the spectral flames had died. "Will you drink, Dafydd? Will you eat?"

"I… can't." He knew he couldn't, no matter how badly he wanted to. Gwyn nodded, as though he had suspected it.

"Then you must leave this place before the sun sets in your world today. In Colorado, not in Wales," he added with a small smile. "We've some hours yet. Wilt spend them with me, Dafydd?"

"Yes." God, yes.

"Then we shall go to my home. You will be comfortable there." He took David by the hand and led him directly into the nearest hawthorn bramble. David winced, expecting the thorns to scratch him, but instead he stepped through the bramble and into a great hall. Tall, narrow windows let in daylight, and the stone walls were covered with brilliant tapestries. The floor was laid out in a mosaic, marble in red and white and black making patterns that entranced David. There was a large fireplace at the far end of the hall, and long, polished wooden tables spanned the length of it. A slender young woman was sitting in a chair by the fire, her fingers strumming expertly over the strings of a large harp, but when she saw them she stood and smiled, hurrying toward them.

"Gwyn! A rare hunt, this time!" Her eyes, bright and green like his, took in David curiously. "And this the mortal who led it. I am Creiddylad," she said, curtsying. "Welcome to my brother's home."

"I thought you were his wife," David said, wondering if he was confusing his legends.

"Sister, and better for it." She cast a sly glance at her brother. "This one would drive a wife to distraction. He's no need of one."

"Enough, meddlesome creature." Gwyn waved a hand at her. "The hounds will soon return, bringing our newest arrivals with them. Make them and their kin welcome. I will greet them properly later."

"As you say, brother." With a last, curious glance at David, Creiddylad darted around them. Gwyn pulled gently on David's hand. "This hall is for revelers. We haven't much time, and I don't mean to waste it in longing. Come with me." David nodded, and Gwyn led him through a door and down a small, dark corridor. There was another door at the end of it that led to a large, circular room. The floor was strewn with skins and the furnishings were made of horns and antlers and bone, cleverly worked together and comfortably padded. The bed was another hawthorn tree, this one a wide, low trunk that spread out into hundreds of tightly-woven branches, supporting a mattress with, surprisingly, no skins but what looked like clean linen sheets instead. A fire was lit, and there were torches burning in three sconces set in the walls.

Gwyn let go of David's hand and removed his helmet. Beneath it his face was… just a face. A sharp, strong face that made David want to take it between his hands and kiss it, but the otherworldliness had vanished. Gwyn laid his grey cloak down and removed his armor, and in moments the king was gone, and only a man remained. He turned back to David and asked, "Are you disappointed?"

"Nothing about you could ever disappoint me," David breathed. "You look… god, you look amazing. Better than I had imagined."

"'Tis well you think so, beloved. It would be damned difficult to make love whilst wearing that helmet." They both laughed, and then Gwyn stepped forward and ran his hands over David's shoulders and down his back, pulling them close. He was only wearing simple, tied linen pants now, and when their groins pressed together, David could feel the evidence of his lover's want hard against his own. "Waited for you," Gwyn murmured in his ear, rubbing warm hands slowly beneath David's T-shirt and up his spine. "Wanted you, beloved. For so long now. A mortal capable of leading the wild hunt, a mortal who could look on us without fear. Beautiful and brave, a true hunter. Someone to share Annwn with. After my lord Arawn lost the Battle of Goddeu and retreated into peace with Achren, I wondered how he could bear to leave Annwn to me. When you are with me, I know the solace she gives him."

"I love you," David said, his voice shuddering with want and sincerity. "I have forever."

"Yet you will leave me." David opened his mouth to defend himself, but Gwyn kissed it closed. "No. Forgive me. I know you carry burdens, debts of love that must be paid before you can be mine."

"I'm yours right now," David said, desperate to feel Gwyn's lips on his again. He got his wish when his lover leaned in and kissed him. Not a brief, silencing kiss like before, but a clinging kiss, a slow and moist and loving kiss that made David melt into Gwyn's embrace. No anger, no fear, no fire except the need they felt for each other.

"Dafydd," Gwyn breathed against his mouth. "My own." He backed them up to his briar bed and lay David down on the pale sheets. They looked like linen but felt softer than silk, and soothed his feverish, needy skin. Gwyn straddled his thighs and crouched above him, just staring at him for a long moment. David would have felt embarrassed if anyone else had looked at him like that, but with Gwyn he just felt languorous, and gloriously sensual. "Too beautiful to be mortal," Gwyn murmured, his fingers pressing up the edges of his sweater and T-shirt until they were bunched at the top of his chest. David sat up for a moment and pushed them off onto the floor. "Stunning." Gwyn leaned over him and licked delicately at a long, slender scar on his chest, just below his left nipple. "How did you win this, beloved?"

"It's not a good story," David said abashedly. "I was rappelling without a shirt on and I screwed up. The rope slipped and cut me."

"Arrogant," Gwyn chuckled, licking it again before moving on. "Every part of you tells a story, written into your skin. 'Tis nothing to be shy over, Dafydd. You are every part of you, and I do not fear your darkness any more than I worship your light. I love all of you equally." He brushed his hands over David's jean-clad groin and grinned. "Though I may be convinced to love certain parts of you more specifically, my own."

David took the hint and unbuttoned his jeans, pushing them and his boxers down his legs and off his feet with Gwyn's eager help. Once he was naked, Gwyn stood up for a moment and took his own pants off, and David had a too-brief moment of seeing his perfection in the flickering torchlight, the smooth whiteness of his skin glowing with a more earthy radiance than when he led the hunt. Then he was back on the bed, stroking David's legs apart and sliding between them, bringing their naked bodies into contact. David groaned as Gwyn devoured his mouth, the ease vanishing as the need grew stronger.

"The sun is flying, beloved," Gwyn whispered. "And I have need of you now." He pressed his hardness against David's, not quite rutting yet. "I ache for want of you."

"You have me," David promised. "I'm yours, however you want me."

"I want you in my hand." Gwyn reached between them and captured David's cock in his long fingers. His grip was firm and sure and wonderfully warm, and David pressed into it, already frantic to come. Gwyn stroked him for a few more moments, then kissed him and said softly, "I want you in my mouth."

Gwyn slid down his body, not releasing David with his hand until his lips were poised over his head. When Gwyn took him into his mouth, David cried out with the wanting of it, and the wonderful, desperate way it made him feel. He couldn't look at Gwyn, couldn't see those perfect lips sliding over his flesh, because if he did he would come instantly, and he wanted to wait for Gwyn. His lover didn't see it that way. He pulled off long enough to whisper, "I want your release," before engulfing David again, and there was no fighting it now. David's hands smoothed over his lover's shoulders and tangled in his hair as he came in that beautiful, hungry mouth, his world dimming around the edges as the pleasure became too intense.

Gwyn slowly pulled away from him, slinking back up his body with a movement that surely had to be illusion, because it was totally crazy that someone could be so sexy that it made his newly spent cock twitch in interest. "The joys of resilient youth," Gwyn said with a smug grin as he settled his full length against David again. He felt his lover's need now, hot like a brand on his sweat-slicked skin. "In you, Dafydd," Gwyn said firmly. "I want to be in you."

"Yes, oh please," David said with a whimper. "I want that too." They kissed again, hard and lingering. Gwyn said he wanted him and David could feel that, but at the moment it felt like all he wanted was to kiss him, over and over, tongue dipping inside his mouth to taste him and tangle with his own. They kissed and clutched at each other's bodies, hands roaming freely over quivering flesh, anxious to feel as much as could be felt in the time they had. When Gwyn's hand pressed between his legs, David moaned with inarticulate satisfaction and pulled his knees farther back, welcoming his lover's touch. Gwyn's hand was light against his skin, fingertips brushing carefully over his reviving cock and soft, smooth sac, and just barely touching his entrance.

"I could be drunk on you," Gwyn whispered in his ear. "Drunk on just this. You are so much, Dafydd."

"I want to be more," David begged. "Please, Gwyn. I need you."

"You'll have me," his lover replied. There was something off about his voice. David pulled back from his embrace and looked him seriously in the eyes. Gwyn wasn't frowning, but his smile was gone as well. He looked... sad.

Gwyn tried to smile when he read David's concern. "So much more I would do with you if I had time to savor you, beloved. So many things we could do together." His smile became a little more real. "But were I to waste what time we have now on melancholy, you would truly be wroth with me."

"Yes, I would," David affirmed with a grin. "So let's avoid that."

"Let's." Gwyn reached over to a small bowl set on a pedestal beside the bed and wet his fingers. He came back and curled one teasingly around David's tightly furled skin, pressing and withdrawing and pressing again before finally sliding inside him. David welcomed the intrusion with a broken groan, pulling his lover's face down to his again and kissing him desperately. He wanted to do more, to reach and touch with his own hands, slaking his own hunger for Gwyn's body, but he didn't want to distract him again. Fortunately Gwyn seemed as intent as David was, and his solitary finger was quickly joined by two others, twisting and churning inside him, striking sparks of pleasure from his prostate that made him clench and moan.

He was hard again, completely hard and open and ready and why the hell wasn't Gwyn inside him yet? David withdrew from their kiss to complain, only for that to be the moment that his lover raised his legs to his shoulders, positioned himself, and entered him in one long, steady glide. David was left speechless, which was probably good, because he had no idea what he'd be saying if he were capable of it. Probably something embarrassing.

"Dafydd," Gwyn hissed as he slid home. He turned his face and kissed the inside of David's knee. "Dafydd, beloved, my own…." He started to move then, pulling back and pressing back in, his movements accompanied by sweet, lilting words in a language David didn't understand, but didn't really need to. He stared into his lover's bright green eyes and wonderfully handsome, human face and watched his expressions raptly. David was feeling pleasure, of course—Gwyn was huge and hot and amazing inside him—but no one had ever seemed to get so much pleasure out of being *with* him before, in him. Maybe David had just never given anyone else the chance. He wondered if he could make it better for Gwyn, and pulled him down closer. David was practically folded in half, but the stretch felt good. Gwyn's stomach was rubbing against his cock now, and he could feel himself getting closer and closer to coming, but that didn't matter. Gwyn thrust into him faster, kissing him and laving the side of his neck with his tongue, his words breaking into gasps and needy moans as his own orgasm neared.

"I love you," David murmured, threading trembling fingers into his lover's white-blonde hair. "I love you, Gwyn."

"Dafydd!" Gwyn thrust hard and stayed deep as he began to come, leaning his forehead against David's and panting warm, sweet breaths against his lips. Watching his lover's rapture was enough to tip David over the edge, and he fought to keep his eyes open and staring into Gwyn's as he pulsed between their bodies, slicking their stomachs with come.

They stayed like that for a long time, breathing in each other's sighs until David's body began to cramp, and Gwyn gently slid out of him and set him down. They lay together quietly for a time, legs entwined, lips and tongues exploring salty, delicious skin. David felt completely satiated and wrung out, and his mouth was becoming dry.

"The sun is flying," Gwyn said softly. "And your needs are growing." He entwined their fingers and raised them into David's field of vision. His hand was sepia-toned now, not yet the warm colors of living flesh but no longer flat shades of grey. "We must get you home, Dafydd."

Of course. Right. Home. Except it was hard to think about home right now, hard to even remember that he had a home that existed outside of this wide, welcoming bed and the loving arms of the man who held him now. Gwyn saw the confusion in his look. "Not my home, beloved. Not yet. Someday." He sat back and helped David to his feet, grabbed a wet cloth out of a silver basin of water that David didn't remember seeing before, and wiped his body clean. The water was wonderfully cool, and David felt so hot and thirsty. He turned his lips toward the cloth as it bathed his neck, just wanting a drop or two to ease his parched throat, but Gwyn pulled it quickly away. "No, beloved. Not this time."

"I need it…."

"You need to go home more, Dafydd. When you return to me, we shall feast, and you will taste everything that Annwn has to offer you." He finished cleaning him and helped David back into his clothes. David let himself be led, pliant and content in Gwyn's care. If only he would give him something to drink… but no, no, he couldn't. Not yet. He knew there was some reason for it, some reason to go back. His family… his mother….

"Oh, god!" David's sudden exclamation startled both of them. Gwyn slipped his own clothes on quickly and looked at his lover with concern.

"What is it?"

"I ran out… I just ran out. My mother, my family, they think I've abandoned her, I just ran and left her there." David's panicking eyes met Gwyn's resigned ones. "I have to get home, now."

"I know it." Gwyn kissed him gently once more, and then turned and picked up his helmet. He slid it on, and the change from ardent lover to regal lord was immediate.

A few moments later they left the room, walking silently hand in hand back down to the great hall. When they entered the room, the crowd went silent, all the laughter and merriment dying away at the sight of their king's obvious displeasure. They moved past the guests quickly, Gwyn giving Creiddylad a look that had her hastening to her harp, to fill the uncomfortable silence with music as the two men left. A moment later the magic had them emerging from the hawthorn again, and Gwyn's stallion was standing in the field alone, waiting for them.

Gwyn mounted quickly, and then reached down and helped David up behind him. The horse snorted uneasily and danced a bit beneath them. "I know," his master said, stroking the stallion's neck. "Just once more now, and then a true rest for you. Hold fast to me, Dafydd."

David wrapped his arms around Gwyn's waist and they headed out at a trot, quickening to a canter in moments. By the time they left the field behind and emerged from the portal to Annwn, they were moving at a gallop, racing against time. The sun was low on the horizon, but they had no trouble keeping pace with it.

David closed his eyes and buried his face against Gwyn's back.

The magic of his earlier ride, the wild joy he'd gotten as they soared through time and space, it had all drained away. He felt tired now, deeply satisfied, but also deeply hurt. He hated thinking about what he'd put his mother through, running out of the house and vanishing into the snow. He hated contemplating what he was about to put his lover through just as much. The fact that he had to leave didn't make David feel better about it.

In far too short a time they had stopped. The stallion stood stock-still, reading the somber mood of his riders. David slid down from the horse, reluctantly letting go of Gwyn as he did so, and stepped back. It was like a fog suddenly lifted from his vision. The cold he hadn't been feeling swept over him, and with a startled shudder he realized it was snowing. The sun was just setting now.

He turned around and saw the cabin a little way up the street. Home again. Except it wasn't home anymore. David remembered the warmth of Annwn with a pang, and the softness of their bed with a feeling far more frantic. He stared up at Gwyn, desperately unhappy and uncertain. "Don't forget about me."

"Never, Dafydd," Gwyn said gently.

"I want to come back to you."

"To that I hold you, then." David could see the edges of the smile he craved, easier when the wild winds of the hunt didn't blur his vision. "Tend to your mother now, beloved."

In another moment he was gone, no thunder or fury to mark his passing, and David felt tears threaten to freeze in his eyes. Turning slowly, he trudged back up the snow-caked sidewalk to his house, opened the door, and stepped inside.

"David!"

"Uncle Davey!"

"You little *shit*, do you know how much I had to pay to get Simon treated at the ER?"

David heard everything but it didn't really register. His eyes were locked on his mother's face. She looked wan, paler than he'd left her, but her big blue eyes lit up when he looked at her. Wordlessly, she held out too-thin hands to him; wordlessly, he sat down in the chair next to her bed and took them.

"I was worried you wouldn't come back," she finally whispered, ignoring the rest of their family as easily as he did.

"Don't worry." David lifted her hands to his lips and kissed her knuckles softly. "I'm not going anywhere." *Not yet.*

Questions about David's disappearance and abrupt reappearance were politely stonewalled. He didn't apologize for sending Simon to the emergency room, not to Simon or his irate Aunt Anne. Simon moved out three days later, having successfully hit on the nurse who'd treated him and more than glad to give his crazy cousin a wide berth. Anne decided Colorado was too cold for her and took off to New Mexico again, so it was just the four of them.

Megan started dating someone, a journalist at the local paper. David immediately offered to look after Wendy when she wanted a date night. "I'll be here with Mom anyway," he said with a shrug. He'd stopped guiding for now, living off his savings to stay at home and take care of Claire.

"That's not fair to you, David. You need a break too."

"The hospice nurse helps a lot."

"That's only for an hour a day. You need to get out, honey, you need to live a little. Maybe you need to go on a date yourself. Find whoever you went to the last time…."

She left it hanging, cringing a bit. No one had gotten a straight answer from David on where he'd gone on Halloween, but that didn't keep Megan from being curious. Did he think they'd be ashamed? It wasn't like David had ever been in the closet.

"I'm fine, Meg."

You're not fine, she wanted to shout at him, but she knew it wouldn't do any good. David let you in when he was good and ready or he didn't let you in at all. If he didn't want to explain himself, no amount of badgering on her part would make him.

Claire lived long enough to celebrate Thanksgiving, but died on Christmas Eve. She and David were alone when she passed, Megan and Wendy having gone over to her boyfriend's place for the holiday. David woke up from a sound sleep and was by her side in moments. The hospice nurse had warned him about how she might go, how some people who had barely moved a muscle for weeks would suddenly become active, writhing in bed, shouting or yelling. Claire simply grabbed onto her son's hand and held it tight, her skin so hot it felt like he was holding a flame. She held him and he held her, and after half an hour of silent, loving possession, Claire died. David sat and held her hand for another few minutes, numbed by the reality of it, before finally motivating himself to get up and call first the nurse, then the funeral home. He saved Megan's call for late on Christmas Day. There was no reason to ruin her holiday.

Claire Evans was buried next to her husband the day after New Year's. David sat through the service quietly, ignoring his Aunt Anne's sniffly tears and the vague overtures of sympathy from people he barely knew. His mother had been a teacher, and her funeral was well-attended, but he'd never really gotten to know any of her friends. Simon didn't come, but Harry did, and David was surprisingly glad to see him. He let Megan organize everything, and when she asked him how he was, he would only say, "I think it's going to be a long ten months."

Ten months. Ten months until the next Halloween, until he could see Gwyn again, until he could finally go and leave this world behind for Annwn. David felt guilty about leaving Megan and Wendy, but they had people here who cared about them; they didn't need him. And when it came down to it, all he really needed was Gwyn.

The loss he'd felt when he left his lover, compounded now by his mother's death, was overwhelming. He painted and sketched and carved, constantly shaping his lover's face, tableaus of him leading the hunt, of him alone on his stallion, of him, half-naked, standing beside a wide hawthorn bed and smiling hungrily. David papered his room with pictures of Gwyn, constantly trying to relive their too-brief time together, trying to remind himself that it had really happened.

He drew simpler pictures for Wendy, of the horse and the dogs and the happy people of Annwn. Wendy was excellent company because she never asked questions; she just accepted the pictures as people and enjoyed them. Because she never asked, David felt more comfortable sharing certain things with her.

"It's always summer there," he told her on Valentine's Day as they sat at the kitchen table together, drawing. Megan was on a date and Anne had yet to make good on her threat to kick him out of the house, since she had no interest in coming back and watching Wendy. "The fields are filled with flowers, and the trees are covered with white and pink blossoms with small red fruit."

"Like a valentine," Wendy grinned, holding up the elaborate pony-shaped card he had made for her.

"Yes," David agreed, wishing for a moment that he could see that living valentine again. Wishing like that depressed him, and he pushed it back ruthlessly. "Just like that."

"When you go back, can I go too?"

"No," David said. "Once you go there it's very hard to leave again. Almost impossible. You'd have to leave your mommy and Jack behind, and all your things. You wouldn't be happy like that."

"No," Wendy agreed, "I don't want to leave Mommy and Jack. But I'll miss you." She got down from her chair, came over to his, and waited for him to lift her into his lap. Once he did, she hugged him tightly, and he stroked her curling golden hair and closed his eyes.

"I'll miss you too."

Winter was long that year, and while the trees were doing their best to bud in March, heavy frosts made it impossible for anything other than pine trees to stay green. When the snow finally stopped falling every week and the sun made more than a cursory appearance, people's spirits picked up.

David couldn't explain why, but he found himself filled with a strange, nervous energy. He was constantly on edge for the entire month of April, and spent more and more time by himself, hiking over the mountains. He resisted every attempt of Megan's to get him to go out and socialize like a normal person, and when his contract came up for renewal as a guide, he turned that down as well.

"David!" Megan said exasperatedly as she packed herself and Wendy up for a long weekend in Denver with Jack. There was going to be a May Day parade and a festival, and while David had been invited by Megan and Jack both, he'd politely refused. "Aunt Claire wouldn't want you to live like a monk for the rest of your life. It's just a weekend away, you can be gone that long. Maybe it'll help you relax some." She laid a hand on his shoulder. "You know, we never really celebrated your birthday. The big Two-One! Come on, we can go to Denver and you can hit some bars, meet some people…."

"No thanks," David said shortly. He was anxious for them to be gone, to just leave already. It was as though he was waiting for something to happen, except he had no idea what it was. He made an effort to be kind when he saw his cousin's worried expression. "Go ahead, Meg. You guys'll have a great time without me, and I'll be fine. I promise."

"You always say that," Megan muttered, but she slung her duffel bag over her shoulder with a sigh. "Arguing with you is like fighting with a force of nature. I can talk all I want, but it doesn't get me anywhere."

"Have a good time, Meg."

"Yeah, we will." She kissed his cheek, then went outside to where Jack and Wendy were waiting. David watched them go with a sense of finality, which he hoped wasn't a bad omen.

The next day was the windiest since winter's end, blowing shingles off roofs and cracking tree branches. David found it impossible to stay inside despite the wind, and he spent the morning and early afternoon outside, feeling well-matched internally to the unsettled weather. He climbed the fire-scarred, nameless peak behind the cabin and paced its summit, staring out toward the west for no good reason.

It was an hour before sunset when David sensed a change in the wind. His breath came faster as he heard the distant cries of the hounds. *Please, please….*

The Winter King thundered toward him, his paleness marred by dark, seeping blood. His armor was scarred from battle, and his stallion's coat was stained black where his wounds dripped onto it. The hounds were there, restive and snarling, but there was no train of spirits this time. There was only Gwyn, and his spectral eyes were fierce with exultation. When he stopped in front of David, he held out a gory hand.

"I have only now finished with Gwythyr," he panted. "My power diminishes too greatly after Calan Mai to reach you until Nos Calan Gaeaf, and I cannot be without you for so long, beloved." His fingers clenched on empty air for a moment. "Do I frighten you, Dafydd?"

"No, Gwyn," David breathed. "You don't frighten me. I'm ready to go with you." He took his lover's hand and mounted up before him. The stallion pranced on the mist and the hounds closed ranks around them. In moments they were gone, racing the sun back to the entrance of Annwn and the life together that waited for them in the Otherworld.

CARI Z. is a Colorado girl who loves snow and sunshine. She and her husband are living abroad currently and trying to feel good about taking showers with nothing more than a bucket of water, soap and a handy ladle. She's trying hard not to envy you right now.

Check her blog at http://carizerotica.blogspot.com for updates on current projects and upcoming releases.

The Light of Foreign Places

Rodello Santos & Damon Shaw

IN THE Year of the White Dervish, the snake-city of Striyn crossed the great desert in its endless, holy mission.

Heart hammering, his nerves taut as the hemp tendons of the city itself, Jai Honrein Sandalwood Morningsun clutched the balcony rail of his cabin and searched for the lights of foreign places. The night air sped by him, cool and calming. Surely such balmy air should bring rest and lazy half-smiles in the darkness? But Jai was young, and thrummed that night, his nerves afire. Standing next to him, his lover Honeysmoke thrummed too, but for reasons more to do with the dream-weed in her pipe. The purple wisp she exhaled was snatched by the wind.

Striyn only sped thus when its destination was close, and all within the wooden walls of the snake-city were on vigil: the ropemakers in their rigging; the tattooists and costumiers on Spine Street; the gardeners in their airy, silk-screened vivariums; even the belly rollers of the snake themselves, deep beneath the sewage pipes, sang as they rolled ever forward.

Nobody yet cracked open the crates of dried flowers, or snapped the top of even one flask of festive wine. The Captain, Long may Striyn Preserve Her, had forbidden excess noise or waste. Who knew, besides their centuries-old captain, when the snake would stop? Who knew who might be listening out there in the jasmine-scented darkness?

Jai knew someone was out there. On horseback, perhaps, cantering on hooves of velvet over the grass. Grass! Green and wasteful and wet, mashed by the belly rollers, smearing the planks.... Jai shook his head, unbelieving. He had thought sand would grate behind his eyelids forever.

"What are you complaining about now?" Honeysmoke said at his side. She was taller than he and older by a decade. The sweet-sharp smoke of her pipe burnt Jai's nostrils.

"Complaining?" He blinked at the glow near her lips. "I didn't even say—"

"I can't protect you if you go," she said, her voice both calm and vibrant. "The Goddess dances, and Striyn, Her city, stirs. Would you leave me now, abandon me to the years?"

Jai hated the vague ramblings brought on when she smoked. "No," he said. "No." But he dismissed the question, the argument, the weeks of sullen silence, the joy and the shout of her before the words left his lips. *Something* came ever closer.

"Look, Honey, look," he whispered. "Lights. A city. Look!"

Stretching across the horizon, a mist of yellow and orange lifted above the plains. Above, the sky shone, uplit in gold.

"Ramsha'hla," she said. As daughter of the High Soothsayer, she was privy to such knowledge.

A thrill slid up Jai's spine at the mention of the fabled city. What pleasures he might partake in. What pleasures he might offer in the name of the Snake Goddess. "I'm going upside," said Jai.

Without waiting for an answer, he stepped onto the balcony rail, and swung around to grasp the ladder that stretched up the side of the snake. The oiled wood, smooth under his palms, was as alive as the city itself. The smell of Striyn always made him pause; wood and hemp and a constant sweet perfume from the very pores of the planking. The adrenaline rush shook his chest and made him yawn for extra air. Again he shook his head, this time to clear it, and pulled himself up the ladder in the darkness.

He heard Honeysmoke following, and wished she had stayed below.

On the back of Striyn, between the gauzy fins of the dewcatchers, Jai braced his knees against the constant slow heave of forward motion and peered ahead. Unlike others who had been recruited this last year, Jai had found his snake legs immediately, his body intuiting each lurch and sway. It was as if he had been born for this.

Honey bounded off the ladder and ran up the side, the fingertips of one hand brushing the woodwork. In her mouth, her pipe glowed in the wind of Striyn's passage.

The cooler air raised goose bumps on Jai's naked shoulders. Out of the yellow glow ahead, red sparks emerged. Green chains of pinprick illumination, tiny blue flames, even ranks of minute windows, piled high in buildings that Jai thought must touch the clouds. His birthtown would fit in the foothills of this towering jewel of a city.

Neither he nor Honeysmoke broke the night with arguments. Even the constant creaking and whispering of oiled bearings far below seemed hushed. Jai could hear the liquid warble of night birds in the grasslands below. The head of Striyn swung across the city, blocking out seven, then five, then three square miles of the crammed lights of thousands, no, millions of people.

"Ai, me," said Honeysmoke beside him. Though they came here only to recruit converts and celebrate, it was in her nature to see danger hand in hand with the unknown. She sounded so subdued that Jai took her hand. They watched as the city became districts became streets became buildings, then the fragile glow of tents amongst trees, and Jai thought his heart might crack and split open like a pomegranate as he realized the snake was slowing. Tomorrow would be carnival, the biggest brightest carnival he, perhaps *any* snake dweller, had ever seen.

Horns blew far ahead, the twin-toned melancholy song of the priests in the Maw of Striyn. The voice of the Captain, May Striyn Keep Her from the Long Road, emerged from holes in the roof.

"Citizens," she began, her ancient voice a melodic drawl. "Darling girls and fiery boys, crack open the casks, swathe and drape and flag yourselves. Bathe and rut and sing with joy, for tomorrow we hold carnival!"

It was the Captain's signal to them: let Ramsha'hla know the city of the Snake Goddess was at their doorstep. The silence was torn by cheers and the thunder of feet on bulwarks. Fireworks burst overhead, causing the black sundrinker jewels along Striyn's back to glitter darkly under their shroud of frosty steam. Rockets and paper lanterns lifted like sparkling pollen into the sky, and Jai Honrein Sandalwood Morningsun and Honeysmoke Kalray Silverydusk kissed like their first night all over again.

He woke the next morning to joyous shouts and whistles, and the decking under him trembled from preparations. Without opening his eyes, he savored the sounds and his own eagerness. Half-asleep, he thought his own tension pressed down on his chest until he realized Honeysmoke's arm lay over his ribs, pinning him. He slipped out from under her, hoping not to wake her, but her sleep-fuzzed voice rumbled from under the blanket.

"Stay," she said. "Let the other seducers do the work. Stay with me instead."

Jai smiled at the absurdity of the request and dressed, putting on his earring—a golden ourobouros—as the last touch. He stepped onto the balcony. The city of Ramsha'hla was equally spectacular in the morning time. Jai gaped at the sun-sparkled minarets soaring to meet the heavens as a flock of pink birds swept past the tallest spire.

On the ground, Striyn had arranged itself like a horseshoe near Ramsha'hla's eastern gate, the snake-city's body defining the arena of the carnival.

Jai shivered with glee. He returned to the room, to the hanging storage baskets, for his plumage, the tokens of Striyn honor. He wove the feathers roughly into his hair while Honey blinked at him from her cushions, her fingers groping for the pipe on her nearby stand.

When he was suitably adorned, he gave Honey a token kiss and left. In his excitement, he could not help the door slamming louder than usual, nor keep from skipping as he ran along shaking walkways and slid down snag-runged ladders until he dropped down through the roof and into the stink and bustle of Spine Street.

Because of her father's rank, Honeysmoke had cabins high in the flank of the city, but prophecy was not Striyn's main aspect, and many dancers and artists had much higher honor—and cabins—than she. So Jai began his journey to the mouth of the snake, passing through Deep Girth, where the discs were smaller and joined only by rope bridges. As he ran along Spine Street, many people spotted the orange feathers in his hair and stepped aside for him. Being a seducer, even a junior one, had its privileges. In Center Girth, however, the plumes grew longer and closer to crimson, and Jai had to duck and jump and sometimes wait for agonizing minutes while higher-ranking snake dwellers proceeded toward the fangs.

In Center Girth, railed walkways joined the discs of Striyn's body; the paths grew wider, the shops more exclusive, the fashions more extreme, as Jai got closer to the Maw. The street curved to his right, hiding the daylight, but the wet smell of grass filled the Spine, pulling him onward.

The queues at the Anointers made him long to slip past, but the preparation rites had to be observed. Their religion had a reputation, after all. The allure of Striyn was legendary amongst the desert towns, and this new city must be impressed at all costs.

So Jai scuffed and tapped and crept forward and eventually came to the immense arches of Striyn's jaw hinges. Between the columns of the fangs, above the throng that crowded the tongue, he saw a scrap of sheer blue, and his heart raced at the thought of stepping down again onto solid ground.

A tinge of jealousy shot through him as the nonseducers bypassed the Anointers. He was ushered by the guards into a booth, where he rubbed his wrists over the polished nub of wood of Striyn's perfume glands. Several other seducers already crowded there, a few catching his eye and smiling, all anxious to get outside and work. The scent of perfume hung in the air in loops of orange haze. By the time Jai would step outside, though, the perfume would be undetectable, absorbed beneath the surface of his skin until he chose to release it.

He left the room shaking and dizzy, and he realized he had not yet eaten. He could grab a kebab or a sweet spiced roll outside, he told himself. As soon as he was done in the booth, he ran, swerving past a trapeze artist with yard-long feathers and translucent, furled wings. He jumped over a flock of sand lizards being led in jeweled harnesses, pushed past a gaggle of the Captain's eunuchs as the light brightened about him, and finally jumped to the grass—grass!—in a place so far from home, he might as well be dancing on the moon.

It took him less than seven breaths, less than five, than three, to know something was wrong.

The citizens of Ramsha'hla had already arrived, but instead of the open mouths, the delight and amazement, they shrank back, tentative and judging. They walked in pairs, and Jai blinked as he realized every pair was made of one man and one woman. The men, glowering behind their veils, swaggered and never touched the steaming cups of spiced wine, nor returned the winks and smiles of Jai and his fellow seducers.

The women took Jai's breath away. Poised, with many copper and gold rings about their necks, they smiled, aloof, raising eyebrows and murmuring to their men in calm and amused tones. They kept their hands in their sleeves, and touched nothing. None spoke aloud, none showed excitement. They looked puzzled, faintly amused, and the brightly decked-out snake dwellers seemed garish in comparison.

Jai bit his lip. How could he convert, if no one walked alone? How could he seduce, if no one would meet his eye? Around him, jugglers, red-faced, dropped their fire clubs, tattooists doodled across empty stools, trapeze artists warmed up in lieu of even trying to impress this jaded crowd.

Their reserve baffled him. Perhaps another of the animal cities had visited recently—the tiger of the war-god Anket or the turtle of wise Hanuma or any of the other religions seeking more followers. Even so, Jai could not imagine their attempts to recruit would be more spectacular than the carnival of Striyn, born of the Snake Goddess, Matron of love and lust, of new delights and second chances.

Yet the citizens of Ramsha'hla seemed immune to wonder.

Flautists played an enchanting mantra of notes, and Jai was pleased to sense a subtle shift. The crowd paused, changed stances, couples leaning on each other as they listened. The tune grew, wove around its own counterpoint.

But Jai studied the faces of the audience, and feared their interest would be fragile and fleeting. Already, several pairs of feet shifted, anxious to move on. Jai pondered what to do to keep their notice, to stoke it. He would have sung, had he a sweeter voice, or joined in the music, if he could play an instrument.

And then the veiled stranger came, striding, dreamlike, *alone*, into Jai's vision and world. She—no, *he?*—for despite his height and grace, his hands were not hidden as the women's were—spun with arms akimbo, plain khaki robes lifting slightly with the whirl. He seemed of age with Jai, newly a man. His veil, securely hiding his face, could not conceal the agate-sparkle of joy in his eyes.

Amusement lit the faces of the city folk, perhaps at seeing a familiar dance set to foreign music. The steps were simple enough: toe right, spin, a sideways skip, knee-bend and kick-hop. But with those simple steps, this lone dancer was razing the invisible walls between their two cultures.

Heart quickening, Jai leapt in.

The stranger's mouth was hidden behind the veil, but by the crinkle around his eyes, Jai knew he was smiling. His approval sent a flash of heat to Jai's face, made him stumble a step. He swallowed and paused, then reentered the dance with a vigorous spin in synch with the stranger.

The change happened at once, like a sudden desert storm. Pairs of folk joined in, first from Ramsha'hla, then Striyn, until they formed a full circle. The tune sped, faster with each repetition, and at the merry end, the dancers seemed refreshed and breathless both.

The new mood sparked the snake dwellers to double their efforts; the buzz of voices rose and the calls of vendors rang with more confidence. Fire jugglers spun their clubs, swift and high. Sand lizards showed clever tricks at their trainer's behest. And despite themselves, the folk of Ramsha'hla responded. The carnival was coming to life.

"Thank you," Jai said, removing an orange feather from his hair and offering it to the stranger.

"It's beautiful," the stranger said in surprise. His voice was rich and resonant.

"From the fire hawk, who mates for life. As the years pass, the feather turns golden. It is a badge of fidelity for the dwellers of Striyn." He did not share that the feathers had been gifts from Honey.

At the mention of Striyn, the stranger eyed the massive snake-city, almost a fifth as large as Ramsha'hla itself. "The tales I've heard do not count fidelity a virtue for your Snake Goddess. I thought She cared more for fleeting pleasures."

Jai had visited enough towns to know the reputation of his religion, and so was not offended. "What is your name?"

The stranger hesitated before answering. "My name is Duphal."

"Duphal, do not believe all you hear, for some tales deny the truths of Striyn and some do not do them justice. Rather, open yourself to the *new*, as you did when you danced." Jai stepped closer, allowed the smallest hint of the snake's perfume to reach Duphal with its subtle magic. It was only fair, given how everything about Duphal—his nearness, his scent, his *mystery*—enflamed Jai.

Jai had lost count of those he had seduced, both men and women, in the many towns that littered the desert's edge. Duphal was the first, though, to affect him so, to make him dry his palms with hidden gestures, to make him rein back a heartbeat that wanted nothing more than to gallop free.

"Why do you stare at me so?" Duphal asked. He twirled the stem of the feather between his fingers.

A dozen compliments came to mind, but they were the rehearsed lines of a seducer. Instead, he said, "Because you are everything I am not. You are born of a grand and ancient city, the Jewel-beyond-the-Desert, as Ramsha'hla is called. I have heard tales of your city too. Here, they say, each man is a hero waiting to birth a legend."

When Duphal spoke, he looked upon the fangs of Striyn's gaping gateway. His eyes were as striking and beautiful as any woman's. "What did you say about believing all the tales one hears?"

The tone was light, but Jai saw a longing in his dark eyes, and a thrill of hope shivered up Jai's spine. He grinned. "So you do not race rocs around the minarets at twilight, and feed prisoners to the victor? This they swear in far Deilan."

"No." Duphal raised one eyebrow. "At *dawn*. And we use visitors, not prisoners, for the rocs prefer foreign cuisine."

Jai laughed. "Would you...." He stopped, unable to finish, for the words that longed to break free were "*lift your veil and let me see your lips...?*"

A heady dizziness overtook him, and he swayed.

Duphal placed one hand on his arm. "Are you well?"

"I'm... hungry," Jai managed to say. He attempted a smile, but found he could not meet Duphal's gaze. He feared he would fall through those smoke-ringed pupils and be lost. "I have not eaten."

"I am hungry myself."

Jai nodded and led them to a canvassed stall of pastry charms. Duphal paid for the apple-and-clove-stuffed pastries—shaped to resemble camels, hares, and eagles—with a pinch of salt crystals and a small copper ingot. Jai found the pastry almost too dry to swallow, thickly powdered as it was with cinnamon.

They strolled and ate, passing opium tents, whirling soothsayers, auctions, and stilt walkers. Jai was pleased to play the tour guide.

"This is much different than Anket's tiger-city," Duphal said.

"They were here?"

The youth nodded. "Several months ago. I regret to say they were better welcomed than your city. But in Ramsha'hla, warriors are bestowed great respect. Even my father was impressed, but he feared they would recruit his best soldiers—"

Duphal's body stilled, and he fell silent.

"Your father?" Jai asked, before realizing he should have kept the silence. "Oh. *Oh*. You're royalty?"

Duphal's eyes grew wide, and he snorted. "No, no, and thrice no! It's...." He paused, and his tone turned sour. "It's worse. My father is the general of our army. You must promise to tell no one."

"Why?"

"If I were seen here, it would be scandalous. It is said that your people are decadent."

"Decadent? Yet you came to see us anyway?"

"That's the *reason* I came." The two youths burst into laughter, draining some of the tension away.

When their laughter subsided, Duphal confessed, "There is another reason too." He paused again, but this time Jai knew enough not to interrupt.

"When the tiger-city came, they set up a massive stage between the front paws of their city. Those who would convert to the religion of war lined up at the stage and signed their names. But I've heard that your folk do it differently."

Jai understood now the reason for Duphal's hesitation. "Yes."

"It is rumored that one merely needs to... lie with one of your people in order to convert." The waver in Duphal's voice belied his effort to speak casually.

"That's not exactly true. We offer the Goddess's blessing even to those who do not wish to convert. And not all our folk are responsible for converting, only the seducers."

"Those who wear the earring of a serpent swallowing its tail?"

"Yes," Jai said.

"As you do?"

"Yes."

"And you convert... only women?"

Jai placed a hand on Duphal's shoulder, slid it down his arm. When he reached the youth's hand, Jai grasped it gently. "All are welcome. Do not worry. I do not know your people's taboos, but among the snake dwellers, it is dishonorable to share another's secrets. What adventures you seek will be private." When Duphal said nothing, Jai added, "I should mention taboos are my specialty."

Duphal's voice dropped to a whisper. "I'm glad to be veiled. It is stifling, but at least no one will recognize me."

With those words, Jai found himself overcome with the desire to see Duphal's face. "Follow me," he said and led him to the soothsayers' tent, pitched in the shade, right against the massive bulk of Striyn's side.

The huge tent was partitioned into smaller rooms, and outside each room, a flautist played so that prophecies were not overheard.

They went into an unused room, and as if he had read Jai's mind, Duphal half-turned and removed his veil. Jai stared at the flattened grass, catching glimpses of jawline and soft cheekbones as Duphal dampened a cloth with dew from the shadows and pressed it to his forehead.

"The sun burns this fierce, in the far South?" murmured Duphal.

Jai shook his head and his gaze snagged on the smooth curve of Duphal's mouth. "Fiercer," he said, but could say no more, as the stranger, a man Jai had met less than seventy—no, fifty—no, thirty minutes ago, floated closer, a startlement that Jai recognized in his eyes.

In a cinnamon-scented breath, they kissed.

Something opened in Jai's chest. He felt it distinctly, like a red-petaled flower opens, revealing ever deeper petals behind, red shading to bronze, to gold.

Duphal broke the kiss, so Jai leaned in to recapture it. He slipped an arm around Duphal's back to prevent retreat, and for an infinite moment, the world shrank to that one kiss. Just as Jai thought he could feel Duphal's doubts melting, the other youth twisted away.

"I... I...."

"Me too," Jai said.

"I need to return... I have duties—"

Jai frowned. "But we've hardly begun. Do not be afraid—"

Duphal stepped back, and his military bearing rose up like a spiked shield. "I'm not. My absence will be noticed. If I linger more, I will have no excuses to give my father that will make sense."

He affixed his veil, and it was like the closing of city gates.

"Will I see you later?" asked Jai.

Duphal nodded. "I'll try. But I can't say when. How long will you be here?"

"Six days, or until your city tires of our decadence and declares war."

Jai's jest was ignored. "I'll see you before then," Duphal said, but the hesitance in his tone did not reassure. "Thank... you."

Then he hurried away, leaving Jai frustrated, jubilant, and alone with the thrumming of his heart.

THE rest of the afternoon bore no fruit. The folk of Ramsha'hla still traveled in pairs, and the moment they spotted any serpent earrings, their attention pointedly focused elsewhere. When Jai passed fellow seducers, they shared the same tale.

He longed to enter Ramsha'hla, but the city had not extended any invitation, formal or informal.

A short rest, then, he decided and headed back to Striyn's Maw and to his quarters.

Honey was there, gazing out from the balcony, and when she saw Jai, a slow smile dawned on her face. "Back so soon? None seeking the Goddess's blessing?"

When she embraced Jai, he returned it out of reflex. "It is only the first day."

"Still, a pity. And a surprise. No birds drawn to such a lovely worm." Her hand slid down his chest, then toward his navel. He gasped, despite himself, when she reached her intended destination.

Honey pressed her body tightly against his, pushed a kiss against his lips. She herded him to their bed and undressed him.

He closed his eyes, imagined it was Duphal's hands—strong, inexperienced, yearning—that glided on his skin, that it was Duphal's stroke, not Honey's, that coaxed him to grow. She lay on her back, pulling him with her.

"Hold me tighter," Honey said, and Jai wished she would keep silent.

She squirmed beneath him. "Pretend I'm a wayward soul, in desperate need of conversion."

"Yes, Duphal."

Honey's body became stone under Jai, and her expression darkened. Impossibly strong, she pushed him off her.

Jai flushed with guilt, then anger that he should feel guilty.

"What did you call me?" Honey hissed.

"You know what I do, my role. I am constantly meeting new people."

"Out there, yes, in the carnival of Striyn. But in here, within this room, I will not share you, not even with the Goddess. You are mine, only mine!"

She was raving, almost blasphemous. Jai knew there was nothing to say when she was in these moods.

"Leave!" she said, grabbing her pipe from the floor.

Frustrated even more, his body trembling from the brink of pleasure denied, Jai picked up his clothes and strode from the room.

JAI did not return to the cabin that night or the next, electing to stay in the seducers' tents outside. Worse, he saw no sign of Duphal in that time. The tents were quiet, barely used, for the Ramsha'hlites unstated practice for the carnival seemed to be "look, but not touch."

On the third evening, one of the fire jugglers found Jai and told him he was being sought. With a knowing grin, the juggler described the veiled strong man with agate eyes.

"Where is he?" Jai asked.

"Still searching, like a pup that's lost his tail. We spoke by the featherdancers' stage."

Jai ran.

The featherdancers had just finished for the night, and Jai saw only strangers in the dispersing crowd.

Heart racing, his nerves sparking, Jai paced through the surrounding tents. When he saw Duphal outside the soothsayers' tent, a smile blazed out of him.

Duphal was looking about, nervously, and when he saw Jai, he gave a little start.

Duphal's face was hidden behind the damnable veil, but Jai could read the eagerness in his movements. "I could not find you, so I returned here, to the place we last met."

"So that our path may continue from where we paused?" Jai asked. Duphal's laughter was like rain. But when Jai went to take his hand, he pulled away. "Not here. Let us be away from others' eyes."

Jai nodded. "Follow me." He led Duphal back to the seducers' tents. They did not speak as they walked, perhaps conserving their energy.

Inside the privacy of the tent-room, Duphal said, "I'm sorry. I have not been able to get away from my training."

"Training?"

"Drills, and studies of battles." He took off his veil, and Jai lost his breath upon seeing his handsome face once more.

Jai drew closer, as did Duphal, and there was only the slightest pause—a shared gaze—before they kissed.

Caress by caress, all hesitation faded, and a tender ferocity stole over them. It seemed to Jai that Duphal opened a cage within himself, a dark prison where he'd hidden every forbidden need, every unthinkable hope, out of fear, out of shame.

Jai learned something in those moments. Of how passion might grow greater for being denied. Of how the guarded love raged brightest when finally freed. Again and again he learned this, and each time, he released Striyn's perfume from his skin, heightening their rapture.

Afterwards, eventually, they lay quiet, smoldering.

They kept the silence for a while before Jai began to ramble about the simplicity of his early life. He told a tale: the first moment he had seen Striyn slithering out of the wilderness toward his little town. The other townsfolk fled, terror-eyed, but he could only stand and stare at the miracle.

"What was it like to leave your family?" Duphal asked.

Jai knew, or at least hoped he knew, the reason for his question.

"I never knew my parents, and the aunt who raised me had seven children of her own. Not that I was ungrateful, but I knew I was a burden she was glad to see go. It was difficult to say good-bye, but I have not regretted it since. Many of the other snake dwellers were happy to leave their old lives as well. Most of them, though, were born on Striyn. My lover, Honeysmoke, says her ancestors were among the first to inhabit Striyn, when the gods sent their living cities to find them followers."

Duphal propped himself on his elbows. "Honeysmoke? You have a lover? A woman?"

Jai rushed to explain. "It is tradition for a snake dweller to open his or her chambers to a new seducer. When I first came to Striyn, Honeysmoke took me to her room."

"But... you love her?"

"No. I mean I do, but it's not the same as I feel for you."

"Am I just another convert to you?" His questions were coming faster.

Jai laid his palm upon Duphal's face, but the other youth turned away.

"I need to return," Duphal said.

Frustration made Jai raise his voice. "Must you?"

Duphal replied with equally growing anger. "Don't be ignorant. Just because you take freedom for granted, it doesn't mean everyone else does. If my father knew I had lied to him, that I had... I had... with you...."

Jai stood. “You can do it well enough, but you can’t say it?”

Duphal was about to answer when the door flap to the tent opened. Marya, a senior seducer in charge of the tent, stood there, her expression between concern and reproach.

“I heard voices raised… and not in pleasure. Is all well?”

“Yes—” Jai began, but he heard a gasp from Duphal. The other youth quickly spun away.

Jai looked and noticed another pair of men standing beyond Marya in the main room: a seducer and a short Ramsha’hlite, whose eyes where wide in fear.

No, Jai realized, not just fear. *In recognition.*

“Everything is fine,” Jai hurriedly assured Marya and moved—too late, he knew—to shield Duphal. With a final frown, Marya departed.

Jai put a hand on Duphal’s shoulder and turned him around. His face was pale.

“Who was that?”

“My cousin.” Duphal said. “If he tells my father he saw me with another man....”

“But he was here as well, for the same thing, no doubt.”

Duphal’s agitation grew. “You don’t understand. The sentence for this crime is death by burial. He will sell me out, fearing I will do the same.” He snatched his clothes and dressed. “I have no choice, I must hurry back and tell my father.”

“But you can’t know your cousin will betray you. Speak to him first. There’s no reason either of you need to die.” Just mentioning the possibility of Duphal’s death sent a jagged ache through Jai.

Duphal stopped and shouted. “What do you know of our culture? This is your fault.”

“Stay,” Jai said, his heart not daring to believe his own desperate request. “Stay here, and leave your life behind.”

He expected Duphal to scoff or snort in disgust. What Jai saw in his eyes was far worse. Despair.

“I can’t. It’s impossible.”

With his veil once more in place, Duphal left Jai a second time.

THOUGHTS awhirl, Jai considered staying overnight in the tent. But the need for familiarity, for some anchor of sanity, was too strong, and he found himself returning into Striyn, back to his room. Perhaps Honey's anger had spent itself in the last few days, or better yet, she was already asleep. The hour was certainly late enough.

But when he opened the door, he found her kneeling before a bronze augury tray filled with multicolored sand. Suspended above it, three candles swung on independent pendulums.

Jai was surprised; he could count on one hand the number of times he had seen her soothsay in their room. From what she had once explained, the future was revealed by reading the patterns of fallen wax, and the colors of sand in those clumps. Honey's gaze was intent upon the reading before her.

"Stay," she said, just as the thought of leaving came to him. "I have looked into your Path," she continued.

He started. "You what? I gave you no permission!" A man's future was as sacrosanct as any secret he might keep. A flush of heat came to his face.

"I saw him. Your 'Duphal'. If you choose to be with him, his Path will entwine with yours... and strangle it. I have seen what occurs if you pursue him—you will both walk down the Long Road."

Jai had opened his mouth to argue, but stopped at Honey's last words. The Long Road was the most feared place within Striyn, the tail end, where one was brought when death claimed him.

Was she lying? He had never seen her as angry as that last time they had fought. *Of course she is lying.*

"I can't protect you if you go," she said, and for a moment her words stirred a memory that Jai could not place.

"I don't need your protection. Duphal and I will protect each other."

Duphal would return, Jai told himself, and when he did, Jai would do whatever was necessary to make him stay. "Keep your auguries with your dream-weed. To yourself."

"I love you, Jai. If you leave me now, the Long Road awaits you."

He left the room, needing to escape Honey's doom-filled words.

IN THE small hours of the night, Jai was awakened in the seducers' tents by unseen rustles. He sat up, blinking, unsure if it was a dream before him or if Duphal had actually returned… eyes wet, approaching, kneeling, his voice soft and cautious.

"I c-couldn't," said the dream-Duphal.

Jai reached out, embraced him until the heaving sobs and heat of Duphal convinced him this was not a dream at all.

"I couldn't," Duphal said again.

"What? Were you able to speak to your father?"

Duphal buried his face in Jai's shoulder, so that when he spoke, Jai could feel the resonance of the words. "Yes. But not before my cousin had reached him. When my father asked if it were true, all I had to do was deny it. He would have believed me. But I couldn't. Because it was the truest thing, ever, in the whole of my life. I couldn't deny you."

Jai waited, let him rest on his shoulder. Duphal's confession stirred hope in Jai's soul, more strongly than any declarations of love. With their bodies so close, Jai could feel the tempo of their hearts.

"What happened after?"

"I left, and he allowed it. But I can never return."

Jai relaxed, knowing Duphal was at least safe. The father could easily have sentenced him to death, if their laws were truly as barbaric as Duphal suggested.

"I wandered the streets of Ramsha'hla, but I had nowhere to go."

Jai ran his fingers through Duphal's hair. "As long as I'm here, you will always have somewhere."

"What should I do?"

Jai winced at how lost he sounded. "For now, nothing. We rest, sleep, and tomorrow will shine with answers."

Duphal nodded, and they lay, embracing. Duphal fell asleep at once—exhausted, Jai knew, in body and spirit. Soon, Jai closed his own eyes, knowing all would work out, all would be perfect, now that Duphal was with him.

WHEN Jai awoke, Duphal was already up, head bowed and sitting beside him.

"Did you sleep well?" he asked, and Duphal flinched in surprise.

"I slept. But my dreams circled back and again, dreams of skeletons pursuing me."

Jai edged closer, placed a kiss on his shoulder. "You will feel better when you have eaten. Come, you will find no skeletons beneath the morning sun."

Duphal surprised Jai with a brief, gentle kiss. Jai hoped it would last longer, but Duphal stood up and affixed his veil. Only now did Jai realize Duphal had not worn it during the night.

Together they ventured out of the tent to find the carnival had already awoken. A sand lizard had broken free and trailed at their heels. Jai knelt and patted its head, and, with a gravelly purr, it stuck out a long forked tongue to lick the side of his face.

"Aren't they poisonous?" Duphal asked, alarmed.

"Yes, but there is nothing that comes from Striyn that we need to fear." He remembered being told such when he had first been converted.

Duphal crouched down, placed a tentative hand upon the lizard. Jai was touched to see Duphal's show of trust.

He was about to say so when he saw Duphal looking beyond, his brow furrowed and eyes troubled. Following his gaze, Jai saw two large men—less than twenty paces away—in military garb. Red circular shields hung upon their backs and glinted in the sun.

When the soldiers turned, Duphal quickly grabbed Jai's wrist, pulled him away in the opposite direction. "Ramsha'hlite foot soldiers. My father must have sent them, and there can only be one reason."

"But he let you leave—"

"He's had a full night to change his mind. Those men will not have come alone."

Jai took the lead. "Follow me." His first plan was to lie low in the seducers' tents, but he stopped short—Duphal crashing into him—when he reached the tent and saw four soldiers already there.

Jai cursed himself. Given what Duphal's cousin saw, the seducers' tents would be the last place to hide.

Duphal whispered, "If my father wishes to find me, he will find me. Perhaps it might be better if I—"

"Do not even consider it."

"If he learns you are helping me, you might be arrested. And that is something my conscience would not allow."

Jai had not considered the danger to himself, but the thought only spurred him. "Neither of us will be taken. Striyn's captain will defend us, if necessary." At least he hoped she would.

"Your captain would not be so foolish."

"There's one way to find out," Jai said, fighting against Duphal's despair. "I shall ask her. Follow me."

"Your captain's a woman?" Duphal asked, but Jai was already moving toward Striyn. A few times they altered their route to avoid nearby soldiers.

"There," Jai pointed, as they neared the fangs. Duphal's brows furrowed as he stared at the entrance, but his pace did not slow. They were not far from the plank of the tongue when Jai felt a weight, invisible but undeniable, fall upon him. His intuition had never been so acute, and when Duphal saw him pause, he looked around as well for trouble.

Someone was watching, Jai was sure, but it did not feel like the practiced search of soldiers. Too much emotion welled behind it.

Only when he looked up did he spot the source. Upon the balcony of her room, Honey stood, a statue distant and alone. Jai's heart twinged for love once felt. The weight of her regard left him, but he knew it had shifted to Duphal.

When the other man flinched and turned to stare at her, Jai knew now that it was not some supernatural intuition on his part that had felt her gaze. Honey wanted them to know she was watching. She was warning him, one last time, warning him to leave Duphal or share his fate.

Shouts erupted—soldiers interrogating entertainers, from the words Jai could overhear. "They're close," Jai said, and he and Duphal hurried toward Striyn.

"Who was that woman staring at us?" Duphal asked.

"A friend," and a second twinge of pain wrenched Jai's heart when he realized that might no longer be true.

"WHERE Spine Street widens, we will find a side staircase that leads to another. That one ascends for a while, then becomes a ladder to the High Temple. The Captain will be there."

Duphal nodded, but his attention kept being snared at every new site they passed. "What was that room, with the orange smoke seeping out?"

"The Anointing room, where the seducers absorb perfume from Striyn."

"Ahhh," Duphal said, no doubt remembering, as Jai did, the heady fragrances from their lovemaking. Jai's body reacted to those memories, but he kept his focus, leading Duphal further into the snake-city.

They reached the first staircase and climbed without incident to Striyn's second level. The landing opened to a hall from which other hallways branched out at irregular intervals.

At the second staircase waited an old priest in stark white robes and a feathered necklace. With him stood two eunuch guards.

Jai clasped his hands and bowed. "I seek audience with the Captain." It unnerved him when the priest showed no surprise at what Jai assumed was a rare request.

"Your appeal is denied, young seducer."

"Forgive this humble servant, but it is a matter of—"

"All is known," said the priest, whose gaze shifted to Duphal, then back to Jai. "The holy city is here for converts, not runaways."

Jai was surprised when Duphal spoke up. "And if I choose to convert?" The words thrilled Jai's heart.

"If we do not return you, your father will declare war upon us. That cannot be allowed."

Jai gaped, and the light left Duphal's eyes. "How did—"

"All is known," the priest replied, and Jai knew at once that Honey had already foreseen this, had asked her father to convince the Captain not to help.

The priest signaled the guards with a raised finger. "It is unfortunate, but they must escort your lover back."

"No!" Jai shouted, but the guards acted swiftly. One gripped his wrist, meaty fingers like a thick manacle. The other struggled to restrain Duphal.

"Run!" Jai shouted, but Duphal made no attempt to flee.

Duphal struck the guard in the groin, but the intended effect was understandably muted against a eunuch.

Jai clapped his free hand against his captor's nose and released a concentrated cloud of Striyn's perfume. The guard's eyes rolled up, and he slipped to his knees in a euphoric trance.

Jai leapt, clawed at the second guard's face, and repeated the tactic, expelling all of the perfume still within him. The eunuch slumped back, lost in dreams he would never achieve.

"Surrender, young seducer," the priest said, his expression one of sorrow. "There is no place on Striyn you can hide."

The truth of the priest's words stung Jai, but every burning instinct pumped through his legs.

"This way!" he yelled to Duphal, who raced behind him down the hall.

Jai knew these hallways well enough, for there were long months when he had nothing else but time to explore Striyn. Alas, he doubted the guards knew them any less well.

He turned sharply at an intersection, Duphal's footsteps thudding close behind. A few turns and several ladders brought them to a long, thin bridge that spanned the eastern vivarium. The green scent of leaves and sharp spices tickled Jai's nose.

"Don't look down. You are not afraid of heights, are you?" A fall from the bridge could cripple, even kill, them.

Duphal's voice was tight. "No. Except in times of stress."

Jai could not tell if the jest was truth. "Focus on my back."

"It is a lovely back," he agreed.

Jai, nervous at Duphal's unexpected quips, kept the pace quick but steady. The bridge swayed, ever so slightly, with their steps. Jai could hear Duphal's nervous breathing, but their progress remained steady. When they were halfway across, stern voices called from below, commands full of anger and authority.

"Just gardeners," Jai said, hoping Duphal would believe him.

"I am sure. They sound very upset."

"We must hurry our pace. You live in a city of towering spires, surely this is not as high?"

"We do not have to walk such thin bridges between them!"

"I see the landing ahead. Here, I shall sing a song. Just repeat each line after me." Jai sang a tune he had learned from one of Striyn's belly rollers, and was relieved each time he heard Duphal, voice cracking and off-key, repeat the verses.

When they reached the other side, Duphal held him, tightly. Jai matched the strength of the embrace. "You are safe. You are safe with me."

"I know," Duphal said.

Though Jai wanted nothing more than to let Duphal rest, he knew the guards were already hurrying to head them off. "We must move on. We can cut through the artists' cabins, from there climb a ladder to get to Striyn's back. They will not expect that." Or so Jai hoped.

Duphal followed, silent now as they ran and climbed. Soon they were running in the open air, atop Striyn's scaled hide and down the snake-city's massive body. Above them the dewcatchers snapped and rippled in the wind. Jai's ears caught more shouts and arguments far below, and he knew the clash between soldiers and snake dwellers was escalating.

"Jai?"

He turned around and saw Duphal farther back than he thought. "Are you okay?"

"Jai. If I do not surrender, your people will find the armies of Ramsha'hla upon them."

"Striyn can defend itself."

"It sounds as though your Captain has already decided. Her guards here will find me eventually. Where are we even running to? There is nowhere to hide."

Jai realized with dread the direction they had been heading. But with the fear came the solution.

"There may be one place they will not look for us. The Long Road, where our dead are brought."

Duphal grew even paler than he had been on the bridge.

"They say it is governed by a man, the Warden of the Dead," Jai continued, "who is beyond even the Captain's orders. If we are granted sanctuary, the Captain will have no choice but to order Striyn away from here, and however fleet your horses, your army will not be able to catch our city." Of his statements, Jai was only certain about the last. For all he knew, the Warden of the Dead was but a legend.

"And if we are not granted sanctuary?"

Jai had no answers, or at least none he could bring himself to speak. "Then we will make our own escape," he said, and turned away.

A SECOND accessway allowed them entry back into Striyn. From there they found the wooden hallway that marked the Long Road. No adornments or writings decorated the walls, only plain wood resembling planks for coffins.

At one point, the passage took them between long side chambers. The doors to the rooms were of a dull black metal, engraved with snakes—or perhaps, Jai shuddered, worms.

"The Farewell Rooms," he explained. "Here the dead are prepared, and those left behind say their good-byes until they meet again."

The air thickened, the deeper they delved; the smell of dust and mildewed wood grew overpowering. Jai offered his hand, and Duphal took it. The only light sources were wall lanterns, and soon the distance between lanterns grew, forcing them to travel long stretches in darkness.

Soon, no lanterns appeared at all, and the two walked the dark for what seemed ages. "We've been moving a while now," Duphal said, the echo strangely cavelike. "Why have we not reached the end of your city?"

"It is said the Long Road is a place between worlds, and cannot be measured. Do not let the darkness consume your thoughts. Think of bright flowers and golden feathers. The shine and heat of sunlight." But even as he spoke, Jai found it a struggle to recall colors, as if the dark had erased even their concept.

Jai stopped when the wood beneath his feet became sand. The air felt water-thick, and he suffered a fleeting panic at the thought of drowning. He heard Duphal gasp at the change in their surroundings.

A disembodied voice shook the world around them.

"You should not be here."

The voice seemed to come from miles above them.

"Are you the Warden of the Dead?" Jai asked, his own voice sounding tiny. "I... we have come to ask for sanctuary."

"A boon your Captain denied. All is known. Would you turn the head of the snake against the tail?"

Jai swallowed. "If the head is blind, and the tail is deaf, then the snake only dooms itself."

The voice grew thunderous. "The living must not dwell here. Return whither you came, children of blood and light and flesh."

"If we do, we shall die," Jai cried.

"And then would I welcome you."

Jai felt the gentle squeeze of Duphal's hand, right before his veiled lover spoke. "Please. I was told your Goddess is one of love and second chances. We are in love. We wish to start anew."

Jai wanted nothing more than to kiss Duphal at that moment. "My lover speaks truth. We ask only what the Goddess has offered, the Goddess that we both serve."

The darkness was a whirlwind around them. Jai pressed close to Duphal, they pressed together, back to back.

The voice rang closer now, so close that if Jai reached out, he feared he would touch the speaker. "The only sanctuary I can grant does not come without price. Are you willing to shed your old lives, to lose your past for the sake of each other?"

Jai thought of his birthtown, of his aunt and cousins, but he had said good-bye to them a long time ago. He thought of Honeysmoke, of better times, of the love she might once have felt, now replaced by the fetters of her need.

He felt Duphal turn and embrace him. Their answer came together.

"*Yes.*"

The whirlwind about them sped ever faster, a shrill choir of voices, ripping at their clothes. A low, harsh light emanated from the very wind, and through squinting eyes, Jai saw that the sand below them was multicolored, like Honey's augury tray—pastels and deeper hues shifting, swirling around their ankles, their legs, their waists, higher and higher.

The vortex vanished so abruptly that they fell, still clutching each other, Jai draped upon Duphal.

"Where?" Jai asked, but his voice rebounded around them, remote as if calling back from some distant tomorrow.

"Look!" Duphal pointed to a tiny speckle of light. They got back on their feet and approached it cautiously. Soon, it became clear that the light's size was an illusion of perspective, its dimensions shrunk by distance.

A thin glow arose from the chromatic sands, and above, streaks of starlight blurred in the sky, as one might view them through tears. The sand pulled at their feet with a sucking sound, each step they took.

The trek felt endless at first, but soon Jai felt as if each step traversed impossible distances.

No, his heart told him. Not distances, but centuries. Slowly the speckle of light grew edges, filled out, until Jai could see the lines that described a doorway.

A prickle of fear itched his skin, and he wondered where the light might lead. When he looked behind him, only pitch darkness remained in his wake.

"Come," Duphal urged. "Let us not look back."

And then the doorway was seventy, then fifty, then thirty paces away. A gauzy shimmer obscured what was beyond, but Jai could make out figures spinning to exotic tunes, heard male laughter, inhaled the scent of grass wafting through, beckoning, the clean, fresh earth, ripe with promise.

"Wait," Duphal said. In a single swipe, he ripped away his veil.

Jai smiled, and thought he had never seen anything more divine.

"Now, I am ready," Duphal said.

And in one giant leap, hand in hand, they broke through the light to find a world undreamt of.

RODELLO SANTOS was abandoned as a baby in a New York Cineplex. He was raised by kind ushers who fed him overpriced Milk Duds and weaned him on butter-flavored topping. Despite this colorful childhood, he now lives a relatively boring existence working in human resources for a nonprofit agency. Nonprofit, by the way, is not a misnomer. Writing allows him to vent his excess quirkiness. His work fluctuates between dark and light-hearted fantasy with frequent visits throughout the speculative continuum. In 2008, he garnered an honorable mention in the *2008 Year's Best Fantasy and Horror* (Datlow, Link, and Grant). His more humorous stories can be found under the clever pseudonym "Rod M. Santos."

DAMON SHAW trained as an actor, his work winning both an Evening Standard and a Time Out award. He slipped into theater design, directing, and puppetmaking and was enjoying carving out a career as a designer when he abruptly fell in love with a Spaniard and moved to Lanzarote in the Canary Isles. Since then he has occasionally worked as a puppeteer and theater designer, but his attention has been focused on carpentry, cats, dogs, and domesticity.

He currently cares for his partner and runs a market stall where he sells his more-profitable wooden designs to the endless stream of passing tourists. He has invented a lunar tide clock, was commissioned to make a set of six-foot-tall wooden machines in the style of Leonardo Da Vinci, and most recently began to write short fiction.

He met Rod Santos in an online crit group called Liberty Hall. They have collaborated on two stories so far and hope to enjoy many more.

Visit Damon at http://damonshaw.livejournal.com/ or on Facebook as Damon Shaw.

Night and Day

Rowan Speedwell

THERE'S an address over the door, but no sign, and you might have just passed by except for the bouncer sitting out front. He's got a couple of battered crates piled in front of him and he's playing solitaire on them; you can hear the slap of the cards as you cross the street. It's Cerberus at the gate; he looks like a pair of extra heads would fit fine on that thick neck. In deference to the heat, he's wearing just an undershirt over his dark trousers, and a straw boater. He doesn't look up when you pause in front of him.

You flatten out the crumpled piece of paper in your hand and read the penciled address. It's the same as the one over the door, but the bouncer doesn't move, doesn't even acknowledge your presence. You don't blame him; you look just like all the other derelicts in town, and probably smell just as bad. Washing up in a public restroom sink doesn't do much for the problem, and you're wearing the same clothes you've had on for three days.

"Help you?" he finally asks, not looking up from his game.

You look down at the spread. He's already fanning out the three cards for the next draw but you say, "Black five on red six."

Now he glances up. "Say what?"

"Five of spades. Six of hearts. Then you can open up the stack with the four of diamonds."

"Huh," he says, and turns back to the spread. The move opens up what looks like a nice run, but he's polite enough to hold off on it to ask you again, "Can I help you?" The voice is less begrudging this time.

"I'm here about the job."

He frowns, shakes his head. "No jobs here, pal. They aren't hiring."

Your stomach wrenches and you say, falteringly, "But Harry said…."

This time he blinks before talking. "Harry sent you? Why dincha say so?" He frowns now, seeing you for the first time, seeing the battered brogans, the worn wool of the trousers, the jacket with the patched elbow. Slowly, he says, "Go on in, I guess. If Harry sent you. Rick's the one you gotta talk to." He shifts just far enough out of the way for you to squeeze through; you see his nostrils flare as he catches a whiff of you, but he says nothing, just turns back to his game.

Inside the first door is a small vestibule, hot and stuffy and probably why the bouncer's sitting outside. The door on the opposite side is dark-blue velvet, padded and tufted, and in each little tuft is a rhinestone, so the door sparkles like a night sky. It's pretty, and lush, and everything you don't have anymore. But there's a handle, and it opens, and you go inside the club.

The lights are on and the mystique of the nightclub is by day just tables and chairs and an empty bar. Ceiling fans circle slowly overhead, putting the ghost of a breeze in the air to cool it down. But the place isn't quite abandoned; over on the low dais of a stage is a piano, gleaming black and sleek, and a man is sitting slouched on the bench, noodling around on the keys. He's long and lanky and, like the bouncer, is wearing a tank-style undershirt, but it's over pin-striped slacks and he's got a striped tie looped and knotted loosely around his neck. He's wearing a fedora and has an unlit cigarette stuck to his bottom lip. As you watch, he leans forward and makes a notation on the sheet music in front of him, then goes back to his noodling. Another moment, another notation, and he leans back and tilts the fedora back from his face and you get a good look at him. He's young, you think, and handsome; clean-shaven, the way you like, and with a face that looks like it enjoys smiling.

You make some movement, some reaction, and he notices you. One dark eyebrow lifts and a grin spreads across the wide, mobile mouth. He takes the cigarette out and drops it in an ashtray on the piano, then says, "Didn't see you come in."

"I'm here about the job," you say again. You're feeling even less confident than you were before you stepped through the door.

The eyebrow lifts again and he says, "The singer?"

You flush, and mutter, "Harry sent me. He said you'd give a listen. That's all I want, is someone to listen."

"Baby, that's all any of us want," the man says. He rises and slouches over toward you. You wonder if he's capable of standing upright, then realize that he's very tall, probably six-four or six-five—he probably slumps so he's at eye level for normal people. You don't think you've met anyone that tall before. "I'm Rick Bellevue. I own this place."

"Nathan Pederowski," you say. He holds out a hand for you to shake; conscious of the embedded grime in your skin, you do so gingerly. He doesn't seem to notice, just keeps hold of your hand and tugs you toward the stage. "Let's hear what you got. What kind of stuff you like to sing?"

"What kind of stuff do you like to hear?" you shoot back. You immediately kick yourself mentally; smart-ass shit isn't going to feed you when the guy kicks you out.

But he's laughing and saying, "Practically everything, but for now let's stick to recent stuff. You know 'Night and Day'?"

"Who doesn't?" you retort. He grins again and plops down on the bench, running through the opening bars of the Cole Porter song. You listen a moment. It's in the right key, and you close your eyes, letting the music roll you like a street kid rolling a drunk. "Like the beat-beat-beat of the tom-toms, when the jungle shadows fall…." The intro comes out like a Gregorian chant, mystical and religious, and when you swing into the first chorus it's like bells chiming on Christmas. "Night and day, you are the one…."

Once you're in the music, you can open your eyes, but you don't see anything; you're blind with love and passion. It's as pure as a homecoming, as hot as sex; it's everything you need and have lost and found again. "And this torment won't be through, 'til I spend my life making love to you, day and night, night and day…." You let the passion burn through you until there's nothing left, and the notes of the song drain from you whatever has been keeping you on your feet for the last three days.

You fall back against the piano, but there's so little left of you it doesn't even shift; instead it holds you while you slide down the polished leg onto the floor. You sit, numb, blank, empty.

"Zeus fuck!" Rick says as he drops from the bench to kneel beside you.

"Richard," a woman's voice says reprovingly, and then, "When was the last time you ate, Nathan?"

"I don't remember," you admit. "I ate at a soup kitchen a day or two ago, but it made me sick, so I didn't go back." You look up but can't see faces; things are gray around the edges and there's a buzzing noise in your head.

Something presses against your lip and you open obediently, like a baby bird. Sweet warmth flows in; you swallow and recognize coffee, loaded with milk and sugar. Too much sugar; it makes you gag. "Sweet," you manage to say.

"You need sugar, and probably salt," the woman's voice says practically. "Richard, go have Mario make up a bowl of soup for Nathan."

The coffee is foul, but it works; the buzzing goes away and your vision clears. The woman is holding the cup to your mouth again and you swallow. She puts the cup on the floor beside you and straightens, looking down on you. "Better?"

"Yes," you respond, wiping your palms nervously on the thighs of your filthy trousers. She makes you too aware of your unwashed state. Women like her don't need to be in the company of bums like you. You wonder why she hasn't thrown you out already.

She brushes an invisible lock of hair back behind her ear. It's blonde, paler than blonde, almost white, and is tucked up in a neat chignon. She's wearing a navy suit, silk stockings, and heels, and the jewels sparkling in her ears are probably real diamonds. A class act. Beautiful, too, as you understand those things. Her face wouldn't be out of place in a painting, and not those weird ones you saw in Paris twelve years ago. "Your singing is spectacular," she says, her voice still that practical, matter-of-fact tone. "Why haven't we heard of you before now?"

"I haven't sung professionally before," you say stiffly, knowing that it doesn't matter how good you sing. There are other elements to performance, and both stage presence and name mean a lot. The stage presence you think you can remember from the conservatory and your lessons, but both were a long time ago. The name means nothing.

"Here, Coco," Rick says, and sets the tray on a nearby table. He reaches down and pulls you to your feet. You stagger a little and he slips his arm around your waist to support you. It feels so good, just the touch of a hand, an arm, an embrace, no matter how impersonal. He leads you to the table and sits you down in one of the chairs, then pulls one out for the woman. Only after she is settled does he sit down and push the tray in your direction. "Eat up."

You glance uncertainly at the woman, not sure if it's rude to eat in front of her.

She smiles back. "Go ahead. I'm Corinna Bellevue, by the way, Richard's sister. I co-own this club. I'm used to people eating in my presence, believe me. Besides, Richard and I have both had lunch, and you haven't. Richard, I would like a drink, though."

"Coffee?"

"That would be fine."

He disappears, but you're too deep in the bowl of soup to notice where. The soup is chicken, rich and thick with cream and vegetables, almost more of a stew. You try to keep from gobbling it, but the spoon doesn't hold enough and you can't move fast enough to get it all down.

A basket of bread and a dish of butter pats appears beside your plate and you pause in the soup-slurping to butter a piece of the still-warm bread. It melts in your mouth, and you let out an involuntary groan of pleasure.

"Beautiful," Rick says behind you, and sets a coffee service on the table before pouring himself and his sister each a cup. He sets a tall glass of ice water next to you. "Mario's a good cook."

He could be the world's worst cook for all you care, but he isn't. The soup is delicious, the bread equally so. When you can breathe and think and talk again, you say so, and Rick grins in pleasure. "I'll tell him," he says. "Especially about the orgasmic groan."

"Nathan," Corinna says, ignoring his rude comment, "there are a few things we need to go over before we sign any sort of contract."

You've just put a piece of chicken in your mouth; you freeze a moment, then chew it carefully, letting her words sink in. A "contract"? Does that mean you're hired? Or is she just talking generalities? You swallow and nod.

"First of all, the Starlight Lounge is a private club. This means that no one comes through the door unless they're a member or are an approved guest of a member. We're careful to maintain good relations with the public and the police, but there is no advertising, no publicity. We don't need it. Membership is carefully vetted, and potential members must be recommended by an existing member. Therefore, the club is a safe place for all kinds of people—and you will see all kinds of people here. Some of them may surprise you, but we don't ever want our members to feel uncomfortable, so if you can't accept people as they are, you may want to reconsider employment here."

"I'm not in a position to judge people," you say bitterly.

"Secondly," she continues, nodding, "do you drink?"

You look down at your hands. The nails are filthy. "No," you say, "not anymore."

"Will working around alcohol present a problem?"

"No. I'm not a drunk. I don't even like the taste of booze. I used to drink because everyone did, but I don't miss it." It's true enough, as it is. You don't tell them about Bertie. It doesn't matter anyway. That was a long time ago.

"Very good. Coffee and tea are always available at the bar. This time of year we also stock lemonade, and there's a fountain for soft drinks. The club serves food until eleven p.m., and is open until two. You'll do two sets a night, from nine to ten and eleven to midnight. From twelve to two the regular band does instrumental work. You're at liberty to continue with the band, of course, if you and they agree. Any tips outside your regular sets will be split with them. Tips during your sets are yours in their entirety. You're entitled to dinner here, and if for any reason we need you in during the day, lunch then as well."

"During the day?" You frown. What if you got a day job? Then you wonder: *Why are you so concerned about a day job when you haven't had one for months?* All you need is enough to pay that rat bastard of a landlord so you can get your room and your traps back. The pay for two hours a night wouldn't be much, but there was that promise of tips too.

"Yes. We sometimes have private parties during the day that involve entertainment, usually things like wedding showers and business luncheons. Those occasionally will involve outsiders. After six, it's members only. But on those occasions you'll receive overtime pay, plus your lunch. We may also occasionally require your presence at meetings or to work out some new element of the entertainment."

"I'm a little confused," you admit. "You've only heard one song. All the other auditions I've gone on, they've asked for three or four at the very least."

"We only needed one," Rick says. He's been quiet during his sister's commentary, leaning back in his chair and watching you. You've known that, although your surface attention has been on Corinna. His watchfulness has been a bug on the back of your neck. "The Starlight needs certain people. She knew you when you came in the door. The rest is just window-dressing."

"Ignore him," Corinna says. "He's fanciful. If you'd like to do a few more songs, be my guest. We're both relatively sure that you're what we're looking for, but if you'd be more comfortable with our decision after you've shown us a little more of what you can do, then by all means. Finish your lunch, first."

A thought occurs to you. "You said 'all kinds of people'. Are you talking about, what—politicians? Gangsters?"

Corinna laughs. "Oh, a few of each, but not too many. We're not connected. No, the kind of people who come here are just not the kind you'll see at other clubs around the city. Not all of them are rich, for one thing. For another thing," she leans forward, her hands on the table, "we don't separate people based on their skin color or ancestry. You'll see Negroes, or Orientals, or Mexicans here."

"And queers," Rick said with a grin. "We have queers, too."

There's a rushing sound in your head and you put it down on the table. A cool hand lights gently on the back of your neck. "It's all right, Nathan. No one will judge you here."

"How the hell did I end up here?" you murmur.

"Because you belong here," Rick says.

Corinna's fingers are slim, but strong, and they knead the tension out of your neck. "Harry sent you," she says, "because he knew we were looking for a male singer who would fit in with our clientele. Who are not the usual run of people, but are still people, and who still deserve a place where they can enjoy themselves and feel safe. You'll see mixed race couples, and yes, homosexuals, and occasionally cripples who love the music even if they can't dance, or can only dance awkwardly. Other places would turn them away, or only let them in to laugh at them. Starlight's not like that."

You don't lift your head until you hear Rick at the piano again. He's playing "I Surrender, Dear" and it makes you laugh even when you really want to cry. "I keep waiting for the punch line," you say, and stand up.

And the roaring sound is back, and then, nothing.

WHEN you finally open your eyes, you're someplace else. You're not sure where—it's not the dingy little one-room apartment you were locked out of three days ago, but it's not the airy room you'd once had at your folks' house either. It's small, but clean, and there's a window fan purring along happily. There are no water marks in the ceiling, it doesn't smell like mildew, and the bed is comfortable.

"It wakes," Rick's voice says, and you look over to see him in a chair, tilted back against the wall on its back legs, his fedora over his eyes.

"How did you know?" you ask curiously.

"Shift of the bed springs, change in your breathing. I'm a musician. I notice sounds." His voice is low and lazy, an odd contrast to his sister's crisp, businesslike tones. "Coco deals with the business end, I deal with the artists. We both deal with the drunks. Dealing with the collapsible is a new one, but I'm the one with the muscles, so Butch and I won the draw. We're upstairs of the club."

You sit up and swing your legs over the side of the bed. You're in stocking feet; your battered shoes are set on the floor beside the wooden dresser. Your head aches, but you feel more stable than you have for twenty-four hours. "Thanks," you say, feeling it's inadequate.

Then you notice the tan suitcase by the door. "That's my suitcase," you say stupidly.

"Yeah. There was a late-payment notice in your coat pocket and Butch went down to deal with it. He said the place was a dump, so he packed up all your stuff and brought it back with him. You can stay here until you find a better place. Unless you *liked* that one?" Rick's voice turns suddenly uncertain.

"Hell, no," you assure him. "But I can't stay here. It's not right." You go to stand up, but you lose your balance and sit down hard.

"Easy, baby," Rick says. He drops the legs of the chair onto the floor and comes over to sit down beside you. "You're pretty messed up, Coco says. Been too long without food."

You put your face in your hands. Your elbows feel like blades on your knees: sharp and mean. "It was either eat or pay rent," you say wearily, "and so rent it was, until there wasn't anything left. I tried to find work, but there's nothing. I didn't know what to do. One of the guys where I applied for work saw that I had voice training and gave me Harry's address." You look up then and you know your expression is fierce, and so is your voice. "I can't stay here," you say. "I don't take charity."

Rick isn't offended. He snorts in amusement. "This ain't charity, baby. This is an investment."

It's your turn to snort. "Investment in what? Yeah, I have a voice, and I'll work hard to entertain your guests. But unless you do professional management on the side and have an in with some record company, that's all I'll do for you. It's not like you seem to even want to bring in more business, what with your 'nobody but members and vetted guests of members' baloney."

"And if we did want to manage your career?"

"What career? Harry's a manager and he sent me to you. So I guess he doesn't think I have much to offer him, anyway."

Rick drapes an arm over your shoulder. He means it comradely; he can't know what it means for you to be touched like that, like a human being. It's weight and warmth and comfort all at once. "He knows you need experience, Nate. You could be the next what's-his-name, the Crosby kid, but Gary Conservatory or not, you don't have the background in performance you need to get anywhere in this business. You'll get that experience here. And it'll be experience like anywhere else—just 'cause we're a private club doesn't mean we don't have problems with drunks and hecklers and asses. We get the occasional fight here, even. And melodrama—God, do we get melodrama. You'll see."

He gives a gentle squeeze to your shoulders and stands up. "In the meantime, Coco wants you to come down and see what you're up against. You won't perform tonight. Tomorrow, if you're feeling up to it. Tonight, though, you come down for dinner, you schmooze with the clientele, you get introduced around. If you feel like it—and only if you feel like it—you can sing a song or two with the band, just to get the sense of it."

"I don't have anything to wear...." You're starting to feel panicked.

"God, you sound like a woman." Rick is laughing. "There's a monkey suit in the closet. It's mine, so it'll be a bit big on you, but if you come downstairs early enough we'll have one of the girls stitch up the pants hems. I'm a giraffe." He points at a door I didn't notice before. "That's the bathroom; there's towels and that sort of thing in there for you to use. I'll bet a dollar to a doughnut you'll feel better after a shower."

"Oh, my God," you say with feeling. "A *shower*...!"

He laughs again, then bends down and gives you a quick kiss. His lips are warm and firm on yours, but gone too quickly; he's halfway across the room before you even realize what's happened. "Come down in an hour or so," he calls as he leaves. "For dinner."

And he's gone, and you're left in the empty room, your mouth tingling from the kiss and the shower waiting. A shower. You feel the grin spreading on your face and get up, slowly this time, so you don't go all dizzy again, and find your way into the bathroom. It's beautiful: white and clean and equipped with fluffy white towels and soap and a razor. The water is hot and, despite the heat of the day, feels wonderful. You stand under the stream, scrubbing, until the water that sluices down your body isn't brown anymore, and then you do it again, just for the luxury of it. You wash your hair twice for the same reason, and when you step out to shave, you're wrapped in a towel so thick you're dry almost before you get your face soaped up. The blade is sharp and cleans your whiskers so well you can't even feel it, and when you're done, the face that stares back at you from the mirror is ten years younger. It's thin, with cheekbones like knife blades, and the eyes are too large and too deep-set, but it's your face again. You run your hand over your smooth cheek, and smile.

The "monkey suit" is a tuxedo, with a black cummerbund and a pleated shirt. The shirt's too big, but the cummerbund's adjustable, so you fix it so they both lie neatly before shrugging into the jacket. Not much you can do about the fit of that. There are black silk socks and garters folded on top of a pair of black dress shoes, so you put those on too, and then the tuxedo trousers. The pants are long, so you turn up the cuffs until you meet the girl who's supposed to fix them, and slide your feet into the shoes. They fit. When you look at the man in the mirror over the dresser, you almost don't recognize him. Then you run your hand through your hair in your habitual gesture, and the locks fall into place, and it's you again. You need a haircut.

DOWNSTAIRS, the place is no longer empty and cavernous. Instead, a half a dozen waiters in black and white scurry around, setting tables; another half-dozen waitresses are folding napkins that the waiters snatch up as soon as they are finished. Three bartenders are sorting through the bottles and glasses, and a trio is setting up on the dais, drums and a bass joining the piano. You had wondered if Rick ever stood straight; now you see he does. He's tall and elegant as he gives directions to a pair of cigarette girls. He's wearing white tie and tails; his dark hair is brushed back from his forehead and brilliantined, making him look like a film star, but a stray curl dips over his brow, giving him a rakish look. He's beautiful as he laughs at something one of the girls says, and you know you're in trouble. You know from bitter experience that just because a man kisses you, it doesn't necessarily mean he's queer. Some men are just ebullient. But Rick doesn't strike you that way; he's too laconic and deliberate.

Corinna comes in and she's beautiful too, but where Rick is earth and fire, she's all air and ice. Her gown is white and glitters faintly in the light; she's so pale the white should wash her out, but it doesn't, it only makes her look like a snow princess. The hair is up again, but more softly, and a spray of more of those diamonds is clipped to the side of her head. The men in the room all look at her as she enters; you can almost hear their sighs.

She's beautiful, but not your kind of beauty. Your eyes go again to Rick, in his black cutaway and white waistcoat, sleek and elegant and powerful, so different from when you first saw him this afternoon. Only to find that he is looking back at you, his dark eyes unreadable.

Then he smiles, and the moment's gone, and he's walking across the club to the stairs you've just come down, holding out his hand for you to shake. "You look great," he says. "The jacket's a bit big, but only if you know to look."

"The pants need hemming," you say. He doesn't release your hand right away but stands smiling at you just a moment too long. Then he's taking your elbow and steering you toward a table. He pushes you gently into a chair and gestures; a young woman in a waitress uniform comes over with a sewing kit in her hand. "This is Billie," Rick says, "our costumer."

She snorts inelegantly and pulls out another chair, setting it between the two of you. "Here," she says, patting the seat, "put your tootsies up here and I'll fix those hems."

You obey, and while she's tacking up the hem, she's talking a blue streak to Rick about her boyfriend, the weather, the state of the Union, her landlord, her landlord's Pomeranian, and an argument overheard on the streetcar. After a while you tune her out; her voice is just background music to the hum and clatter of the club getting ready to open.

"…think he's asleep," she says, and you open your eyes and look at her.

"Who, me?" you ask, and she and Rick laugh. You hadn't even registered when she'd had you switch legs, but now you do remember it, vaguely, and she picks up her sewing kit and trots off toward what Rick informs you is the employee lounge.

"Ready for introductions?" Then he pauses and asks, "You crazy about your name?"

"Nathan?" you ask in puzzlement.

"No. The Pederowski part."

"You want to change it to something like 'Peters'?" That would be okay; I went by "Peters" for a while when I was trying to make it in New York.

"Nah, nothing so banal. I'm thinking something like 'Petroff,' something a little more exotic. You got cheekbones sharp enough to slice, and those dark eyes. You look Russian."

"I probably am, somewhere back a ways," you admit. "Polish, Lithuanian, Scottish... a regular Heinz 57, me."

"So 'Petroff' or 'Pedrov' or something? Coco?"

She comes across the room, gliding.

"What do you think about Nathan Petroff?"

Oddly enough, she seems to know what he's talking about. I get the feeling he's like this all the time and she's just used to translating. "I like it," she says decisively. "It suits him, and it's more marketable than plain Nathan Pederowski. It won't bother your family?"

"Ma'am," you say bitterly, "I haven't got any family to be bothered."

"You do now," she says matter-of-factly and glides away.

You're breathless with shock, staring after her. Then there's a hand on your back and Rick's voice in your ear. "It'll be okay, Nate. Now, let's get you some supper."

Over her shoulder, Corinna calls, "I had them set your meal in the office; go over the details and have him sign the contract, Richard. We're too busy out here."

"Oh, right," Rick says, and he moves his hand down to the small of your back, not quite pushing, but guiding you back to the stairs and up to the first landing. There's a door there marked "Office," and he edges you in. It's like Corinna, all white and polished and elegant, with silvery metal and white leather. The desk is silver metal and glass. Even the phone is white.

But the food that sits on the glass table in the corner is steak and red boiled potatoes with parsley and fresh green beans, and the smell is overwhelming. You close your eyes a moment, just inhaling.

Rick says, "God, will you *stop* that?"

You blink. "I'm sorry," you say, confused. "Stop what?"

"Stop *lusting* like that. You look like you're about to come."

You flush, embarrassed. "Oh, Jesus," you swear. "I'm sorry. I don't mean…."

"It's okay. No, well, it's not okay, but it's not your fault. Sorry." For the first time since you've met him, Rick seems at a loss. He shakes his head, and then says, "Siddown. Eat. I'll talk, then when we're done eating, we'll sign the papers."

"What papers?"

"The contract. It's standard boilerplate for performers." Rick gestures for you to sit down, and you do. The meals are already plated, with sprigs of parsley for decoration; a far cry from the unidentifiable gray mass you'd tried to eat at the soup kitchen. And it's delicious—the steak rare, the beans crisp, and the potatoes buttery and just-soft-enough. "With the exception of a privacy clause. You have to agree not to talk about the club to anyone. All interviews, questions, inquiries, anything like that comes directly to me or Coco. For convenience, we also ask that you don't take any job outside the club without clearing it with me or Coco." He gives a quick grin as he takes a bite of steak. "We'd *prefer* that you don't take any job outside the club, but some people have extra expenses."

"I'd thought to get a day job," you admit, "for security, you know. I mean, I'm not stupid. I know that these gigs don't always work out, and I want to find someplace, I mean, someplace nice to live, and two hours a night, even with tips, won't cover that, and…."

He reaches out with his fork and touches the tines gently to the back of your hand. You stop talking. "If what we're paying you doesn't pay for a nice apartment," he says levelly, "then your standards of 'nice' are a helluva lot higher than mine. And as for the security—this is a *contract*, Nate. We're asking you to commit to us for three years. At the end of that time we expect you to move up in life, not down. You'll leave here with a recording contract, a nice nest egg, or not at all."

"*Why*?" Your cry is heartfelt and confused. This can't be right. This can't be happening, not after everything you've been through. You're too used to being on the bottom for this to even make *sense*. "What do you get out of this?"

"Are you kidding? Baby, when you sing, you make *magic*." He takes the fork from your hand and drags you to your feet. "Leave this a minute; we'll come back when we're done. Come on." And he drags you out the door by the hand, down the stairs, and up onto the dais.

The musicians look up curiously. "Remmy, Jake, Rob, this is Nate. He's the singer. He's gonna sing right now." He looks in your eyes. "Nate, I need you to sing for these guys. For us. Before the customers come in, just us, right now. Can you do this?"

You blink, dazed, and nod.

"What do you want to sing?"

The words come out of your mouth without you thinking them. "'But Not for Me'," you say.

Rick snorts, and then says, "Okay. Guys, you know that one?"

"Gershwin, right?" The guy at the piano plunks out a few notes. You nod. He starts playing the intro and you start.

"Old man Sunshine, listen you; never tell me dreams come true. You try it, and I'll start a riot. Beatrice Fairfax, don't you dare try to tell me she will care; I'm certain it's the final curtain. Don't want to hear from any cheerful Pollyannas, who tell me love will find a way—it's all *bananas*."

You're angry now, at Rick's high-handedness, at this lovely dream of a possibility that can't possibly be real, at this vision of what life could be like, and the venom comes out in your voice.

"They're playing songs of love—*but not for me….*"

Your gaze is basilisk-like, locked on Rick's startled dark eyes, holding him paralyzed with your anger, your voice, your music.

You're vaguely aware that the others in the room have stopped moving too, but it doesn't matter. Nothing matters but the beautiful man standing in front of you that you know you can't have, no matter how kind he is; he's so far out of your orbit he might as well be that film star he looks like. Or a real star, somewhere up in the night sky, scintillating and lovely and untouchable. Even if there were a chance he might want you, you know he'd grow bored and move on—you have nothing to offer such a bright being. And having once had him, to lose him would be unbearable.

"It all began so well, but what an end. This is the time a fella needs a friend—when every happy plot ends in a marriage knot, and there's no knot for me."

Anger dismissed by loss, you try to make him understand the ending words of the song, make him understand you.

When you finish, there's silence in the room, and you're as drained and exhausted as if you'd never had the lunch or the nap or the half-eaten steak dinner upstairs. The applause and whistles come as a surprise, and you look up, confused.

Only Rick is still, unmoving, his expression shattered. You stare at him until your eyes get blurry, then you step off the dais, push past him, heading for the stairs and your suitcase, desperate to get out of your borrowed finery, your borrowed life, into your own filthy clothes, away from here, away from him.

He catches you up halfway to the stairs, his fingers hard on your upper arm. He jerks you around and his other hand grabs your other arm, so that he's holding you still. "Where are you going?" he snaps.

You can't answer. You don't know. His face is dark with rage, flushed and angry and hurt. You didn't mean to hurt him, you only wanted to push him away, to save yourself the grief you knew was coming.

The tears spill over then, and you curse yourself and you curse him, and you curse God for making you like this, and for taking everything away from you so that you have nothing to offer this man, *nothing*. But the only thing that comes out of your mouth is his name.

"Rick…."

And then his mouth is on yours, and it's not the friendly peck he'd given you earlier. No, this is a kiss, hot and hard and hungry, and hands dragging you into an embrace that's less about affection or comfort and more about need. This is lust. This is heat. This is desire.

And God save you, you reach for him with both hands, digging into his brilliantined hair, yanking him down and kissing him back just as hard as he kissed you.

In front of a room full of witnesses. In front of his *sister*.

Who, when you come up for breath, dazed and lost and aching, says, "Now that you've gotten that out of your systems, will you sign the damn contract so that I can put you on the payroll?"

And Rick throws his head back and bellows with laughter. "It's not just me," he tells you. "It's *her*. And she gets what she wants." He turns you around so that you're facing the room, the wait staff and the cigarette girls and the bartenders and the band. His body is solid and warm behind you. "Look at them," he whispers in your ear.

White flutters all around the room as people wipe their eyes or blow their noses. A waitress sobs into the breast of one of the waiters. Two other waitresses are weeping on each other's shoulders. "One little song," Rick murmurs. "One little song—not even a long one—and they're yours. You made them cry. You made them feel. I haven't seen magic like that since, since *Orpheus*."

You know who Orpheus is, but the classical reference confuses you. "I thought he played the lute," you say.

"The lyre."

"Right. He wasn't a singer, was he?"

He snorts. "Yeah, he was, but what's the difference? He made magic. So do you. Zeus fuck, baby, why the hell hasn't anyone seen that before?" His hands are on your shoulders, squeezing. "Now do you see why we want you? Why all it took was one song for us to know you belonged here?"

You shake your head. When he turns you back toward the stairs and takes you back up to the office, you obey blindly, too tired to argue.

He sits you back down at the table and makes you finish eating before taking out the papers to look over. You think maybe you should have a lawyer look at them, but you can't afford a lawyer, and don't know any anyway. Still, they seem pretty straightforward, no small print, no confusing lawyerly language. No more complex than a lease, or the application forms you filled out at Harry's. A thought occurs to you. "How did you know about the Gary Conservatory?" you ask. It's the first thing out of your mouth since the scene downstairs.

"What?"

"The Gary Conservatory. You mentioned it."

“Oh, yeah. While you were napping, I rang Harry and asked him to send over the stuff you gave him. Your education was in there.” He’s quiet a moment, then says, “You’re older than you look.”

“Is that a problem?” You give him a level look.

“No, not at all.” He shrugs. “I’d have pegged you at late twenties, but thirty-five isn’t exactly old.” He folds some papers back into an envelope before going on. “I was surprised to see your war record.”

“Why?” you ask. You can’t quite keep the bitterness out of your voice. “You figure because I’m queer I’m a coward as well?”

His laugh is low and humorless. “No. Not that you were a soldier. But that you served for over two years, won half a dozen medals, and still got a dishonorable discharge.”

“That’s what they do with queers,” you say shortly. “I went in with the Brits in ’16, but when the Yanks got in the next year, I transferred over to an American battalion. Should have stayed with the Brits.”

“Why didn’t you?”

“Long story.” You don’t want to tell it; don’t want to even think about it. So instead you grab the fancy fountain pen and scrawl your signature recklessly across the bottom of the contract. “There. You’ve got me—I’m yours for three years.” You cap the pen carefully before tossing it back across the table to him; even angry, you can’t bring yourself to mar the virginal whiteness of the room. “What next?”

“Well, you get the grand tour. Since Roosevelt signed the Cullen-Harrison Act this spring, we can officially sell 3.2 beer and what Coco refers to as ‘the ghosts of grapes’. Of course, that’s only officially.” He stands, and you follow suit. “Leave the dishes; someone will clean up in here.”

You follow him downstairs. Corinna comes up and regards the two of you with a raised brow, eerily like her brother despite the difference in coloring. “Contract is signed, Coco,” Rick says, “and Orpheus is ours.”

“‘Orpheus’,” she echoes thoughtfully. “The lamenter, he of the darkness, the orphan. The singer of magic. Acolyte to Dionysus and Apollo. Dionysus, in jealousy, had him murdered by maenads.” She muses a moment, then adds, “I’m not sure if he was jealous of Orpheus’s talent or his love for Apollo.”

“I know which I’d wish for,” Rick says.

She gives him that raised-eyebrow look and retorts, "Murdered is murdered, whatever the cause. And afterward there is only vengeance left."

She's sweet, and delicate, and fairylike, and the words in her angelic voice freeze you to your bones.

"He's here, and he's ours," Rick says, "and nobody's going to murder him for whatever reason. Unless you have enemies we don't know about?"

This question is directed to you, and you shake your head. "No one," you say, "only…" *Bertie* "…one, and he's not an enemy, just… no longer a friend. No enemies, no friends, no family. Footloose and fancy-free."

"Not anymore," Rick says. "You have a contract, and we've got you. Come on."

He shows you the rest of the place: where they hide the good booze if they get raided (The place used to be a speakeasy, until the spring; then they turned it into a legal supper club to take advantage of the easing of the Volstead Act. Rick tells you Prohibition will be repealed by the end of the year. He's so certain you almost believe him); the room in the back where the games are (All straight, even the roulette wheel; Rick tells you Corinna has an obsession with justice, and while she's not above breaking the law, she won't cheat an honest man); the fiery kitchen with the dark-browed Mario in command (He has a clubfoot but that doesn't slow him down; his knife flashes in the dim, steamy heat, the fires under his pots giving the place the reddish glow of a furnace. Or maybe Hell. But it's a well-organized Hell; his assistants are quick and sure and seem to almost read his mind. It could just be fear of his knife. You don't think you've ever seen one as long that wasn't stuck on the end of a rifle).

Rick takes you through the kitchen out to the alley, where he lights up a cigarette and stares at the sky. It's coming on dusk now; you can hear the sound of automobiles out front as they disgorge the early arrivals. He stares at the west, where the sun is already out of sight, the clouds gone purple and rose and gold against a sky going indigo. "And so it ends, and begins," he says softly, and turns his back on the sunset. "There's the moon. She's almost full tonight."

You don't look. How many nights did you and Bertie gaze up at her beautiful serene face from the filth of the trenches, lying close in mud, watching the moon rise behind the forward emplacements? There were moments then when you didn't mind the mud, didn't mind the sound of the guns, didn't mind the stench or the cold or the wet. Moments when Bertie's hand would touch yours, trailing a finger across your wrist; or when he'd shift so his hip brushed yours, or his shoulder. And you knew that later you and he would be crawling into an empty, abandoned side trench, trying to find a dry spot where you could fuck each other in hurried silence under that same moon, sometimes not even unbuttoning your damp wool uniforms, just rubbing up against each other, the only skin that touched being your hands and your mouths.

"Oh, well," Rick says quietly, "I like the daylight better myself." And he opens the door and you go back inside.

WHEN you wake it's still dark, and you lie in silence and confusion, not sure where you are. Then you remember, and stretch luxuriously in the clean sheets, in the clean if threadbare nightshirt you'd pulled from your suitcase. You can't have gotten more than a couple of hours of sleep, but you're as rested as if you'd slept for days; it's not a challenge to rise and go to look out the open window. It faces east, and while it's not quite dawn, there's a lightening of the sky that matches the lightening of your mood.

You're staring at the dark sky when you hear the footsteps in the hall, going past your door: quick, but not running. Curious, you go to the door and open it and look out into the corridor, but all you see is a flash of dark cloth in the dim light of the wall sconce by the stairs. Dark brown, maybe, or purple; you'd bet purple because you have a suspicion of who it is, and he's just the sort to wear a purple silk dressing gown. Not a robe. A dressing gown.

And it's not quite a suspicion, but more of an instinct. Your body thrums like a sympathetic tuning fork when he's near, just as it did with Bertie.

You let the door close quietly behind you and follow him, up the stairs instead of down, to a door that stands open against a sky still spattered with stars. Silently you creep up the stairs and stand looking out the door at him. He has his back to you, his face turned toward the paler sky in the east, his feet bare on the tarpaper of the flat roof. There is nothing else here, just the furnace chimney and the low, dingy brick walls that frame the roof. Just him, and you, and the dawn sky.

The first edge of sunlight creeps over the horizon, and he drops the dressing gown, letting it slither down his body to lay in a tumble at his feet. Your breath goes still in your chest.

He stretches his arms out as if he is basking in the watery light. His shoulders are taut with muscle, his arms long and strong, his lean back leading down into a dimpled firm bottom and long, powerful thighs and legs. He is completely nude, standing with his arms spread like a king, like a sacrifice, his head thrown back. In the dark of the club, his hair looks black, but now you see that it's brown and bronze, and the sunlight as it moves across the roof raises sparks of red and copper. And it's long, down to his shoulder blades—it hadn't been that long last night, certainly not. It fits him, somehow; not Rick the club owner, lazy and laughing, but this creature, this king, this worshipper.

And then he begins to glow. First a soft, subtle gilding of his skin that makes no sense; he should be dark and silhouetted against the sun, but he is golden, glowing. Brighter and brighter he shines until the sun has cleared the city horizon, and by then he is incandescent. And finally, light explodes around him, white and painful and glorious.

When you open your eyes again you are back in your bed, and it's only the ceiling that you see, this time in the pale light of very early morning. You blink, confused, and then realize you must have dreamed going up on the roof, dreamed seeing Rick shining like an arc light, taking in the sun as if it were sustenance.

There's a light knock on the door and Rick himself sticks his head into the room. "You're up," he says in surprise. "Thought you'd still be asleep. You were dead on your feet when you came up last night."

"I'm awake," you acknowledge. "And I feel fine. Hungry."

"Throw some clothes on and I'll meet you downstairs in ten minutes. Mario doesn't come in until noon, but I know a place not too far away that makes an excellent breakfast. Coco's still asleep; she loathes mornings, so I don't often have company." Then he's gone, the door closing with a quiet click.

You get up and go to the closet, to find that some kind brownie has cleaned and pressed your shabby clothes and hung them up on the rod beside a handful of Arrow shirts in your size, and fine wool trousers folded over pants hangers. There is a white linen suit hooked on the back of the closet door with a note pinned to the lapel that reads, "Wear Me." It makes you laugh, but it would look stupid with your battered black lace-up shoes, so you reach instead for your second-best trousers, your first-best having been the wool ones you wore for three straight days and never want to wear again. But there is a pair of white and cream shoes on the floor of the closet beside your brogans, and you crumble to the silent pressure of the Bellevues' generosity and your own desperate need to look good for Rick. A five-minute shower and shave and a brush of your teeth with the new toothbrush in the glass, a quick process of dressing in new clothes from the skin out, and you're only a minute late meeting Rick.

He's waiting by the front door of the club, a straw fedora on his head and another in his hand. He tosses it to you and you put it on. "Ready?" he says.

"Yes. Thank you. For the clothes and things. And the bed. And…."

He laughs, and opens the door. "Consider it—"

"An investment," you finish for him. "Yes. But I'm still grateful."

There's a car waiting at the curb, a beautiful golden Lincoln Model K, with its low, sweeping lines. The interior is white leather, and it occurs to you that the Bellevues must have their fingers in more pots than just a little supper club that caters to oddball types. And the people you met last night were oddballs, all right, not just in their social or racial or physical characteristics, but something much deeper, much less clear. You're not quite sure what it is, but you push it to the back of your skull to cogitate on later, when you have the inclination.

For now, you want to enjoy this moment, the ride in a sleek, high-powered car beside a sleek, high-powered man, on a cool, clear morning with empty streets. You shoot him a quick sidelong look and are oddly comforted to see that his hair, while definitely brown, is not electric with copper sparks, and no longer than it was last night.

"It's not far, and at this hour, before the traffic, it should only take about twenty minutes. If you're desperate, there's a Thermos flask full of coffee under the seat. I made it earlier. But that's the extent of my cooking ability."

"I can wait," you say.

The car is open, so you both are quiet, silenced by the wind of your passing as he speeds through the city streets. It is only a matter of minutes before you have left the city behind and are tooling along rougher country roads. There aren't any mountains within a hundred miles of the city, but the river cuts through bluffs to the west, so the road climbs in switchbacks up to the higher ground. You arrive at your destination, a small restaurant on top of the bluff, and Rick pulls into the gravel lot. The sign says "Delphie's." As you climb out of the car, the front door opens and a small woman comes running out to leap into Rick's arms. He laughs and hugs her; she plants a loud kiss on his cheek before dropping to her feet in the gravel and giving him a good, solid punch to the upper arm. "Four weeks!" she yells at him. "Four *weeks*!"

"I've been busy," he says weakly. "She's been good?"

"She's fine," the woman says, and then turns to you. "Hullo. I'm Delphie. You're…?"

"Nate Petroff," Rick says. "Our new headliner."

She doesn't say "Never heard of you," but the phrase is loud in her skeptical look. But she shakes your hand anyway. "Meetcha," she says, then to Rick, "Come on in. You can visit her while I'm fixin' up your breakfast. Coffee's ready, on the sideboard."

The restaurant is tiny but clean, and the coffee is hot and black and perfect. Rick takes the cup you pour him and leads the way through a door at the back and up a short path to an even tinier cottage. He raps on the door once, and then pushes it open.

The little living room is redolent with the sweet smoke of marijuana, but it's not a jazz musician or flapper holding the joint. It's a little old lady in a rocking chair, her eyes vague and filmy. "Hey, Auntie," Rick says softly.

"Don't you call me 'Auntie', boy," the woman says. "When you don't hardly come to see me no more."

"I'm sorry, Auntie. I brought you a present." Rick reaches in his jacket pocket and takes out a brown paper-wrapped package.

"Better be the weed," 'Auntie' says.

Rick laughs. "Of course."

"I suppose you want me to look at him?"

"If you like." Rick is noncommittal, but he glances at me.

The woman is crotchety, but little and frail. She doesn't scare you until you sit on the hassock in front of her rocker and she leans forward. She smells of lavender, soft and powdery, and of pot, sickly sweet. Your empty stomach roils and you clench your coffee mug.

She says nothing, but stares at you a long moment. Then she turns to Rick and starts speaking very fast in a language that sounds Greek or Turkish or something Middle Eastern. He listens, going still, and then finally nods, slowly, as if unwilling to hear what she says. She winds down eventually and turns back to you. "It's as well," she says to you, as if you have a clue what she's talking about, then sits back in her rocker and raises the joint to her lips again.

"Come on," Rick says, and leads you back out of the smoky cottage.

"She has severe rheumatism." His voice is apologetic as you walk back down the short path to the restaurant. "I bring her the marijuana because it eases the pain. She's very old."

"She's very strange," you counter. "What did she say? And what language was that?"

"It's a Greek dialect. She's from the same little village my family's from. Of course, we've been in America for a long time."

Delphie is waiting at the door with a big basket, which she hands to Rick. "Too nice a day to sit indoors. You go on up to the picnic spot."

Rick gives her a buss on the cheek and you follow him across the gravel lot to a stand of trees. Just past the trees are a wooden table and benches on a place near the edge of the bluff, overlooking the river. Rick sets the basket on the table, then turns to you. His face is serious, but the hand he reaches out to brush your jaw is gentle. "It wasn't anything important. Just a crazy old woman's ramblings. I shouldn't have subjected you to that, but she has so few amusements. Ready for breakfast?"

There are rolls, and omelets in steaming bowls, and crisp bacon and spicy sausage. And more coffee, in a vacuum flask. And slices of melon in multiple colors. You and Rick eat silently, but when you've finished and set down your fork, he says, "What happened after the war?"

You blink. "After the war?"

"After you were discharged. What did you do?"

"I went home to Michigan for a while. I'd gotten a scholarship to the Gary Conservatory, which they'd deferred for anyone who was fighting in the war, so when I left Detroit, I went there."

"They didn't look at your war record?"

"Of course they did." Your voice is sarcastic but you can't help it. It hurts. "They asked me why I was dishonorably discharged."

"What did you do?"

"What would you do? I *lied.* I told them that someone else had made advances to me, but that when I rebuffed them he went to his officers and said I was the one. I had no proof, but neither did he, and so I told them that the officers chose to believe him."

"Is that what you told your family?"

"No. I told them the truth. Which is why I left Detroit." Your voice is shaking, so you take a moment to bite into a Danish. The thick, sweet, raspberry goo drips on your chin and you wipe it off, licking your finger. When you look up, Rick is staring at your mouth.

Angrily, you say, "And then when I failed there, I went to New York and tried to get work there, and failed, and Philadelphia, and failed, and Boston, and failed, and took a job as a longshoreman, and then lost my job when the market crashed, and now I've come here and you think I'm not going to fail again and you're *crazy*, you know that? I don't know what you want of me, but I *suspect*, and I don't like it." You drop the rest of the Danish onto the plate and say, "So if that's what it is, we can just say forget it. Drive me back to the club and I'll get my stuff and get out of your hair."

"You give up too easily," Rick says, and eats a piece of bacon. It's his turn to lick his fingers, and you stare just as helplessly at him as he did at you. "You think," *slurp* "that just because," *slurp* "I want you," *slurp* "that I don't think you can sing? You saw the staff yesterday. You know you can sing, but you're afraid, and I won't tolerate fear of failure. Fear of *me*, that's okay." He wipes his fingers on his napkin, and cocks his head at me. "Who's Bertie?"

There's only the sound of the breeze in the little clearing and the faraway rush of the river below. "He was my lover," you say numbly. "In France."

"Auntie says you left your heart on the battlefield and what came back to the States was only your shell."

And just like that, you're back there, crawling over the mud and bodies and scraping your hands on stones and fallen barbed wire, the night sky exploding with lightning and rockets, the air red and misted. He is out there, wounded, not dead; you would know if he were dead, but they wouldn't let you go until after night fell, not that night is any cover, any comfort. But at last they send the corpsmen out with their wood and canvas stretchers, crawling over the ground like so many red-crossed ants, trying to find the merely wounded among the newly dead, and you go with them. For Bertie.

You find him, by luck or God's grace or maybe by the humming recognition in your soul. He is torn and battered but alive, and you get him on a stretcher and, crouching, drag it like a travois back to the trench. It is hours and you are terrified the whole time that he will die out there under the red and exploding sky. You don't dare look back at him, just reaching behind you to touch his shoulder to make sure he's still on the stretcher. You ignore the ache in your back and the ache in your thighs from half-crawling. You ignore the rain, and the rockets, and the shriek of tracer bullets, and the crunching thump of the guns.

One last stretch of barbed wire, and it tears your shirt and leaves a scar on your back, but Bertie is in the hands of the British corpsmen, and they are carrying him back away from the lines. You can't follow; you're not hurt, much, and they shove your Winfield back into your hands and put you back on the line.

"He was injured. I brought him back to the trench." You are quiet a moment, then say, "I met him again in New York. I was working as a waiter in a fancy restaurant. He came in with his wife. He didn't know me." The words are flat, meaningless.

"Do you still love him?"

Do you? You think of him as you saw him in that restaurant: polished, urbane, with that stupid little mustache; fawning over the narrow-faced bitch who wore his ring like a trophy. He looked at you blankly when you said his name, and was merely polite. Coldly, uninterestedly polite.

Then when you'd gone out in the alley for a cigarette, he'd come out and offered you money not to say anything to his wife. Even offered "favors" if you'd agree. He was drunk, stinking, his breath reeking of gin, and he'd tried to kiss you. The smell of the gin made you sick.

You'd left him in the alley with a bloody nose, his money fluttering in the evening breeze, and gone back in and quit.

"No," you say now. "I did once, but now—no." Not that Bertie. The sad, lonely little Bertie of the trenches who adored you and needed you and loved you. That one. That one you'd loved.

"Like Orpheus and Eurydice," Rick says. "My analogy was closer than I thought." He gets up and moves around the table, reaching down to take your hand and draw you to your feet. You stand there a moment, and then he takes you into his arms, kissing you.

You're tired of pushing him away when you want him like fire, and so you go with him, lying with him on the tablecloth he's thrown down there on the grass, in the sunlight. There's the usual awkward scramble to get out of your clothes, but he's never awkward and seems to imbue you with some of his grace. You lose yourself in his hands and mouth and warm, strong body. He coaxes you up and over and in the glory of it you see him again as he was in your dream, golden and incandescent and godly.

Something about that, about this, makes you laugh and he stops what he's doing and stares at you again. "What?" you ask.

"Do that again."

"Do what?"

"Smile like that."

So you do, and he literally lights up with his own laughter and amazingly, impossibly, you go over again and this time he follows.

When you open your eyes and sit up, the tablecloth is ash except for the outline of your body. The grass is scorched. Rick is lying on his side, watching you with careful eyes.

"Well," you say, "that's interesting."

"It's a side effect of lying with someone like me," Rick says.

"It wasn't a dream this morning, was it?"

After a moment, he shakes his head. "No."

You sit up, wrapping your arms around your bare knees. "So, what are you? Besides hard on sheets."

"Long story. And not so much with the sheets; it's the sunlight that does it," he says with a faint smile. "You're very calm."

"Would you prefer me to run screaming?"

"No. Not you. You might clobber me, but not the screaming." He sits up too. "We should probably go on back. Your first rehearsal with the band is at one."

"Is that it then? We're done?"

"For now? Yes." He gives me a quick grin. "I hope there will be an encore later, maestro."

You throw a handful of ash at him. He laughs.

DRIVING back into the city he's quiet again, as he was this morning, concentrating on weaving through the increased traffic, of both the foot and automotive kind. You're stopped, waiting for a streetcar to pass, when he reaches over to touch the back of your wrist. "I hope I haven't frightened you," he says in a low voice.

You shake your head. You don't know why you're not frightened. You should be. But every time you think that, you see him as he was when you walked into that club, lazy at the piano, in that silly undershirt and tie combination, and somehow all the fire and heat and sun in the world can't make you fear him.

But when you get back to the club there's a man standing outside with a pair of goons flanking him, and *him* you fear. He's not very large, but there's a presence about him that's intimidating, more than can be accounted for by the goons. Dark unruly hair and eyes bright green and a little crazy stare at you as you get out of the car.

"So this is the new canary," the man says.

"Dion," Rick says warily. "What can I do for you?"

"Introduce us." The guy has the accent of the streets and his hands are gnarled like grapevines. He's talking to Rick, but his dark crazy eyes never leave you.

"Nathan Petroff, meet Dion Winyard. He owns The Vinery over on Port Street."

“Get it?” Dion chortles. “Vines? Winyard? Port?”

“Got it,” you say. “God of the grape, no doubt.”

The silence is loud. Then the man says in a different voice, “Smart boy. Did you figure this all out yourself or did Golden Boy here let you in on the secret?”

You shrug.

“It’s not that simple,” Rick says, and his voice is irritated.

“It’s always that simple,” Dion says. “Let’s go inside and talk about it.”

“I can’t stop you,” Rick says. “But the goons stay out. You know that.”

“The goons stay out,” Dion agrees.

Corinna is waiting when you get inside. Her suit today is black, pin-striped, and chilly, reflecting her expression, and there is no sign of the staff. “Hello, you drunken bastard,” she says, her voice uninflected.

“Hello, you frigid bitch,” Dion responds in the same tone. “Beat it. This don’t involve you.” He turns back to Rick and jerks his head at you. “What’s so special about this loser?”

“None of your business,” Corinna says.

“I said beat it, bitch.”

“The day I take orders from a drunken Johnny-come-lately like you, Dion,” Corinna says serenely, “is the day Zeus rises and kicks your filthy ass.”

Dion ignores her, his attention on Rick. “Another one of your hard-luck cases? Zeus fuck, Ricky, this place is full of them. What d’ya need one more for? I’ll take him off your hands. The Vinery could use a new warbler.”

Your blood runs cold, but Corinna says dismissively, “He’s too good a performer for a whorehouse, Dee.”

“He’s staying here,” Rick says. His voice is quiet, uninflected, but Dion grins.

“Is he? We’ll see.”

The place is still after he leaves, all of you standing frozen until after you hear the sound of the door closing. Then Rick whips off his hat and hurls it to the floor. “Son of a bitch!” he swears. “That’s all we need is that bastard trying to lure Nate away. Or worse.”

“It was bound to happen eventually,” Corinna says calmly. “He would have heard of him sooner or later, and you know he always wants what you have.”

Rick puts his hand on your neck, threading his fingers through your hair. “I’m sorry, Nate. Dee’s a pain in the ass, but don’t let him shake you.”

You just nod and close your eyes at the luxury of his hands on your skin. “It’s okay, Rick.”

Corinna says, “You two have about ninety minutes until the band gets here for rehearsals. Nathan, I’d like you to do at least one set tonight, if you feel up to it, so focus on working with the band on some standards you’re comfortable with. As time goes on you can build up your repertoire. Rick, get him relaxed; he’s stiff as a board and I want him ready to work when the band gets here. You too.”

“Yes, ma’am,” Rick says, and takes you upstairs again, where he proves conclusively that he’s no harder on sheets than any other man.

You open the set that night with “Embraceable You,” and you sing it to Rick.

DION keeps away, but Harry shows up the second night and congratulates you on your performance. He tells you you’re not the first singer he’s steered Rick’s and Corinna’s way, and he names two people that you’ve actually heard of, one a big band singer and the other a rising Broadway star. He says when your current employers think you’re ready, he’ll take over as your manager and steer you straight up the charts. He’s easy to believe, especially because he’s clearly fond of the Bellevues. You’re becoming pretty fond of them yourself.

So you keep singing, and keep loving Rick, and neither activity ever begins to pall. You open a bank account, but somehow it’s so much easier to keep living at the club, close to Rick (Corinna apparently has a flat somewhere in the city; you never see her before noon). On the nights when Rick sleeps with you, he’s gone in the early predawn dark, but you don’t follow him again. Instead you just wait for him to come back and roust you out for breakfast. After a few weeks, though, you discover in yourself a heretofore unexpected ability to cook, so the two of you dare to raid the irascible Mario's kitchen and make your own breakfasts. That requires, however, making sure you replace the food you eat before Mario gets there at noon and comes after you with his machete, so a couple of times a week you visit the local market and do grocery shopping together. It's positively domestic, and the kind of thing you dreamed about with Bertie.

Rick doesn't seem to get bored of you, either. He'll sometimes play when you're on stage, but doesn't sing himself unless you're alone with him. Then it's odd, minor-key songs in that Greek dialect you don't know, and they usually put you to sleep. Other than that, you go on long drives in his gold Lincoln, and work on new arrangements of songs, and sometimes read the latest novel from Fannie Hurst or Edna Ferber. He is an enormous fan of Mary Roberts Rinehart's supercriminal "The Bat," which you tease him about mercilessly. And of course you go to the movies, usually matinees. He prefers Garbo to Crawford, but you both agree on Gable. And Harlow. Corinna rolls her eyes at your taste in melodrama, but the two of you just laugh at her. All three of you love the Marx Brothers.

And then, one morning the police come to the club, and Rick has to go downtown and bail one of the waitresses out of jail for solicitation. It's strange, because the waitress is Billie, and she's the least likely person you know to wander from the straight and narrow like that. Well, excluding Corinna, of course. You offer to come with him, but he just tells you to go on to the market and replace the dozen eggs you'd used up in the monstrous—but delicious—omelet you'd made for him earlier.

So you do, and it only occurs to you halfway to the market that it's the first time you've left the club without Rick in—is it six weeks already? The few blocks to the market retrace the same route you'd walked all those weeks ago on your way from Harry's, but you're not the same sad sack that came down that pike; you've money in your pocket, new clothes on your back, and a song in your heart.

So that when you see the shabbily dressed woman with the toddler in her arms, holding out a battered man's hat for people to drop coins in, and no one dropping coins, you have to stop. The woman isn't pretty; she has the sad, drawn face of the hopeless, and the child has her own face buried in the woman's shoulder, but she's thin and wasted under the worn pinafore.

You stop and pull your wallet from your pocket and take a five-dollar bill out and put it in the hat. "Buy the baby something to eat," you say gently.

The "baby" turns to look at you and you step back involuntarily. Those round black eyes have no whites, and instead of a nose, there's a red vertical slash. When the creature grins, it flashes teeth that are sharp with ragged points. "Gotcha," it says in a growly voice, and puffs a breath in your face. This time the step back is more of a stagger as the world goes fuzzy.

The woman isn't shabbily dressed anymore; she's not dressed much at all, just a bloody animal skin draped over her like an apron. She laughs—cackles, really—and drops the "baby," who scampers off into the woods that have suddenly appeared around you. The woman, her knotted hair exploding from the neat bun she'd worn before, follows, laughing wildly.

The city is gone. You're standing in a clearing, in the middle of a circle of stones surrounded by wild woods. Above the trees you see mountains. Your heart pounds in your chest and you spin around, blinking. "This can't be right," you say aloud, and the fright in your voice makes you all the more scared.

"It isn't right," another voice answers. You've heard that voice before, but you have to turn around to be sure.

Dion Winyard is sitting in a stone chair, almost a throne, just outside the circle of stones. He's wearing the same kind of outfit the crazy woman had on, an animal skin draped over one shoulder and wrapped around his waist. A crown of vines circles his head and a leather wineskin is in his lap; as you stare at him blankly, he takes a swig from it. "It's not *right*," he repeats, "but it is the way it is. Only here is the way it should be. Out there—it's all wrong."

"I don't understand," you say blankly. "Where am I? What is this place, and how did I get here?"

"See, that's the problem," he says, pointing the mouth of the wineskin at you. "You *live* with them, and you haven't a clue who they are. They're part of the problem! They just go along with the way things are. They don't get it—if we don't fight, we're gonna end up just like the others. They think if they change, if they go along with how the world wants them to be, then that'll be fine. They think just because they've lasted two thousand years this way that *they're* the survivors. Them and their 'music'." His sarcasm puts the quote marks around the word. "Do you even have a clue who they are?"

You glare at him, but he just waits. "Yes, of course I do," you say. "I'm not *stupid.* I went to school. I know about... them. I don't know *why*, of course. Or how they survived... whatever it was they survived."

"The death of the Great Pan," Dion says. "The death of everything. I know what they teach you in schools, mortal. They cleaned it all up, organized it like they were damned Hesiod, for Zeus' sake. Crammed us all into nice, clean little niches, god of this, goddess of that. But that ain't the way it was. Ain't the way it is, or should be, for that matter. I'm the god of the vine, whoop-de-do. I ain't the fucking god of the vine. I'm the god of madness, of drunkenness, of lewd behavior, of *fucking*, for Zeus' sake, and they've got me emasculated as god of some gods-damned *plant*? And Ricky? They turned him into a faggoty sun god or crap like that. Twenty thousand years the god of the hunt and the chase and the scalding desert, and now he rides his little chariot across the sky and mentors mortal musicians. *Jazz*!!" He says the word like a curse.

"What do you want from me?" You try to be brave but it was easier facing the guns in a charge across the bloody plains of France than this man. Or god. Or whatever he is.

"They're the only ones left, except the little godlings, the ones who *are* actually gods of plants and shit like that. And the leftover monsters. Those don't matter. But *they* do. They've turned their back on who they are—who they *were*. They were once among the oldest and strongest of all of us, but they've forgotten. They've gone weak. I haven't, but I can't go on alone. The three of us can rule the world again, once I do this."

"Do what?" You've backed as far away across the clearing as you can, but there's an invisible wall or something you're plastered up against. Behind you the trees rustle, as if inhabited by more of the crazy pelt-wearing females, but your hands touch only solidity.

"Bring them back into their godhead," Dion says, his voice low and wicked. "Force them to take it up again. Then—when it's three, and the best of us—then we change the world. Cast down their plaster gods, their pallid, bloodless saints of sacrifice, make them worship us again as they did before. And you, little man, are just the one to do it."

"Me?" you squeak.

"You. You're the closest thing to a worshiper Ricky has."

The invisible wall dissipates behind you and you stumble back, right into the arms of the wild women. Filthy hands with nails like thorns grab you, scratch you, clutching arms, legs, dragging you across the clearing to where Dion stands. He raises his arms and there's a rumble, and a stone slab appears in front of him, waist-high. The wild women throw you up onto the slab; you try to scramble away but they've got your arms again and haul you down onto your back, hanging onto you. Dion draws a long knife, curved like a scimitar, and slices open your new shirt, the tip sliding along your breast and belly and leaving a thin line of red.

At the sight of the blood the wild women howl. Dion grins. "First blood," he cackles. "This is how it will go, Nate." The sound of your name on his lips is terrifying. "You are the worshiper, the devoted, the sacrifice. I dedicate you to the sun god Utu, the god Shamash, the god Nergal; to the god Inti, the god Istanu, to Agni and Ravi, to Helios, to Aten and Khepri and Ra, to Huitzilopochtli, to Malakbel, to Igbo, to Magec, to Ngai. To the gods of light and justice and punishment, of fire and war and the daylight hunt. To the eagle, to the lion, to the wolf. And through this sacrifice to the sister of the Sun, the Moon, Mayari, Astarte, Isis, Bendis, Selene and all the other crap names of that crazy woman. By this sacrifice do I bring them to their godhead…."

Vines have sprung up all around you, binding you to the stone. The knife is poised above your breast, glittering in the dappled light of the clearing, a drop of blood quivering on the tip. The women are crouched around the makeshift altar. Your mouth moves as you whisper silent prayers—to whom you're not sure, maybe the God of your childhood, the God of your parents who drove you out, begging for forgiveness, not rescue, because you know there's no hope, not anymore. Your hope is down at the police station, bailing Billie out of a trumped-up charge—and you know now who it was that accused her, to get Rick out of the way while he pulls this crazy stunt. You take a breath and close your eyes, bracing yourself.

Someone screams and it's not you.

Your eyes shoot open and you stare up at Dion, who's got a stick growing out of the center of his chest. He drops the knife and it lands on the stone beside you with a clatter. "Zeus fuck," a complaining, *beautiful* voice says, but the vines have twisted around your head and hold it immobile, so you can't see.

"You shot me, you bitch!" Dion accuses angrily.

The wild women are screaming and, from the sound of it, running away. Rick comes closer and touches the vines; they shrivel up and fall away. He's got a bow in his left hand, the arrow still nocked, but his right hand draws you up and against him. "Are you all right, baby?"

"I'm okay," you say into his shoulder.

"Of course I shot you." Corinna sounds mildly aggrieved, which, after a few weeks of acquaintance, you know means she is *furious*. "What the hell were you thinking, Dion? Nate is a *mortal*. You bring him here as a *sacrifice*? You're breaking all the oaths we took when we were permitted to remain."

"Of course he is," Rick says. His voice is a comforting rumble in your ear. "He's nutty."

"He said he would bring you into your godhead," you mumble.

"Like I said, nutty. We gave all that up, you moron." You know he's not talking to you. "We *agreed*. *You* agreed."

"It isn't enough!" Dion roared. "To have to live among those petty little minds, those little lives? To see them bow down to these new gods?"

"They are the gods they have chosen, Dion," Corinna says. "They are the gods who fit what they are now, the gods of this age. Our time has come and gone. To them, we are nothing more than the shadows of their ancient past, the gods of the field and the hunt and the physical world. We are not the Written Gods. We are the Dreamt Gods. Our time is *done*."

"So I'm supposed to just give in, let myself die like Zeus and Hera and Osiris and Woden and all the others?"

"No," you say, turning back to him. With Rick at your back you feel braver, strong enough to face this man, this god. "Go on the way Rick and Corinna have. Find your niche and your worshippers among the ones who are left." You snort. "You know Rick says they're about to repeal Prohibition...."

"Huh," Dion says. "Prohibition has been a gold mine for me."

"You're a gangster, and a successful one, so you know how it is. People will always drink. They'll always go crazy. They'll always…" you glance at Corinna and modify what you're going to say "…have carnal relations. Find your worshippers there. Corinna's right—this isn't your time anymore. And your idea wouldn't have worked, anyway. Rick's not a god to me. He's just a man. A man who sets things on fire occasionally, yeah, but still just a man."

You feel Rick's hand fall away, feel the coolness at your back where he had been standing. You glance back to see his face blank. And then you think… *oh*.….

And you add, "The man I love." But you say this to Rick, not to Dion. Dion doesn't matter anymore. "I don't care if you're Apollo or Vishnu or Buddha.…"

He's laughing now. "I'm not Vishnu or Buddha!"

"…it doesn't matter. You're Rick Bellevue, and I love you."

"Finally," Corinna says.

THEY leave Dion there, trying to get up the nerve to yank the arrow out of his chest. "It won't kill him," Corinna says as she and Rick escort you to the gold chariot that waits in the trees. "It'll just hurt like the very devil. We can't be killed by ordinary means. We can die, we can kill ourselves, but a mere arrow is nothing."

"She left the killing arrows at home," Rick says to you in an aside.

"Of course I did. He's an idiot, but he's still family."

Rick sets his bow down on the floor of the chariot at his feet and picks up the reins. Corinna somehow looks right with a bow in her hand, even in the filmy white dress she is wearing, but he looks plenty strange in his white seersucker suit, holding a bow. Of course, the *suit* looks plenty strange on a man standing in a gold chariot and driving a team of four white horses. Not even white, really; more incandescent, like Rick the morning you'd seen him on the roof.

A road opens up through the trees, and as Rick drives the chariot, the air gets fuzzy again; something whacks you in the back of the knees and you sit down hard on the back seat of the Lincoln, and Corinna pulls out a filmy white scarf and wraps it around her hair. "You lost your hat," she says over the back of the front seat, and hands it to you. You put it on, but you feel ridiculous with your sliced-open shirt, the edges stained with blood.

"Are you all right?" Rick asks again.

"Okay," you respond. And you are. The cut stings a little, but not much. "Where are we?"

"I want to make a stop," Rick says.

The road starts to look familiar—or rather, the switchbacks do—and you see up ahead the little restaurant on the bluffs. This time when he pulls into the parking lot, there's no Delphie to come running out to meet him. "Come on," he says, and opens the door for Corinna. "You can leave the bow—I'm not going to kill either of them."

You follow them up the path to the little cottage. Delphie's waiting outside on a bench, with Auntie in her rocker in the doorway. The restaurant owner's face is set.

"You listened in, didn't you?" Rick asks her. "When Auntie spoke about Nate."

"Yeah," she admits. "And told Dion. Sorry. It's just hard to say no to him, y'know?"

"Yeah," he agrees, "but you're my employee, not his. Next time he asks you to do something like that, you tell me, okay?"

"You aren't mad?"

"Oh, I'm plenty mad," he says, "but where am I going to get someone to watch over Auntie?"

She lets out a breath of air in relief. He adds softly, "But that doesn't mean you aren't getting punished."

"Oh, crap...." And suddenly it's a baboon crouched on the bench. It howls pitifully.

"You get your real form back when I think you've been punished enough," he tells it. "Plus this way you can eavesdrop all you want and not have to worry about anyone pressuring you to blab."

"What did Auntie say?" you ask finally.

"That you were the perfect sacrifice if I wanted to get back what was lost to me," Rick says distantly, his eyes on the roof of the house. "That you were the key. You were wrong, you know, back there, when you stood up to Dion. It *would* have worked." He drops his eyes to mine. They're dark and sad and *human*. "But I would have lost you. And, my Orpheus, I love you."

"Finally," Corinna says.

YOU'RE not unchanged by your experience. When the usual crowd files in the next night (you and Rick take that night off, you to recover from Dion's tender mercies, Rick because he can't bear to be away from you), you see scattered among them not ordinary humans of whatever shape or color or gender, but the small gods and monsters Dion referred to. Some have horns, and webbed hands, and cloven hooves for feet; they're brown and green and gray and some of them have leaves growing out of their head, and one woman has snakes for hair. (You'd wondered why she'd always worn sunglasses even inside the dimly lit club.) And when you walk down the street, some of the people you see aren't exactly people. But you're still human. And so is Rick, more or less… just a little more than less.

"You won't live forever," he told you that night as he ran a hot thumb over the tear from Dion's knife, sealing the cut with just his heat, "but you'll live a damn long time, and you'll stay young and healthy that whole time. I can still do that much. Will you stay with me until then?"

"On one condition," you say lazily, running your hands through his hair as he kisses your belly. "Put Delphie back the way she was. It's not fair to her or to Auntie to leave her like that. She couldn't help that Dion scared her; he scares me and not a lot does anymore. And she's just a woman."

"Don't let Coco hear that," he murmurs, and starts kissing his way back up your chest. "Well, I was planning on leaving her like that for a year, but I guess I can compromise to six months."

"A week."

"Four months."

"A week."

"You'd dare argue with a god, puny human?"

DELPHIE is human again a week later.

An unrepentant biblioholic, ROWAN SPEEDWELL spends half her time pretending to be a law librarian, half her time pretending to be a database manager, half her time pretending to be a fifteenth-century Aragonese noblewoman, half her time… wait a minute… hmm. Well, one thing she doesn't pretend to be is good at math. She is good at pretending, though.

In her copious spare time (hah) she does needlework, calligraphy and illumination, and makes jewelry. She has a master's degree in history from the University of Chicago, is a member of the Society for Creative Anachronism, and lives in a Chicago suburb with the obligatory Writer's Cat and way too many books.

The Flower Boy

Belinda McBride

I

Valentine's Day, San Francisco

PHILIP YEOH stood at the intersection near Third and Harrison with a bundle of red roses in each hand and several flower-stuffed five-gallon buckets at his feet. He smiled at the drivers of expensive cars as they crawled along in San Francisco's mid-afternoon traffic, hoping desperation didn't show on his face as he tried to make eye contact with indifferent commuters.

He was set up too close to the business district, yet not close enough. If he'd nabbed a spot there, his flowers would look a bit more desirable against the backdrop of tall buildings and manicured façades. Here, at a trashy intersection, they just looked cheap in contrast to the kiosks and businesses that the drivers were leaving behind.

He lifted a bouquet, held it to his nose, and inhaled deeply. Damn hothouse flowers—barely even had a scent. He'd invested every last dime in the flowers in a desperate gamble to make the upcoming rent. Grants and patchy scholarship funds just didn't cut it when you were a semi-employed art student in San Francisco. He deftly rearranged the bouquet, but there was only so much he could do with rubber bands and cellophane wrap. If he'd had vases or some containers, he could have made magic happen.

He sighed, shivered, and smiled winsomely as the traffic shifted, moving along just yards at a time. Pulling up the hood of his jacket, he was able to block some of the drizzle coming from the foggy sky. His heart picked up pace just a bit as a window opened and a hand emerged, extending a ten-dollar bill. He made the exchange, feeling a little better about the day. It wasn't the rent, but it was a meal.

His mother would never have believed he'd be starving while he was in college. His stepfather wouldn't have cared. Philip's eyes burned at the thought. His stepfather had held Philip and his artistic abilities in contempt. He'd managed to get out before it was too late, but he'd left his mother behind. When the old man took himself out while driving drunk, he'd taken Lily Yeoh Jackson along with him. They'd left their son nothing but memories and a pile of debt.

What would his birth father think of him? Would he swoop in and rescue Philip from the drudgery of his life, or would he look at his unknown son with indifference? Philip pulled his mind away from thoughts of those who were now dead and lost. His birth father had been some poor Chinese boy his mother had left behind when she came to America. But still, he sometimes ached to know the man. He sighed, noticing the air smelled of peaches. Peaches and something else....

"*Ni hao!* Would you like to buy some flowers?"

He whirled at the sound of the musical voice, eyes wide with shock, and then with anger.

"This corner's taken!" He wasn't a particularly militant sort of man, but like a beggar, he'd defend his patch of concrete to the death. Well, maybe not that far.

He blinked at the person who was approaching him down the concrete traffic divider, for truly, he wasn't certain if it was male or female. A blue knit cap was pulled down over black hair, with several long black braids escaping and hanging down his shoulders. He... or she... wore a pale blue tunic with a ratty wood-fiber belt hanging low on slender hips. A large yin yang pendant dangled from a jute cord around his neck. His shorts were loose and simple, baring pale, elegant legs. Oddly enough, he wore only one shoe, while the other grubby foot was bare. Philip shivered in sympathy, but he didn't seem affected by the cold winter weather.

He, Philip decided, for there was the hint of a package at the V of his legs. But then he looked at the face and changed his mind. Ivory skin and ruby lips and sparkling almond eyes spoke of femininity.

"I was asking if *you* wished to buy a flower." Indeed, the young person carried a woven bamboo basket over his arm. It was loaded with all manner of wildflowers: daisies and chrysanthemums, poppies and sunflowers. All brought a smile to Philip's lips, and they made his roses look drab.

Frankly, the kid looked more destitute than he did. What could it hurt?

"How much?"

"One dollar per flower."

He dug into his pocket and fished out the ten-dollar bill. "I'll buy one then. That Shasta daisy."

The youth's ruby lips curved up into a smile. "I have no change."

So it was all or nothing. Philip sighed. "What's your name?" The youth looked him in the eye with a guileless smile. He couldn't help but smile in response. Something about him made Philip simply feel good.

"I'm Lan Caihe. But you can call me Lan." He bowed slightly, clasping his hands together in front of his chest. Automatically, Philip bowed back. Some habits never died, not completely.

The name was vaguely familiar, but Philip didn't know enough Mandarin to translate. His mother would have known.

"Well, Lan, I hope your flowers bring me luck." He handed Lan the money, extending it with both hands. He had rice in the cupboard and some broccoli in the freezer. He'd put in a few hours at the florist, helping out for the upcoming spring weddings. He'd make it to the end of the week, when his check arrived, and somehow he'd get his share of the rent.

Lan formally accepted the money with both hands and carefully picked out a variety of flowers, handing them to Philip with a flourish. With a smile, Lan tucked the white daisy down into the center of the bouquet he held. It looked like a drop of snow against the vivid red background.

"Thank you, sir."

"Philip."

The youth bowed slightly. "Philip." His rosy lips turned up in an impish smile.

A car horn beeped, startling him from his fixation on Lan's face.

To his gratification, the driver bought the bouquet, smiling at the quirky daisy that nestled in the midst of the flowers. He paid the ten, plus a tip. Philip quickly picked up a new bouquet and tucked another of Lan's flowers into the bunch. Within just minutes, he'd sold every bouquet with a wildflower, and one hundred dollars warmed his pocket.

He glanced back at where Lan squatted on the concrete divider. His flower basket was still full.

"Would you like to buy the rest of them?" Again, an enigmatic smile played over his full lips. Now he was certain that Lan was a male. There was a husky edge to his voice. His long braids swayed in the breeze from the bay, and suddenly Philip didn't want his flowers: he wanted Lan. Erotic images clouded his thoughts: he and Lan making love, misty ribbons of clouds surrounding them, golden light illuminating their naked bodies....

He blinked. "Lan, I know you probably need the money as badly as I do...." He turned to hand a bouquet to another driver. They were still selling, in spite of the absence of Lan's wildflowers. He looked down at the bill in his hand and extended it to the youth.

He was gifted with another radiant smile. "I will sell them, but not for money."

Philip tilted his head a bit. Was Lan propositioning him? He occasionally dated here in the city, but he'd avoided relationships. Between school and work, he simply didn't have time. He loved San Francisco, enjoyed the sexual fluidity that flourished here, but hadn't really found his niche. He had roommates and casual friendships among his fellow students, but no deep connections. Perhaps this was the beginning of one. He'd never have considered hooking up with someone like the androgynous flower boy. Philip preferred his men to be masculine, and his women to be girly. Lan was an anomaly.

"How do you want me to pay for them?" He was unable to look away from Lan. Oddly, the traffic must have come to a complete stop, as their surroundings were nearly silent. He could hear horns honking and the revving of engines, but it was in the distance. He noticed how Lan's face reminded him of a flower, perhaps a peony. Maybe he was both boy and girl. That made Philip's heart race a little faster.

"You can buy the rest of my flowers with a kiss."

"A kiss," he repeated, as if he hadn't heard correctly. "I can do that."

"Very good. Very lovely." Lan moved nearer, and Philip was overwhelmed with the fragrance of flowers. Not one single fragrance but multitudes made up the perfume wafting around them. Lan brought up his hand and gently stroked his fingers along Philip's smooth cheek.

"You are such a handsome young man. Tell me, Philip Yeoh, what do you study in school?"

Something was odd about the words, something that tugged at Philip's subconscious. Sounds and words and names from long ago. Had he given the flower boy his name?

"Art and design. I go to the Academy of the Arts."

Cool, gentle fingers trailed over his lips. "You are so warm; your skin is golden, like sunshine." Lan moved closer, his slender body nearly touching Philip's. Heat radiated from them both, mingling and blending with the light perfume of flowers and fresh peaches. "You have a strong face, Philip."

Those intoxicating fingers trailed over his cheekbones. Philip gazed into Lan's face and was surprised; he hadn't noticed the slender, arched nose and the delicate, black brows. His face was a pale oval, while Philip's was triangular with broad cheekbones narrowing to a sculpted jaw. His stepfather had been white, but like his mother, Philip was all Chinese. Yet he looked far different from Lan and his delicate beauty.

Lan leaned closer and their lips touched. The delicate flavor of peach filled his senses like nectar. Philip's eyes dropped closed as the Earth fell away from beneath his feet and he was lifted into the heavens. The kiss was delicate at the start, and then, as their mouths opened to each other, tongues met and bodies touched. His arousal was so intense that Philip could hear only the rush of his heart. Dizziness overwhelmed him and he sagged a bit, finding himself caught in surprisingly strong arms. The kiss broke, and he gasped, his eyes fluttering open.

II

PHILIP staggered in shock. The cars were gone. There were no streets, no buildings. Golden mist filled the air and showers of flower petals rained down on his face. He went limp and fell back, landing softly in drifts of snowy blossoms. Their perfume rose all around him, making him suck in air just to savor the fragrance.

Lan stood before him, still the same and yet… different. So very, very different. He lowered himself to his knees, fairly glowing in the pastel light reflecting up from the flowers. He now wore flowing robes, much like those a woman from old China would wear. Pale blue layered over white; the silk was embroidered with large silver chrysanthemums.

One foot was garbed in a delicate slipper, while the other foot was bare, ivory-colored and slender. His silken black hair was caught up at the crown of his head in a ribbon-wrapped bun, while the rest of his hair tumbled in a black sheet down his back. Yin yang symbols were embroidered into the fabric that held a carved wooden belt around his waist. The basket of flowers hung from a simple wooden hoe he carried.

Philip struggled to sit upright and gaze at his surroundings. Rugged mountain peaks thrust upward through the mist; otherwise, he'd have believed that he was in the very heavens. Perhaps he was; perhaps he'd been struck by an out-of-control vehicle in San Francisco's rush-hour traffic. He was probably lying by the side of the road, invisible to the drivers who were intent on returning to home and family.

He looked up. Clouds traced through the sky and Philip gaped in shock; great, golden dragons twisted and played through the wispy clouds floating overhead. Delicate laughter rang through the air, and he looked back to Lan. He was setting tea out on a rock that was more beautiful than the most exquisite table in the mundane world. He knelt, holding back the billowing sleeve of his robe as he poured.

"Tea and poetry and discussions of love and beauty. There is no greater way for young men to spend an afternoon."

Philip glanced down at the layers of robes falling over his loose trousers. He reached up and felt the cap of a scholar upon his head. He opened his mouth to speak, and then closed it again. The words coming from Lan's mouth were in Mandarin. It was an ageless dialect, and Philip understood everything he said. When he spoke, the unfamiliar words tumbled out without effort.

"Are we in Heaven?"

"This is my home, Philip. I thought you needed some time away from that harsh life you lead." He smiled, offering tea in a paper-thin porcelain cup. Philip knelt on the flower-covered ground and bowed slightly, accepting the cup with both hands.

"I know little of poetry."

"Your very existence is poetry. I've seen your paintings and sculpture. I've seen the art you make with flowers. You *are* poetry, Philip. If you don't know the words, we will simply speak of beauty and love." Lan smiled over the edge of the cup and sipped. Philip did the same, knowing as the tea touched his tongue that this was magic and he truly was in Heaven. Lan was an angel sent by his mother.

He cradled the cup and bowed his head, watching the swirl of golden-green tea in his hand. "Thank you."

Lan smiled and lifted the cup to his lips. He tasted and then looked at Philip, who knew what was coming, yet was still surprised when Lan asked.

"Would you make love with me, Philip Yeoh?

WOULD he make love with this fantastical, glorious creature? Philip blinked, staring at him. Why would someone so magical wish for the attention of a being as common as himself? Philip was aware of his appearance. He was good-looking, if your taste ran to young Chinese men of average height and build. In his case, living poor had led to better health. Before his mother's death, he'd been lamentably out of shape, the legacy of too many hours of screen time.

Living in the city, he'd learned to do without cars, without junk food, and had honed his body biking and walking through the hills of San Francisco.

His straight black hair used to be immaculately styled, but monthly haircuts were a thing of the past. He wore it long, tied back in a loose ponytail. Reaching up, Philip discovered it was neatly arranged in some sort of knot underneath the cap.

Perhaps this was only a dream? If he was dead, would he be in the heavens, being seduced by what could only be a god? With a jolt, he remembered.

"You are *hsien*. Lan Caihe. You are one of the Eight." The Eight

Immortals of Taoism. His mother had called Lan the Yin Yang god—both genders, and neither. He was the patron of beggars and flower sellers. Of course he'd be the deity of choice for someone like Philip Yeoh.

Lan smiled and shook his head. "I am simply Lan Caihe. Yes, there are seven others I travel with at times." Lan sipped his tea, looking completely at his ease. Now that Philip had made the connection, the *hsien* suddenly appeared larger… more. He swallowed, fear mingled with awe and amazement. Lan had asked him a question. He owed him an answer.

He spoke; his lips were paper-dry in spite of the excellent tea. "You honor me."

"No, Philip, I am enchanted by you, and simply wish to spend time in your company. You charm me with your sweet kisses and gentle gaze." He leaned forward a bit, his pale fingers resting on Philip's hand. "You bring kindness and beauty to all you encounter."

Philip flushed with embarrassment, yet at the same time, Lan's words brought a warm glow to his chest. There were times when his life was so painful and frustrating. Often, he wished to go back to the way it had been before, even with his ugly home life. Lan's words gave him hope.

"Then yes. I'll make love with you. We'll speak of poetry and art. We'll drink tea and look at the beauty around us."

It truly was beautiful. The dragons still scampered through the clouds, and as the mist broke up in places, he watched them careen from the sky, diving to the ocean below. To one side of him, a perfect peony rested on a teakwood bench. The pale blush of its petals was sublime, and the beauty was a painful balm to his eye. Immediately Philip knew he'd never be able to translate all that he saw onto canvas. He felt small next to the surrounding grandeur. He inhaled, feeling the pain of inadequacy ripple through his heart.

As though he understood exactly how Philip felt, Lan spoke. "That is how you should feel when confronted by the reality of nature. We are merely small travelers through the wonder of the Earth." Lan was gazing up toward the mountains, an awed expression on his delicate face. He fit into this setting like a beautiful, rare jewel.

Philip set the cup down and rose to his knees, reaching out to touch

Lan for the first time. His fingers stroked along silken skin; they tangled in the ebony length of his hair. He felt the breath of Lan's sigh against his cheek. They drew closer, and lips brushed, teased, and finally engaged in a kiss.

This time the world didn't vanish. When he opened his eyes, Philip was still surrounded by beauty, still in Lan's surprisingly strong embrace. The immortal smiled down at him and drew him close again, lifting Philip to his feet. In a moment of supreme grace, he moved them both to the teakwood bench. Looking up, Philip saw a cherry tree burst into blossom. Petals showered down where they lay. He rested against Lan's body, letting his eyes drift shut as the other man explored him, stroking down his arms, teasing his nipples through fine, silken cloth.

Lan's fingers were white and delicate. Philip rested his own hands over them and saw the rough skin; his short nails had paint embedded underneath them. Lan's hands slipped away, gliding under the silk of his robes, slipping into the waistband of his trousers. Philip kicked off his slippers and let the pants slip from his legs.

His lower body was bare; his outer robes fluttered, moving as though the breeze gave them life of their own. Soft hands stroked along the tender skin of his hips, his outer thighs, and finally they cupped his testicles, drawing a shiver that ran down his entire body. He shifted, feeling Lan's hard erection against his lower back. He twisted his head, burying his face into the fragrant skin of the *hsien's* throat. Once again, he smelled peaches. He moaned, lifting his body so that Lan's hard shaft slipped free of its silken prison.

As he stroked Philip's cock, Lan began to thrust, his penis stroking up between his parted legs, nudging alongside Philip's cock and balls. The velvety head kissed his skin, bumping gently over the rose of his ass.

Philip wanted Lan inside his body. He wanted to be taken, invaded and completely overwhelmed. With one hand the immortal caressed his chest, pinching and teasing his nipples, strumming him up to a rare pitch of arousal. With the other hand Lan gently pumped his cock, pausing to spread a bead of slippery precum over Philip's cockhead. He once again moved Philip's body with ease; he seemed to be even larger, even stronger than before. He possessed Philip with gentle power, his strokes speeding up until the climax began to build and twist up Philip's body. He murmured a protest, and Lan nipped his ear.

"You don't want me to do this dry." His tongue slipped into Philip's ear, drawing him even closer to the edge. "Don't worry, we aren't finished."

With that, he added a twist to the stroke and Philip came, crying out with a choked, broken voice. He felt his seed spill again and again, caught in the warm grip of Lan's palm. He panted, forcing his eyes open to watch. Lan's white hand was filled with milky seed, and he slicked it over his own erect penis until it glistened. When a slippery finger pressed against Philip's entrance, he went stiff in resistance. It was always a bit frightening with someone new.

"Relax, my peach." Lan's finger slipped in, stroking Philip back to an impossible arousal. Soon enough, the finger was replaced with the blunt tip of his cock, and Philip let out a breath, stunned at the ease of the other man's entry.

A dream. This entire experience was a dream. It had to be... he pulled his face from Lan's silk-covered chest and gazed at the sky, watching as the dragons danced and great, fiery birds coasted through the clouds.

Lan moved into an easy pace and they lay back on the platform, which Philip now realized was a bed. The lay on their sides and Lan's arm slid under his knee, lifting him open. Philip was stripped of all power, all thought. He existed simply to reside in this beautiful place, making love and drinking tea and speaking of poetry and art.

Well, they hadn't really gotten to the speaking part yet.

He ached to watch Lan's beautiful face, and again, the immortal anticipated Philip's needs, withdrawing from his body, and gently rolling Philip to his back. Philip pulled his knees up high, hissing between his teeth when Lan pushed in again. He was still slick and slippery, which seemed impossible, but as this was a dream, there would be no pain or discomfort. There would be only sublime bliss and joy in the act.

Lan paused to open Philip's robes, while he remained fully clothed. Watching him, Philip wondered just what lay under his silken gown. Did his male body share the features of a woman? Did he have soft breasts as well as a hard cock?

Lan's hair spilled forward, tickling the skin of Philip's belly and chest. His beautiful eyes went half-closed in pleasure. Braced over Philip's body, there was no question that the immortal was cleanly balanced between his yin and yang. His face was still touched with femininity, his touch was gentle, but testosterone made him dominant and aggressive with Philip. Perhaps he was as fluid and everchanging as nature herself.

He began his steady thrust into Philip's body. His breath sounded like music and smelled like sweet rain. When he bent to steal a kiss, his lips tasted like peaches. When he tried to pull away, Philip fisted his hair, licking at his mouth, trying to catch the taste and scent and feel of the immortal. He studied him, committing every feature to memory. He vowed to remember every moment of this fantastic adventure, because even as the bliss of orgasm threatened to steal all thought, Philip knew the moment was only fleeting. He needed to remember. He needed to carry this back into his life and his world. Somehow, Philip knew that the flower boy was the key to his future.

Lan's face grew dreamy, and then intense. He took his climax and played it like a musical instrument. It rose and ebbed, singing out to the heavens. Philip felt his own orgasm pressing in on him; he pulled Lan down into his arms, feeling the weight of the immortal over his body, pressing his cock between their sweaty bodies.

Even as Lan moaned into his orgasm, Philip shattered, feeling as though he was now one of the falling drifts of cherry blossoms floating toward the ground. He was trapped beneath Lan's body, barely able to catch his breath.

Lan panted, his face flushed, his skin dewy with sweat. He looked down and gazed into Philip's eyes. The emotion in his eyes was indescribable. He… loved. He loved Philip.

"Sleep." His voice was mesmerizing. He reached up, caressing the hair that had fallen loose from Philip's cap.

"No. I can't… I…."

"Sleep." Lan placed a gentle kiss on his lips. "Sleep and be whole. I will always be at your side."

Philip felt the ground move underneath his body, and wind whipped his hair and clothing. Rolling his head to the side, Philip saw that they were on the back of a giant, snowy crane. They angled through the sky, climbing up past where the dragons endlessly played in the clouds.

Through heavy eyes, Philip watched as heaven faded away.

III

They stood in an unfamiliar office in an unfamiliar city. Chinese people moved around them, clearly unable to see Philip and Lan, but never once walking into them. He looked up at the immortal; Lan stood at his side, back to his familiar, androgynous appearance. His clothing was tattered but clean and the basket of flowers dangled from his arm. He was wearing shorts, though it must be cold outside. The thought made Philip smile.

"You are the patron of flower sellers."

"That's you." Lan smiled at Philip. "And of beggars."

"I'm not a beggar, Lan." He'd done many things out of desperation, but he'd never begged, and he'd never sold himself. He'd even slept on the street a couple of times, but always found a way to get by.

He looked around the office. The building was old, but the office was modern and well-equipped, though not upscale. He saw no windows, but wondered if they were in Hong Kong, or even Taipei. He tipped his head, hearing both Mandarin and Cantonese being spoken as several people chattered on telephone calls. He'd lost the ability to understand.

"Walk with me." Lan placed a hand on his arm. Philip followed.

They moved through a corridor until they finally came to a small office. Philip looked around, trying to identify the business, but everything was written in Chinese. He barely remembered his days at Chinese school as a child. Maybe when he finished school, he'd take the time to learn Chinese again.

There was a desk in the small office, and bookshelves. Lan stepped forward, plucking a business card from a holder on the desk. He handed it to Philip, who frowned and then noticed that the card was written in English as well as Chinese. It read: *Lan Caihe Benevolent Association. Philip Hu, President.*

"This is a charity for the homeless," Lan explained.

Philip looked at Lan. "You are also the patron of beggars. The homeless aren't necessarily beggars, but charities survive by soliciting donations."

Lan took the card from his hand and stuffed it into the front pocket of Philip's jeans. "You are a flower seller. Your father is a beggar." His smile was sly and he turned away, trailing fingers along the battered wood of the desk. "He begs on behalf of those unable to care for themselves. He is a man of great honor and kindness."

Philip looked at the bookshelves. There were family photos displayed on the shelves: a handsome, middle-aged man posed with a pretty wife and two children. He moved along the shelf, looking at time in reverse as the subjects in the photos grew younger.

He then arrived at a grainy shot of the man with an infant in his arms. He was young, barely out of his teens. His clothing was poor and ragged; he was skinny but clean. He awkwardly held the baby. Their beaming smiles were identical.

"That's me." He reached out and picked up the photo. "I have one just like it, but all three of us are in the picture." He set the photo back on the shelf, and then looked at the portraits again. A father, siblings. A family he'd never known existed. His throat suddenly felt tight. He swallowed before speaking. "She never talked about him… her family moved to the U.S. when I was just a baby. Did he want me? Do you think he misses me? Lan?" He looked around, realizing that the room was growing dim. "Lan?"

"Look for me in the eyes of the flowers. Seek me in the faces of the poor." He felt a soft caress on his cheek, and a kiss on his lips. A tear fell; he tasted it as it dropped onto his mouth. It tasted like peaches.

"Lan… no…."

As he drifted into darkness once again, Philip felt his heart break for the second time in his life.

THE strident sound of a car horn jolted Philip back to awareness. He looked down at the bouquet of hothouse roses clasped in his hand. In the center, a pink peony brought the bouquet to whimsical life. Numbly, he held it out to the customer, taking the bill and stuffing it into his bulging pocket. How much money was stashed in his jeans? Hundreds… maybe more. They'd been handing him tens and twenties, never waiting for their change. One businessman paid with a hundred-dollar bill, waving away the money that Philip held out to him.

He turned, looking for Lan, but he was alone save for dozens of cars on either side of the traffic divider. His buckets overflowed with flowers, bouquets of lilies and chrysanthemums, roses mingled with daisies in a riot of color. All around him, the fragrance of flowers rose into the air. As fast as he was able to collect the money, he sold Lan's flowers. When he looked down, the buckets were always full. He sold his flowers and smiled through the tears in his eyes.

When at last he was weary and the buckets were empty, Philip gathered his belongings and trudged to the Muni stop. He reached into his pocket for change, but instead came up with the embossed white business card. He took his seat and stared at the card.

Lan Caihe Benevolent Association. Philip Hu, President.

There was a phone number and a street address.

He rode the bus and forgot to get off at his stop. He rode until it reached the end of the route and then he got off and took another bus that led back the way he'd come. He got off the bus and began walking, looking at the address on the card.

Not China… not Taiwan… but right here in San Francisco's Chinatown. Absently, Philip walked, not even noticing the awkward bulk of the empty buckets bumping his legs. When he finally stopped at the address, the Chinese writing dancing over the doorway matched the writing on the card.

There was a single light on inside. The door was locked, so Philip stood back, nonplussed. There were offices on the ground floor; up higher, there were residences. He looked to the side and saw a girl crouched in the shadows. Homeless and poor and desperate, she watched him cautiously.

"They're closed. I was too late tonight." Her face was peaked with hunger and the chill of the evening must have been hard for her, as she had no coat. Philip shrugged out of his cheap jacket and handed it to her. He glanced down at the nest of buckets and saw that the top container was filled with flowers. He looked at the girl and smiled.

"Would you like to buy a flower?"

She gazed at him, and then over at the flowers that hadn't been there a moment before. She reached out a trembling hand. "This is all I've got." It was a grubby five-dollar bill.

"Don't worry, I've got change." He took the bill and handed her the bucket, smiling as she got up from the ground and peered in at the flowers. When he handed her a wad of bills, she didn't even look to see what he gave her.

"All these for a dollar?"

"Yeah. I'm finished and they won't keep overnight. I'll bet if you head on down to Broadway, you'll find plenty of tourists."

She hefted the bucket and started in that direction. She paused and turned, and for a moment, her visage was suddenly radiant. The fragrance of peaches and flowers filled the air.

"He'll be back for you soon. He loves you."

Arms circled him from behind, and for a moment he was wrapped in warmth and love. He leaned back his head, smiling as a kiss brushed his cheek. When he turned, nobody was there.

The glow diminished and the girl stood on the sidewalk, blinking in surprise. She turned away again, hurrying down the street. Philip smiled when she paused and put a brilliant poppy into the hands of an elderly woman.

Look for me in the eyes of the flowers. Seek me in the faces of the poor.

Joy and relief swept over Philip in a rush. So was this what it was like to fall in love with an Immortal? Obviously, their relationship would be far from normal. His hands ached for a paintbrush and the zeal of artistic fire ran through his veins. Tomorrow he would buy canvas and new paints. He would paint what he'd seen and felt there in the heavens. He would do his best to bring that joy to the inhabitants of this world.

Philip turned back to the locked door and rang the bell. Footsteps echoed within as someone trotted down a stairway. The door opened. "We're closed, but you came by just at the right time."

The smile on the man's face was as beatific as Lan's. This was a face that had known suffering and joy, love and pain. The smile faded as he saw himself reflected in the young man outside his door. Recognition settled over his face. His lips trembled. He reached out to touch Philip's face, and then his hands dropped to his side.

Philip reached out, clasping those hands, holding them tightly. He didn't try to hide the tears in his eyes.

"I could not find you. I looked, but your mother vanished so many years ago." His brown eyes were full of tears. "We moved here to find you, and yet it seems you have found me instead." He blinked, and the tears rolled down his cheeks like dewdrops. "I prayed. I prayed every day I would find my son!"

As he looked at the face of his father for the first time, Philip smiled and reminded himself to buy incense and an altar. He knew that when his prayers rode the smoke to Heaven, Lan Caihe would be listening.

BELINDA MCBRIDE was born in Inglewood, California, but grew up far to the north in the shadow of Mt. Shasta. While her upbringing seemed pretty normal to her, she was surrounded by a fascinating array of friends and family, including a polyamorous grandmother, a grandfather who is a Native American icon, and various cowboys, hippies, scoundrels, and saints.

She has a degree in history and cultural anthropology, but in 2006 made the life-changing decision to quit her job as a public health paraprofessional and stay at home full time to care for her severely disabled autistic niece. This difficult decision gave Belinda the gift of time, which allowed her to return to writing fiction, a dream she'd abandoned years before.

Belinda's hobbies include soap making, collecting gemstones, travel, and martial arts. She has two daughters, six Siberian Huskies, and a menagerie of wild birds that visit the feeders in the front yard.

As an author, Belinda loves crossing genres, kicking taboos to the curb, and pulling from world mythology and folklore for inspiration. She was a finalist in the 2010 EPIC competition in the erotic science fiction category and a CAPA winner in 2009.

Visit Belinda at http://www.belindamcbride.com and http://www.belindam.blogspot.com. You can contact her at belinda@belindamcbride.com.

Look for these anthologies from

DREAMSPINNER PRESS

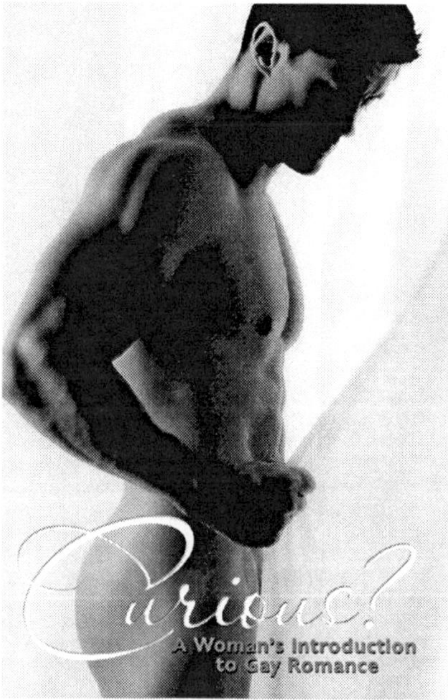

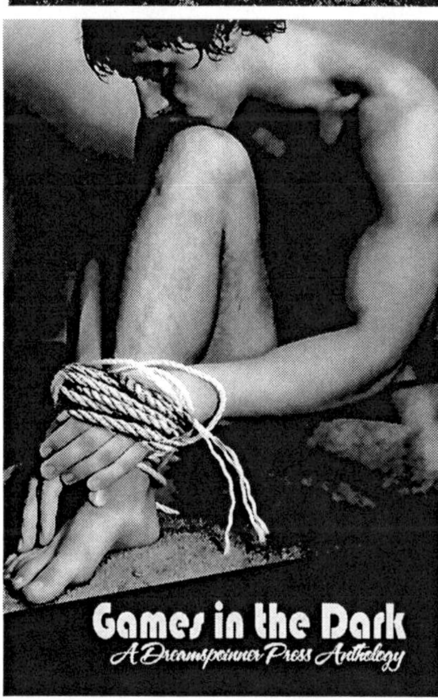

http://www.dreamspinnerpress.com

More romantic anthologies from

DREAMSPINNER PRESS

http://www.dreamspinnerpress.com

Dreamspinner Press
For more of the best M/M romance, visit
Dreamspinner Press
www.dreamspinnerpress.com

Breinigsville, PA USA
21 October 2010
247814BV00005B/4/P

9 781615 813728